PRAISE FOR ALI ROSEN

The Slow Burn

"Immersive and uplifting, at once swoony and reflective and deeply emotional, *The Slow Burn* is the perfect summer romance! The descriptions of Italy made me feel right at home, and I gobbled up this book in a single holiday afternoon, as voraciously as I would fresh pasta. Ali Rosen has written an empowering, unputdownable story that celebrates the people who want it all and who are determined enough to reach for it with open arms. A fantastic summer read!"

—Ali Hazelwood, #1 *New York Times* bestselling author of *The Love Hypothesis*

Unlikely Story

"*Unlikely Story* is the book equivalent of finding the perfect tomatoes at the farmers' market."

—Ali Brady, *USA Today* bestselling author of *Battle of the Bookstores*

"Ali Rosen captures the complexities of coming into your own. [*Unlikely Story* is] a therapy session and a love letter to New York, all in one book."

—Julie Soto, *New York Times* bestselling author of *Not Another Love Song*

"I adored *Unlikely Story*—Ali Rosen packs every page with heart and humor. Featuring lovable and relatable characters, amusing scenarios, and thought-provoking insights, Rosen's slow-burn romance is proof that love can be found in the unlikeliest of places."

—Lauren Kung Jessen, author of *Red String Theory*

Alternate Endings

"A complex story of a woman at a complex part of life—Bea's story is told with humor and care, and the romance Rosen crafts for her is gentle and tender and so satisfying."

—Kate Clayborn, *USA Today* bestselling author of *The Other Side of Disappearing*

"I adored Bea and Jack's second-chance love story. Their chemistry and banter are top-shelf, Rosen's prose is witty and insightful, and the Irish setting is gloriously realized. I'll be the first one at the table for every story Rosen wants to tell."

—Emma Barry, author of *Chick Magnet*

"Ali writes the kind of characters I want to be friends with in real life, and gives them the beautiful love stories they deserve. *Alternate Endings* is the perfect blend of sharp wit, delicious tension, and breathless romance that will have you yearning from the onset and thinking of long after you've reached the end. A must read!"

—Tarah Dewitt, *USA Today* bestselling author of *Savor It*

Recipe for Second Chances

"As a reader and a writer, I am always over the moon when I find a new author with a refreshing, wonderful new voice. Such is the case with *Recipe for Second Chances*—I couldn't turn the pages fast enough. When I got to the last page, I felt sad that the story was over. I wanted more. To me that is the mark of a really good writer."

—Fern Michaels, author of 153 (and counting) *New York Times* bestselling novels

"*Recipe for Second Chances* is the ultimate 'one who got away' romance—especially for lovers of lusty chemistry, glamorous locales, and decadent cuisine. A heartwarming, escapist treat!"

—Tia Williams, *New York Times* bestselling author of *Seven Days in June*

"*Recipe for Second Chances* is a sweet, utterly charming romance that swept me away to the Italian countryside, and I never wanted to return! [With the book's] lush settings and mouthwatering food, I absolutely loved every delicious morsel."

—Lynn Painter, *New York Times* bestselling author of *Better Than the Movies*

Ali's Cookbooks

"Ali Rosen is saving our dinner parties one dish at a time."

—Carla Hall, chef and television host

"A necessary and delicious addition to any collection!"

—Kwame Onwuachi, James Beard Award–winning chef, *Top Chef* judge, and executive producer of *Food & Wine* magazine

"Ali's got us, and I'm so glad that she does."

—Dorie Greenspan, author of *Baking with Dorie* and *Everyday Dorie*

"I want to give Ali Rosen a big high five for writing this book."

—Pati Jinich, James Beard Award–winning and Emmy-nominated host of *Pati's Mexican Table*

The Slow Burn

OTHER TITLES BY ALI ROSEN

Unlikely Story

Alternate Endings

Recipe for Second Chances

Cookbooks

Modern Freezer Meals

Bring It!

15 Minute Meals

The Slow Burn

ALI ROSEN

This is a work of fiction. Names, characters, organizations, places, events, and incidents are either products of the author's imagination or are used fictitiously. Otherwise, any resemblance to actual persons, living or dead, is purely coincidental.

Published by Montlake, Seattle

www.apub.com

EU product safety contact:
Amazon Media EU S. à r.l.
38, avenue John F. Kennedy, L-1855 Luxembourg
amazonpublishing-gpsr@amazon.com

ISBN-13: 9781662535963 (paperback)
ISBN-13: 9781662535956 (digital)

Cover illustration and design by Liz Casal

Printed in the United States of America

For my mother,
the role model who showed me that a woman can be
both deeply caring and unapologetically ambitious.

And for every reader who seeks out those role models in
the pages of their books.

Living is moving. Nothing is learned by standing still.
—Dominique Crenn

I'm so pathetically intense. I just can't be any other way.
—Sylvia Plath

Chapter 1

If I wanted to be charitable, I would assume John didn't know about the fire when he dumped me.

I'm not sure it's in my nature to be charitable, though.

I didn't anticipate walking into my apartment and seeing his bag packed while the only thing that mattered to me was burning down.

The excuses started instantly. They were the same excuses I'd always suspected he'd use on me when he eventually left.

I'm only holding you back.

You don't have time for me anyway.

You don't need anyone else, and I respect that about you, but I need more.

I wanted to ask whether this breakup was actually because my restaurant was on fire, which might make me less impressive arm candy now.

I wanted to ask if it had anything to do with the hostess at his newest restaurant, the one who's always fawning over him.

But I didn't. After all, he's not wrong that I never have time for him anyway.

So now, as I'm sitting at a diner with Anita the day after, my head feels on the verge of imploding from the copious amounts of tequila I consumed once John closed the door on us.

Normally at night I would've been at the restaurant, but of course last night, my restaurant was in the capable hands of the New York City

Fire Department. Standing there, watching my favorite place go up in flames without any ability to stop it, wasn't exactly something I could handle. I left to walk the two blocks to my apartment and wallow. And get dumped, apparently.

So. Tequila. A fitful, mostly blacked-out night of sleep. Then Anita throwing a bucket of ice water on my face, into my bed, at ten o'clock in the morning, saying she was dragging me to brunch. *Ugh, brunch,* I thought, even as she was pulling me out the door, *every line cook's nightmare.*

"Look at this as a blessing in disguise, Kit." She's practically inhaling her pancakes, her usual mile-a-minute, Italian-accented verbal pace barely affected. "No one needs a break more than you. Insurance money will pay for the restaurant. Take the summer off, let the management team rebuild, and you can come back stronger."

"No."

I'm in denial. I fork a piece of her fluffy diner pancakes, even though my eggs and tea are still sitting untouched in front of me.

"Go to a resort on the beach. Soak in the sun and ignore everyone. It'll be great. You haven't taken a vacation in the fourteen years I've known you—this is a great excuse."

"I hate the beach," I retort.

"Doesn't have to be the beach," she continues undeterred, her dozen bracelets clanging and her colorful attire hurting my hungover eyes. "Go to Tokyo and eat your way around the city. Wander through vineyards in France and drink yourself into oblivion. Just take some time off. There's nothing you can do for the restaurant by wallowing in your apartment for months on end."

She doesn't even know John broke up with me yet. I can't help but think that maybe there *was* a problem with my relationship if my best friend is suggesting I leave the city for months and she hasn't even considered what would happen to my boyfriend.

I push that thought out of my mind. It's not important now.

"I could keep busy by working for you?" I ask hopefully.

Her dark eyes stare at me with so much force I worry I'm about to disintegrate. At least that would eliminate my drunken headache.

"I'm perfectly happy at the trattoria with my two line cooks and simple prep. I left that fine dining shit behind me, and *you* are not going to fuck up my happy place—"

"You know some people might say it's rude to imply that having your best friend working with you would be—"

"A best friend who I worked with already. Thank you, but no thank you," she says, cutting me off. "There's a reason you have Michelin stars and profiles in *Food & Wine* and I don't. You're the only executive chef who actually shows up seven days a week at her restaurant. Even T. K. took a day off in the heyday of French Laundry."

I take another piece of her pancakes without looking up. I can't argue with Anita.

We met as lowly line cooks at New York's seafood mecca Le Bernardin right after we'd both graduated culinary school. She was untethered petals blowing in from Italy on a warm breeze, ready to learn something new. I was a determinedly rooted succulent, stoically primed to survive without sunlight, who just wanted to plant myself in the most prestigious restaurants I could find. After a couple of years, Anita abandoned fine dining and went to work in a series of simple but perfect Italian restaurants, until she opened her own. Think four fresh pastas, two meats, and a smattering of appetizers that people go crazy over. She's managed effortless in an always-booked restaurant, and I love her for it.

But that simplicity has never been my goal. I went from Le Bernardin to Masa to learn Japanese technique and then on to an acclaimed French spot, where I was noticed as the chef de cuisine. I wanted to win, whatever "winning" means to a workaholic chef. And I have.

A few years ago I was tapped to become the executive chef of a new restaurant from one of the city's leading hospitality groups. They'd found the ideal space for their vision, inflected with New American,

French, and Japanese influences, and I was apparently the chef with the perfect training to execute. I'm not an owner, but it's still my name and recipes on the menu. It's the kind of opportunity an ambitious chef covets, and it's lived up to every dream, instantly becoming one of the most renowned and hardest-to-get-into restaurants in the city. I've thrived calling the shots. I look forward to every single day.

Until today, I suppose.

"Come on," I harangue Anita, undeterred. "You know I go insane if I'm not busy. I'll keep my mouth shut. I was a sous for years. I can take instructions." I pause, because I'm not looking forward to admitting the one thing that might convince her. "You know I can't ask anyone else."

She snorts—the thought of me approaching any other chef is laughable. My precision, my dedication, my competitiveness, and my fastidiousness are all assets in my kitchen, but they haven't exactly given me a reputation as being collaborative. I never ask anyone for anything. No one would believe that I could shut up and take instruction, even though I lived that hierarchy for a decade before having a space of my own. But I could do it again.

"You're spiraling a little bit, you know that?" she asks, in what has to be the most obvious statement ever made. "You don't need to slum it at someone else's restaurant to be busy."

"I wouldn't say 'slumming it,'" I mutter.

"Yes you would." She shoves the last of the pancakes in her mouth before I've even touched my plate. "You're mourning and in shock simultaneously. But the restaurant will reopen. You'll get a plan together and expedite the work, and you'll be back up and running by the fall. There's nothing you can do about it now, so use the time for something fun."

"It's not that simple."

"It is, though," she says with a shrug. "John'll have some construction crew he overpays working discreetly on nights and weekends to get it done for you as quickly as possible."

Now I'm the one shoveling food in my mouth. I guess my appetite disappearing no longer matters when I need to avoid the ability to speak.

"John and I broke up," I finally say with my mouth full. If I'm not looking at her and can obscure what I'm saying, maybe I'll be able to avoid her incredulity.

But no such luck. She stills.

"What did you just say?"

"You don't even like him," I mumble. It's the defensive equivalent of *I know you are but what am I?*

"When did you break up?"

"Last night."

"Last night after the fire?" Her voice is getting loud.

"Well, *technically* I think the fire was still happening."

"So you were losing it over the restaurant and got in a fight and dumped him?" Her voice is getting louder by the second, and she hasn't even heard the story.

"He dumped me," I say as casually as possible.

"Wait . . . John dumped you while your *restaurant was on fire*?"

"Maybe he didn't know about it."

I look up right as a bread roll comes flying at my face. It hits me in the jaw with a sweet little thud. At least the bread here is soft. I wonder what bakery they get it from?

Anita snaps her fingers in my face at my distraction. "'He didn't know about it'? He's head of one of the city's biggest hospitality groups. He's a personal investor in your restaurant! You think he was hanging around your apartment without a heads-up that everything was going to shit?"

I weigh that thought—one I haven't really had time to consider, with the tequila and the blacking out and the morning headache.

"Well," I say, "he needed a reason to finally admit he was sick of me, so I guess maybe this was as good as any."

Anita's hackles go down, and her whole face softens. I hate that she's always been able to catch my tiniest flecks of weakness on the rare occasions when they leak out, like a restaurant inspector who spots the one out-of-date product in the entire walk-in. No one else clocks those lapses, because at this point everyone else assumes my products are immaculate. Only Anita ever seems to poke at me to prove I'm human.

She's quieter now but still as serious as stone. "Your value has never been tied to that—"

"Save it," I growl, desperately hoping to avoid a pep talk.

"—show clown who love-bombed you and introduced you to his contacts so you'd feel like your value was tied to his skills as a restaurant investor. He didn't elevate you. *You* elevate you. Your talent. Your skills. Your work."

"I'm also pretty good at sex," I quip, trying to throw her off.

But she's not taking the bait. "You don't get to think he's better than you. You've always had the ability to do better than him, and I can't *believe* that little shit dumped *you* when you're a star and he's an empty suit."

"Stop being so nice and just give me some honest feelings, why don't you," I reply, sarcasm dripping while I take a long sip of my tea.

"Kit." My name sounds like a warning coming out of her mouth. But after we stare at each other for a few moments, she clearly decides to drop it. "Are you okay?"

"About John?"

"I guess?" she says.

She's always hated him, so I'm surprised she's not doing a victory dance.

"I'm . . ." I sigh, because I think I know the answer and it's hard to admit it out loud. I bite my already-chewed nails but then rub my hands through my short hair to try and stop myself from succumbing to my least favorite habit.

But with my whole life imploding, I guess it's an acceptable time to be slightly more exposed in front of my best friend. "No one else is ever going to want me for me. I'm not sexy or fun. I'm obsessed with work. I have no other hobbies—happily! I *like* that about myself.

John understood that. He didn't need me, and he never pushed our relationship. We never had to live together; he didn't need date nights; we went to industry events, we had sex, and when we talked, it could be about the restaurant. Maybe that's not like some amazing love story, but it's all I can handle."

You know the poster of *Get Out*, where Daniel Kaluuya's eyes are as wide as humanly possible, conveying both terror and sadness simultaneously? That's what Anita looks like right now. And *this*, this right here, is exactly why I don't share my innermost thoughts with people. They're abnormal and no one wants to hear them.

But before I can let that depressing realization settle, Anita grabs my hand.

"I'm sorry, I really didn't know that's how you saw things," she finally says, and I hate the quiet pity in her voice. "But honey, that's not it. It's fine if you don't need a partner, but love shouldn't ever just be that."

I know she's thinking of her husband and the gooey way they look at each other. It's not that I don't believe in love—I see it. I see *her*. I know people build lasting relationships and that love isn't some farce we're all fed. But she's wrong about me. That *isn't* me. I only love cooking and New York like that—and I've always felt really damn lucky to have two things I *do* love that much.

But there's no way to explain that to someone who can check her passion at the door at the end of a shift and would live wherever life took her.

"I don't want to talk about John, okay?" I say, and she nods, knowing I need to change the subject back to safer ground. "But I do know enough to know that I can't sit around for months waiting for my restaurant to get renovated."

She sits back, and the smile that curves onto her face scares the shit out of me, because I know she thinks she has a solution, and there's no way to stop Anita once she has an idea in her mind.

"I actually have the perfect plan for you," she says, predictably.

"Is it working with you?"

She ignores me and continues. "You want to work. I want you to get away. What about Italia?"

"What about it?" She's spent fourteen years trying to convince me to travel home with her, and I wouldn't have expected her to want a vacation now.

"Nonna needs a summer assistant. Her usual person is out on maternity leave, and it's been a bit chaotic. Why don't you go work for her?"

That wasn't what I was expecting. "Doesn't your grandmother run like a tiny restaurant in a random town in Tuscany?"

"Yes," she replies, daring me to say anything against her beloved nonna.

I try to be as delicate as possible. "Didn't you just say to me that working in *your* restaurant would be slumming it?"

"Yeah, but I don't need help. She does. And besides, she's a legend. You'd learn more from her than you did at Alinea."

"I was shucking oysters and tweezing dill for the entire summer at Alinea, so I don't actually count that as a real culinary learning experience."

"Exactly." Her smile is smug, and I'm panicking a little; after begging for something to do mere moments ago, I now have no legitimate excuses. "You can't pace around the city all summer like a caged tiger, waiting for your restaurant to reopen. And with this, you'd actually learn how to make pasta from scratch, which I still can't believe you ignore as a basic cooking skill."

I roll my eyes at that one. Never get into a conversation with an Italian about food when you were trained on French technique.

"And she won't cut you any slack," she continues. "It wouldn't be a break. She won't care that you have a Beard Award, and she'll be thrilled to work you to death."

It's pathetic how much that thought perks me up.

"You're going," she says, certain that she's got my life all figured out. "Come on, the hard is what makes it great."

"Don't quote *A League of Their Own* at me," I huff. "I introduced you to that damn movie! Italians can't quote baseball things."

"Cooking is what gets inside you!" she gleefully taunts back, doing a pretty terrible Tom Hanks impression and relishing getting under my skin. Or maybe she's relishing lightening the conversation. We've always kept things breezy for each other, and this day has been skating way too close to openness.

"I'll think about it," I finally say.

Outside the diner, we give each other hugs while she continues to yammer in my ear about how her plan is the best idea of all time and I try to ignore the tight feeling in my stomach. Uncertainty is not something I'm used to anymore, and this sudden turn of events has me completely upended.

I walk until I find myself ducking under caution tape around the restaurant and into the burned-out remains of my kitchen.

I don't know what I was expecting, but I'm not prepared for the total disarray that greets me. Everything is either charred from fire or wet from the water that put it out. It's jarring in a place that's usually clean to the point of sterility. Fine dining is nothing if not precision, and the beauty of a perfectly organized stainless steel restaurant kitchen has always been calming. Now, instead, it's anarchy in front of me.

Before today, this room was more home to me than my actual home. It was my happy center nested inside the city that I belong in—the comforting soft interior of a perfectly cooked chocolate lava cake. This room has always been my own personal docking station, where I go to power up, to function, to be at my most potent. Each section is like an extra limb—sauces that I'd hover over to make sure they were perfectly seasoned; seafood that needed to be scorched *just so* to stay deliciously tender; salads that sang with the produce I'd carefully curated from farmers whose numbers I had on speed dial.

And now it's torched.

My phone buzzes with a text, and I pull it out of my pocket. *Ugh, John.*

I already got a call in to our teams in Dubai and Tokyo. I think we could schedule you in three month-long residencies at our properties there and potentially, I'm thinking Singapore but maybe São Paolo could be better. Everyone's really stoked—not about the fire, obviously, but about the opportunity to get you for a chunk of time.

I stare at it, wide eyed. He broke up with me *last night*, and this is what he's texting me today? Like we're simply back to being colleagues?

I scroll down and see I have a text from my dad too.

Kit! I just saw the news! You need a plan of action. How long do they think renovations are going to take?

I cringe as I look at the texts side by side. It hits me for the first time in my life that even though I've worked for everything I've earned, I've *always* allowed a man to clear the path for me. And maybe those weren't the wrong choices in those particular moments, but I hate that that's somehow my default.

This room is suffocating.

I walk outside to get some air, although that's hard to do with an end-of-spring heat wave already making the trash smell. I stand waiting for the light to change and see a guy sitting on the ground with a sign asking for cash. I look in his hat on the sidewalk, upturned and ready for donations, with only a couple of dollar bills and a Korean face mask packet someone's thrown in.

This ridiculous city. I love it so much, even though it spits everyone out. Fast paced, acerbic, funny, intense. So much of it is me.

I pull out a twenty and add it to his pile.

Anita's right. I've gotta get out of here for a little bit; I can't handle my beloved New York with this much ambiguity. I wouldn't survive, even if I called in a favor and worked at someone else's restaurant. The boredom would eat at me. The speed and energy of the city would taunt me. I want to work and do what I'm good at, not think about logistics.

Anita's plan floats to the front of my mind, like a crystal clear door number two. It's a lighthouse tempting me across an ocean. There's a thrill to the idea of rejecting the path everyone assumes I'll embrace. Perhaps the double whammy of losing my restaurant and John is the jolt I actually need to take control and do something that's entirely my decision, suggested by the one person who's never treated our relationship as a transaction.

I want this feeling to go away, and Anita's offering a tailor-made solution.

So I do the first impulsive thing I've ever done in my life. I take out my phone and book a one-way ticket to Rome.

Chapter 2

Magic for me has always been in a kitchen. It's the sound of a sizzling pan. It's the satisfaction of a perfect flavor on your tongue.

I've never found a *landscape* enchanting, for crying out loud.

But looking out the window of the taxi as we wind through southern Tuscany, I have to admit that there's something beguiling about the countryside here.

It's a landscape of pointy conifers, undulating low hills, sunshine-dappled sunflowers, and the silver-green breeze of the olive trees. Top-heavy, thin-trunked trees lean, as though they're deciding whether to follow the wind. Wild brush lines both sides of the road, stretching up as though trying futilely to touch the sky.

My image of Tuscany was always fancy vineyards and cities like Florence or Siena. But Anita explained to me that southern Tuscany, Maremma, is more cowboy and cattle country than an elite enclave. It's farms, olive groves, and wooded preserves flowing south from the base of the volcanic Mount Amiata. It's bracketed by wild rocky seashores and ancient walled Etruscan towns on the hilltops.

An hour and half out from Rome, we reach the town of Manciano, and the drive starts to become comically hemmed in. I'm surprised this tiny car is gunning up these inclines and navigating sharp turns around stone walls that look like they've survived a millennium. But somehow, the taxi driver makes it, and we come to a stop in front of a small house. It's made of patched brick and has an imposing filigreed wooden doorway with a modern doorbell, surrounded by vines covered in bluebells.

"Andiamo," he says as he gets out of the car, then pulls my single giant suitcase from the trunk. I guess this is the address.

I look on the door and see an envelope taped to the front, with *Kit Roth* scribbled in hurried cursive. I open the envelope, and inside is a set of keys: a large one for the front door and another labeled only "#3."

Is this place really so rural that you can leave keys taped to a doorway and no one thinks twice about it?

I say "Grazie" to the driver and open the door. Inside, stone steps lead up an unlit stairwell. I haul my suitcase until I'm on the third-floor landing and unlock the door marked #3.

The apartment is small but clean. The floors are a gray tile, and the walls are covered with framed posters of old Italian films. Anita's cousin has a friend who has a friend who's been looking for a subletter. Apparently this apartment is around the corner from the restaurant owned by her nonna, Gia. For a hastily planned escape, this is as good a place as any to crash.

A door in the living room opens onto a small balcony that puts the whole neighborhood in perspective. That entire gorgeous landscape we drove past opens up in front of me, with low hills dotting the distance. I can see across a lot of the town now, all the burnt orange roof tiles topped with satellite dishes, a stark contrast of old and new. The air is clear, and the memory of the smell of New York is already fuzzy.

I'm some mix of exhausted jet lag and wired adventurer, so I figure I should get outside before I fall asleep. Even with my dislike of coffee, I bet a jolt of caffeine from an espresso would do wonders for me. And then maybe I can find my way to Gia, since Anita said she would be in the restaurant all day.

Sure enough, around the corner is a building with **PASTA FRESCA** written in bold red letters on a white sign. But I figure I'll walk around town for a bit and get my bearings before going inside.

Manciano is quiet, and the small streets are a serene place to meander. The town is beautiful, but it's not a fairy-tale fiction. It's lived in. It's ancient stone next to dented stucco. Wisteria and those bluebells line so many of the buildings, but they also exist next to a neighbor with seventeen kinds of cacti out front in an array of overwrought pottery. It's not the Disneyland frozen-in-time vibes of so many of the small but overtouristed European cities these days. It's charming because it's imperfect and still alive.

I grab an espresso at a coffee shop counter, downing it in one sip to avoid the flavor.

My phone buzzes in my pocket. Fucking John again. I didn't reply to him a few days ago when he texted, but apparently he didn't get the hint.

São Paolo is interested. Give me a call when you have a sec.

Maybe it's the jet lag, but I don't have the patience to ignore him anymore. I hit the call button, and he answers on the first ring.

"This isn't normal," I spit out.

"Good morning to you too," he says. It's early morning in New York, but he's always awake and sharp, like a shark who never stops swimming.

"It's not normal to break up with someone and then the next day start talking about work like nothing happened. You're assuming I'm just . . . fine?!"

There's a moment of silence. "Aren't you?"

"No!"

"You want us to give it a real go?"

I open my mouth, surprised. "No?"

He chuckles, affectionate, and it makes me want to claw his eyes out. "The reason you're not fine," he continues, "is because of the state of your restaurant, not because you're upset about us breaking up. You're pissed at me because you don't like being dumped. But that's not the thing that matters to you here."

I stay silent because it stings that he's being so harsh *and* that it's so true. But I hear him sigh, and I know from the tone of it he's not looking to pick a fight. It's another reason we always went along so smoothly—we never had enough skin in the game to need to fight.

"It's fine, Kit," he says softly. "I knew who you were when we got together."

"What's *that* supposed to mean?" I snap.

"The fact that I could even use the phrase 'give it a real go' after *five years* should be enough. You've never been in it."

"Oh, and you were?"

"I did us both a favor," he says, and I'm surprised to hear a glimmer of sadness in his voice. "People shouldn't simply coast along because it's easy."

"That's not—"

"We're not in love with each other. So *can't* it just be fine? Can't we call it and keep working together and do what we do best? Because that's the part we both actually *do* love, and we're damn good at it." He pauses, but I'm too stunned to say anything. So he barrels on. "Let me figure out getting the restaurant fixed. Let me figure out places for you to work this summer so you're not bored. The restaurant group will get a chance to promote you and bring attention back here when you reopen."

He lets the silence sit now. And I feel . . . *gross*. Because the truth is, he's not wrong. About any of it.

And that's the part that feels the grossest. Did I let passion for my work completely overtake the need for passion for anything else? Did my ambition and my love of New York let me autopilot other parts of my life to the point where the assumption is I'll steer wherever I'm told?

I look around the town surrounding me, ancient and opposite of everywhere I was mere hours ago. And I've never been more convinced I've made the right choice.

"You can get the restaurant back in order," I finally say, determination steeling me. "But I'm not doing bullshit pop-ups for a bunch of rich dudes across the world so I can be paraded around like a company asset. I'm working for Anita's grandmother for the summer."

"Anita's grandmother?" I *so* wish I could see his face right now. "Where the hell is she? Some random town in Italy?"

"I'm going to learn how to make pasta."

"Oh, this is some *Eat, Pray, Love* bullshit?" he says, all the kumbaya rationality of his previous attempts to placate me clearly torched by my refusal to go along with what he wants. "You can't force it, Kit. You're not going to suddenly find peace in a pasta bowl."

"You're such a condescending asshole," I retort. "Let me know when my restaurant is ready for my return. Until then, don't text me again. I'm in Maremma."

"You're already—"

But I don't wait to hear him finish. I gleefully hang up the phone and make my way back through the town.

Until I'm standing in front of Pasta Fresca again.

The door is open when I arrive. Anita wasn't kidding when she said it was simple. There are two small wooden tables outside and six inside. The walls are all that same mismatched, slightly crumbling brick I've seen on so many buildings here. There's a big fan, ugly mustard-color curtains, and bottles of wine lining racks on the wall. Drying ingredients like salami and garlic hang from the rafters like extra decor.

"Are you coming back, or what?" I hear a forceful voice call out from the kitchen in an Italian-inflected accent, but with clear control over her English.

I walk over to a swinging door and peek my head in. The smallest, oldest woman I've ever seen is rolling out pasta dough on a long wooden table that's dusted with flour. A hand-cranked pasta machine is bolted to the end of the table, and rollers and stamps for various pasta shapes are strewn around. There's one large gas range, a lot of hanging pots and pans, and more bags of flour than I've ever seen, stacked on every shelf and in every corner.

"Nonna Gianna?"

"Just call me Gia," she says curtly, then takes a moment to divide the dough into sections. "So, you made it in one piece?"

"Yup."

She stops working and looks me up and down. "You don't look like a great chef," she mutters, as much to herself as to me, wiping her hands on the weathered white apron she's wearing that goes almost to her knees.

I like that she's already giving me shit. That, at least, makes this tiny room feel like a kitchen. "Not up to your standard?" I give back.

"Anyone ever tell you you kind of resemble a bug?"

I snort a laugh. "Any bug in particular?"

She actually takes a moment to think about it, and I respect that. "What do you call those ones, the long ones with the big eyes that pray?"

"Praying mantis?"

She snaps her fingers and points at me, like I've solved the mystery.

I have to admit, from that level of bluntness, she's a real chef. So there's only one way to play this and survive.

"Maybe I look long to you because you're so short?" The tone is saccharine, but the intention is clear.

She shrugs and starts to take one section of dough over to the pasta machine. "You're still tall for a girl, even if I *am* a raisin at this point."

At that, a laugh can't help but burst out, and she rolls her eyes, as though I'm enjoying this too much. To prove the point, she immediately hands me a bag of onions.

"Dice these, as small as you can. Your station can be over there." She points to a small table crammed in the corner. It's even lower than hers, so I know she's aware it'll be too short for me.

But I'm okay with a bit of hazing. This is nothing.

I pull a wooden cutting board toward me (there's no plastic anywhere, and I'm definitely not going to be the fool who asks her) and lay out my knife roll. I pull out my chef's knife and quickly sharpen it on my steel. Then I get started.

As I dice onions (then tomatoes; then pick thyme; then shell pistachios), I watch her work. Her knobbled fingers must be hurting, but she shows no sign of slowing down. She's a machine. She hand cranks pasta into perfect flat sheets. She stuffs and stamps out ravioli. She extrudes long noodles from another hand-cranked machine. She watches over sauces that are slowly simmering on the range, richness and fresh herbs colliding to permeate the heavy air.

We pass a few hours like that, listening to a radio tuned to a classic station of Italian songs from another era. She only speaks to me to give me a new task.

The funniest part is that occasionally I hear people walk into the restaurant and open a fridge that must be in the dining room. They shout some version of "Thanks!" in Italian and then walk out without coming into the kitchen to bother her.

I guess I'll have to figure out what that's about on another day, since she doesn't seem inclined to say anything about it.

Finally at around six she looks up at an old clock on the wall and wipes her hands on her apron.

"Customers come starting at nineteen o'clock. Now we take a break and I smoke."

She walks out, and I hurry to wash my hands and follow her. She sits at one of the outdoor tables and beckons me to do the same. It's still warm outside, even if there's a shadow from the sun beginning to dip down.

"So what's the schedule?" I ask, shaking my head no when she offers me a cigarette. I've never understood chefs who smoke—why would you possibly want to dull your palate?—but so many do. It's funny seeing this tiny, overworked little grandma smoke, though.

"I come in at noon sharp. I make the pasta for pickups and also get some of the dough ready for later. Then we do dinner prep, as you saw today."

"Oh, so you take orders for fresh pasta to go as well?" Maybe that explains the fridge raiders.

"There's no orders," she scoffs, her deep voice now making more sense, as a smoker. "I make what I make and that's it. People come and look in the fridge, and whoever gets it first gets it. They leave cash in the drawer. Then we do dinner and we cook until we're out. Simple."

"What if someone has a request or an allergy?"

She scoffs again and then takes a big drag of her cigarette. "We don't do this here."

I get the sense there's not going to be any more explanation than that. So I change the subject.

"Do you live in this neighborhood too?"

"No. Cassero's not for me. Too busy. I like the countryside."

"Cassero?" I ask, sidestepping the humor of an almost entirely empty area being described as "too busy."

"Si. Manciano has different rioni . . ." She pauses, clearly trying to come up with the English word. Her English is so perfect that aside from her accent, I've almost forgotten I'm in another country. "Neighborhoods? Or districts? I don't know. Anyway, the rione inside the medieval walls is called Cassero, after the large tower."

"Is it a good area to live in?" I ask, the realization hitting me of how little I actually know about this place I've moved to for the next few months.

"You know, the old town of Manciano has historically been called the 'Spy of Maremma,'" she says with a smirk, butting out her cigarette on the ground as she stands up. "It's because from up on this hill, you can see practically all of Maremma, all the way to the sea on one side and all the way to Mount Amiata on the other. But I think the name's more fitting because everyone's in everyone else's business all the time."

At that she gets up and walks back inside.

I guess break time is over.

Chapter 3

For the next week, I forcibly shake myself into a new routine—like mulching over weathered crops to make room for whatever new ones need to come up. Being in a kitchen where I'm not in charge isn't as strange as I would have thought; I did it for years, and I can do it again. I might still be numb from my entire life imploding, but on the plus side, there's something satisfying about showing up for work and being treated like an automaton.

Gia hasn't let me touch anything related to pasta dough yet, but I'm glad, since in any new kitchen it's always necessary to start with grunt work. And I'm damn good at passing whatever tests are placed in front of me. I prep ingredients, grab supplies, scrub down the kitchen, and even buy her cigarettes once when she runs out.

Being reliable for Gia is the only thing I'm focused on. I don't need to find myself on an Italian adventure of self-reflection, or whatever bullshit John tried to lob at me. I want to get to a place where I actually learn something about my craft from an elderly expert (fine, yes, after tasting her pasta I can confirm she's as absurdly good as Anita said). I'm going to focus on that for the rest of the summer until my restaurant is fixed. This is all I need.

In the mornings I sit on my balcony, read food books I've wanted to catch up on, and drink tea (since I'm guessing drinking tea in espresso country would get me the side-eye at any café). From noon until around eleven at night, I'm in the restaurant.

And okay, sometimes I'm in before noon too. It doesn't hurt to keep things spotless in a kitchen.

Which is how I find myself at 11:30 a.m. standing on a ladder, rocking out to Olivia Rodrigo's healthy dose of man angst while cleaning off the high shelves that store the giant bags of flour.

I've decided it's necessary because dust and flour obviously look similar. And I'd bet anything that Gia never actually has anyone clean these shelves off. She's probably had some lumbering delivery guys stacking these fifty-pound bags for decades, without ever looking at what's accumulated. So in the interest of being the kind of proactive, helpful chef that I am, I'm making good use of the dustpan and brush to clear away years of potential contaminants that have probably been infiltrating Gia's perfect pasta.

The only thing I haven't anticipated is someone touching me.

With my (stupid, I'm now realizing) noise-canceling headphones, I didn't hear anyone come in, and the shock of a light touch on my ankle jolts me. I automatically grab at the most stable thing I can find, which, unfortunately, is a bag of flour that happens to not be particularly stable.

I crash onto the floor, followed swiftly by the giant bag of flour that explodes on contact, creating a cloud that expands into the air and lingers while I'm flat on my ass like a total idiot.

I take out my headphones and am immediately bombarded with an apology from a figure I can barely make out through the smoky hanging flour. Or at least I think it's an apology, based on the tone and speed of his words.

"I don't speak Italian," I cough out.

I see him nod through the haze.

"Right, right, you're Gia's new chef, yeah? I'm *so* sorry." I know I haven't met this man, because his accent is unfamiliar—he's somehow both Italian but clearly a native English speaker. "I was looking for Gia and you didn't respond and I didn't realize your headphones were so . . . all-encompassing? You were sort of singing along and I didn't want to startle you if you saw me, but now I'm realizing I startled you even more."

I wipe my face and look up. You've *got* to be kidding me.

I'm covered in flour, I got busted for screech-singing at work, my ass is probably going to have a bruise the size of a melon on it tomorrow, and the guy this all happened in front of is *extremely* good looking.

Let's leave aside the fact that he's jacked and seems to be so tall that he's noticeably taller than me (which happens *so* rarely), but his oval face is curtained by the kind of dark, flowing devil-may-care hair that a nineties boybander would've killed for. His jaw is lined with perfectly unperfect day-old scruff, and right above his upper lip is a small beauty mark I can't tear my eyes from.

I think maybe now I'm staring?

Did I hit my head? Why am I *noticing* so much?

I see hot men all the time—I live in New York and I run a high-end restaurant, for crying out loud. So it's surprising how much this guy is affecting me just by looking at me. It's unsettling.

But maybe this is what happens after getting dumped and then having a moment away from my routine in a new country, on a new learning curve. I'm probably noticing *all* men more.

He, of course, isn't contemplating anything about me other than how he's going to get this bedraggled, flour-covered beanpole off the floor. His brow is furrowed with concern, and it would be cute if it wasn't aimed at my complete ineptitude, which I have a deep urge to explain is very unusual for me.

I ignore the throbbing pain of my side and try to stand up with as much dignity as I can muster. Or as much dignity a person can have while brushing off fifty pounds of flour surrounding them.

"It's fine," I say with a casual air that probably doesn't fit how ridiculous I look. "I'm Kit Roth, by the way."

I hold out my hand, and he takes it, still seeming suspicious that I might actually *not* be fine. But my brain zeroes in on how much I feel his hand envelop mine, and the sensation sparks right into my veins.

My hands have always been stronger than people expect—calloused, burned, and scarred from years in the kitchen. It makes most men grip hard. They always subconsciously have something to prove with a woman like me. But his hands are as rough as mine on the surface, strong, but the grip is gentler. It's firm, but open. My body seems to absorb every place he's touching me.

Our hands stay clasped for a beat too long. He's watching me and I stare back, both momentarily transfixed. Maybe he's watching because he's concerned that the woman who fell off a ladder has a concussion, but I can't stop myself from looking into this man's dark eyes.

"I'm Nico Ruspoli. And, uh . . . I'll help you clean this up," he says, finally breaking eye contact as my pulse continues to boom inexplicably. But I must be going completely insane, because I'm rooted to the floor while he's moving again, grabbing a kitchen towel and then wiping off the flour I've gotten all over him.

Right. Cleaning up. Shit. Who the hell am I in this moment? It's pathetic and extremely unlike me. Gia's going to come in soon, and this definitely does not live up to the example I want to be setting.

I pull myself together and get the broom while Nico grabs a trash bag. We silently sweep up, and for a minute it seems fruitless—that cloud of flour still hangs in the air with every attempt to get it into the bag. But eventually we start making progress.

"How are you liking working for Gia?" Nico asks, once we're nearing the end of the cleanup and our focus can stray enough to talk again.

"I've only been here a week," I deflect.

"Meaning?"

"Oh . . ." Here I was thinking this was small talk and it didn't matter. "I don't like to pass judgment too early. She's still testing me out. I'm a glorified kitchen scut at this point, so I'm happy to pay the dues."

He nods, taking that in.

"You're living in Matteo's apartment?"

Well, I guess Gia wasn't kidding about everyone knowing everyone else's business.

"Yup," I reply, realizing my reputation is probably preceding me all over town, but I know nothing about this guy. "Do you live in Manciano too?" I ask, trying to pry just enough that he won't notice.

He's wiping his hands off again, and it's frustrating to be unwittingly jealous of a dish towel.

"No, I live outside town. Near Gia, actually. I never wanted to live inside these walls, you know?"

These people really seem to think this tiny town is some giant metropolis.

"Well, I haven't ventured outside the walls yet, so I wouldn't know. Have any advice for me?" I ask.

"Oh, you'll love visiting all the farms and producers around here," he says, his eyes on me again.

"I'll love that, huh?" I quip with a smirk.

"I thought you were a chef?" he says, a small amused smile blooming. The look he's giving me is pure—interested—delight.

Is he flirting? I can hardly tell what flirting might look like anymore. Working in a kitchen makes me so used to everyone's bluntness and teasing that I would barely register it. I only talk to men to yell at them about things like whether an order is being fired. The best part about being in a relationship was getting to be completely oblivious to any man's interest.

But his eyes flicker to the curve of my mouth, and it's a look that could stun an elephant. That slight movement has my heart pounding in my chest again. As though the silk of his look alone is worth more to my body than running a mile.

"I thought you were a . . ." I come up blank, all my mental energy working to keep my internal flutterings from showing on my exterior. "Sorry, I have no retort to that," I say, and his laugh is a burst that's all exhale, surprised by the honesty but filled with joy. It puts me at ease even as my pulse still races. "I actually have no idea who you are, Nico Ruspoli."

I'm drawn in to the way his lips rise, amused, curious. The way his smile goes the whole distance to those eyes that are watching me so pointedly.

But before he can say anything else, we're interrupted. "He's my grandson-in-law," Gia grunts, "and he's here to bother me and distract me from actually getting work done." She blusters into the room and puts down a bag of herbs that look like they came straight from her garden.

Oh, *shit.*

Grandson-in-law.

This must be the husband of one of Anita's many cousins. And that instantly halts any thoughts of flirtation, like one of those steel security gates you noisily pull over a shop to close up at night. I might be a lot of bad things, but home-wrecker isn't one of them. Damn Europeans and their frequent disinterest in wedding rings—that always throws me. Whatever vibe I must've been getting from him clearly only had to do with my lonely, horny brain and nothing from him. *So much for having any game post-John whatsoever.*

And as if to put the point on it finely, Nico only has eyes for Gia now, leaning over her table and smiling in her space while she bustles, getting organized.

"I wanted to swing by to tell you about the importer I met who wants to see my filter. Someone gave him my info, and he stopped by the frantoio. It was a really interesting conversation, and I wanted your advice."

"I'll come by tomorrow. Right now I'm cooking," she says, and she swats at him, although it seems to come from a well of affection rather than annoyance.

He salutes her like a private taking instructions from his general and then turns back to me. "It was really nice to meet you, Kit Roth," he says, my name slow and deliberate. "I hope I see you around—and I promise I won't tell Gia about the bag of flour we destroyed."

With a wink he walks out, and I barely notice as Gia rolls her eyes, because I'm trying so hard to be the normal version of myself that should be rolling my eyes too.

Chapter 4

Monday is the only day Gia closes the restaurant. I have the whole day off, since my offers to come in and do cleaning or prep work were met with a terse locking of the front door and instructions to not come back until Tuesday.

My usual morning of sitting on my balcony and reading cookbooks with tea suddenly isn't enough. Maybe it's knowing the whole day is stretching in front of me with nothing to do. I guess I eventually have to stop pretending that I'm living my normal life with a normal restaurant job.

I should go out.

But baby steps. I walk outside the main walls of the town and see a street lined with little shops. A few older people sit on plastic chairs, animated and gesticulating. It reminds me of people on stoops in New York, only they've pulled over their own chairs instead of having one built in. It projects a certain rustic charm that has me waving at everyone. They wave right back—and look at me gleefully in a way that makes it clear they know who I am.

The shops are all lovely in their simplicity. The flower shop, named Piante e Fiori, is next to a cheese store named Casa del Formaggio. There's an alimentari on the corner selling produce and other groceries. Across the street on the edge is a pasticceria named Belpagna.

I could certainly go for some pastries. I walk into Belpagna, and a small bell chimes above the door, but none of the customers sitting at small tables with café chairs even notice. It's busy but in a muted way, like this is the calm place where everyone can gather.

I notice reams of awards and magazine articles lining the wall. For it being such a small-town shop, I'm surprised this place has garnered so much attention.

"Would you like something?" I hear a voice say behind me in English, and I turn to the counter. A woman with a dark bob pulled back with a blue top-knotted bandana is staring straight at me. Her angular face is a sharp contrast to the twee hairstyle.

"How'd you know I speak English?" I say, curious.

She raises one eyebrow with a sly look. "You haven't figured out yet that everyone in this town knows you, even if you don't know them?"

I laugh and walk closer to the counter, surveying the case filled with pastries. "I *have* noticed that, yes. It's a bit jarring."

"That's what happens when a famous chef comes to a boring town with nothing else to talk about." Now it's my turn to raise an eyebrow, but she immediately volleys back: "What part of that do you disagree with? Maybe you haven't ventured enough to know we're boring yet. But you of all people aren't going to argue with 'famous chef,' no?"

I like how she's baiting me a bit.

"Not going to argue with anything," I say with a smile. "I'm mostly interested in eating whatever you're making, since it seems like you're a bit of a hit yourself." I gesture to her wall of accolades, and she grins. I wasn't going to pretend I don't know I'm a well-known chef (in the circles that care about chefs), and apparently she's not going to downplay her own success.

I like her already.

She pulls out a plate and puts three items on it. "Sugar bombolone, pistachio cream–filled sfogliatella, and a slice of apricot ricotta cake. My husband Antonio makes all the gelato—do you want an affogato?"

There it is. I knew there was no chance I could make an Italian acquaintance without immediately being shunned for not liking coffee, even if it is poured over gelato. But might as well bite the bullet and be honest.

"Actually, I was wondering if you have tea."

I brace for the reaction, but she simply says "Of course," then grabs a tea bag and pours hot water over it.

"I thought Italians only drink coffee?" I ask, wondering about her nonresponse.

"Eh, most do, but you aren't Italian, so what do I care."

I nod, enjoying the backhanded acceptance, and pull out my wallet. "What do I owe you?"

She waves me off, as though I'm insulting her.

"Please, I'm glad to have you in my pasticceria. Sit at that counter and eat your pastries so I don't have to feel bad when I make you commiserate with me later."

"Thank you . . ." I pause, but she catches on quick.

"Emilia."

"Thank you, Emilia."

I do as instructed and pull my plate over to sit at one of the stools against the counter. I take a bite of the sfogliatella and practically melt. Each little layer of the pastry is like a light fluff of carb heaven, brought together by the velvet airiness of the pistachio cream inside. The whole thing is gone in under a minute.

"You really aren't messing around here," I say with my mouth still a bit full. "This is incredible."

"Coming from you, that's a real compliment," she replies, leaning against the counter opposite me.

"Have you spent any time in New York?" I ask. She seems to be more familiar with me than I would expect of any chef in Italy.

"Oh yeah, I love New York. I grew up in Milan, so it's a bit of a kindred spirit. I ate at your restaurant a few years ago, and it was practically a religious experience."

I'm used to people complimenting my food, but there's something about this woman and her no-nonsense demeanor paired with really fucking incredible pastry skills that makes the compliment particularly satisfying.

"I appreciate that. One pastry in and I might say the same for you."

She smiles that sly smile again, confidence brimming. She wanders over to her espresso machine and makes herself a small cup and then comes back to the counter. No one else is currently ordering anything, so she can take advantage of the lull to have a break of her own.

"I was sorry to read that your restaurant had a fire. But I do have to ask why you decided to spend time in Manciano of all places?"

It's the fairest of questions. I think no one else has asked me yet because I haven't allowed myself to speak to anyone other than Gia for more than a minute at a time. But for some reason, now I want to. I find myself explaining it all to her—and not only the sanitized version I would've expected, but the whole thing. I tell her about John breaking up with me, and Anita pushing me out the door to Gia. I give her the rundown of the scut work I've been doing since arriving, and she seems to enjoy that part the most.

"Gia doesn't cut anyone slack, so I'm not surprised she hasn't let you touch the pasta yet. But I bet you like working for someone who isn't impressed by you." She finishes the espresso and eyes me.

"Yeah, I think it's actually my more natural state, to be proving myself." I shrug, caught, but sort of thrilled to be able to speak honestly. "I like to work and I like a challenge. So this was better than any New York kitchen where there would be expectations."

"Do you like living in New York?"

I try to think of how to possibly explain my relationship with my city. "So," I start, "there's this comedian, Billy Eichner, who does these abrupt, sort of rude-man-on-the-street interviews. And one time he goes up to this woman and is like, 'How does it feel to be an elitist, New York piece of shit?' And without batting an eye she goes, 'It feels awesome.'" Emilia laughs, and the sound makes me smile. "And that's kind of how I see my life. I know New York is a weird city and we're all sort of snobs about everything, but we work hard and we *are* good at whatever we do, so it's kind of great if that's what you're into."

She nods along, a smile still playing on her lips, but she seems to not be surprised in the least. "Yeah, it's a special quality of New Yorkers that you share with the Milanese. But we're ruder I think. We wouldn't even answer someone accosting us on the street. Now in *Manciano*, phew, your Billy Eichner would get pulled onto a chair and have someone talk his ear off for an hour about the pros and cons of life." There's tenderness in both observations, as though both locations hold a key to her heart. "So you're a New Yorker, then."

I nod. "Yeah, I've lived there for almost twenty years now. I didn't grow up in New York, but I've always known in my bones that it's my place. My demeanor fits it. I'm blunt, but I'm not complicated. I say what I mean. I don't go back on my word. I gain energy from crowds. I feel like that's a pretty good summary of a New Yorker."

"But you needed a break?"

"Forced into one," I say dismissively.

"So when they rebuild, it'll all be the same as before?" she asks. "Your kitchen, your menu?"

"I'm sure I'll have a few new things to add that I've learned here," I say, that familiar itch to create always present.

"But always NYC for you," she says with a smile.

"Yeah." Even though I'm enjoying this town, nothing warms me like the thought of home.

"And then what?"

"After I'm back?" I ask.

"No." She shakes her head. "I mean later. Like, in five years."

I fidget with a napkin. "Well . . . I hope eventually the restaurant group will make me a co-owner in something I get to design," I say, surprised by my honesty. I haven't even admitted that to Anita. But something about Emilia's bluntness makes me comfortable handing over my story the same way she's easily handed over her sfogliatella. "But that goal really is years away—I'm still paying my dues."

"That's like the final video game level for you," she says, understanding.

"And I'm just happy to be in the game," I chuckle.

"Winning the game on double speed," she counters. But then tilts her head. "Well, maybe with a side quest after a fire."

That knocks a real laugh out of me. "You get it."

I take a bite of the bombolone and have a similar reaction as with the first pastry. A delectable dusting of sugar tops an airy ball of dough. I'm in love.

"Shit, where did you learn how to do this?" I ask, staring at the remains on my plate like they hold the secrets to the universe.

She laughs. "I went to culinary school in Roma. And everybody has a nonna, but mine was a better cook than others."

"I don't have a nonna," I point out.

She shakes her head. "You have Gia now. Anyone who's schooling you that hard has intentions of being your adoptive nonna."

I think she's reading too much into it, but I'm not going to say that to the one person here who I could possibly see myself hanging out with and/or stealing pastries from.

A customer comes in, and Emilia wanders away to help them, but soon she's back, leaning over the counter again and ready to chat. I'm surprised to be so relieved. But I guess I'm used to chef chats in my restaurant, and without a big staff it's been unknowingly missing from my life.

"So did you get a bike or something for while you're here?" she asks.

I take a sip of my tea. I want to answer diplomatically. "I'm not exactly a bike kind of gal. I don't really see myself pedaling along the countryside."

But Emilia laughs again. "No, I meant like a scooter or Vespa of some kind. Unless you plan to buy a car. How're you getting around?"

I pick at my short nails, a little embarrassed to not have thought anything through. "I'm not really."

"Not what?"

"Not . . . getting around. I've been in the restaurant and I've been in my apartment and I haven't left the town."

"That's pathetic," she says before wandering away again to get gelato for a customer. When she comes back, she levels me with a look. "You can't live here without some mode of transportation. It's mental suicide. You have to be able to get out and explore when you have time off."

"I don't want time off," I grumble. I get another stare, and I'm guessing that's a pretty effective tactic with her husband and whoever else she deals with on a daily basis. Her dark eyes are naturally a little downturned, so she has an air of dubiousness that radiates off her naturally.

"You can't live in this ridiculous tiny place and not take it in a bit."

"You think a scooter is the answer?" I ask, considering the thought. It *would* be pretty badass. Emilia nods her head and keeps staring me down. "I wouldn't even know where to begin, though," I say honestly, probably encompassing more than just my lack of transportation.

"Flavia!" I hear Emilia bark across the room to a small older woman, followed by a string of Italian I obviously can't follow.

Flavia has an animated response to whatever Emilia is saying, and after a bit of back-and-forth, they both turn to me.

"Okay, you can rent Flavia's husband's scooter for the summer if you want," she says, the casual solution as much a foregone conclusion as it is a surprise to me.

"Won't her husband miss it?" I ask.

"Oh no, he either died or is pretending to have died, so he won't need it anymore."

I . . . don't really have a response to that, but I guess it's probably better not to ask.

I see Flavia pop up and walk out, and I have no idea whether I've offended her or if she's happy about whatever is happening.

"She's going to grab it," Emilia explains.

"Now?" I say, suddenly not quite sure I'm ready to lose my main excuse for being a hermit.

"Sure. She says you can cook her dinner a few times and call it even."

"I can't just take someone's scooter."

"Why not? You're related to Gia."

"I'm not *related* to Gia."

"Yeah, but in the context of everyone here, you are. It's fine, he's not using it, and it needs some new juju. And I think so do you."

An argument is on the tip of my tongue, but Emilia is shooting me that same look from earlier that clearly is her go-to when she wants to get her way. And I *do* need to figure out how to get around eventually. I can't argue with the convenience of someone's estranged husband's abandoned scooter. I certainly understand the sentiment of wanting to rid yourself of someone else's memories.

So I suppose I can just go along with it.

"Okay," I say, trying to muster the appropriate enthusiasm for someone who's instantaneously solved one of my most externally apparent issues. "That's quite a convenient solution for me, so thanks. What else can we manifest? Can you help me go frolic in an olive grove? Because those trees have been calling my name."

The bell above the door rings again, and I see glee written all over Emilia's face. "I think you really are making things happen today!" she says.

I turn and stop short when I realize who she's looking at. Nico has sauntered in, and I hate that his presence makes the air crackle to attention instantly. He's looking, once again, like a snack left out on the counter to tempt me. *Great.*

"Vorrei un caffè, per favore," he says to Emilia, who immediately bounces over to start his espresso. Nico turns to me, and a smile takes over his whole face. "Hello again."

His expression is so earnest. His energy radiates calm, and yet all he does is make me edgy. I should say hello back, but I think his presence has stunned me into silence. I should've figured I'd run into him again, but I've been trying to *not* let my mind wander in the direction it keeps wanting to go. He's wearing beat-up jeans and a flannel shirt with the sleeves rolled up in a way that clearly was haphazard but now has the effect of accentuating everything. I have to look past him so I don't stare. Whatever this man sets off in my body, I need to ignore it.

I'm saved by Emilia, who sets the small espresso cup in front of Nico with panache when she returns. "Kit was just saying to me how she wanted to see some olive groves, and you walked right in. Do you have time to take her?"

"Sure, of course," he says back, with a nonchalance that's hard to fathom. "It's summer, so you know there's barely anything happening."

"Uh, hello?" I interject. "I don't even have a way to get anywhere yet."

But at that moment Flavia walks back in and tosses me a set of keys. She says something in quick Italian and then wanders back out.

"Your ride is parked outside," Emilia translates.

I look out the window and see a matte-marigold scooter haphazardly parked on the street, its character etched into all the nicks I can see even from a distance.

"I . . ." This is a lot for one day after effectively being in solitude for a week, outside of Gia. I turn to Nico. "You really don't have to show me anything. I was simply making small talk with Emilia."

"You're not interested in olive oil?" he asks, leaning toward me and fixing me with that same focused, still gaze that's been running in my mind on a loop ever since we met. His proximity and his attention make me feel like a fish being lured in. He's magnetic, and yet the worst part is, since that earnest expression is back, he clearly doesn't even know it. Hot men who don't know they're hot are true kryptonite.

But I imagine, if he's married to one of Gia's granddaughters in a town where everyone knows everyone, no one flirts with him either. So maybe he doesn't even realize how much the way he watches me feels like interest.

"Oh no, I am," I say, still attempting to ignore whatever his eyes are doing to my insides. "But I just don't want to bother you. I don't even really know what you do?" It's a weak excuse but not inaccurate.

"He makes the only olive oil worth a damn here," Emilia cuts in.

A small blush rises on Nico's cheeks, and it makes him even more endearing. Most men would've said it themselves if it was remotely close to the truth. And even with my limited knowledge of Emilia, one thing is clear: She certainly wouldn't proclaim it if it wasn't accurate. I wish I could pretend like I don't want to know more, but I do.

And thankfully Emilia keeps talking. "He's so rigid during production you'd think he was managing a nuclear bomb. It's like the steadiness of a chef handling an ingredient, but with a mechanical engineering degree. And last season he engineered his own filtration system to reduce particulates even more than any other commercially available one."

Okay, now I'm intrigued on a professional level, which means I'm better able to shake off my inexplicable physical nonsense and actually focus on excitement of the food variety. "I didn't even know most producers use a filter," I say. "I thought they racked the oil and let the particulates sink down?"

I'm not immune to the excitement that takes over his face when he registers that I might actually be able to nerd out on this with him. Damn, this man wears every emotion so visibly.

"Most rack, yes, but a lot are also filtering. We actually do both, even though most people who filter just do that from the start and move on. We rack for a week before using the filter, and I believe it's created a smoother product. I'm mostly grateful that Emilia agrees with me, because I'm not sure I'd trust anything if she didn't."

He gives her a warm smile, and she pats his hand, like a proud friend. The blunt demeanor she wears naturally seems to slide a bit when she's talking to him, like he tugs at everyone's tough edges.

"So yours is the one Gia must use?" I ask, putting two and two together. I know she uses something local, since it comes in unmarked jugs, but she said so little about Nico the other day when he stopped by that I've had no idea.

"Obviously Gia wouldn't use anything else," Emilia cuts in again. He blushes a little more, and I wish I didn't notice the way it creeps past the stubble of his face and ever so slightly onto the curve of his neck.

"So you want to come see the groves?" He's deftly changing the subject, but I understand why.

"Sure," I respond, my curiosity to learn about olive oil production overtaking my innate twitchiness around this particular man. Maybe it's against my better judgment, but if he's Gia's grandson-in-law, then I'm going to have to get over this little giddy attraction real quick anyway. Better to start now.

"Can you actually drive, though?" he asks, nodding out the window to the scooter waiting for me.

"Only one way to find out, right?"

Chapter 5

It turns out that riding a scooter is *not* like riding a bike.

Poor Nico. This guy clearly has the patience of a saint. My little marigold scooter is not as sweet as she appears. Figuring out how to go forward without going *too fast forward*, and turning enough but not *too much*, is a process. It's a process that takes me at least twenty minutes to practice enough where I'm comfortable going on a real road.

I'd guess it normally should take less than ten minutes to drive to Nico's farm, but I'm grateful he's not in a rush, because having me accompany him has stretched that time significantly. When we finally pull up into the driveway of a small house, I take off the helmet Flavia left with the bike. It was kind of her to include it, even though it's clearly made for a large man who's never used it, and seems more like a liability than a safety measure. I guess finding a store with a helmet that fits is my next activity in a day that's been much more eventful than I initially hoped.

But when I remove the key to get my rumbly new ride to turn off, all those thoughts dissipate as I'm blanketed by the quiet here. Nico's house is like an entryway; fields with olive trees as far as the eye can see stretch behind us. But it all starts at a little friendly stone cottage with a rounded wooden door. It's more whimsical than the houses in town: more bowed and singular. There's a beaten-up wooden outdoor table with chairs off to the side, and a few boulders that seem to be for sitting and staring into the groves. It's all so beautiful in its simplicity, tucked away from town like a shell you find hidden on a beach.

"You feel okay after that ride?" Nico asks, and I turn back toward him.

"Oh sure," I bluster. "Once I got the hang of it."

"You did great," he says kindly. "It takes a bit of practice to get used to anything new." *Ain't that the truth.*

"Is this all your land?" I ask, changing the subject.

"Yeah, it is now," he says as he starts walking around the house. I follow, and we walk for a few minutes in companionable silence until we're deeper in among the trees. He projects a stillness that fits with the seemingly unending nature of the grove. And the setting makes my body calm down a little bit around him, which I'm exceptionally grateful for.

"So," he finally says. "This is sort of all there is to an olive grove. There isn't much action here." His words are unnecessarily modest. No one would need action here, since it's so incredibly beautiful.

Weedy, vivid green grass lines the sloping ground, and every few feet is a gnarled bushy olive tree. They look like a character you'd fall in love with from a Tim Burton movie—slightly gangly and awkward in their stance but impossible not to feel affection for. Maybe it's the fact that their leaves are almost like needles. It gives the trees a dichotomy of being lush and thinned. And their silver-green color makes them seem muted next to the vibrancy of the grass surrounding the trees.

Up close, the trunks are a lighter ashy color, more bent and rippled than the typical base of a tree. And across every defined spindly branch are tiny globes, waiting to ripen, grow, and become recognizable as olives.

"I've never looked at olive trees this close before. They're kind of unusual," I remark.

He gives me a soft smile, seeming to understand that it was a compliment and enjoying my realization. "Yeah, there really isn't anything else like an olive tree. For one, they grow all over the world, in many climates and soils. And second, they're true survivors. They don't need humans or any special intervention to make them thrive. If there's a drought, they don't die; the olives are just a bit smaller that season. They're pretty incredible plants, really."

"So what exactly do they need you for?" I rib.

He barks out a laugh and gives me a mischievous grin. "I think that all the time. There's not much to do here eleven months out of the year, other than watch the trees grow. We can't do anything more than leave them alone, and whatever the weather is that year, then that's what it is. Some of the oldest trees here are eight hundred to a thousand years old, so it would be ridiculous to think we're actually doing anything."

"Which ones?" I ask, curious. He starts walking, and I naturally follow.

We get to a more open field, with the trees spaced a little farther apart. These trees are a bit wider, more pocks and winding roots, the age showing in the beauty of their curves. "Do they still produce as many olives?"

"Oh yeah," he says. "There doesn't seem to be much of a difference once they've reached maturity."

"So seriously, what's the point of you?" I cheekily press, and he gives me that loud barking laugh again. It does something to me, that laugh, as though it fills me up with its joy and makes me want to get it out of him another time.

"None, really. My job is all in making the oil. I think that's where the real differences come in, frankly. The olives are important but not as important as what you do with them to get oil."

"How often do you make the oil?"

"We basically do everything in one month."

"That's it?" I exclaim. "For the whole year?"

"Yeah, in October we harvest our own trees and we get in others' harvests to the mill, and we're making the oil for about a month. That's our oil for the year—we have a distributor who sells it once it's bottled. But yeah . . . there's not much more to it."

"Nice life you have here," I say, and he shyly grins in agreement.

But as if the whole thing couldn't get more charming, a small tan dog runs up to us as we keep walking. He's so excited to see Nico that he's jumping and spinning at the same time, yipping with glee, his tiny stub of a tail whisking back and forth so wildly it's become a blur.

If I thought I saw Nico's smile before, the arrival of this little rascal elicits a whole new category. He crouches down and lets the dog lick every inch of his face. They're a study in opposites that fit together—Nico a stoic, unmoving giant with a quiet expression, and a tiny, playful, solid mass wriggling with his tongue everywhere, his emotions bursting from his whole body.

"This is Luce," he says, finally picking up the dog, who's now breathing heavily and happily from his exertion.

"Loo-chay?" I ask, trying to pronounce it properly.

"It means 'light.'" He's looking at Luce with adoration, and I can see how this firecracker creature could be a shining beacon for someone.

Luce looks over at me, his eyes bright. He has a face so cute it reminds me of a stuffed animal, covered with short, wiry light-brown fur. He's the same color all over except for a bit of darkness around his nose and on the tips of his tiny flopped-over, V-shaped ears. If I was going to make a cartoon dog to appeal to small children, this is probably how I'd draw him. He tilts his head joyfully, as though he's checking me out.

I put my hand out for him, and he immediately licks it, the wetness of his black button nose and the whiskers on his chin tickling me.

"He's kind of goofy," I admit.

"He's extremely goofy," Nico concurs, the grin still in place as he rubs Luce's head.

"Where did he come from?"

"In general or right now?"

"I meant right now, since he seemed to pop in out of nowhere, but also generally."

"Well, he's a border terrier, so he's an English breed, but he's fully integrated into his Italian lifestyle," Nico explains. "Which means he has full run of the fields and loves to bound around, making sure everything's in order. He thinks he's in charge, and maybe he is."

"Maybe no one's told him there's actually nothing to do most of the time."

Nico snorts a laugh. "Yeah, he's still under the delusion that we might have some control over things here."

He puts Luce down, and we start to slowly meander after him.

I'm uncomfortable with how much my brain refuses to stop seeing this whole scene as attractive. If my instinctual reaction found the rolled-up sleeves enticing before, he made the sensation multiply by cradling a small dog. And walking alongside him, our long strides matching up, feels so effortless. *He's* effortless. I'm imagining his wife must be as offhandedly elegant as he is, the way I know Anita is too. And that rational thought helps me shake the rest of it off.

We stop at a wooden fence that's clearly more decorative than useful, since the gate that accompanies it is open. On either side are cows unlike any I've ever seen. They're a whitish-gray color, with two horns sticking out, curved into a half moon and close to horizontal. Their shape is a little more streamlined than the cows I'm used to.

"So this is the fence between my place and Gia's," he explains.

I'm surprised to not have realized. "You're neighbors?"

He nods, his grin turning more mischievous. "Oh yes. This was my grandfather's farm, and he and Gia's family have buttressed against each other forever. But she and I have always been simpatico. I let her cows graze on my fields, and she lets Luce bother her in the few moments she's actually at home. It's a perfect symbiosis for both of us."

"What are these cows?" I ask, still unable to stop looking at the ethereal gargantuan beasts dotting the fields.

"They're Maremma cattle—they're a local breed. Historically, the breed used to feed on marshlands in the wild, but now people keep them because they do so well in the harder terrain. We use them for beef, of course, but also to help us keep this feral land under some level of control."

"Why do you need to keep the land under control?"

He tilts his head, unknowingly mirroring Luce's look earlier. "It's not as lush here as in other agricultural regions of Italy. It can get very dry in July and August, and sometimes we can have fires. There's a reason why all the olive trees have so much more space between them than you'd typically see in most agriculture. Fires can't spread as long as the brush is clear, and cows can help with that."

"How do you deal with a fire once it starts?" I ask, trying not to think of my restaurant and its charred remains.

"Sometimes your only option is to hit it with fallen branches and hope for the best."

I stare back at him. "Hit the fire?"

"Sure." He says this like it's no big deal, but the image is hard to shake. "As long as there's no brush to catch, it stays pretty contained."

"Except for the giant trees surrounding you!" I exclaim.

"Yeah, true. One time it melted the rubber base of my work boot when I was trying to stamp it out." Okay, *that's* another image I won't be able to get rid of. He might be taken, but nothing's going to stop my mind from fully imagining him, sleeves rolled up, battling a fire. I try to ignore it.

"So there's *some* drama here in the other eleven months," I say with a chuckle.

He rubs his hand along the fence and nods, catching my eye and holding it for a second too long. "I guess you're right."

The depth of his voice makes me shiver.

I never react this way to anyone, but there's just something about this man that unsettles me and soothes me at the same time. I know I can't want *him*, but his demeanor makes me want *something*. I've never wanted anything but my work. I don't yearn for men, especially the kind who wouldn't put up with someone like me. That want is unsettling.

I remember a workplace therapist once encouraging me to face distress by breathing in through my nose like I'm smelling flowers and exhaling through my mouth like I'm blowing out candles—so that's what I do in the face of my unfortunate attraction to this extremely off-limits man and whatever bullshit he's stirring up.

We walk again, along Gia's fence, and then start to loop back. At the edges of the fields, where the land slopes a little more, you can see all the hilly distance surrounding us.

"Do they grow olives everywhere here?" I ask, shaking off all my internal thoughts and getting back to what matters.

"Olive trees can handle a wide range of weather but not altitude. They only grow up to six hundred meters here."

"What grows beyond that?"

"Chestnuts up until eight hundred meters. And then birch."

"And you use it all here?"

"Oh yeah, we use everything. My wife—well, she's gone now—but she always said people in Maremma find a use for everything, even the sticks."

"Oh." The whole sentence jars every assumption I had—when Gia said "grandson-in-law," I assumed his wife was around. But there's a small melancholy that's slipped under his sunny exterior. Has Anita ever mentioned any cousins who passed away? *Shit.* I'm so insensitive here. I have no idea what to say.

And I hate the small part of my brain that has now lasered in on the fact that maybe he's *not* taken.

What. Is. Wrong. With. Me? I've been single for all of five minutes, and what I do not need is to be sexualizing some recent widower. Obviously this weird mental state I'm in isn't about him—I'm probably still about one hundred steps from even acknowledging whatever emotional wreckage is living inside me. There's a time bomb waiting for me to acknowledge that my relationship ending hurts somewhere, and eventually it'll probably all explode.

Maybe that's why my body is inventing some palpable one-sided physical attraction with an unavailable man. I bet my subconscious is just loving pretending like I'm open to life when really I'm only running toward locked doors.

He doesn't seem to notice, though. He's lost in his own thoughts again as we walk along, Luce trotting at his heels.

"Thank you for showing me," I say as we come back to where we started. I put a hand on my scooter's handlebar, as though I need a tactile reminder of my getaway vehicle.

"Sure, anytime." That brief melancholy is gone and replaced again by those watchful eyes, as though he's got a zipper to my brain and he's slowly pulling it down and reaching inside. "You should come see the frantoio, if you're interested."

"You're going to have to forgive my ignorance on that word," I chuckle.

"Right, right," he says. Nico's hand reaches down to pet Luce, who's hopping as he scrounges for attention, but those eyes never leave my face. "The mill, I mean. 'Frantoio' is the Italian word for 'mill.' As beautiful as the olive groves are, the mill is actually where the more interesting part happens."

"You're just saying that because it's the only thing you have control over."

"Don't I know it," he says softly, one side of his mouth curling up.

"I'd love to," I say, redirecting, even as my mind screams that I have to leave before my insides tie themselves into knots so tight even the most experienced sailor couldn't loosen them.

"We can do a Monday again," he asks, "since that's when you're off?"

"Sounds great," I reply, nodding, hoping the timing comes across as noncommittal as I feel.

I swing my leg over the scooter and put the key back in the ignition. Nico absentmindedly runs a finger along the handlebar, where my hand had just been resting. But then he balls his own hand into a fist and knocks twice on the scooter, a little auditory permission to get going.

Right. "See you round," I say.

"Like I already told you, in this town, no one gets to avoid seeing each other, I'm afraid," he says, that small smile back.

I give him a little wave, like the dork I apparently am with him, and I skid back, even though I mean to go forward. I can see he's holding in a laugh, which I appreciate, but geez, I wish I could be like ten percent smoother right now.

I take a deep breath and start again. With a jolt forward, I make my way back down the road to town.

Chapter 6

Two weeks after my arrival in Italy, Gia finally lets me make a batch of pasta alongside her. She insists that there's no pressure because she's not going to sell it to anyone. I'm determined to change her mind.

We start with strozzapreti and cavatelli, because Gia says those are the least likely for me to mess up.

I've never watched a person so precise and yet so free all at once. She makes everything from memory, so I follow her around surreptitiously with a scale. When her back is turned, I weigh the flour and semolina and eggs to try and get a real grip on the recipe, even though I know that's not the point. Everything for her is feel. She moves dough across the ridged pasta board with the agility of a violinist streaking their bow across their instrument. It's an extension of her hand. She eyes me, unimpressed, as we go along, silent except in the moments when she redirects my hands ever so slightly to fix something she deems incorrect.

It's an unlearning of sorts for me. Everywhere I staged in my career was an excess of technique. It was cutting edge; it was tweezers; it was pushing the boundaries. The technique here is all in the rustic precision. The pasta is perfect because Gia knows exactly what the dough should feel like, no matter the humidity outside today or the elevation of where she's making it. She knows what the salinity of the water should be. She knows the exact moment when undercooked turns into al dente and the amount it will keep cooking from the moment it leaves the pot until you pick up your fork to taste it. It's sensory repetition. Measurement can only take you so far.

I'm surprised by how much joy I'm taking in the simplicity of it all. It's not that I'd grown stagnant at home exactly—I truly love my restaurant and look forward to going in every day—but I hadn't realized how much I'd stopped learning by being the person in charge, by always pushing forward. I'm supposed to have the ideas, but I never travel or take time to observe others. And being here with Gia is making me admit that perhaps I should get out more. I don't want this forever, but there's a soothing perfection to watching this old lady's hands work dough the way she has for thousands of days before.

Obviously I haven't shared this part with Anita. She would roast me in an instant. Every day, her texts are the same.

Anita: Are you fully obsessed with Italian food yet?

Kit: I'm obsessed with figuring out why the fuck everything is called Pecorino here.

Anita: yeah, Americans really muck that one up. Any sheep's milk cheese is a pecorino. Not just the Parmesan alternative you guys make it into.

Kit: "you guys." Like I created the American culinary linguistic choices.

Anita: I just hope that now you become as grumpy about Pecorino labeling as I am.

Kit: Probably not my highest priority when I come back.

Anita: Stop thinking about coming back and enjoy the moment!

Kit: I'm enjoying the moment.

Anita: probably because you and my nonna love to work too much.

Kit: I plead the fifth on anything that could incriminate Gia.

I don't want to admit to her yet that I'm begrudgingly enjoying it much more than I expected. I don't want to explain that every morning I climb up to the top of the stone steps in the middle of town that look out over the square, and I stare into the distance beyond the town and the olive groves all the way to the ocean, silver and hazy against the sky.

There's a poem carved in marble next to the bench I sit at, and it says *Ti Amo Maremma. Fin Dove al Mar Ti Sposi e Ti Vesti di Tramonti.* I try to translate it, but beyond loving Maremma, it says something about marrying the sea and wearing sunsets, so the poetry has been lost along the Google Translate road. Still, I can't help but be somewhat charmed by a place that has stone ramparts clothed in poetry.

I haven't shared *any* of that with Anita.

I'm also glad that Anita and I never talk about desserts because then I'd also have to admit that the best pastries I've ever had are apparently Italian. I've swung by for tea and breakfast a few times at Belpagna. When I've walked through the door, Emilia's skeptical resting face immediately turns into a knowing smirk, set off by whatever colorful topknotted bandana she's always wearing. After the first few visits, she's now started to pour a cup of tea before I even walk over. She hasn't yet let me pick which pastry I'm getting. But I appreciate that that forced decision also has allowed us to go off on the kind of chef-obsessive tangents about technique or produce or supply chains that I'm already missing from home.

I've tried not to overstay my welcome, even though I know it's a place where others seem to hang around for hours. This town isn't a place where I need to plant roots; as a reality show contestant might say, I'm not here to make friends.

But it's nice to have someone to talk about cooking with. A lot of days Nico pops in, too, and he'll join whatever ingredient-focused conversation Emilia and I have going. The more I get to know him—the more his booming laugh and his food science tangents start molding into familiarity—the more I'm able to shake off whatever attraction I feel and start to enjoy the company.

I'm surprised by how much seems normal, even if I'm still hesitant of the whole situation. I would've expected to have a crash at some point—from losing John, the restaurant, and my routines all in the span of a day. It hasn't come, though. Instead, I can tentatively admit that I've started to relax slightly into the grooves of this place, like a new pair of shoes you haven't quite broken in but feel are on the way there.

I don't need Anita finding more reasons to gleefully tell me she told me so.

Besides, I have Gia busting my chops enough already.

"You need to stop mincing the garlic so much," Gia says, standing over my shoulder today.

"This is just regular mincing," I reply.

She responds by shooing me over and starts slicing the garlic with her knife, as exact as a mandoline.

"When you mince it to death, it releases all the sulfur. You're altering the flavor. Slicing it and then chopping finely keeps it intact."

"I would've thought you'd want more garlic," I poke, since she seems to add a hefty amount to everything.

"The Roman poet Horace said that garlic is the essence of vulgarity. And I think he was right—we can all stand to be a little bit vulgar, but at some point it's too much."

I snicker. Gia clearly isn't easy for everyone to get along with, but she's a known quantity for me. She's a chef to the nth degree. That is, until she decides she wants to pry.

"Are you the youngest in your family?" she asks, now rolling out dough without even looking at it.

"Why?" I ask suspiciously.

"You have a chip on your shoulder," she states matter-of-factly.

"So do you," I retort, like the teenage contrarian I secretly still am inside.

"Right. I'm a youngest child. I had everything to prove."

She's daring me to argue and clearly never going to let anything go. I'm destemming thyme, so at least I have the bandwidth for a conversation.

"My sister is the oldest, then my brother, then me," I say, taking the bait because I want to prove her wrong. "We're all only eighteen months apart, so we were always compared. But they're both pretty soft, like our mom. My sister was athletic and didn't want to pursue it, and my brother had no interest in *anything* competitive. So I didn't need to prove anything to them because I was always pushing myself. And my dad found me easier to deal with—he's competitive, too, so he was always at my crew races and helping me plan what was next. If anything, I think it made me more driven and sure of myself. That's the *opposite* of a chip."

"If you say so," Gia snorts, and I hate that she thinks she's got me figured out somehow. It makes me bite my already-short nails even shorter. A nervous habit I should most certainly break.

"What do *you* have to prove at this point?" I finally ask, giving it back and seeing if she can take it.

"Oh, I've proved it all. My father preferred my brothers, always. Then I lost my first love young. And then I had a really boring, pointless marriage until he died when I was in my forties. So I get to do things my own way now," she volleys back.

She doesn't seem to want to elaborate on any of those bombshells that she threw out casually, so I respond with, "I do things my own way too."

"Clearly," she scoffs, with a hint of amusement in her voice.

I know prying more isn't going to lead anywhere, but I am finding that I like talking instead of our usual silence. "Why is your English so good?" I ask, changing the subject.

"I really loved reruns of *The Golden Girls*," she says without a hint of irony, which makes me laugh. "What other simple questions have you got?"

"Why are there so many stray cats?" It really has been a big question on my mind. They seem to be *everywhere*. And ever since Nico and Luce, I can't stop noticing how many animals are around. Not that I'm thinking about that duo specifically.

"They breed like rabbits," she says bluntly, "and people are too generous with their table scraps. Don't feed one, or you'll be stuck with it forever."

"Duly noted," I say with a smile.

"I mean it—women getting over breakups always want to cling on to some animal. Don't be a cliché and take in a cat."

Well, that makes me look up. "How do you know I'm going through a breakup?" I ask.

"Your friend Anita isn't exactly a vault."

I snort out a laugh, because she's absolutely right. She starts stamping out circles for ravioli, and I love watching her like this.

"You know," she says, eyes on the pasta but her demeanor relaxed, "I get the sense you think you're fine because you weren't madly in love with the guy anyway—"

"Who said that?"

"Please, Anita talks my ear off. It's like she thinks she can make up for not being here by boring me to death with everyone in her life's little inane dramas. Anyway, I was going to say just because the man was kind of worthless doesn't mean you're fine. You need to wait before you pick yourself off the ground. Healing's important."

I huff, mostly because I hate how much she's trying to negate everything I thought I was doing so well at. "No offense to your bullshit town where everyone seems to know what each other had for breakfast, but this isn't going to be a place where I'm dating."

Gia shrugs and starts filling the ravioli with their stuffings, little jewels of ground pork and herbs. "Yes, by all means, ignore what I'm actually saying."

"Work heals me," I throw out. I've moved on from mincing garlic to chopping onions, and the repetitive motions actually *are* soothing.

"I've always thought that, but maybe I'm not the best example," she says nonchalantly.

"Oh, we're admitting I shouldn't see you as my next life role model?"

She snorts, and it's *almost* a laugh. I can't help but feel pleased whenever I even get close to amusing Gia. "Maybe not. But in pasta, absolutely yes."

Even with this conversation, she's still laser focused on the ravioli, impenetrable, and as much as she wants to downplay things, her life choices look pretty great in my book. She's determinedly herself. She's herself and content *without* a relationship. Maybe I can learn from her mistakes and skip over the losing a first love and enduring a pointless marriage and simply get to the good part where I cook all day, have friends, and enjoy my tranquility. I don't need more than that. I'm lucky to not need or *want* more than that.

Yet like always, Gia's here to burst my bubble. "Just don't be like Nico and leave it too long," she says, finally looking up and pointing at me. "His wife is gone, and he's taking too much time to get over it."

I wish Nico's face wouldn't come so fully to my mind at the sound of his name. But I push the thought aside. If *she's* leaving it, why can't I? Hell, if her husband died in his forties, it sounds like she's left it for the entire second half of her life. And she seems perfectly happy with that choice.

"When did you become the town relationship expert?" I toss back.

"Please," she says, rolling her eyes. "Everyone would be better off if they let me make their food and give them advice about how to run their lives."

I laugh because she truly seems to mean it. In her mind, everything could be solved if we all listened to Gia more often—do as she says, not as she does.

I think about all the old people in this town sitting outside all the little shops on their plastic chairs, gossiping, but also trading what they view as their hard-fought wisdom. It's no wonder so many of the young people leave, when they feel that burden of attention.

"Just don't take in a cat," she says again, pointing a rolling pin at me like there's nothing more serious. But in a second, she's changing the subject again. "Do you know how to debone a fish?"

"I'm a fucking Michelin-starred chef. I know how to debone a fish," I mutter, grabbing the fish she's proffered to me before setting back to work.

Chapter 7

Much as I've tried, by the third week here I've now fully succumbed to not living my mornings in isolation. I still climb the stone steps once I'm up to get my body moving, but I've stopped pretending that swinging by Belpagna is only an occasional activity. It's daily now. Even within a few weeks of being here, I have to admit it's become an essential balm in my life.

What can I say? I'm a control freak who needs a routine.

I like to think it's because Emilia doesn't give me shit about my tea, and her pastries make me want to kidnap her and drag her back to my restaurant when we reopen. But for now, I'll settle with parking myself at her counter and peppering her with questions between customers. To be fair, she gives as good as she gets, because she has her own unending questions and minutiae to lob at me. We're two food nerds with no hobbies except our jobs, finding a way to spend even more time being nerds.

And now most days Nico comes and sits next to me and joins in the peppering. His presence still makes me physically on my guard, but there's something about the melancholy I saw that day at his groves that subsequently made it easier to view him head on. And I like the camaraderie of this morning, food-obsessed friendship trio. In New York, my days are all spent in my kitchen. While I have friends at the restaurant, I'm everyone's boss, so the dynamics are different. Outside of that I have Anita, and I always had John around, but neither of them wants to get into the molecular structure of butterfat content.

So instead of holing up in my room and reading technical treatises, I'm discussing them with two humans.

"Modernist Cuisine has done a lot of work on studying that, you know," Emilia is saying to us with enthusiasm as we debate the merits of whole wheat. "Whatever nutrients are found in the bran aren't really doing anything for us, so we might as well just eat white bread."

"Says the person currently pushing white flour–filled pastries on her entire town," Nico teases.

I look at him, my mouth stuffed full of a bombolone, with sugar clinging to my lips, and try not to laugh. "I appreciate the pastry pushing," I say in Emilia's defense. It's a bit muffled from the carbs taking up residence in my mouth, but I think I've still gotten the point across enough that Emilia looks pleased.

"I'm merely pointing out that the higher price point is a racket," she continues, undeterred. "Did you know when they did fecal analysis and blood tests, they saw our bodies don't really absorb any extra vitamins and minerals in whole wheat anyway?"

Nico puts his head in his hands. "We're talking about fecal analysis at breakfast?"

A customer comes up, and Emilia seems delighted to step away.

I swallow the rest of my bombolone and turn to see Nico watching me. "You didn't ever come see me at the frantoio," he chides with a small smile.

"I don't bother people," I say, brushing his comment off as simply as I brush the remaining sugar from my hand.

The truth is, the more I've gotten to know him, the more I'm dying to see Nico's mill and learn about the olive oil process. Nothing could be more obvious, based on the amount of time we spend delving into the tiniest details of food.

But there's something about the ease I've found with Nico in these mornings that I'm afraid of rocking. That day we walked alone together unsettled me, and I very much do not need to be unsettled; a widower related to both my best friend and my current boss is quite possibly the worst person to be inconveniently attracted to.

Although, maybe now that we're friends, it wouldn't matter as much. Now that I've seen him as a fellow food nerd, those sparks have probably faded. I've never actually been attracted to anyone who's shared my interests.

"That's very kind, Kit, but you're really never bothering me," he responds. "It truly is the slowest time of the year. I think you'd love seeing it."

His modesty is so disarming. Most men I've known—especially most chefs, my god—want to beat you into submission over how lucky you are to have one second of their time. Nico's actually making something extraordinary, and yet all he wants is for me to enjoy seeing it. It's hard to not say yes to that.

So that's how I find myself late on a Monday afternoon parking my scooter next to Nico's mill (with a much smoother parking job this time, if I do say so myself) before wandering inside.

"Anybody home?" I shout. Complex steel machinery stares out in front of me. There's a conveyor belt that leads to a cylindrical structure that must be twenty feet long. It feeds into more equipment, and I can't quite tell from here what the order of operations is.

Nico walks into view, and that beam of a smile wallops me.

Damn it, he just *is* cuter out here in his element. He's in one of his many flannel shirts, again rolled up at the sleeves, and this time, adorably, it's buttoned one button off, so the shirt is sitting a tiny bit askew. He's almost breathless with excitement at the prospect of showing off his beloved mill, and I need to ignore how much that passion for his work makes my heart stutter.

"You came!"

"I told you I was coming today, didn't I?" I ask, although any worry that I'd gotten the wrong message is placated by his clear happiness at my arrival.

"You did, but I'm excited to show you." That part is clear enough from how he's practically bouncing on his toes. "It's not very often I get someone in here who will actually appreciate it. Growers bring me their olives and dump them in crates without a second thought. Importers or investors just want to know the stats behind our scores at international competitions and what the end product could mean for them. My crew is wonderful, but they've been doing it forever and nothing is novel to them. So it really is a treat for me."

He puts his hand on my shoulder, which should read as friendly, but all I can think is how *big* his hand feels on me. It lingers even after he moves it, like ice on a burn that stings as your skin comes back to its normal temperature.

I take a deep breath and shake it off. Thankfully he doesn't seem to notice any of my weirdness, because he's already standing in front of me, a ringmaster ready to let his performers show off.

"Okay, so the thing you have to realize about olive oil," he starts, "is that it's long and then an instant. You take a year to grow the olives, but making it takes only a single day. You can harvest in the morning, take the olives to a mill, and by that night, you have oil."

"Like magic," I say, wanting to lean into his enthusiasm.

"Truly," he replies giddily. "But that day is everything. The miller ensures the quality much more than the specific olives."

"Says the miller," I retort, with a light nudge on his shoulder that makes him grin.

"I'd say it's about eighty-twenty."

"You're saying the olives—the olives you spend the entire year growing—are only worth twenty percent of the process?"

He shrugs, his eyes full of that endearing mischief that's waiting for me to argue. But I'm not going to bite.

"So each machine you see here has a different role," he continues, easily shifting the subject. He walks over to the first one, which looks like a conveyer belt, and gives it a pat. "It starts with washing and removing leaves and debris. Then this is the malaxer." We walk over to one of the more cylindrical machines. "That crushes the olives and stirs them into a paste. Then there's a separator that removes all the excess materials and then a centrifuge to extract water from the oil. Then we filter."

"And Emilia thinks your filter is better than anyone else's," I point out. He shrugs again, but a small blush warms his cheeks. His humility always startles me—I've noticed it in all our conversations, whenever Emilia and I get going at Belpagna. Nico doesn't speak half as much as we do, but when he has something to say, it's always incisive and measured. Yet the man can't take a compliment whenever we praise his well-earned insights. It's an unexpected quality in a man so assured in every other aspect of his life.

"Well, the filter has helped, yes," he continues, deflecting. "But so much of it is just watching the machines. The speed, the temperature, the time . . . it all changes, depending on different olives. There are hundreds of parameters that change all day long."

I suddenly realize how close we're standing. In a mill the size of a large soccer field, we've ended up at a small panel of screens that measure and showcase all his "parameters." And as he talks, we slowly drift, static balloons that somehow find each other. I can feel the rub of his shirt against mine, and even through the material he feels so *solid.* We're close enough that I can smell the way the outdoors mixes with his simple soap. He's once again unnerving my insides.

I clear my throat. "It's like being a chef," I finally say, looking at the machinery instead of him, because I'm trying to swallow back whatever his nearness is doing to me and focus on what he's saying. "The ingredients are the start, but then the difference is in the technique."

"Exactly!" he says, jubilant at the understanding.

I turn toward him and try to avoid his eyes, but I'm close enough to see that little freckle above his lip that I try so hard not to notice.

I'm always trying *so* hard.

But when I look up, his gaze has found mine, and it's clear he's also realized how close we are. Despite the cavernous space and cold machinery surrounding us, the air suddenly holds a heaviness to it, like rain clouds about to break.

I hadn't noticed before how quiet it is in here. I imagine in the fall during production, this room must be roaring with life when every machine is at full speed. But for now it's empty. It's blue skies coming through the glass windows, blocking out all sounds from outside. Only our breathing registers, and I wish I could hide the nakedness of how much deeper I currently need to inhale.

Although when he swallows, I wonder if he's thinking the same thing, even if I can't read his expression.

I can feel his hand lingering right next to my waist—close enough he'd only have to move an inch to brush against me. He's so close I can practically hear his pulse racing as fast as mine is. But some spooling tension is holding him back. I rub my hand on my pounding heart to try and calm it down, but it's not working.

I wonder if I should close the gap.

I'm trying to remember all the reasons why this is a bad idea.

"Nico!" a loud voice calls, and we jump apart, scalded before ever touching.

A large man the shape of an oversize bowling ball is shouting rapidly in Italian and striding toward us. I use the convenience of the noise to take the deep breath my body's been needing and blink to shake off the haze that overcame me.

Nico's stance is completely changed—maybe I only imagined that heaviness before, because now he's entirely on guard. His voice is sharp when he starts talking again. He always sounds distinct in Italian, looser. But this feels different. Even without the words making sense to me, it's clear this person isn't someone Nico wants to see.

They go back and forth for a bit, the tone oscillating between civil and openly hostile. Then the man finally looks at me.

"Bonjourno, chi sei?" he says, eyeing me up and down.

"I don't speak Italian," I reply, unsurprised by the coldness in my tone. There's something about this guy and the way he's speaking to Nico that has my hackles up. Nico is among the mildest men I've ever met, so how could I not be suspicious of someone who's put him on edge?

"Ah, you're the American," he says, looking amused, and I throw up my hands. Seriously, does *anyone* have *anything* else to talk about around here?

"I'm sorry, I'm not sure who you are," I respond.

"Tommaso," he says, holding out a hand. I skeptically shake it back. "Nico and I were just discussing boar hunting season. I was reminding him again of how important it is this time of year to the town's economy."

Nico's expression is thunderous, and I almost want to laugh because it's such an unexpected look for him. But maybe it's naive to think that spending a few weeks chatting over pastries could make you know someone.

Still, I feel strangely compelled to show which side I'm on, even if I have no idea what that side's supposed to be.

"I'd think Nico has a pretty good grip on the town's economy," I say, trying to be as dismissive as possible over something I know nothing about.

Nico puts his hand on my shoulder, and I can't tell whether I'm helping or hurting. I wish I didn't once again notice his hand so much.

"Tommaso, you need to leave," he says quietly but firmly. "My stance on this isn't going to change."

Tommaso ignores him and turns to look at me instead. "You tell Gia she doesn't get to order everyone around, eh?"

And then he storms right out.

Nico's eyes are closed, his hands on his hips. He reminds me of a preschool teacher trying to gain back his composure after dealing with a roomful of toddlers.

"What was that about?" I ask. He gives himself a moment to take a heavy, deep breath, but then opens his eyes.

"Want to come on a walk?" he asks, a hopeful note in his voice.

"Of course."

He shuffles into an office, and I hear him throwing something in a bag. He comes out, and apparently we're on our way.

Chapter 8

Nico is walking so rapidly it's hard to keep up. He's lost in his own thoughts as we make our way through another olive grove. Luce noticed us the minute we came out of the mill and bounded over, thrilled to tag along. Nico still reaches out to pet Luce every time he jumps up, but his mind is elsewhere.

The grove clears, and we start walking up a hill covered in untamed grass. It's a gradual slope, and it's hard to make out what exactly is waiting for us at the top. But based on the way Luce is hopping excitedly and running ahead and then back, it's clear we're going to a stop they've been to many times.

As we approach the top of the hill, I start to make out something at the edge, but my eyes don't really believe it until we're standing in front of it.

"This is . . . a couch," I say, looking at this old-fashioned, weathered, leather-ish beige couch perched on the top of a hill.

"Yup," Nico says as he plops down onto it, Luce following immediately into his lap. He brings his bag up, reaches in, and pulls out a small clear bottle, its contents a fiery red. He opens the top and hands it to me. I take a sip—it's a premade Campari and soda, fizzy bitter perfection bottled in glass. He pulls out another one for himself and downs it practically in one go. It looks so small in his large hands.

I turn around and sit down, suddenly realizing why we're here. At the top of this hill you can see the sun starting to set rose pink across a sky with clouds that look like painted wisps. The grass in front of us is slowly absorbed in the distance by olive trees and then more wavy hills, one of which contains Manciano perched high. I wonder if, when I'm looking out my apartment window, I'm staring directly at Nico's couch hill.

The view is stunning, even if it's a little incongruous to be sitting on a piece of indoor furniture plopped at the top of a grassy knoll.

"It's quite a different seating arrangement than in town, where all the old people just pull out plastic chairs," I finally say. He chuckles at the thought but doesn't disagree. "How did you even get a couch up here?"

"I was going to get rid of it anyway, and a friend helped me carry it up," he says casually, as though walking with a couch up a hill is no big deal. "It's serene up here."

He grabs another drink from his bag and sips it more slowly this time, facing out toward the sunset and not looking at me. I always find his stillness disarming. I'm all movement, but he's just as strong by being still.

"You know," he says, "one thing I love about these trees is that every year their yield is different, and there's no rhyme or reason. Sometimes, only twenty meters apart, you'll see one tree with tons of olives and another with practically none. The weather is the same, so who knows why it happens. It's its own little mystery; it's kind of romantic knowing not everything has a reason."

I wait before responding. Whatever happened with Tommaso is clearly still roiling inside him, and I know enough to give him the space to decide what he wants to tell me.

He absentmindedly pets Luce. "The boar hunting is impossible. There are all these weird old Italian laws—or maybe Tuscan laws, I suppose—that give ridiculous rights to hunters. If you walk on my property without a gun, I can obviously have you arrested for trespassing. But with a gun, in hunting season, you have a right to be in any area where the municipality decides you can hunt. Boars love digging around olive trees, so our land always falls into a boar area. During harvest, the boars stay away because there's too many people, but in the summer you see them a lot. There's a few weeks in the summer where the hunters can come, and they're allowed onto the land with like twenty or twenty-five people. And in recent years they do it at night because they think it's easier to surprise the boars."

"What does that have to do with Gia?" I ask, curious how this became about her.

Nico lets out a deep sigh. "What doesn't have to do with Gia?" His lips curve with a sad smile as he finally tilts his head toward me, and I get that sense again, when our eyes catch, of something intangible roiling between us. But he looks away again as quickly as he started. "No, it's not her fault at all, really. For years she's been sleeping outside with her cows and a rifle whenever they come on her land."

"I'm sorry?" I say, suddenly turning my whole body toward him because *that* wasn't where I thought this was going.

"About a decade ago, the hunters accidentally shot one of her cows. Her farm has always had cows, and she treats them like her children. She loves them." His laugh is wistful. Seeing him around Luce makes me think he could understand anyone's attachment to any animal. "So since then, she's slept outside with her rifle. Only I don't know if you've noticed, but she's getting quite arthritic."

I've certainly noticed the way she has to take a moment for her hands when she's working pasta dough. But since I never knew her before, it wouldn't have occurred to me that her current rapid speed has been slowed down. Maybe that's my error for underestimating anything about Gia.

"Her doctor said this year she can't sleep outside the way she's been. He's been saying it offhandedly for years, but he really put a fine point on it this year. So over the last few months, Gia did everything she could think of to get our land made into a reserve, so the hunters couldn't come. But they fought it. Bitterly. She accused them of a lot of underhanded tactics, and it got pretty ugly."

"I certainly wouldn't want to go into battle against Gia."

Another one of his small smiles curls up again, and he rubs his hand through his hair, tousling it and letting it look even more wild. "No, neither would I. Tommaso doesn't care about anything but the rich people he brings up on expeditions from Rome, so it's hard to know whether he defeated Gia fairly or not. But the result was the same. Starting next week, they'll be back."

"And what's Gia going to do?" I ask.

Nico cringes. "It's not so much Gia, as me."

I nod, the realization sinking in. "You're taking over for her," I say. It's a statement without question, because I already know the kind of man Nico is. He's not going to let Gia hurt herself.

"I am," he says quietly. "And I guess Gia just told Tommaso that. He was counting on her bowing out this year and having unfettered access to the land. But having a person sleeping against a tree with a rifle isn't exactly appealing to a bunch of tourists looking to sneak up on an animal in a place they want to pretend is fully wild."

"I'll do it with you," I say, surprising myself as the words tumble out of my mouth. But the minute they do, I know I want to. I *want* to show up for Gia.

He pauses. "You don't have to do that." I hate the resignation in his tone. It bolsters the thought.

"I'm stubborn as all hell," I say. "I normally run a restaurant on my feet seven days a week. I can handle a little bit of sleeping outside."

"But you don't *need* to."

"I feel like I'm part of this now," I admit. I'm surprised how true that already feels after such little time. "Gia has taken me in at a . . . well, a particularly hard time for me." I pause, but Nico doesn't say anything. He's clearly not surprised—the town talks, after all—but he gives me the same space to finish that I gave him. It's discomforting, the ease I feel in this town, with these people. But this solitude up on the hill is doing something to my insides—like this is a place where secrets can be shared without consequence.

"I'm trying to just go about my days here like this is all a normal break for me, but the truth is, I haven't really faced anything happening at home. I ran away from my restaurant burning down and a breakup. I'm waiting for all of it to wallop me in the face at some point."

"And that point is going to be sitting outside in the middle of the night, carrying a rifle?" he ribs, an attempt to lighten the burden of the words I'm spitting out.

"*No*," I retort. "The point is that Gia took me in. She had no reason to trust me, other than Anita said she should. She gave me a job and found me an apartment and kicks my ass every day. So I want to help her."

"Why do you like someone kicking your ass every day, if you don't mind my asking?" For someone who's spent a lot of our conversation tonight looking away—as though if we catch each other's eyes again, we might have to reexamine whatever almost happened back at the mill—he's watching me now. That earnest face, wanting to understand.

"Tough comes easily to me," I admit. "Gia keeps pointing out that I'm the youngest, so she thinks I had to be scrappy. But I think I always would've been scrappy." I look back out at the view. It'll be too much to admit if I have to see how my words affect his expression. "It's always been easier for me if things are clear cut. I rowed crew in high school and college, which was really the first time I felt like I belonged somewhere. It started because I was tall, but eventually the rhythm took over my life. I fed on it—the competition, the strength, the discipline. Being a chef is like an extension of that. I've always thrived on hard work. And I've always sought out environments that didn't mind women like that."

"Women like what?" he asks softly. Luce moves to put his head on my lap, and it's like he's an extension of Nico, reaching out when things are hard to say.

"I don't know . . ." I blow out a breath. This is the thing I've always known about myself that's hardest to admit. The lack of femininity. The abrasiveness. It's what people want from a chef, unless that chef is a woman. And it's hard to articulate a divide that no one admits to. "I guess I'm a little more . . . assertive than a lot of people."

"People or women?"

"Well, I know a lot of chefs who are women, so I don't see it as any difference."

"But other people do," he says, understanding.

We're both silent for a few minutes, watching the light-pink sky turn an inkier purple. "Yeah," I finally say.

I don't know why this is finally the moment where my grief over losing John comes roaring to the surface. I've never felt sexy—I've always been *too much*. I know I'm considered attractive enough, but my personality has never been appealing to most men. John was the first man who ever really pursued me, who made me feel desired and special. But I never actually thought it would stay, and he proved me right by leaving. Maybe I accepted mediocrity, but it was my choice to accept it—a glove that perhaps wasn't my style, but it fit enough to keep me warm.

And then that acceptance went away.

I think it's why I'm so comfortable with Gia. She's actually starting to accept me warily over time, now that she's seen me. And that earned acceptance feels more real.

"Gia took me in too," Nico finally says, his deep voice a comforting tether back to the world I want to be focused on. With Luce now fully in my lap, it feels easier to turn back and watch him. The tactile necessity of patting Luce is an essential buffer.

"Yeah?"

"Yeah. I didn't grow up here, actually. Everyone treats me like I've lived here my whole life because this was my grandfather's farm, but I actually grew up in Rome. And my mother is British, so I spent a lot of the summer there."

"Is that why you have a British dog?" I ask.

"My mum got him for me a few years ago," he says with a smile. "She thought I might need someone around, and she grew up with border terriers, so I guess the joke's on me, because I didn't realize how *constantly* around he'd be."

I scratch Luce behind the ears. He's perked up, almost like he knows we're talking about him and is proud of it.

I wonder if Nico got the dog when his wife passed away. But that's not my place to dig into.

"So how often did you come here?" I continue.

"I came up a lot on weekends. But especially in the fall, I was always around for harvest. I'm the one who convinced my grandfather to actually build the mill. He never had one until I was a teenager."

"You convinced your grandfather to start making olive oil himself when you weren't even out of high school?" I love thinking of data-driven, persuasive but calm Nico as a kid, tall and lanky before he grew into that height.

"He always had the land, but he never wanted to bother with the machinery, so he took his olives to be milled at another place a few towns over. But once I started following along that process, I was convinced we could do better."

"When did you start following along?"

"I was probably eight or nine."

"Eight or nine?" I repeat.

It's getting darker, but I can see he's blushing a little again. He opens another small bottle of Campari and soda and takes a sip, shrugging it all off.

"I just mean that's when I started going with him to the mill and became interested in the process. He didn't actually start building his own mill until I was fourteen or fifteen. It's expensive to build a mill. We had to run the projections on how long it would take to pay off the equipment—"

"*We* ran the projections. Meaning, like, ten-to-twelve-year-old *you*."

"Yeah," he says simply.

"Maybe the people in town treat you like you grew up here because you saved them from having to drive an hour to get their olives milled."

At that I get one of his booming laughs, and it makes me feel warm inside. I've never heard a friendlier laugh, despite its sonic decibel levels. It makes Luce stand up at attention.

"Maybe," he finally says. "My dad loved being in Rome, and I don't think my mother could've handled living out of a city. There's a great British expat community there, and this is much too rural for her. And over time I had . . . more attachments here. So when my grandfather died, it was only natural I took over."

"Did you *want* to take over?" I ask hesitantly.

He thinks about it for a moment, like the thought has never occurred to him. As though his family's needs were what they were, and he never considered his own. "My degree is in mechanical engineering, so I always wanted to tinker with machinery and devices. It's easy to do that from here. I have plenty of time for that, since so little happens outside of the fall. It's how I've been able to perfect my filter." I don't point out that that's not really a direct answer. But he keeps going. "And I love it here. At every age, no matter where I was in the world, when my grandfather was alive, I always came back for harvest. Everything feels hopeful; everything is moving at full speed; you create something beautiful so quickly. I really love it, and Gia makes me feel like I still have family here."

"Sounds perfect," I say, the joy in his words seeping into me.

"Yeah, it is." He pauses, seemingly lost in thoughts of his favorite time of year. But then he just as suddenly snaps back to it. "But you're serious about sleeping outside? Protecting the cows?"

"Hell yes," I say, sitting up a little straighter so he can see my resolve. It's a welcome bravado after letting my past get the best of my mind earlier. This version of me—the woman who takes care of her own—that's who I want to be. Not the woman who gets flustered and chatty while sitting on a couch. "Besides," I continue, "it'll probably take two people to equal one Gia."

He grins. "That's for sure. Well, I'm glad we're now in this together."

"Me too," I reply, only a little unsettled by how much I like that thought.

Chapter 9

"Gia's still putting mine in a separate fridge drawer with a sign telling people my pasta is free of charge." It's hard to convey how serious I am when Emilia's already howling with laughter. "I've been here over a month, and it's like nothing I do matters."

"A month isn't very long to someone in their eighties," Emilia points out as she wipes away a tear from her eye.

"It's good, though. My pasta is *really good.*" I'm not able to let this go. I've always had a superb learning curve. And I have taste buds. I know my pasta's good.

"Definitely not as good as hers, though," Emilia retorts.

I huff, a stubborn horse whose reins are being pulled on. "I'm not saying I'm as good as Gia. But it's certainly good enough to not give away *for free*!"

Emilia seems endlessly amused by my frustration. "She's probably doing it to keep pissing you off," she points out.

I hate that she's probably right.

Emilia fills a little bowl with scraps and walks it outside to a waiting stray cat. When she comes back in, I know how to change the subject. "Gia says if you feed those cats, you'll never get rid of them."

"I don't want to get rid of them," Emilia counters.

"So you're just going to have a lost cat dependent on you for the rest of their life?"

"Sure," she says, shrugging. "And maybe they don't consider themselves lost. Maybe they like being free; have you considered that? We can be friends to strays too."

I have no apparent response, so instead I pick at my nails. I'm still annoyed that she laughed at my pasta humiliation.

She goes over to help some customers who've walked in, and I look at my phone.

I have a series of texts my dad sent me last night. I don't think he totally understood my decision to do this for the summer, but now that I'm here, he's embracing it. He always moves forward—his base mode is "What's next?" So lately it's: What's next with learning about pasta? What's next for the restaurant renovations? And the perennial, What's next in whatever teams we follow?

I also have a more recent text from Anita, who uses any excuse to troll me while kindly checking in to make sure I'm okay—her insomniac late nights in New York are now my Italian mornings, so this has often been when we catch up.

Anita: Admit that pasta is the best

Kit: It's not a competition.

Anita: How can you be learning Nonna's pasta and not be freely admitting that it's the greatest food out there?

Kit: Because I'm not exceptionally biased? Because while pasta is great I haven't been completely Italianized after a single month?

Anita: Two months then?

Kit: I wouldn't count on it.

Anita: How about counting on your menu having pasta when you come back?

Kit: That I might admit to.

Anita: Huzzah!

Anita: Anyway I'm not only texting to harass you about pasta today.

Kit: Oh yeah? Something else higher on the harass list?

Anita: Nope! I've also decided to come visit!

Well, that has me sitting up. I'm a little surprised by how emotional the thought makes me.

Kit: Really?

Anita: yup

Kit: Need to see Gia?

Anita: I need to see both of you, ya dingdong. I love you too. I have to make sure everyone's treating you properly.

Kit: Does that mean you can convince Gia to stop giving away my pasta for free as though it's literally worthless?

Anita: Probably no chance of that.

The bell above the door chimes, and I look up to see Nico walking in. By now, after a month, I've softened into our friendship. That frisson still remains, yet mostly when I see him it makes my heart happy instead of just pounding.

But that growing familiarity also means he immediately clocks my expression. He points at me and circles his finger around.

"What's with the giant smile?" he asks.

"My friend Anita's coming to visit!" I say without thinking.

"Ah," he replies, and I'm reminded from the look on his face that of course he knows Anita. I immediately regret saying anything.

"I forgot . . . well, yeah, Gia's Anita . . ." I stumble, realizing too late that of course Anita's related to his wife. But he waves me off.

"That's so nice for you," he replies, completely ignoring my bumbling and putting on his most genial expression.

I sort of . . . hate it? He's always so expressively open, and this is one of the first times I've ever seen him appear fake. But I guess I can't blame him for not wanting another reminder of something that's clearly sad for him.

We're saved from any more awkwardness by Emilia emerging from behind the customers and gesturing to Nico.

"Espresso?" she says, and he nods. He sits next to me at the counter as Emilia quickly grabs a small cup for him.

"I actually have a favor to ask you," he says to her. "Gia's doing the fundraising dinner for the Cassero Palio team, and she wanted to know if you'd do the desserts."

Emilia waves it off like it's nothing. "Of course."

"What's a Palio?" I can't help but ask.

"Ah," Emilia says, slapping the table with elation. "It's just about the stupidest thing anyone could imagine, but it's all anyone talks about come August."

"Okay . . ." I say, knowing she's dragging this out for my benefit.

"So, in Siena, they've had this annual horse race since the sixteen hundreds called Il Palio, and it's a competition between the neighborhoods. And every neighborhood has their own clubhouse and history dating back hundreds of years."

"That doesn't sound stupid—" I start, but Emilia cuts me off.

"Manciano decided in *2010* to start their own Palio. But because of animal rights or something, we race barrels instead of horses. And now everyone is obsessed with it as though these have been blood feuds for eons rather than a modern nothing race that's been run a handful of times. It's a bunch of men racing barrels around the streets for an hour in order to literally win a cloth."

"There's a women's team too," Nico amusedly points out.

"With a ridiculous pink trophy," Emilia scoffs, even though her bandana today is pink with flecks of gold sparkles.

"But now at least with the honor of the same barrel size," Nico points out. He's goading her, and I exhale a breath at seeing the lightness back in his eyes.

"It's completely ridiculous, and I want no part in it," she says with a flourish. "Except I obviously have been forced to join the Cassero team and would do anything to help them win."

"Naturally," I reply. I turn to Nico. "So why does Gia care about Cassero if she lives out of town?"

"Gia loves a competition," he says, and then he gives me a knowing look. "I can't think of anyone else like that who might get into the Palio this year . . ."

I lightheartedly smack him on the chest, and his booming laugh echoes off the small space.

"I don't actually live here," I reply.

"Oh, I bet you anything they ask you to participate for the women's team. The only rule is you have to live here or be related to someone who lives here, and every team stretches those rules as far as they can go to get their strongest team."

"I appreciate you acknowledging that I would absolutely be a strong teammate," I reply, acquiescing to his competitive taunting.

"Is Gia already set on convincing you to participate again this year?" Emilia asks Nico.

"Wait," I say gleefully, fully turning to Nico now. "*You* roll a barrel in this thing?"

"Well, me and seven teammates," he mumbles.

"But you don't live in town, *and* you don't have a business in town!"

"I like that you're already in the Palio competitiveness spirit," Emilia says with a laugh. "But he's on your team, so maybe don't fight this battle. Barrel rolling is all about strength and height, so at least four teams out of the six always try and convince Nico that he technically belongs to their district."

His beautiful blush is back, and I can't help but wonder how far down it goes below his shirt. He's so easily embarrassed whenever anyone gives him a compliment, which I'm never going to be able to not find endearing. Well, endearing and exceptionally hot. That thought is probably making me blush too.

"No one can say no to Gia," he says. And both Emilia and I nod, not arguing an irrefutable point.

"Hence why I said yes about the pastries for the fundraiser," Emilia points out.

"Good, I'll tell Gia," he says as he stands back up, then drains his espresso in one go. He turns to me, and the angle catches my breath. I'm sitting on a stool, and he's towering over me. I'm not really able to stop Emilia's comment about "strength and height" from running on repeat in my head.

"I'll see you tonight at the grove?" he says to me.

Right. The first night of permitted boar hunting is this evening, so we're sleeping outside. "Yup," I say, unwavering. I don't want him to even consider changing his mind.

"Okay." And with a tap on the counter, he's gone.

Chapter 10

The air is a perfect summer evening temperature when I pull my bike up to Nico's house. He's waiting outside, Luce hopping along beside him, spinning in circles of glee.

"Are you sure you want to do this?" he asks, for what has to be the twentieth time.

Nico's hesitancy is comical next to the overt enthusiasm from Luce. You'd think he was experiencing the greatest excitement of his life, based on the wiggly joy emanating from his little body, rather than an evening out in his own backyard.

"I'm here. I'm wearing white as requested." I motion to my outfit, and he nods.

"Good. I've also got reflector vests." He tosses me a yellow vest that's noticeably too large. "I don't want to take any chances of them not seeing us."

"Do you think Gia would be more or less upset if we got shot instead of a cow?" I tease.

Nico puts his head in his hands. "No joking about getting shot."

"Maybe for you," I argue. "But if we're really going to sleep outside to try and thwart aggressive boar hunters, I'm gonna at least need to be able to joke about the absurdity of it all."

"That's . . . fair," he says, handing over a rolled-up sleeping bag. I notice he has a much longer, stiffer bag that he's slung over his shoulder. I don't want to guess what's inside.

He starts walking into the grove, and I follow, Luce bouncing at our heels.

"We can take shifts when we need to sleep," he says as we make our way toward Gia's gate. "I brought two chairs out this morning so we have somewhere to sit, but with the sleeping bags, we can lie down if we get too tired."

"Sounds like a good plan," I reply, wanting to sound like I'm taking his instructions at least *a little* seriously.

We reach the gate, which is closed this time. I've never seen the cows penned in, but I guess that makes sense if he and Gia want to keep them safe and accounted for. We go into their area, and sure enough, two camping chairs are leaning up against a large tree.

But Nico hasn't mentioned anything, because he's examining a hole in the fence. "Someone ripped a piece of this," he says, crouching down to give it a closer look. "It wasn't like that earlier . . . I wonder if they already came by and are trying to send us a message."

"You think they're vandalizing your property?" I counter. "That's a pretty big step."

"I don't know what to think anymore," Nico says resignedly.

He sits down with a heavy sigh and opens up his bag. He pulls out a battery-powered lantern, some beers, a bag of snacks, and a rifle. It's like something out of a scene from a Western by way of Italy.

I sit down next to him. "What happens if you're asleep and they come and I need to shoot the rifle?" I ask.

He looks up, startled at the question. "The rifle isn't loaded, Kit?"

"Well, what's the point of it then?" I ask, flabbergasted.

"To scare them a little if they come near us!" he says in a tone that implies I should've found this obvious. "I'm not going to actively point a loaded rifle at someone, especially someone who technically has a right to be on the land."

"Oh." Right, that makes much more sense.

Okay, maybe I'm not the best partner in crime for this particular activity. They don't teach you how to ward off potentially dangerous hunters at culinary school in Manhattan.

"Gia's experience—and my hope—is that just by knowing we're doing this, they won't even come on our land. But if they *do* and they see us, they'll quickly leave. Tommaso talks a lot, but all the people he's hunting with aren't from around here, and they're paying him to go on an expedition. Tangling with angry local people wouldn't look good for his business."

"That's a relief," I reply honestly.

He opens a beer and hands one to me. Our fingers brush, and I hear him inhale softly. I quickly move away and try not to focus on it. It's going to be a *long* night if I'm grumbling internally about my embarrassing attraction to this man I've somehow volunteered to sleep next to.

We sit for a moment with the sounds of an outside evening—crickets chirping, wind rustling in the leaves. It's soothing. I'm too wired to even think about sleep yet.

"Tell me more about your grandfather," I finally say, wanting to soak up the stories of this place as we pass the time here. When we're at Belpagna with Emilia, we usually talk about food or the town, but I know that anytime I can bring up Nico's grandfather, he's especially happy.

"Well, he lived in the house I'm now in," he says. "I know I should update it because some parts are a little ridiculous—there's a bathroom with no door, just a curtain. The heater is fully powered by olive residue." He chuckles, and I love that the warmth of this topic makes any lingering awkwardness immediately dissipate. "And his decor consisted of a lot of dream catchers, even though he never actually went to the US or a reservation."

"He had a vision."

"He certainly did." His smile is soft. "Every time I think I should change something, I can't bear to lose the memories associated with the space as it is. I love his warped table where we had meals together. I love this photo he has on the wall from when I was finally old enough and trusted enough to get up on a ladder and rake the olives. There's an old, run-down chair with a falling-apart ottoman that I know I should get rid of, but it's where we sat and talked about so many important things. It's where I convinced him to open the mill, despite his total lack of interest in the machinery."

"It makes sense you don't want to let go of important parts of your foundation."

He nods, reflective. "What about you?" he asks, turning it around on me. "Did you start cooking with your family when you were little?"

I shake my head. "Not really," I answer honestly. "But I think I honed my drive as a kid, and that's been a huge part of my career. I'm focused like my dad. And he saw that early on, so he pushed me. When I started rowing, he became sort of obsessed with it. He'd train me when I wasn't in practice, always thinking I was beyond what my coaches could provide."

"Was he right?"

"Probably," I sigh. "I mean, I don't think I would've gotten as far as I did if he hadn't been stretching me to be better."

"What did that look like?" He opens another beer, ready to listen.

"Well, in the beginning it was extra practices, mostly. Summers at camps, getting on the radars of top coaches. In high school I got picked for the junior national team, and so my dad really laser-focused in on technique after that. But it was worth it in the end—we won Junior Worlds, and then in college my team won the national championship." I pause, not wanting to get into more than that. "Then I discovered cooking, fell in love with it, and went to culinary school in New York."

"And you think sports helped with that?"

"It made me clearheaded," I say honestly. "I knew how to push, how to win. It taught me how to set a goal and achieve it. And while I liked rowing, I *loved* cooking. The ability to constantly learn, to be creative while also being precise . . . it fit me perfectly. And living in

New York was like I'd found a place that matched my intensity. It's the perfect controlled chaos for me."

"I've always felt that way with Rome too," he says.

"You did?"

"Yeah, I loved growing up there."

"So what made you want to be here for more than just harvests?"

He's silent for a bit, and I wonder what nerve I've hit. He runs his hands through his hair, the habit I've noticed he has whenever he's lost for words.

"I fell in love with my wife," he finally says quietly. My chest twinges at his words, sad for having opened this heartache for him again with my question. "Lorena grew up here. She was a couple years younger than me. We always knew each other because Gia and my grandfather were next door to each other. And while they never really got along, it didn't matter because . . . well, you can see how the fence is never closed and this town is so small. Lorena didn't want to go to college because all she wanted was to take over for Gia. So she was here. And I fell in love with her, and it seemed worth it to me to stay. I loved Rome, but I loved her more. And I truly loved it here too. As I got older, it felt more like home than Rome. It seemed like the perfect life, really."

He takes another long sip of beer. He's staring into the darkness as though ghosts might come out of the shadows. That melancholy is back, and I want to reach out to him, even though I know it's probably a bad idea.

I can't stop myself from asking the one other question I've been wondering. "When did she die?"

He jerks toward me, and I'm afraid I've said something extremely wrong. Weren't we kind of talking about it? Was that taking it too far, though?

But I did not expect the next thing he says. "She didn't . . . die? Why do you think that?"

My mouth falls open. "You said . . . ? You said your wife was gone? And so did Gia? I just assumed . . ." I don't think I could've put my foot further into my mouth. My whole face is heating up, and thank goodness the only light is from this small lantern, because I feel like a complete moron.

"Man, you and Anita really don't talk about family things, do you?" he asks, and I can't tell yet if he's offended or amused.

"I mean . . ." I think about it. "I guess not. Anita hated my boyfriend, so that made us avoid talking about wider stuff." That's a depressing thought, but I guess it's sort of true.

"I always assumed you knew that," he says quietly. "This town is so damn small, I figure everyone knows my wife left me."

The pain in his voice makes me want to stand up and hunt her down so I can strangle her. His wife *left*? What was wrong with her? He's . . . well . . . I don't want to admit that the thought currently crossing my mind is that Nico's one of the best men I've ever met. He's kind and gentle and brilliant and so fucking handsome it makes me insane sometimes.

"I'm sorry," I finally say, "I just find that extremely hard to even fathom."

"Why?"

"Because you're you!" I blurt out, and I'm once again grateful for the lack of light because I'm cringing at my total lack of tact. I mean, I never have tact, but usually it's in the context of being everyone's boss in a kitchen. Not delving into the personal lives of sweet men who don't need me making them feel worse.

But he chuckles softly, almost as though what I'm saying is so ridiculous that he finds it funny. And that makes me so sad it aches. How can I look at him and see someone so wonderful, while he truly believes there's no surprise in someone falling out of love with him?

"Seriously, I know I haven't been here long, but come on. Something must have been deeply wrong with her," I finally say, wanting desperately to forcibly banish the seeds of doubt his wife left him with.

"It wasn't her fault," he says, and that cracks my heart even more. I'm ready to start yelling at him, to make him believe he's better than that, but he senses my rising indignation and holds up his hand. I wait. I can see he has more to say but that maybe it's hard to. He sweeps a hand through his hair again, another gesture of trying to find comfort somewhere.

That longing to help is palpable. It's such an unusual feeling for me, that kind of desperation to solve something for someone else. But I force myself to give him the space he clearly wants. Until finally, he speaks again.

"Staying felt easy to me once we were together. I loved the land, I loved my grandfather, and I loved her. It never occurred to me to live anywhere else. But we *did* travel a lot, showcasing the oil internationally. And she'd never really done that. I think the more she saw of the world, the more she realized she didn't actually want this small life. And it just happened that she came to that realization right around when my grandfather died and I was taking everything over. I *couldn't* leave. And she couldn't stay."

"So she just . . . left?"

"I don't blame her," he says. And that makes me the saddest of all. "At least Gia was pissed enough at her that she's kept me on as a surrogate grandson. I didn't lose everyone."

He goes quiet again, and I know the only thing I can do for him is give his misery some company. "John left me, too, if it makes you feel any better," I share, surprised once again that words I keep in with everyone else slip out around him. "The breakup that just happened. We'd been together for almost five years, and I thought things were fine. I mean, we didn't live together and we didn't really have much in common outside of work, but it worked for *me*. My job's a little insane . . . Anyway, my restaurant caught on fire, and he decided that was the moment to dump me."

"That's pretty shitty," he says with a sigh.

I pick a stick up off the ground and fiddle with it. "Is it clichéd if I also say I don't blame him?"

"It's not clichéd if it's true."

I nod, recognizing that this conversation has become a safe space for us both now.

"I always thought he would leave," I admit, now tracing patterns in the dirt so I can keep fidgeting. "And I wasn't the easiest girlfriend. So without a restaurant, I can get why our relationship wouldn't have worked anymore."

"Something must have been 'deeply wrong' with him," he says with a small smile, purposely echoing my words back to him.

"Unlike you, I'm not going to argue with that," I reply with a laugh.

But I'm stunned into silence when he reaches out a hand and takes mine. His is warm and rough; my hand fits completely inside his. He moves his thumb over mine, like it's the most natural thing in the world, like he doesn't see or care that mine are as calloused as his.

I can't help but stare transfixed, burning up from the contact. It feels so *intimate*, this little piece of comfort he's gifting me, or that maybe we're gifting each other. Two abandoned souls finding solace in each other and in the purity of protecting the animals around them. The indisputable chemistry that exists between us makes it hard to breathe. It makes me wonder what he's going to do next.

But something shifts, and he gingerly disentangles our hands. We're silent for a long time, as though that silence can help us ignore the hand-holding and confessions, if we just give it long enough.

"You're really kind to me," he finally says, and I wish I could reach back out to him again, but I get the sense that the moment is gone. "I'm extremely grateful we're friends."

I know he means it as a compliment, but the word "friends" lands with a thud between us.

"Me too, Nico," I whisper. Because it's true, even if after only a month of knowing him, I already feel like he's so much more; that word feels so small compared to the lifeline that his friendship is for me right now.

"Promise even when you go home at the end of the summer, we can still be friends?" he says. "I don't think I'll find anyone else to talk to about olive yields depending on water alkalinity."

I snort a laugh at that. We *did* spend the better part of an hour debating that the other day.

It's hard to shake off the confusion of everything that's unsaid. Whatever tension sits with us whenever we're together, whatever the spark is that I constantly feel with him, whatever kernel of truth sits inside every conversation we have . . . he deliberately ignores it.

And maybe it's better that way. I don't need to suddenly turn into the kind of person who pines and confesses my woes to a new friend—someone I didn't even know a month ago. Being in a new place doesn't mean I need to go completely soft.

I'm here for the summer, we *are* friends, but I need to get back to my regular version of myself that doesn't need to say so much.

So we sit. We sit up and protect Gia's cows. We take turns sleeping in the night. And when the sun rises, we've got a whole new day ahead of us.

Chapter 11

By Monday I'm tired. The restaurant is always busy, but weekends feel more lively and we always close later in the evening. Now is also the most popular hunting time for tourists, so Nico and I have been sleeping outside for a few nights in a row.

He and I feed the cows every morning after waking up. He isn't comfortable enough yet to let them roam around his land again—not because the hunters wouldn't see them during the day but because he's become convinced that Tommaso and his allies have been messing with the fence, and he doesn't trust them not to stage an "accident" to get back at Gia. If the cows stay fenced in, Tommaso would have no excuse.

But that means I'm arriving to the restaurant at eleven after a poor night's sleep with just enough time to grab my tea and shower (and okay, yes, still shoot the shit with Emilia and Nico over that cup of tea. Because what, am I not allowed to live?).

I tried explaining the scenario to my dad, who told me not to get behind on my "pasta studies." It made me realize it would be impossible to explain this place to anyone who isn't here. How do I get into the fact that my "pasta studies" include loyalty to an elderly woman whose cows are in trouble?

I decide these evenings with Nico don't need to be mentioned again.

And in another twist on "things that are wasting my time," I also spent a large portion of the week arguing with Gia over her boar ragù. Yes, it's a classic dish to the region—ragù di cinghiale—and she serves it over a polenta that is somehow crispy on the outside and pillowy soft on the inside. But my argument that we have to hit the hunters where it hurts found no purchase with Gia. And honestly, I've got to respect someone so old school that she could have a blood feud with some dudes but still not let that touch her culinary integrity. She's hardcore.

So this is all to say, maybe I'm not in the best mood when I get in the car with Nico to go get new fencing to patch up the spots that are broken.

I've tried to convince him that since they're dramatically too small for a cow to get through, it doesn't matter. But Nico likes to live on principles, which I can't fault him for. And apparently our principles include not letting Gia's fence "sit in ruin" (his words, not mine). So since he once again made it about Gia's honor, I insisted on going with him on my day off.

But now that it *is* my day off, I'm a little cranky.

"I would've thought enough of Emilia's pastries would solve anything for you," he jokes as we pull out of Manciano, heading toward Saturnia, another nearby town.

"Apparently they're not as all-powerful as we thought," I pout.

"There's a good pastry shop in Saturnia; we could double down."

My mouth drops open in shock. "We're not going to *cheat on Emilia*!"

"You think I've never eaten breakfast anywhere in this entire region other than Belpagna?" he asks. I'm silent because I want to answer *Yes*, but I know rationally that's absurd. "Do you think I also only ever have dinner at Pasta Fresca?"

I scrunch my nose and try to think of something pithy to say in retort, but I'm too tired. I'm saved by the bell of the GPS voice blaring out from my phone saying, *In five hundred meters, turn left*.

But Nico doesn't make a move to turn. "Are you so distracted by cheating on all your most loyal and beloved women that you're going to make a wrong turn?" I ask.

"That's not the right way," he says offhandedly.

"If you keep going straight, it adds four minutes to the drive!"

"Who cares?"

"Why *wouldn't* you go the faster way?"

"Because I've done this drive a hundred times," he points out.

"But maybe you've just been doing it wrong for twenty years, and you never knew because you didn't turn on your GPS."

He sighs, and I'm shocked when he flicks on his left blinker and makes the turn.

I'm, again, without a comeback. I'm so used to fighting with men after drawing nonsensical lines in the sand and having them be just as unwilling to back down as I always am. It's a habit you *have* to form as a female chef. You can't show weakness or compromise because you'll always get run over. It's a callus that forms over itself every time you try to be conciliatory, only to have it backfire on you.

But Nico simply made the turn.

"Okay, where to now?" he asks.

My mind is still practically going through a hard reboot, but I manage to say, "You're on this for a couple kilometers, and then you turn right, and that takes you straight into the center of town."

"Really?" His tone always surprises me. It's never dubious. He's always curious. He practically exists to be curious and have his mind changed. Although, from a work perspective, I guess you can't aim to upend production protocols if you aren't open to trying new things.

"That's what it says," I respond, looking over the map one more time.

We turn right, down a smaller road. "I guess this must be a shortcut I never knew about," he says gamely, driving along even as the road turns to dirt and starts narrowing.

We're only about a minute in when I start to suspect I've made a mistake. We're on a road, sure, but it's looking less and less like one the farther we go. A dirt path stretches in front of us, caged by trees that lean in, making the road look like it has a tented canopy. All the vegetation makes it hard to see where the road might let out. And as we keep going, the dirt becomes heavily scattered with rocks, with some of them large enough that the car goes over them like they're speed humps.

Nico keeps going, but he's slowing down. There are increasingly more rocks, and the trees are tightening in. When I see branches start to scrape the windows, I have to speak up.

"I think . . ." I start, fighting all my instincts. "I think I was wrong. You need to stop the car."

He slowly stops and then looks over at me. "Did we take the wrong turn?"

I hand him my phone and show him Google Maps pulled up on it.

"We did take the turn it says we should take. And it's still showing that we go straight. But . . . I think it's an error in the map. I don't think we can actually go this way."

"Do you want to try and go a little farther to see?"

I appreciate how, even in the face of overwhelming evidence that this is absolutely a disaster, he's still letting me make the call.

I put my head in my hands. "I'm kind of worried about the rocks puncturing your tires at some point," I admit. My voice is muffled, and I'm so embarrassed. He knew how to go, and I stupidly thought I knew better—or, to be fair to me, that our overlords at Google knew better. But still.

"I'm so sorry, Nico. I shouldn't have insisted."

I start to feel my heart speed up, and not in a fun way. I'm not used to being the fuckup. I'm the person who executes. I'm the person you can count on. I'm the person who will work ten times harder to get us where we need to go. And, unhelpfully, this total screwup suddenly brings forward everything else I've screwed up lately—I wasn't good enough for John; I couldn't protect my restaurant; I don't have anyone other than Anita who chooses to be my friend outside of work. And now I'm trapped in a forest where spiraling seems like the only rational option.

But Nico gently takes hold of my wrist with one hand and lifts my chin up with the other, snapping me out of it. "No one could have guessed the map was wrong, okay? It's not a big deal."

Normally when Nico touches me in any way, all I feel is that undeniable spark between us. But this time it's so tender I want to cry. No one has ever treated me with care the way he does. I pull my hand away and bite my nails so I won't keep going down the path of turning into a basket case.

But that doesn't go unnoticed either.

"Please stop hurting yourself, okay?" he asks quietly. I put my hands down, and I can see him exhale. I exhale out slowly with him, and then he keeps talking. "Okay . . . we just have to back up, I guess? We got in, so we can get out. We'll take it slow, and eventually we'll get back on the road."

I nod and take a deep breath. He's right. It's a challenge, and we can handle it. I'm someone who knows what it's like to be totally in the weeds on the line. I know what it's like to have everyone counting on you to slowly but surely get yourself out of whatever hole you're in. So this I can do.

I shake out my shoulders and get back into game mode.

"I definitely didn't save us four minutes, huh?" I joke, knowing the best way to get back on track is to fake it until I make it. If I can fake feeling lighter, then eventually it'll be real.

"No," he says with a smile, "but you did get us an adventure."

He puts the car in reverse, and immediately I can see that this is going to be near impossible. The car has a backup camera, but because branches are hitting us from every side, the car interprets them as though we're hitting something at each door. And as a result, instead of showing the image on the screen that would help us line up the tires, it's blaring angry sounds and showing an image of the car with bright red on either side to politely remind us that we're too close to the edges.

All I can contribute is whether he seems too close on my side, but with such little wiggle room, it's impossible to know with any accuracy. I try to open the window so I can look out, but all that gets me is some branches with truly unnecessarily sharp thorns on my arms.

This cannot be the best way to do this.

"Okay," I finally say, "I know I got us into this mess, so please tell me to fuck off if you want to, but can I make a suggestion?"

He stops backing up, parks the car, and turns to face me. Without the car constantly beeping at us, the silence of being stuck in a mass of trees is suddenly deafening.

"Kit. I have no idea why you would think that's what I would say to you right now, or that I wouldn't be open to a suggestion."

He seems almost disappointed in me, which makes me feel like a kid who's about to cry in front of their teacher. "I wasn't saying you *should* tell me to fuck off," I mumble.

"If you want to try and lead us out of here, I'm a thousand percent ready to be your sous chef and follow instructions."

"Even though I don't know what I'm doing?" I ask nervously.

But he chuckles, the sound a beautiful, quiet balm. "I don't think either of us knows what we're doing when it comes to reversing out of a glorified dirt road littered with rocks while tree branches scratch their way across the car," he points out. "So if you have an idea, I'm in. Let's try it."

I have to swallow to stop the shock from roaring back in. I'm not used to patience and consideration. Those are definitely not traits in a working kitchen. It's a strange sensation to have someone like Nico in my life—he's a sharpshooter made to precisely pinpoint every crack in the wall I've built around myself.

But I can't focus on that now.

"I think I should get out and direct you from behind the car," I say. "The issue we keep having is if you go even an inch to the left or right, the road is so narrow that it buttresses you up into a tree. So we've got to be precise about it. I can call you so you can hear me, and I'll direct as you go?"

"Let's try it," he says with a nod.

His expression is encouraging, so that's my cue to take a deep breath and exit the car. I get scraped on every limb, but I'm able to press myself against the car enough so I can squeeze past and then get behind it.

Looking at the car from this angle, it's clear we definitely need to be careful. The "road" is only a few inches wider than the car on either side. And the roots of the trees really buttress up right to the edge, along with some of the larger rocks at points.

I take a deep breath and call Nico. He immediately answers. "How does it look from back there?"

"Do you really want to know?" I ask, and I'm bolstered by one of his loud laughs.

"Nope," he says cheerfully. "Just tell me what to do, and I'll follow."

I try to hold on to some of his confidence as we slowly make our way—we really have to focus on not making any mistakes that could get us stuck. *Just a* touch *to the left there. No, no, no . . . there you go . . . straight . . . straight . . . you're tilting just a little bit . . . whoops, you're too close on the right . . .*

And on and on. The sun is getting higher in the sky, and I'm heating up. The dust that the car has kicked up is fully caking me. The scratches from earlier burn a bit as I let them linger. But we're making progress. It's crazy to think that going forward, this took us only a few minutes, but backing out is a whole other ball game.

Our encouragement and the rhythm keep things steady. The situation does sort of remind me of being in the kitchen with another chef on a night when we're slammed but we still feel like we're a step ahead of drowning. We're simply one foot in front of the other, not looking behind me to see how much farther we have to go and only focusing on each small stretch as we're doing it.

Slow. Steady. Patient with each other and ourselves. We're both making the other better; as the person in charge at my restaurant, I'm not used to having an equal teammate like this. But it's working.

After about half an hour, the road starts to open up again. And finally, we get to a point where he can turn around. Once the car is facing out, he puts it in park and hops out. All that nervous energy I've been holding in with patience has to burst out, and I can't help but run up to him and let out a cheer as he wraps me in a hug.

"You did *so* great," I say, my face buried into his chest, disarmed by how good he smells and how much I like having his arms around me.

He doesn't say anything back, just tilts down so his chin is resting on the top of my head. I can feel him breathe me in too. We linger for a moment. I'm dirty from head to toe, and he's still cool from the blast of the air-conditioning, but we're both basking in the same experience. The adrenaline high from suspense is having its comedown. I'm flooded with a sense of relief that I'm not sure is from getting out of a precarious situation or from allowing myself to hold on to this hug from Nico.

But eventually, as my pulse slowly abates, the fog of excitement starts to clear, and I know I need to take a step back. I've never been so reluctant to leave a platonic hug in my life. I wonder if he is too.

"Well . . ." I say, cringing when I see how much dust I've rubbed all over his shirt and how many scratches are now on his car. "I guess we should go your way to Saturnia?"

He chuckles one last time and gets in the car. I follow suit.

"I'd follow you a lot of places," he says with a lopsided grin, "but from now on, Saturnia's directions are mine, okay?"

I couldn't agree more.

Chapter 12

I wake up a few days later to incessant banging on my door. I pull the covers over my head, thinking maybe if I ignore it, the banging will stop. But unfortunately nothing can deter whoever has decided to make my door their personal piñata.

I get up and throw on a pair of pants. I swing the door open and am momentarily stunned by the tiny, bangled whirlwind standing in front of me.

"Anita?!"

"Surprise!"

"I thought you weren't coming until next week?" My half-asleep brain is still trying to catch up.

"I never get to be one step ahead of you," she teases with a mischievous smile and a pinch to my cheeks.

I can't stop myself from pulling her into a tight hug. As much as she knows I hate surprises—as anyone normally tasked with keeping an expensive ship upright every night would—I'm so grateful to have my favorite challenging pain in the ass in front of me. Maybe she and I don't swap family stories as much as Nico would've expected, but she's there for me in every way that matters. She brightens my rough edges. She always reminds me of that Rolling Stones line—Anita comes in color everywhere. And she knows that if I'd been aware of her arrival, I probably would've fussed and prepped and gone out of my way.

I've got to hand it to her for playing chess when I wasn't even aware the game had started.

She loosens her grip, kisses me on the cheek, and then automatically wanders into my apartment, making herself at home. She grabs water from the tap and curls up onto my couch.

"How do you look so put together after sleeping on a plane, when I'm a mess after a normal night?" I muse as I sit next to her.

"I showered at Nonna's," she says with a shrug. "And she had a double espresso waiting for me on arrival."

"Oh okay, so everyone knew you were coming except for me," I pout.

That smile is back. She's so damn pleased with herself. "I didn't want you to go to any trouble," she says, confirming my earlier suspicions. "I don't need you to do anything for me. I'm here to visit and not get in the way."

"So does that mean you won't be hovering around the kitchen tonight?" I ask, already knowing the answer.

"Of course not," she shoots back. "I grew up on those tables, watching Nonna. Now I get to harass you too? I can't think of anything better."

I grumble and stand, having noticed it's time for me to get moving anyway. But Anita's not letting me stay grumpy. "I brought you something," she says, handing over a box.

"Oh my god, Nosh Sticks!" I practically hop up and down with glee over seeing my favorite American snack food.

"Happy with my surprise now?" she laughs.

"A thousand percent," I say, already ripping open the box to eat one. "I'm getting dressed, and then I'm making you come with me for the rest of my morning routine."

"I love that you have a morning routine here!" she says. "Manciano has really become a little oasis from home for you, huh?" Her eyes practically have hearts in them for how sappy she seems over her master plan working. I want to push back, the way I always do. But something in her expression makes me unable to burst her bubble.

"It has," I admit.

After a quick cold shower to wake myself up and a change into clean clothes, I'm much more able to bask in Anita's sudden presence. We walk arm in arm on my usual route, only this time instead of being alone with my thoughts, I'm getting color commentary from my best friend. Houses I've walked past every day suddenly get a story attached about Anita's childhood antics, small strings tethering me more to the history of this little town.

We climb up the steps until we reach my morning summit. There's a misty haze hanging in the distance, and it's covering the ocean from showing up on the horizon.

"You come up here every morning?" Anita asks, and we plop down on the bench, its black steel always a strange contrast to the ancient knobbly sand-colored stones of the walls surrounding it.

The square in front of us is still empty. It's lovely always seeing the town from above when it's so quiet in the morning; the old marble fountain hasn't even had its water turned on yet. To the right, a person waves from a deck chair on their balcony. I wonder if they slept there or came up with the sun.

"It's peaceful," I reply, not knowing otherwise how to put into words the serenity of my daily ritual of staring out from town to farmland to distant ocean.

"It's very peaceful," Anita agrees. "Although I can't believe you've become a person who can imagine yourself outside the four walls of a restaurant."

I scoff. "That's a very narrow version of my life in New York."

Anita just shrugs with a mischievous smile, the implication clear. I ruffle her hair and take her hand.

"But I admit it's not completely inaccurate." I pause, staring out at the mist as it slowly burns off from the sun getting higher. "When I'm cooking with Gia, I can easily slip back into that."

"So what stopped you from slipping into it completely?"

"The damn woman insists on days and mornings off," I say with a smirk, and Anita chuckles.

"So you've been nudged into not only learning the vast superiority of pasta, but also into finding yourself outside the kitchen?"

"I wouldn't go that far," I say, pursing my lips as I consider it. "I guess . . . with these mornings . . . I've at least realized that when I go home, I should probably widen my world a little bit," I admit. "I hadn't realized how insular I'd become."

She gives my hand a squeeze, and we sit, staring out into the distance a bit longer, letting that admission make its way out of my mouth and into the open air.

In typical Anita fashion, she doesn't make me dwell once she's shucked me open. "I don't think I've ever sat up here," she says, allowing a subject change. I happily take the out.

"Well, when I first arrived, I would just read all morning, since there's so many books I haven't caught up on," I try to explain. "But time stretched a little too much. I had to find some semblance of a routine so I wouldn't get twitchy."

I can see from her dubious expression that Anita knows I'm minimizing, but she doesn't push it. "Well, it's a good routine," she says. "You found a good spot for morning thoughts."

She pats my knee, and I put my head on her shoulder. I shouldn't have worried so much about letting Anita see that this place has been good for me. I shouldn't always shy away from letting anyone see that there's some tenderness in me too.

I notice the poem carved into the wall once again and sit back up.

"I've been wondering what that poem's all about," I say, gesturing to it. "My translation didn't make any sense."

Anita looks over and smiles. "I find that with English, too—poetry is always the hardest medium to translate, because when we convey emotion through lyrical language, there's always something lost when it has to be explained."

She stands up and goes closer, lightly touching the marble that the words sit on, examining the words through feel as much as language. "'Ti Amo Maremma. Fin Dove al Mar Ti Sposi e Ti Vesti di Tramonti,'" she repeats quietly, the melody of her mother tongue making the words sound even more poetic. "It's quite beautiful, actually. That second sentence is hard to translate, but it's roughly like, 'where you marry the sea and clothe yourself in sunsets.' I'd interpret it as people's love for this region is so strong that it's as boundless as the sea, while as beautiful as the sunset. I sort of adore that it's set in stone here because, to me, it's meant to be about enduring love. A connection to a place."

Her fingers are still dancing across each indent where the letters have been made. I wonder how much she misses it here when she's gone. I wonder if she looks out of New York Harbor and thinks of the Atlantic connecting her all the way back to Maremma. I wonder why I've never asked.

But I'm doing a lot of things lately that I never have before.

"Why didn't you want to come back here after culinary school and your internships?"

She turns back around to face me, a small smile in the curve of her lips. "Because I fell in love with Eddie," she says simply. It pains me how much her happy story echoes Nico's heartbreaking one.

I think of her now-husband, as connected to the Bronx as she is to Maremma, and I realize these must've been hard conversations for the two of them. But again, I never asked.

"He couldn't build a full life here," she explains, sensing all my questions. "He doesn't speak any Italian. And I was already in New York. Once we were together, there wasn't really a question of where we should live. I miss it, of course I do, but you can have more than one home. New York and Maremma are both home for me."

"I'm sorry I never really knew what a sacrifice you'd made," I reply, the truth so obvious now.

But she shrugs it off. "It's not what you and I do, you know? That's how I know we're both New Yorkers first and foremost now. We don't dwell; we keep moving. And we both know the other person always has our back. If I'd needed to get emotional about it, I would've told you."

"I'm glad I understand it better now," I say quietly.

"Me too."

She sits back down on the bench, and now it's her turn to rest her head on my shoulder.

"I checked in on your restaurant before I left," she mentions.

I scoff. "You wanted some latent barbecue smells?" I have to joke about it so my compartmentalizing can keep potential sadness out.

"They've actually gotten a fair amount of work done." She sits up to look me in the eyes, so I can see she's serious. "You haven't talked to John about what they're doing?"

"Have I talked to *John*?" I ask, incredulous that she'd assume I'd been in contact with her least favorite person and my current least favorite ex.

"I just mean about the restaurant, obviously. He's gotten a crew in pretty quickly. They've already cleared all the debris out, and the permitting is getting fast-tracked."

"What?" Now I'm really confused. "All I've heard from one of the other partners is that they're working on it and felt optimistic about the end of summer."

"Well . . . yeah, I think because John's made it his personal mission," she says, her face now scrunched in that adorable way she does when she's processing something. "I assumed he had some motive and would've told you."

"Money is his only motive," I say dismissively. "He probably just wants to get things moving as quickly as possible again so his investment doesn't sit empty."

Anita still has that dubious look on her face, and I'm curious what part of this seems so off to her. "He told me to tell you hello. When I was there. He was overseeing whatever they were doing, and he started chatting to me like nothing was wrong. My instinct was to punch him, but I didn't think you'd like that."

I chuckle. "No, I don't think any punching is necessary."

"I just don't like that he's got something up his sleeve that he hasn't told you about."

"Let it go, Anita," I sigh. "The man dumped *me*. There's nothing he wants from me other than to get me cooking again. Being friendly to you is his way to help him sweep it all under the rug."

Anita harrumphs next to me but doesn't say anything else about it. Instead she hops up and holds her hand out to me.

"All right, enough of this sentimentality. I want to go to Belpagna," she says cheerily.

I gladly let her pull me up, and we walk down the stone steps, away from the poetry of words and landscapes and toward the poetry of pastry.

Chapter 13

The bell chimes above the door, and I see Nico swivel around on his stool to watch us walking into Belpagna. I shouldn't be surprised that he's here already—I stayed out longer with Anita than I normally would. He's already drained one espresso and a plate is empty in front of him, except for a dusting of sugar.

He smiles when his eyes land on me, but I see the hesitancy when he spots Anita. I wince, thinking of how he probably also had no idea she was showing up today.

"Anita! *Ciao*!" Emilia comes out from behind the counter and wraps her up in a big hug. Emilia's bandana today has pumpkins on it, which seems hilariously unseasonable for her. She must've gotten dressed in a hurry. But whatever razzed her morning is nowhere to be seen now as she excitedly starts chatting rapidly in Italian to Anita. I take the opportunity to sidle up next to Nico and drop onto the stool next to him.

"So, Anita came early," I say, stating the obvious.

"Are you a person who likes surprises?" he asks, in a tone that indicates he knows the answer already.

"I am not," I chuckle. "But it's Anita, so I'm glad she's here." He smiles gently and nods, looking into his empty cup. "Is it weird for you?" I ask.

He shrugs and fiddles with a napkin. His demeanor is always so easy that I usually forget he's a little stuck in some places too. "Anita and

Lorena, my ex-wife . . . they weren't particularly close, especially because it's been so long since Anita even lived here. But . . . I feel like everyone else in town has moved past it at this point; or at least they don't openly pity me anymore the way they did a few years ago." His small laugh is hollow, and I want to grab another pastry from behind the counter just to add some sunshine and sugar back into his life. But he carries on. "Every time someone related to Lorena comes back, it's like the entire town then gets a fresh excuse to start a new dance around how I'm doing . . . then to ask how *Lorena's* doing, even though I obviously don't know anymore. It's like I have to be in that fishbowl again."

I surreptitiously glance around the room, and he's right—it's hilarious how much everyone is casually watching this scene. Eyes dart from Anita to Nico to see when that little piece of gossip will begin.

"Do you want us to grab something and go?" I ask, searching my mind for any solution to his discomfort. But he shakes his head.

"That's ridiculous, Kit. Other people's boredom isn't a reason to mess with our morning."

I give his shoulder a squeeze in solidarity, hoping to convey my understanding. His head tilts down, his hair brushing my fingers, like an involuntary nuzzle. I can't help but lean into it, which makes me immediately regret touching him. I *have* to stop doing this to myself. Any friendly contact between us instantly lures me in, making me powerless against lingering longer than I should. It's embarrassing how much even his smallest gestures affect me.

I make myself move my hand away. I've got to get a grip.

"I can't believe she was able to pull one over on you," Emilia says gleefully from behind the counter, nodding toward a beaming Anita, who sits on the stool next to me.

"Yeah, if you have to be awoken by interminable pounding on your door, at least let it be your long-lost friend," I quip.

Nico snorts next to me, and both Emilia and Anita turn to look at him.

"Good to see you, Nico," Anita says, reaching out to shake his hand. "How've you been?"

I'm grateful she's being so innocuous. I actually *am* kind of curious about what she thinks of the whole situation. But considering that would make me just as bad of a gossip as everyone else in this town, I definitely file that thought away.

Nico seems relieved as well, and they start chatting about this year's harvest. Anita is obviously well versed in the olive oil process, and they get deep enough in that I finally switch seats with her and look at Emilia.

"I think it's a bombolone kind of day," I say, and before I can even finish the sentence, Emilia has whipped out a plate and shoved a pastry on top of it. She turns around to make my tea and then swiftly places it in front of me.

"I think," she says with that sly look of hers, "the cats outside are protesting your hatred of them, because now I have three on my hands."

I look out the window and see a calico trio pressing their faces to the glass.

"Or maybe," I reply pointedly, "the rest of them got the memo that you're a sucker."

Emilia scrunches her nose with a smile. "I don't know *what* you're talking about."

And then without another word, she walks outside with scraps for the cats.

"I'm going to head out too," Nico says, taking the opportunity to stand. "Anita, it's lovely to see you. Welcome back."

"Glad to see you're well, Nico," she replies.

I catch a little bit of what Nico was talking about earlier in Anita's expression. There's a tinge of pity to it, laced with the discomfort of knowing there's an undercurrent to whatever she says. I can understand why he'd be hesitant to have any reminder of a past he's desperately trying to move on from.

But if Nico's registered Anita's countenance, he doesn't show it. He puts a hand on my shoulder, mirroring my gesture from before, and it takes everything in me not to copy his earlier movement and lean my head into him.

"If you want to skip our stakeouts this weekend to hang with Anita, don't worry about it," he says. "I can handle it on my own."

"No!" I rush, maybe a little too forcefully.

I know I shouldn't anticipate our evenings as much as I do—and certainly my back doesn't appreciate my enthusiasm for an activity that includes sleeping on the ground—but I've started looking forward to our weekend surveillance overnights. I try to convince myself that it's because I like being outside; or that I really do want to help Gia; or that I love the cows (?). But you can't hide untruths from your gut, and my gut covets those unhurried conversations with Nico in the dark.

My whole life has been whirlwinds and pushing and edges. There's a softness I get to have in those evenings that I've never had before. And I want it.

"Okay then," he replies without pushing. Maybe he wants our evenings, too, even if neither of us would ever say so out loud. He lifts his hand off my shoulder and gives all three of us an awkward little wave. "See you guys later."

I watch him walk out the door. When I look back at Anita, there's skepticism lining her face.

"What in the actual fuck was that?" she asks, raising an eyebrow at me.

"What?" I genuinely have no idea what she's talking about.

"You and Nico were . . . looking at each other."

"I look at most people I talk to." I take a long sip of my tea and stare right back at her.

"The vibes were weird."

"I cannot help you if you're asking me about vibes."

She lifts one of her fingers into my face. "What are you and Nico staking out? And why do I get the impression you want to be staking each other out?"

I scoff, like a kid whose hand is in the candy jar and wants to protest a bit too much. And apparently, my salvation will be in babbling. "We're doing a favor for *Gia*. She's in some feud with the boar hunters, and they killed one of her cows last year—they say by accident; she doesn't agree—and so she tried to get them booted off her land, but she lost so now she thinks they're going to retaliate, so on weekends when they're here, Nico and I sleep with the cows to keep anyone from hurting them."

I think maybe I've bamboozled Anita with such a ridiculous story that it's hard to parse out what the hell I'm even talking about. "That's abnormal," she finally says.

"I'll say."

"Even for Gia," she clarifies.

"Eh, I'd guess Gia gets herself into more abnormal situations than most," I counter.

Anita laughs and pats my hand. "You're probably right about that. But it's nice of you to want to take care of her."

I can see I'm off the hook because she's happy I'm protecting her nonna. And Anita knows I'm the kind of person who sets a stake in the ground when it comes to loyalty, especially for another chef, regardless of whether it was for her grandmother or not.

Although I know we just talked about how we can be close without dwelling on details, I still feel an unfamiliar twinge of guilt over not completely letting Anita in. It makes me think of all the other ways I've kept my supposed best friend at arm's length. I wish it wasn't Nico's voice that was echoing through my head right now, but I can't help it.

Man, you and Anita really don't talk about family things, do you?

His words have been sitting with me ever since he said them, in part because it's so strange that I never even considered the idea myself. I've always been able to handle my shit on my own—I'm proud of that—but I wonder if I could talk things through a bit more.

Anita's voice shakes me out of the thought. "I'm glad Nico seems well," she says, as much to herself as to me.

And at that, I can't help but take the opening.

"Yeah, I never knew anything about your cousin Lorena," I venture. "I always assumed if one person was expected to stay and take over for Gia, it would've been you."

But Anita doesn't have a second to respond before Emilia comes back to her perch at the counter and cuts in. "Oh, with Lorena that was always going to end badly," she says, inserting herself seamlessly back into the conversation as though she never left. "That girl had no idea what she wanted, so she latched onto Gia and then onto Nico. She never knew herself well enough to build her whole life around two good people. It was bound to snap."

"I think Gia sort of underestimated Lorena," Anita adds. "She never pressured me to take over because she always saw my wings were wider; I wasn't ever going to stay in Manciano. I think Lorena *seemed* like she was content here. And Gia *wanted* to see that, because she wanted someone in the family to take over for her. But her life became so small at such a young age. She got married, she had her role at the restaurant. Her whole life was laid out, and I think she just freaked."

"Pshh," Emilia says, clearly not on Team Lorena in whatever this story is. "She made her choices and then changed her mind. *And* didn't care about taking down two of my favorite people along with her destruction."

Anita obviously has a softer spot for her cousin because she tilts her head back and forth in thought. "If it's not right, it's not right," she finally says. "Gia's okay. And it seems like Nico's okay now. No one would've been better off with her staying around when she'd already realized she didn't want to."

"It's still sad, though," I say quietly, biting my nails aimlessly and thinking of Nico's melancholy acceptance. *It wasn't her fault.*

"It *is* sad," Anita agrees. "But people heal. When you're dealing with the entire trajectory of your life, you have to be honest. Ends are also beginnings. So, it's the way it was supposed to be."

"Yeah, that's fair," Emilia finally agrees. "Some Band-Aids are harder to rip off, but it doesn't mean we should leave them on forever."

"What about my addiction to the Belpagna gelato?" Anita asks with a smirk. "Can that be healed in some way at the moment?"

And with a roll of her eyes, Emilia takes the cue and goes to get us all scoops of Italian perfection.

Chapter 14

"I really can't even see where the hole was," I remark, peering at the fence and trying to see where Nico patched it. We're both sitting on the ground up against a tree, so we have a pretty good vantage point.

"You're only saying that because you can't make it out well enough in the dark," he counters. "Look at it tomorrow morning, and you'll see it's still a mess." He pauses and takes a sip of beer, considering. Finally he admits, "I think it's better than nothing."

"You mean now that it's fixed, a cow can't wander through it?" I tease.

He pushes his hair back, and I sort of love that my needling makes him mildly huffy. We've been out here for a few hours already, and I'm relishing his company after a few days of missing him in the mornings because Anita wanted to drag me to all her favorite other places.

"I never said a cow could 'wander through it,'" he counters.

"But once the fence has a small hole, there's a chance it could grow?"

"No," he says succinctly, not taking my bait.

"Or the cows might start to wonder if there's a chance to get their freedom back so they start trying to push against it?"

"Obviously not."

"*Or,*" I keep going, trying to keep the delight out of my voice, "smaller animals could come in and taunt them, and then the cows would resent you for keeping them penned up when they're so used to roaming."

His laugh is modulated by his attempt to pretend he isn't laughing. It makes me want to get a full-throated version out of him.

"It's like a reverse Cinderella," I continue. "Instead of the mice and birds helping her get dressed, they come to mock the cows for being hidden away."

"Okay, first of all," he says, finally breaking and now turning toward me, a point ready to be made, "mice and birds can *always* get through or above the fence. They wouldn't need a hole to get in and see the cows."

"Because the unrealistic part of my idea was the way they got in, and not the anthropomorphization of animals."

"*Second of all*," he continues, as though he didn't hear me, "I already told you I wasn't fixing it to keep anything out. It's the principle of it."

"Do the cows know about your principles?"

He puts his head in his hand in feigned frustration. "You're relentless."

I can hear the affection in his voice, and it warms me. I've certainly been called "relentless" and a whole host of similar adjectives by the men around me. But it usually hasn't been meant as admiringly as I know Nico means it.

Even as I know the night is getting later than we'd normally stay up, I can't think about sleep yet. I've loved sitting out here under the stars and trading stories and barbs and playing twenty questions just to pass the time. It's *easy*. It's always so easy being with Nico.

"You know," I say, "this started by me complimenting your fence-mending skills. I was trying to say you did a good job, and you were trying to talk me out of that opinion."

"That's true." He's so unabashedly self-effacing, and it always throws me a bit.

"I think it made the trip to Saturnia worth all the effort, since we did eventually get the supplies," I say, chuckling, and he groans again.

"My car would disagree with you."

"A few scratches won't hurt anyone!"

"They literally hurt a car," he says with a laugh. "The whole point of a car is to not get scratched."

"I thought the whole point of a car is to drive from point A to point B."

He sighs that amused sigh, and I love it almost as much as one of his laughs.

But as though the grove is sighing along with him, a heavy gust of wind blows. I close my eyes against the dust, and I can feel a slew of prickly leaves fall.

I try to brush them off and open my eyes. Nico's sitting close enough where I can see him notice that something is still in my hair.

"Did I not get it all?" I ask, pawing again at whatever spots I seem to have missed.

The side of his mouth curls up, the one with that adorable freckle right above his lip. "No, you've still got a few in there," he says, pointing to one side of my head.

I brush it again, and I can tell from his expression that I haven't made any headway, even if I was hoping my short hair couldn't possibly contain more than I've already brushed out.

"I know I'm going to be sleeping on the ground anyway, but I really don't need to resemble an olive tree," I whine. "Can you help me?"

He nods and leans toward me. He gently picks one leaf out of my hair, then another. A third appears to be a bit more lodged in there, so he's careful about disentangling it.

But when he's done, he's moved into my space enough that we're even closer than before. And he doesn't move his hand.

I can feel my heart rapping against my rib cage at his nearness. I'd been lulled out of the high alert my body always feels around him by our easy evening of banter and lightness. But now, when he's so deliberately close, the feeling's come roaring back, and his hands on me have stunned me into sensory aftershock.

The premise that he's touching me to help me get something out of my hair is rapidly fading as time starts to tick away and we're still not moving.

I want to hear that sigh again, but this time with my name on his lips. I want that hand to stay in my hair while he twines his fingers through my strands. I want his mouth against mine.

I'm trying to remember why this is a bad idea.

Is it a bad idea? Two consenting adults who clearly have some attraction between them—why can't I just kiss him?

But I hesitate, knowing that I've felt this precipice before with him, and every time I've been left wondering if I misread things. Why *has* he pulled away every time it seems like there's something between us? Is it because of his ex-wife? Does he wish she would come back? Is he scared I don't want him? Am I projecting?

Screw it, I'm not a nervous wallflower. Maybe I've become *too* soft while away from my restaurant. I'm never this wishy-washy.

I lean in and press my lips to his.

For a second, his fingers stay in my hair, and I can feel his satisfaction breathing me in, the pressure of our mouths together delicious without even taking a taste. My whole body is fizzy like a carbonated drink.

But then he pulls back from me with a different sigh, this one weary, and I hate the sadness I see written all over his unsurprised face. I instinctively reach out and put my hand on his chest, wanting so badly to comfort whatever I've broken by putting my unfiltered thoughts into action.

He closes his eyes and puts a hand on top of mine. For a long moment, we breathe again together, and I can feel the steadying of his pulse along with the rise and fall of his chest.

Until finally he opens his eyes again, a wistful smile playing on his lips. His fingers slowly push my hair back behind my ear, and he traces its curve and down, until he's lightly holding my jaw.

"The problem for me," he says quietly, "is that if I really started kissing you, I'm not sure I could stop."

I sharply inhale, his words cutting through me with the realization that I've opened a dam, and I'm not sure if we're going to be able to undo it.

"How do you know," I mumble under my breath, as though if I speak too loudly, all my thoughts are now going to come tumbling out.

He reaches up his other hand until he's got my face cradled. I have the strange sensation that I'm about to be broken up with, even though we've barely ever even touched. Why am I aching even more than when I was *actually* broken up with a few weeks ago?

I can no longer tell whether it's my heart beating fast or if I feel his underneath my hand. Or maybe both of ours started feeding off each other while I listened to him say the words he clearly didn't want to, after what I've so bluntly made impossible for him to now not admit.

"You're leaving, Kit," he says finally, and my heart squeezes at that realization of what should have been so much more obvious to me. "And whenever I'm with you, I start to think I could . . ." He exhales, stopping himself before he says more than either of us is ready to hear. He takes a deep breath and starts over. "I really felt invincible once. And then she left. She left, and I broke, and I can't do that again. I'm happy now, I really am. I'm happy with my trees and my dog and this ridiculous town." He pauses again, and I can see that sentiment play out across all his beautiful features. That peace that he's finally found, and how hard-fought it is.

And I want, more than anything, more than even to kiss him, for him to know I would never intentionally hurt that.

"I understand," I whisper, and I have to shut my eyes tight to stop an inexplicable tear that's threatening to fall. He pulls my body into his, wrapping me up in his arms, my head against his chest. I can now hear that steady heartbeat, so alive and so consistent, just like he is.

"Of course I want to kiss you," he says softly. "I want to kiss you so badly that sometimes it seems impossible not to. But I can't kiss you and then watch you leave. Because I really meant it when I said I wanted for us to stay friends. But also selfishly, I want when you leave for my heart to be intact. And I don't think either of those things are possible if I start kissing you."

I pull back to look him in the eyes again. They're searching mine, hopeful that I can somehow close this can of worms I insisted on opening. Me, with my unceasing need to scratch at every itch and fling wide every door. I couldn't just let us be. I could no longer ignore that palpable feeling I knew was coursing between us.

But I've also never had a friend like Nico. I've never had a friend who looks at my tough exterior with admiration and then slides beneath it to find the soft underbelly. At a time when I should've been anxious about my restaurant and raging to get home, he's given me humor and hope, and mornings to look forward to.

I need to close the can of worms.

"I want both of those things too," I agree. "You don't have to explain it."

The sigh I get now is relieved. Whatever weight I placed directly on the center of his chest with my actions has at least been lightened somewhat.

I put my head on his shoulder, and he clasps my hand in his. We sit that way for a long time, backs still up against a tree, holding on to each other, but as friends who can't be anything more. We're friends, because at this moment in each of our lives, we both really need that.

And that's going to have to be enough.

When I wake up in the morning with my head still on his shoulder, Nico offers to show me where he mended the fence. It's a glide away from the secrets we spoke in the night, and I'm happy to play along. And so I go closer to the fence with him and marvel at the talent of putting something back together, even when the seams are showing.

Chapter 15

The rest of the weekend goes by in the regular blur, and then Monday is the Palio fundraising dinner. Which means I get to (happily) work on my day off.

A helpful reprieve when I'm desperately trying to not think about Nico.

I'm not exactly succeeding.

Things haven't been weird, exactly. But there's been a small but distinct shift. I'm grateful that Anita has joined our mornings, because it's created a slight enough buffer that nothing feels *ruined*.

Maybe it's the playfulness that's shifted. There are no pats on the back or secret eye rolls or dipping a spoon in the other's gelato. The can of worms has been shut, yet the seal isn't quite the same; the air's been let in, even if the contents are still inside.

But we're moving past it. Things are getting better. In fact, even if I'm uncomfortable, I'm glad I said something, because now at least I know. Whether he wants to kiss me or not is no longer important. The *wanting* isn't relevant anymore. We're two adults with an attraction who logically know that giving in to it is a bad idea. What happened isn't relevant.

It's not.

I'm really trying to make it not.

So thank goodness for this dinner, is all I'm saying.

Gia's really going all out. Someone brought over extra tables earlier, and the street around the restaurant has been closed off, so we've basically doubled the number of seats we normally have.

She's kept the menu minimalist and very classic. We're starting with a shrimp crudo and burrata, to keep us from having to do much more than plate anything. She insisted we have pici—the regional pasta shape that's like a thicker spaghetti—and she's pairing it with a local pecorino (of course) and a fennel sausage. She's finishing with her boar ragù over polenta, even though her insistence on boar is still cracking me up.

I tried to see if she'd let me make the pici this morning. "It's the simplest pasta," I pointed out. "It's flour and water and then running it through the pasta machine. You know I can handle it."

"That's where your overtrained brain gets everything wrong," she remarked without even looking up while we both deveined shrimp for the crudo. She didn't even need to look at me to casually insult me.

But even if I wanted to pretend like I was offended, I mostly was curious about her reasoning. I'm also lucky to be basically impervious to insults by this stage in my life, between kitchen culture and review culture (Yelp, anyone?).

"Pici is a hard pasta *because* it is simple," she continued. "It's not just about the exact balance of water—and salt, by the way—to the flour. You want the right level of springiness in the dough so you get that toothy bite when you've cooked it perfectly. Pici is thick, so you don't want it to gum up or overtake whatever sauce you're making. The dough needs to be at an exact state to handle extrusion, and then it needs to rest for the right amount of time. It has to cook in correctly salted water, and it needs to be removed from the heat at the exact right time to find the balance of al dente. *Handling it* is not enough."

I tried to think of a comeback. Any comeback. Something witty? Something to give her confidence in me? Something defiant to rile her up and entertain both of us while we prepped double the food we normally would?

But before I could think of what to say, she'd moved on. "I'm going to make the pasta. I want you to place the gorgonzola dolce and chopped rosemary on those figs."

"A task a small child could do," I said.

But instead of responding, she just shrugged, as though saying *Hey, if the shoe fits.*

I swear, Gia must've been a *devastating* teenager. I can't imagine going toe to toe with her in a mean girl scenario. She's cool as a cucumber while cold as ice when she wants to be, and all without saying a word. I wish I didn't love it so much. I wonder if Nico's grandfather ever told him stories about young Gia.

And damn it, there I go again, thinking about Nico.

I watched her make the pici. I plated the figs (like a small child). We got the rest of the food ready for the evening.

A few hours later, when I step outside to say hello to everyone before the dinner starts, I'm surprised by the number of decorations that have sprouted up over the course of the afternoon. I hadn't really known what to expect of this dinner. I could tell by Gia's extra work that this event is important to her, but I don't think I understood how important it is to the whole neighborhood.

Lights have been strung up across the closed street. Banners and napkins and place mats all in the Cassero colors of dark blue and maroon have been festooned across the table. All the streets around us are lined with flags shaped like upside-down medieval ramparts.

The entryway to the restaurant and its surrounding area is now a bona fide party. Unmarked wine bottles from the neighbors' stashes have been haphazardly placed across all the tables and on any available surface. Emilia arrives (today's bandana featuring the Cassero colors) with trays of pastries, and everyone cheers as she ducks inside to put them away. The conviviality of the moment reflects across all the faces ready for the evening to begin, as though the entire neighborhood is reclaiming their little corner of this town and relishing in it. The adults drink wine and chat while kids play soccer in the streets. No one seems to be in a rush to get dinner started, because they're enjoying themselves plenty.

As Emilia predicted, I've already been asked to join the women's team. Apparently Anita shared that I'd been a college athlete, and that, combined with my height, seemed to make me automatically on board. Flavia—the woman whose missing husband's scooter I'm using—is apparently Cassero's neighborhood leader, and she and Martina, the women's team captain, set out to convince me a few days ago. Flavia was thrilled to remind me that I wanted to pay her for the scooter, and this is apparently the only thing she wants. I had no choice but to agree. So the minute I step into the decorated outdoors, I have at least five people congratulating me on my addition to the team. Once again, word gets around fast here.

After begging off all the compliments based on nothing I've done so far, I walk back into the restaurant. I start grabbing plates of the crudo, my mind already thinking about the next course, but I run straight into Nico.

"Oh, hi. Sorry!" I clumsily try to stay upright. It doesn't help that he's so solid he's knocked the wind right out of me.

He reaches out an arm to steady me but then pulls it back. This is the part of declaring *FRIENDS ONLY* that has made everything else feel fraught. He never would've thought twice about reaching out to me before.

I can't look him in the eye, so I look at his arms, and that's a mistake too. His arms are so beautiful they make me *long*, and that's a sensation I'm entirely unfamiliar with. It's like he's scrambled my brain, and now I'm noticing everything. I've been attracted to a man before—I was attracted to John—but he didn't have forearms I found myself pining over.

"Hi," he replies calmly, and I finally look up at him. His face is unreadable. I hate that lately I can't read him.

"Are you helping with the . . . the service?" I ask, trying to stop my brain from overthinking.

"Yeah, Gia said all hands on deck."

I notice Luce is hopping quietly next to him, and I reach down to give him a pat.

"You know Luce doesn't have any hands, right?" I tease.

He smirks and rolls his eyes at me. I wish I wasn't so relieved to have some of that playfulness back, but I am. "He wouldn't be happy alone all night, and he promised to behave."

"Did he now?" I ask, feigning being impressed.

"Yeah, we had a whole chat about it before we left. He said he'd make sure everyone was having a good time and cuddle anyone who wasn't."

"Well, thank goodness he's here," I continue, enjoying the levity. "Because with a perfect summer night, Gia's food, and more wine than anyone could consume, I'm assuming most people will be having a horrible time."

He snorts out a laugh and gives me an indulgent smile. "Exactly."

But right then Anita—who's also been tasked by Gia with serving—comes up behind us. "We should probably grab the shrimp, right? This dinner isn't going to serve itself."

"Oh, right, right, right," he says, momentary distraction now gone. He claps his hands together, brought back to the task at hand. "All right, Luce, let's get these people fed."

The two of them trot after Anita into the kitchen, as though Luce might actually get something done. I can't help but watch Nico talk to Luce as he grabs plates and places them on trays. He's so comfortable in his skin, talking to his dog, helping out his former grandmother-in-law. Like this life is the most natural thing in the world to him.

I like seeing him like this in a kitchen, because that's *my* natural place. I like him at ease in my place.

But I shake it off because, of course, it's not actually my place. It's Gia's. And I need to get a move on.

The night goes by in a blur of action. Everyone's voices boom in excitement over the size of the local shrimp, and about those damn figs

I scooped gorgonzola over. We furiously plate the pici, Gia whacking me with a wooden spoon every time she thinks I'm getting too precious with my presentation. The compliments and cheers afterward are an indication that no one could ever have too much of Gia's pasta. I get distracted by a conversation with the butcher who makes the fennel sausage we included in the pasta—the ratio of fennel pollen vs. seeds—and Anita has to nudge me with a wink to get back to work.

The satisfaction on Gia's face as everyone eats the boar and polenta is enough to make the whole evening seem worth it. The chaos of serving everyone at once; the impossibility of the timing with various speeches and pronouncements and cheers for Cassero; the innumerable kisses my cheeks are flooded with as I'm inundated with grazies from everyone in the neighborhood.

The excitement over the Palio is palpable. I know it doesn't have the history of the ancient horse races in Siena, but it has heart. This community is an ancient town perched above an unchanging landscape, but its core is alive and beating. They want a celebration; they want to band together; they want the mischief of competition.

Anita's been flitting around all night, clearly in her element among her people, and it warms me to see her like this. I wonder if she wishes she could stay until the Palio happens next month. I wonder how many years she's been dragged back to compete.

And it's particularly special to watch Gia in her element. She's living a life of her own choosing—getting to be independent while also taking care of an entire town. It's hard not to think I should aim to be more like her.

After the desserts are placed onto the table, I finally get pulled into a chair by one of the neighbors, the forcefulness apparent even through the slew of Italian, and I'm force-fed some of Emilia's delectable apricot ricotta cake while a glass of wine is placed in my hand. It's hard to complain about anything so perfect.

"Is this the first chance you've gotten to eat tonight?" I hear a voice next to me ask.

I turn and am surprised that instead of the elderly inebriated townspeople I'd originally been sitting with, I'm faced with an attractive man around my age. And he speaks English?

"Oh, I eat while I'm cooking," I say, shrugging it off. "I'm never hungry at the end of a night."

"Fair enough," he chuckles. "But certainly the first chance to sit down, yes?"

I nod. I'm trying to place him. At this point I feel like I know most of the people in Manciano, or at least in our Cassero neighborhood, by sight if not name. It's not that big of a town. But I don't think I've ever seen him before. His face is distinct: good looking but with those marked Italian features I'm more used to seeing on busts in a museum. His accent indicates he's obviously Italian, but his English is better than that of most of the people in town.

"Have we met before?" I ask.

I get another chuckle in return. "Apologies, no! Your reputation just precedes you. I'm Beppe; my mother is Sofia over there." He points out an older woman that I've definitely seen in the restaurant and around town. She's younger than Gia, but they've always seemed to be friends. "I live in Roma, but I came up for the night because I'm always sucked into the Palio."

He laughs, and I understand where he's coming from. This town does seem to have a way of keeping its hooks in everyone, even in the most lovable way. I imagine that the kids who grow up here and want to have a more professional life in places like Rome or Milan still end up always coming back for every festival and event. Manciano has that way.

It makes me think of the sign next to my bench—once you've married the sea and allowed yourself to be clothed in the sunsets, you can't ever quite shake that. I wonder how many people spread across the country and world are always called back to this little town. If it can summon Anita, it surely could summon someone from Rome.

"Does that mean you'll be rolling a barrel for Cassero?" I ask, and he smiles wide.

"Oh, absolutely. I've been roped in every year since it started. Lately, I try to claim I've aged out, but the competitive spirit keeps me returning. Well, that and my mother insisting that I'd bring shame on our family if I didn't show up."

I laugh, and he keeps the smile.

"I hear you're rolling a barrel for Cassero as well," he points out.

"Yes, they got me too," I say, putting my head in my hands.

"Well, you couldn't bring shame on Gia now, could you?"

"Good point," I reply, my eyes lifting to meet his as I take another sip of my wine.

We sit like that for a while, finishing off the remains of the wine left at the table. Beppe works in marketing in Rome, at a firm he founded, so he has a lot of flexibility to come visit his mother when he needs to. He doesn't want to move back, but his affection for his town is undeniable. I'm impressed with the amount of local gossip he's still able to keep up with, and he regales me with some backstories of the various people in town.

By the time Anita comes over to poke at me, I've almost forgotten I was only supposed to be taking a short break.

"Lovely chatting with you, Beppe," I say, standing up.

"You too, Kit. I hope I run into you again the next time I'm here." He stands up as well and gives me the proper Italian kiss on two cheeks. Anita raises an eyebrow and grabs my hand.

"You know, if you start a fling with Beppe," she says quietly as we walk away, "Gia would adore holding that over Sofia, since she thinks her son is the greatest thing to ever come out of this town."

"Hey!" I say, swatting her with a dish towel. "I think somewhere in there is an insult of me!"

"Oh, *absolutely not*," Anita says, parking herself right in front of me so I can see she's serious. "Only that Sofia wants grandchildren and an Italian wife. For *you* I'd say it's an excellent idea. The only way to get over someone is to get under someone else, you know? At some point you'll have to say, 'John who?'"

The words prick at me because I have to admit my head almost swiveled toward Nico when she first started that declaration. It hadn't even occurred to me that she meant John.

How empty was my yearslong relationship that, two months out of it, I don't even remember that I'm supposed to be getting over it? I keep expecting the moment I break—sorrow for my loss; anger about how he left me; fear over what's ahead. But so many weeks later, it still hasn't surfaced. I'm worried that says more about me than it does about the relationship itself. Could I really be so hardened that I can brush a yearslong relationship off? Or maybe worse—could I really have been in a relationship that meant so little to me for so long?

And am I just distracting myself, mooning over someone who's unavailable? It's hard not to wonder if this is less about Nico and more about my own inability to be attracted to someone who might be uncomplicated. If I subconsciously focus on the one guy who isn't available, then I won't have to put myself out there, right?

I look over toward Beppe, who's still watching me. He raises his wineglass in a cheers when he sees me look over. I wave back. And then drag Anita into the kitchen.

"Well, I wouldn't say no," I admit to Anita, whose face lights up so much you would've thought she was a kid on Christmas. "But right now, I'm more concerned with doing the dishes," I say, changing the subject. "Let's get started."

And I turn on the loud creaky faucet so I won't get any more commentary or argument out of Anita.

Chapter 16

A week after the Palio dinner, we've unfortunately arrived at Anita's last day here. I've gotten used to her joining our Belpagna mornings and harassing me in the kitchen at night.

In New York I don't have time like this. I don't give myself mornings with friends, and I don't have any routines outside of work. Catching up with Anita is usually a once-a-month post-midnight nightcap or Tuesday daytime walk with a to-go cup of tea. Between Anita's recent lurking and my now monthslong consistency with Emilia and Nico, I've kind of gotten used to having community around me in a way I never really have before.

So we have to do up her last day right. And since it's a Monday, I'm free to actually get out and see something. Emilia suggested a beach day, and I'd almost forgotten how close we actually are to the ocean, since I've never ventured much farther than the surrounding towns. I pull my little marigold scooter to the front of Belpagna and grab my beach bag off the back.

"On your advice, I actually *did* buy a new bathing suit at the farmers' market," I say to Emilia as I walk in. "And though I didn't believe you that that was a real thing, I now appreciate being part of another bizarre Italian custom. I also bought new sandals *and*, unrelated, an alarm clock."

"I told you," she says with a grin. "And stop calling it a farmers' market. It's just the market. Produce can be sold next to underwear. You guys are weird that you separate it out."

She takes off her apron and bandana (adorned with lemons today) and calls back something Italian into the kitchen. She comes around the counter carrying a large bag full of food.

"I thought you said there was a little snack bar at the beach?" I ask.

"Yeah, but I want to eat good things on my day off."

"Snob."

"Seen a mirror?" she retorts, pushing past me with a grin.

"Yes." I smirk. "Have you seen one now that your hair is out of that scarf?"

"Hey!" she says as she pulls a new turquoise one out of her pocket. "As though I'd want to be like you and let my hair get out of control."

She swiftly ties the new bandana, while I'm left trying to see if my hair is standing on end in all this humidity (and it's not. I should never let Emilia make me doubt myself).

I rush to follow her out the door and am surprised to see Nico standing next to Anita.

"Oh, are you coming?" I ask, unable not to notice that he's wearing shorts (something I've never actually seen him in before) and a loosely buttoned short linen shirt that sits on him as though it was designed to torture me.

His brow furrows at my question, and I'm hoping I didn't come across as too unwelcoming. He can't possibly know that the only reason I wouldn't want him joining us on a daylong activity is because the thought of seeing him in a bathing suit is giving me heart palpitations.

"Is that okay?" he asks.

"Oh, yes!" I reply, a little too enthusiastically. "I'm so glad you're coming! Emilia just didn't tell me. This is going to be so fun, right? I haven't been to the beach here yet. Do you know this beach club we're going to? It's supposed to be really nice but low-key. I think it'll be great."

He gives me a soft smile in response to all my rambling. I wonder if my incorrigible mind's thoughts are apparent to him.

"I'm going to drive my car, so you can throw everything in my trunk if you want to," Emilia says to me, ignoring my nonsense.

"Oh, I'm good," I reply. "It all fits on the back of my scooter."

"Look at *you*, so Italian now!" Anita exclaims, scrunching her nose at me like I'm a cute little puppy who's finally figured out how to not chew on her own tail. "Who would've thought you'd be living that dolce vita life, driving a scooter along back roads to an Italian beach?"

I roll my eyes. "I also gutted some fish yesterday and scrubbed dirt off of produce—want to romanticize that too?"

"Maybe," she says, giving me a kiss on the cheek.

"Nico, are you coming in the car or taking your Vespa?" Emilia asks.

"Vespa," he says succinctly and then turns to me. "It's farther than you've gone on yours before; why don't you follow me, just in case?"

"Thanks," I reply, hating that that small sentiment has me mildly choked up. Nico always seems to toe the line between trying to look out for me while never being patronizing. In New York, everyone assumes I'm solid steel, with no need for any looking out. In contrast, most of the locals here treat me like I can't tie my own shoes because I'm foreign and don't speak the language. Finding that middle ground so perfectly seems like an art.

We put on our helmets and take off. The sun gets higher in the sky as we follow winding roads for an hour. I'm behind Nico the whole way, and the lack of needing to pay attention to directions allows me to breathe and take in the views stretching out in front of me. As we get closer to the beach, the fields turn into palm trees. When Nico pulls over to park, I do as well, and I put my scooter right next to his.

"How was the drive?" He removes his helmet, and that hair really should be illegal. He looks like he's in a shampoo commercial, with that kind of soft, tousled look that you want to run your hands through.

But I'm ignoring it.

"Good," I reply. "Thanks for letting me follow you—it made it a lot easier."

He reaches out and tucks some of my messy hair behind my ear, smoothing it delicately with his fingers. I guess we had the same thought, although I'm jealous he can act on his impulses without the fear of spontaneously bursting into flames. Apparently that's just me.

"No problem," he says, a small smile that feels only for me playing across his lips. He squeezes my shoulder before turning in the direction of the path toward the beach.

I follow him, and we come out on the other side to a pebbly beach covered in Campari-colored striped chairs and umbrellas. Next to the vibrant electric blue of the ocean and the craggy rocks rising from it, the whole scene looks like something off a postcard.

"Our chairs are here!" I hear Anita's voice call, and we swivel around until we see her waving from a corner. They've snagged us four beach chairs under two dainty umbrellas, and we have a perfect view of an imposing rock where everyone seems to be jumping and splashing into the water. There isn't a cloud in the sky, and it's the perfect day to be outside, soaking up sun like empty pages ready to have a story written down.

They call it a beach club, but it's more basic than anything you'd find in the US. Chairs are sardined together to make the most of the space. There's a little row of six cabanas in the same orangey-red hue as the chairs for people to change into their bathing suits. In the corner is the promised snack and drink bar. And that's really it. Some people stay on their chairs; others have climbed high on the towering rocks that surround us and have turned this little patch into its own private cove; and then of course there are all the people swimming, dotted along the water.

It's a casual slice of heaven.

Emilia and Anita have taken the two chairs farthest in, so Nico and I drop our stuff next to each other.

"I'm gonna go change," I say, grabbing my bathing suit before scurrying over to one of the cabanas. This particular suit, essentially a bra and underwear the color of sunshine, seemed like a good idea when I was at the market looking to grab an easy bathing suit. But sitting next to Nico all day, half naked, is not really a thought I'd considered.

I change and come back outside. Anita's placed a spritz on the little table next to my chair, and I take a big sip. I pull out my Kindle (my latest purchase is a new memoir of a chef I know, who's a total dick, but he's admittedly had an interesting life). I focus on that so I won't wonder where Nico has wandered off to.

Left alone, I have a blissful half hour to stop thinking entirely. It's amazing how much you can relax with a spritz in hand, a good book, a comfy beach chair, and a view of crystal clear water in front of you. Tension I didn't even realize I was holding seems to melt away, carried off on the salty breeze.

I know in general I take some days off—but this is really *off.* This is brain off. This is responsibilities off. This is time turning off. This is ambition and what's next and what am I doing OFF.

The email from my dad this morning asking me when the restaurant is opening again can be forgotten. The thought of what I can prep for tomorrow to impress Gia can be forgotten. The recipe development I want to get started prepping for the fall can be forgotten.

I'm in the moment. Why don't I ever do this? Why don't I ever *let* myself do this?

But I can't really focus on that thought because I see Nico come out of the water, and thank goodness I have sunglasses on, because I wasn't really prepared for the sight in front of me. I'm unable to stop staring, like a caricature wolf whose friend turns into a ham dinner once she sees him in another light. For someone who pretends to sit around and tinker with machinery most of the time, he's as solid and expansive as someone whose farm actually requires more than simply waiting for olives to grow. Then, pair that body with someone who's just come out of water—tousled hair, bathing suit clinging, droplets slowly making their merry way down with gravity.

I down the rest of my drink and put my eyes immediately back on my book. Nothing good can come from staring at my friend.

But I feel the bounce of him plopping onto the chair next to me, and suddenly I'm itching to move.

"I'm gonna go jump off the rock," I say with conviction, surprising even myself. I hop up and don't look at Nico. Emilia, oblivious to my internal nonsense, stands up too.

"I'm game." She starts walking toward the path up the rock, and without a glance back I'm following her.

The cliff is not exactly a treacherous height—the jump is maybe fifteen feet from the water—but it looks so joyous. It's mostly teenagers taking turns jumping and then climbing a rope to haul themselves back up. There's a lifeguard who looks like he's at least in his seventies—tanned to a deep burnt orange color, as though he's spent his entire life outdoors. It's comical to think that this man could save any of these robust teens, but I kind of love that no one has taken away his happy place. One of the girls is screaming because the boys are throwing little pieces of bread in the water to make the fish come to the surface every time she's about to dive in. The water is so clear you can see them materialize.

But despite all the teasing, she eventually jumps. And the grin on her face when she pulls herself back up the rope shows it was all worth it.

"You want me to go first?" Emilia asks.

"Nope," I say with an impish smile as I take off at a run. I fling myself into the air and smack the water hard. It's cool but not cold, a thrilling balm to my overheated skin. I'm always grateful for my short hair whenever I go in the ocean or a pool because it's easy to keep out of my face. I feel Emilia come crashing in beside me with a gleeful yelp. When she surfaces, her grin is as large as the teenagers'. We both pull ourselves up by the rope and insist on going again.

We probably do the jump half a dozen times, each one a thrilling moment of freedom that never dulls. The sensation of jumping toward blue sky meeting the water and submerging into quiet is like nothing else. If I was fifteen years younger, I would definitely be on the endless loop with the teens. But there comes a point where I'm happily winded and need a break. After the last jump, we swim back to shore instead of climbing up the rock again.

I collapse, satisfied, into my beach chair.

The one next to mine is empty again.

"I'm going to go get a gelato; do you want one?" Emilia asks.

"Is it terrible?" I reply, knowing the answer.

"Yeah, I'm using the word 'gelato' loosely," she laughs. "You'll be lucky if it's not like a Spider-Man Popsicle or something."

"Anything chocolate I'm game for," I allow.

"Yeah, trashy cheap ice cream sometimes admittedly does it for me too," she says as she wanders away.

Anita's watching me as I towel myself off.

"What's up?" I ask. "Missing me already?" I hate that she's leaving tomorrow, so naturally I'm making light of it.

"Of course I am," she says, waving me away, the happy look on her face muted by some other thought she's not yet ready to share.

"Penny for your thoughts?" I ask, hoping to slyly pry it out of her. Look at me, evolved and asking for feelings.

"Please, a euro coin at least," she tsks. She looks away, like she's deciding whether to tell me or not. But then finally she turns back, and I can see that I'm about to get some Anita opinions.

"Can I give you advice?" she says, and I nod her on, knowing there's no point in arguing. "I don't think you should get involved with Nico."

Seriously? Okay, I was wrong. Innermost thoughts *should* stay inside. "Oh, for god's sake, Anita, who said anything at all about—"

"I have eyes."

"He isn't even here. I literally wasn't doing anything—"

"I don't mean just today, although two people casually sneaking looks at the other in their bathing suits earlier is certainly some peak high school–level entertainment. I mean, all the time. I mean at the coffee shop in the mornings, or stopping by the restaurant, or hello on the street. He's such a good guy—"

"Oh, *thank you* for whatever that makes me? First Sofia's son and now Nico. I'm a real catch."

"You *are* a catch, and you're also a good guy too," she says pointedly. "But you're not a lover, not in that way."

"I'm an excellent—" She puts a hand up to stop whatever snarky thing I'm about to say.

"I know you love me. I know you love your family. But you're not . . . You're good at compartmentalizing. And for you, I actually think that's wonderful. You have your restaurant; you have what you want. That's your focus. And I don't begrudge you that. I hated John, but I got why you wanted something easy. I'm so happy you came here for the summer, and I'm especially glad you seem to have gotten out of your routine. But Nico's not a guy who can do a casual thing. He already had someone who needed the world to be bigger. Don't hurt him, okay?"

"I like how everyone assumes I'm the one doing the hurting," I mumble.

That gets her attention. "Who else assumes that?"

I can practically feel my cheeks going red. I bite at my nails to try and avoid her. It's ironic that Nico's the person who's made me think I should share more with Anita, when now she's the one who's making me feel uncomfortable about him. But maybe he's right that I need to let more out. And maybe the truth can actually stop this conversation.

"For your information, Nico and I have already talked about this. I know we . . . spark . . . as you said." She snickers and I ignore her. "But we want to be friends, for real friends. So nothing is ever going to happen. I'm not an asshole, okay?"

"I *absolutely* never even thought for a minute that you're an asshole," she says with sincerity. "I just . . . look, he's a sexy man, okay? That's hard!"

I laugh as I flick my towel at her. "You're a married woman, Anita! And he was married to your cousin! You're practically related."

"I'm not dead or blind," she mutters under her breath, and I shake my head, unable to contain my smirk.

"It's fine. I'm fine," I say, as much to convince myself as her. "No emotional train wrecks forthcoming. I just got out of a relationship."

"Meh," she replies, even indifferent to John in absentia.

"Love you for sort of standing up for both of us, though," I say, kissing her temple.

I get up again, because even though there's probably some ice cream coming my way, I'm feeling a little raw after more sharing than I'm used to. I need a minute to myself.

I climb up one of the higher cliffs and sit out facing the ocean. There's a plaque with another poem written on it, but without a phone to do Google Translate, I can only guess what someone might've had to say about this view.

It's beautiful up here. You can see all the way to the horizon, the sun high in the sky making the light dapple across the water. I get lost in it, my mind calm again in a way it never usually is. What is it about this salt water and the air and the view that's making me easygoing?

I feel someone sit next to me, and I turn to see Nico.

Maybe it's the satiation in my muscles from all the jumping, or maybe it's just my inherent comfort with him that's never *really* gone, but for the first time all day, I'm glad he's next to me again.

"How was swimming?" I ask.

"It's pretty glorious here," he says, and I nod in agreement. "You looked like you were taking advantage of the setting?"

I grin at the memory of giddy enthusiasm, the over and over and over of having a moment to fly. "Yeah, this is pretty great. I'm a bit disappointed in myself for not getting out here earlier."

"We all take for granted the things that are always around us," he says, smoothing out my own self-judgment in an instant.

"Hey," I ask, remembering the poem next to me. "What does this say? I feel like everywhere I go in Maremma, someone's carved some verse into a rock."

He laughs in agreement. "Yeah, Italians love our words. We like to memorialize our appreciation for pretty much everything."

He leans over to look at the plaque. He studies it, mouthing the words to get their feel. "It's a beautiful poem, actually," he says, looking impressed. "So, okay, it starts with, 'Eterni sono quelli come te, che cammini-invisible sulle onde del mare verso l'orizzonte, lasciando risuonare al vento la tua voce.' It means, roughly, that those like you are eternal, or maybe . . . timeless. And you walk, invisible on the waves toward the horizon and let your voice resonate into the wind. It continues, 'Per incidere nelle nostre anime l'indelebile segno del tuo sorriso e della tua voglia di vivere.'" He pauses here, and my gut unintentionally churns with the loss of his cadence. I hear him speaking Italian all the time, but when a poetic language is used on poetry, it's even more magical.

He switches back to English to continue explaining. "It's hard to really translate perfectly, but it means, again roughly, that you're etching in our souls the indelible mark of your smile and . . . I guess the will to live? I take it all as a celebration of life, and living to the fullest. It's optimistic, filled with hope for optimistic people. Like if you live your life with determination and try to be positive, you'll live forever. Even if not everyone notices."

He's looking at the horizon, and I take the moment to watch him. His hair has a salty curl to it he normally doesn't have, and the way the light drinks him in would make anyone take stock of the optimism in their life. I think of Anita's words—*he's such a good guy*—and it's hard not to see every layer of that on him as he interprets poetry and stares out across the glistening sea.

He's found a way to have what he wants in an imperfect world. He has his work and his passions but also peace and family and community. Maybe I can have that too. Maybe that's what Nico was always meant to be for me. A kindred spirit who could show me that I can strive for more. That that *more* doesn't have to only be professional success.

I thought I was at the pinnacle without realizing I'd been stuck. And I'm starting to think maybe it's possible to stay at that pinnacle but just be a little less stuck in my ways.

We stay, staring out at the hazy horizon line until there's a slight chill in the air from the sun beginning to lower itself in the sky.

"Time to go home, I think," he says, patting me on the leg, his touch once again lighting me up in ways I wish it wouldn't.

We come down from the rocks and see Anita and Emilia packing up as well, so we gather our things and make our way back to the car and Vespas.

The golden hour here takes on another meaning as we wind along the curving road, with dappled light peeking through the initial palm trees and wooded brush and then opening up on the expanse of wheat fields and olive groves.

And it's hard not to feel the beach's optimism seep into me, even when we're all the way back in Manciano.

Chapter 17

I'm annoyed with myself for how much I miss Anita once she's gone.

It's not like we see each other constantly in New York. But I blame Emilia and Nico for my newfound softness; in the span of a few fortnights, they've cracked me open like one of their beloved fresh hazelnuts, and now elements that used to slide right off me have seeped their way into my open crevices. It's like I've forgotten why hard shells exist. It's nagging me that all this openness I've been cosplaying at on this temporary sojourn has turned out to also have a downside. Apparently it's not all cliffside poetry and bomboloni.

So of course the mature and normal reaction is to skip going to Belpagna for a few mornings.

All of Manciano is now decorated for the Palio, even though the event is over a month away. Flags and neighborhood colors adorn every possible lamppost, doorway, and awning. Here in Cassero, the dark blue and maroon covers everything and somehow feels fitting for my immature emo mood.

While the town is already getting into celebratory mode, I'm avoiding, staying home reading, and shoving pecorino down my throat as much as humanly possible.

It doesn't help my mood that one of the cats from Belpagna has taken to waiting outside my apartment and follows me to Pasta Fresca every day, as though she's missed seeing me in my normal routine and she's going to make me recognize it.

But apparently the cat isn't the only one who's not going to let me stay alone.

I arrive at work on Friday to find Emilia and Nico casually sipping espresso on stools in the kitchen. I drop my bags from the market on the counter and give them both a pointed stare.

"The moping is over," Emilia declares, staring right back.

Nico stays silent, tousling the hair on the back of his head, apparently pulled into this ambush against his better judgment.

"I'm not moping."

I turn away from them and start unpacking.

"Are you too sick to walk to the bakery?" I hear the smile in her voice, but I'm not giving her the satisfaction of looking to see.

"No."

"Suddenly allergic to gluten?"

I shudder at even the suggestion. "Nope."

"Discovered that you can boil water and stick a tea bag in a cup without me?"

"I could always do that," I scoff.

She sets her espresso cup down hard on the table, which finally jolts me back into looking at her. "No more being a bambina, okay?"

My hands fly to my hips. "Did you just call me a baby?"

"Molto bene! I see we've been picking up some Italian."

"Emilia!"

At that, Nico stands up wordlessly and comes between us, his tall frame blocking Emilia's attempt to tease me into submission.

All my petty irritation is zapped by his nearness.

He's closer than he's been in a long time, as though he's decided my bad mood is worth breaking the self-imposed frisson of distance we've had ever since the almost-kiss in the field. I appreciate the sentiment, but the gesture comes with the unintended consequence of reminding me what his eyes look like when they're watching me. Like how you don't think about being hydrated until you suddenly find yourself parched. And I'm not sure I needed to be reminded of that at this stage.

But then he startles me even further. "I'm gonna hug you, okay?" he asks.

What?

I could not have predicted that as the direction he would be taking. "Okay?" I say, confused but undeniably warm at the thought.

He wraps his arms around me, and everything softens. All that hard shell I've been building back up over the last few days doesn't need to be cracked—he simply melts it. I breathe him in, and he smells like freshly cut grass and dirt, and the whole effect is more calming than a bottle of wine. My mind is attempting to remind me *friends, friends, friends*, while my body is trying its hardest to ignore the rational thought and just lean into his touch.

"Hmm?" I mumble in response to something he must've said that I barely heard.

I hear his laugh from against his chest, that depth echoing in my ear, and it makes my heart beat even faster. "I asked if that helped."

"Helped what?" I respond, my voice muffled because I'm unwilling to move my face when I'm so comfy against him.

"You seem stressed," he says with a tenderness I know I'm not imagining.

"I'm not *stressed*," I reply, even while my clinging to the chance of a hug from him seems to scream the exact opposite.

He ignores me and keeps talking. "When mammals are stressed, it causes a physical response, and tight squeezes activate the body's parasympathetic nervous system. It helps."

I finally peel myself off of him because I need to look at his face, skepticism now lining mine. "When you say 'mammals' . . ." I start. He doesn't seem to follow. "Is this a strategy you employ on *animals*?"

Emilia snickers next to me, but Nico still doesn't seem to see what the problem is.

I snap my fingers in his face to get him to focus. "I'm asking if you're treating me like one of your cows?"

Emilia is now howling, and I can see things finally registering for Nico.

"Well, Temple Grandin—" he starts.

"Temple Grandin!" I shout. "You're trying to make me feel better by using a tactic that was *actually* developed for cows?"

"To be fair," he says, his soft voice incapable of not sounding soothing even when he's being unwittingly patronizing, "she developed a pressure device for neurodivergent people because she saw how much cows were soothed by being squeezed before being slaughtered."

Emilia is doubled over, tears coming out of her eyes, while Nico stands there with his hands on his hips.

"*What?* It helped, didn't it? It was just a thought that came to me in the moment when you and Emilia were bickering!"

He stares over at her pointedly, like this entire course of action is her fault.

"You really need to spend less time around machines, trees, and animals," Emilia chokes out, still unable to control her laughter.

"I just hate seeing you sad," he mumbles to me, ignoring Emilia.

That wipes the smirk off my face, squeezing my heart from knowing he was doing the best he could. Even if he did it without thinking and tortured me (and probably himself) by coming so close.

But Emilia hasn't clocked any of it because she's now standing there explaining to poor Nico why he shouldn't compare women to cows. He's not listening, though, and is instead focused on something on the table.

"Does Gia have bugs in the kitchen?" he asks me without looking up.

Well, *that* wasn't where I thought this already-confusing conversation was going. "Why?"

He holds up the bottle of bug spray I unpacked on the counter, along with the rest of the items I picked up, before finally catching my eye.

"Oh," I say, waving him off. "No, that's not for here. I'm just getting some mosquitos on my patio at night." His brow furrows. "*What?*"

"You're going to spray this where?" he asks, his face not betraying his thoughts.

"On me?"

I'm feeling less sure by the minute, and the small grin that twitches across his face is confirmation that I'm not absorbing Italian by osmosis as much as I'd hoped I was.

"This is . . ." I can tell he's trying not to laugh. "You bought an insecticide, like if you wanted to murder an infestation. So sure, I guess that would get rid of the mosquitos if you wanted to. But probably also burn your skin off."

"Saying 'murder' is pretty dramatic," I huff, swiping the bottle out of his hands and then looking at it. First he has to discombobulate me with hugs, and now he's laughing at me? What has this morning turned into. "This has mosquitos on it!" I finally exclaim.

"Those are ants."

"*Flying* ants?!" I squeak.

He tilts his head, considering.

"You've been sleeping on the ground in an olive grove, Kit." He gingerly picks the bottle up out of my hand. I'm a little disarmed by how much he's willing to touch me today. "I'd be more afraid of this than any of the bugs you've probably already ingested in your sleep."

I shiver at the thought, which was clearly his intention, and now he's laughing, full-throated.

"Okay how about this," I say, "I'll forget you compared me to a cow if you forget I bought chemical insecticide instead of bug spray."

He grins wide, his amusement the sunshine that's now instantly pushed away all the darkness I've let seep in during the last few days. "Deal."

He holds out his hand, and I wrap mine around his, so confused by all these touches yet unable to contain myself now that I've had a hit. It doesn't help that I can't stop staring at his mouth. That freckle above his lip always gets me, but the joy stretched across his face makes him so eminently kissable. We both hold on a beat too long, and I'm not sure I would've been able to let go, but we're interrupted by a new voice behind us.

"Ciao a tutti!"

I instantly remember myself and let go of Nico's hand. I turn around and see Beppe, Sofia's son, whom I met the other night at the Palio dinner. He's looking more casual today, and I can't help but smile when I see him beaming back at me.

"Nice to see you again, Beppe," I say. "Gia's not here yet—she's grabbing something at the butcher."

But he waves the sentiment away. "Actually, I wanted to stop in to see you."

"Oh?" I shift on my heels, unsure now, and keenly aware of both Nico and Emilia watching this unfold.

"I'm back in town for the weekend, and I was wondering if you'd like to go out for a drink with me tonight?"

"I'm working tonight," I say automatically, unsure why that's stumbled out so fast.

"No, I know," he chuckles. "I wouldn't dare do anything that could get me a scolding from Gia." He smiles conspiratorially, as though as a kid that's *exactly* what he was constantly doing. It's hard not to let my lips curve back up at the thought. "But I meant after work," he continues. "Don't you usually close up by ten? We could grab a drink next door, just casual."

Beppe can't see Emilia, so she gives me an unsubtle thumbs-up.

I can feel Nico behind me. I wish I could see his face, but I don't dare turn around.

I hate that my entire brain is focused entirely on wondering what Nico's reaction is.

I think about Anita's enthusiasm for just this scenario. *The only way to get over someone is to get under someone else, you know?* I know she meant John, but . . . maybe that *is* what I need right now, if I'm more focused on Nico's reaction than the actual cute, available man asking me out. And especially a cute man who doesn't even live here, so he couldn't care less that I'm leaving at the end of the summer. He's asking me out. *Just casual.* The easiest drink I should ever say yes to.

"That sounds really nice, actually," I blurt out, not allowing myself to overthink it now that Anita's voice is back in my head.

I feel Nico still behind me, as though his breathing was a metronome that's been suddenly stopped. I can see Emilia's eyes on him, but they don't betray her thoughts—I'd definitely never play Emilia in a game of poker. She might look cute with her aprons and hair wraps, but she can be stone cold when she needs to be. And if I had to bet all my money on what she was thinking when she looked at Nico right now, I wouldn't have a clue what to say.

I certainly can't turn around and look at him. But that's also for the best because this is *not* about Nico. A nice man asked me out, and I accepted. And now he's asking me what time I get off work while simultaneously pulling out his phone and handing it to me, in order for me to give him my number. He's all movement and confidence and fluidity and no cares in the world. And I've got to get my mind off the stone statue standing behind me.

I input my number into his phone and hand it back. He immediately starts texting something, and a moment later my phone buzzes.

See you tonight! it says, a silent missive from Beppe.

"Okay, well, now I really *do* need to work," I say, shooing everyone away before finally turning back to Nico, who seems to have schooled his face enough to have no discernible expression. Apparently he's off my poker list too. "Emilia and Nico, thank you for cheering me up. Beppe, I'll see you later. I need to make some gnocchi now, that Gia probably won't let me sell."

Emilia and Beppe both wave and then turn and start chatting to each other as they walk out the door. Nico stands there for a moment, his eyes catching mine, the melancholy that flickers almost too fast to miss. But he doesn't say anything—of course he doesn't say anything.

I want to shake him. He's the person who made the rules, and now we're stuck in this torturous loop. We like each other too much to avoid hanging out together, but we *like* each other too much to keep letting this not hurt. The hug made that painfully obvious to me, even if he's still living in some land of denial.

But I can force my feelings down too. I'm a chef, for crying out loud. We're conditioned to ignore pain, ignore problems, ignore exhaustion. I've got to mentally deglaze my pan and pour some wine over the fire to get everything unstuck. I turn back to my station and pull out my cutting board.

I don't look up again as I start to chop onions, but I hear Nico wordlessly leave.

Chapter 18

The precision required of simplicity has gotten me through a lot of nights lately, but it's especially what I need tonight.

Running a Michelin-starred restaurant made me more and more susceptible to gussying up. Why *not* add an impressive ingredient or master another complex technique? Why *not* make the dish that requires extensive sourcing or seven hours of prep? The challenge is exhilarating. It's an ego boost to feel like you're innovating. And the constant feedback loop of social media—which rewards out-of-the-box ideas—makes it seem inevitable that you'll keep striving for some brass ring always just out of reach enough that you push even harder.

But the longer I work with Gia, the more I'm coming to appreciate that stripping down is often more impressive. A perfectly grown local snap pea has a sweetness a grocery store version won't have. Blanching it for the exact proper timing keeps your crunch but still cooks it *just* enough. The right drizzle of olive oil, the right dash of salt, the right cuts on the bias to create beautiful but even shapes and textures—every little piece counts when you're keeping it simple. And when executed perfectly, nothing's more satisfying. Nothing tastes as good as fresh pasta cooked in briny water pulled at the exact right moment, topped with those precisely blanched snap peas and a dollop of local ricotta whose cheesemongers make it late in the afternoon so it's freshest for Gia.

Getting simplicity right is hard.

But I think I'm getting better at it inch by inch as every day goes by.

When I look at the clock and see that it's ten, I peek out into the dining room. Gia left twenty minutes ago, and the only people still here are three friends huddled around a table with empty espresso cups. The kitchen is closed, and they're lingering without a need or care.

I'm out of excuses to be late to Beppe.

I wash my hands and take off my apron. I'm in rubber shoes, a T-shirt, and my stretchy-waisted work slacks. My hair is sticking out on the sides from the humidity of staring over pots of boiling water all night. I've put no makeup on.

I wonder if I should run home and at least freshen up. But then I cringe, thinking how embarrassingly obvious that would be.

With nothing left to delay me, I push myself off the wall and walk the thirty steps to the bar next door that's only distinguishable by a small sign above the entrance that says **Il Bar**. It's the perfect run-down but cozy place that you would expect in a town like this. A long, worn wooden bar with frayed stools gives way to a back area with simple metal chairs and tables, with wine racks covering the side walls. Behind the bar, an elaborate espresso machine sits next to all the bottles of liquor. There's a TV mounted to the wall, playing a soccer match, and a vending machine with cigarettes. Multicolored fairy lights have been strung up haphazardly in one corner.

Have I mentioned I love it? It's the Italian version of every dive bar I went to after a shift in New York.

And I love that on a Friday night deep into July, it's filled with locals ranging in age from sixteen to eighty. There's a whole crew of high school age kids crowding a table while sipping on beers, heads down, showing each other whatever they're finding fascinating on their phones. Gia is sitting with two of the guys who regularly come into the restaurant for pasta and are among the only people she trusts to take mine (without pay I'm still assuming, although I've seen them throw money in the container a few times, either as a gesture to her or to me, who knows. But I'm guessing her).

My stomach drops when I see Nico in the back, swirling a glass of wine with Emilia's husband, Antonio. I don't think he notices me as I come in; his focus is solely on whatever Antonio is saying. I fidget for a moment, wondering if I should say hello, but I decide against it. Not the distraction I need tonight.

Instead, I turn my attention toward the bar, where Beppe is sitting with two glasses of wine. The colored lights are dancing across his face, yet he somehow maintains an air of assurance even in this most unserious of settings. It's hard not to notice his innate rugged handsomeness in this strange neon lighting. I could be into this. I can ignore the other people swimming through my mind.

He waves me over when he spots me. "You look like you could use a drink."

He slides one of the wineglasses over as I sit down on the stool next to him.

"Wow, don't shower me with compliments all at once," I jibe, lifting up the glass and taking a sip of the always-present local white wine I've grown more than accustomed to.

He laughs as though I've told the best joke in the world. "See, this is why I like you," he says, the directness of his laughter and compliment momentarily jarring me. "You're very frank."

I shrug. "I think being a chef does that to a person."

"How so?" He seems genuinely curious.

"It's a pretty hierarchical job," I admit. "You can't have bullshit between you and your coworkers when you're on the line, standing next to fire, trying to get dishes out one after the other in rapid succession. There's no room for platitudes."

"And you like that?"

I nod. "It fits me, I think."

"See, I would've thought the frankness comes from being American," he says, chuckling.

I tap my fingers on the counter, considering it. "Probably both," I admit. "But harder to notice when you're surrounded by each other."

He leans toward me, brushing his hand across my whirring fingers. "And how do you feel around Italians?"

He's flirting, lightly, making it clear he intends for this to not simply be a drink among friends. And it should be working. He's cute. The closer I am to him, the more apparent that is. He's suave without it crossing the line into cheesy, the way I normally write these kinds of men off. But I'm willing there to be a spark that I don't yet feel.

I ignore the implications and barrel on. "Considering the amount of crap Gia *still* gives me after so many weeks, I'm going to assume kitchen culture is the same across all languages."

"I know I said it before, but I really *do* dread a scolding from her." His affection for her lines his words, and it makes me warm to him a bit more.

"I get one most days, but I take it as a compliment."

"And see, that's the kitchen culture you're used to. What would you do if she gave you an *actual* compliment?"

I huff a surprised snort, and I can see how much my reaction delights him. "Not possible."

"You don't think at some point this summer you'll get a 'Nice job' out of Gia?"

I think about her razzing on my pasta even though it's practically perfect at this point. "Not a chance," I say through a smile.

"How'd your gnocchi turn out?"

I'm surprised he remembers that offhand comment from earlier. "Gia took a bite and told me 'Not bad,' so I think it was my best work yet."

He chuckles. "What made it particularly great?"

"I think the ricotta here makes a huge difference," I answer automatically, always ready to delve into the minutiae of food. "We get two types at the restaurant—one is a creamier version we use for sauces and accents. But the other is denser, it has less liquid to it. So it adds a fluffiness to the texture of the pasta but doesn't make it all fall apart once it starts cooking. The whole recipe is really just flour, eggs, ricotta, and parm, with the right balance of salt and pepper. So the type of ricotta makes or breaks it."

"And what did you put on top?" he asks, curiosity still beaming out of him.

"Extremely charred eggplant. I love the smokiness melding to the creaminess."

"But Gia wouldn't use the gnocchi you made?"

"Absolutely not," I laugh.

"But she took your eggplant and let it top *her* gnocchi?"

"She deigned to allow it, yes."

"I'd take that as a win," he says, eyes dancing across me.

I haven't had a man look at me like I'm *fascinating* in a long time. John liked sex (obviously), and he could get deep into conversations about restaurants. But he never seemed to delight in me the way I think Beppe is now. And I've seen attraction wash over Nico; I'm not blind. But there's always a resignation behind it that takes away the fun of his gaze for me. When it's friendly, it's friendly, but when things start to dip into something more, I can see the electric fence go up.

The conversation with Beppe is easy, and we carry on chatting through a few more drinks. He asks me about my life, and it's all so fluid, never delving deeper than I want to go. He shares easily about his life in Rome, giving me a better picture than I got the other night, when we both stayed so focused on the town and the Palio. It's nice existing beyond these stone walls with someone and being reminded of the world outside the vortex of this place. I can imagine returning to New York in the same way Beppe can extricate himself from all this insularity and live fully in a big city, even when a little piece of his heart will always be here.

It's comforting in a way—I haven't thought a lot about what going home will mean, probably because I can't imagine these two places coexisting. Yet this conversation makes me think maybe there's a world where I can have both.

But that nagging sense of absence is lurking through the evening. Not the absence of enjoyment or good conversation. There's an absence of *chemistry*. He's willing it to be there, but it's not. There's nothing shimmering in the air between us. There's none of that delicious tension when you wonder if someone is feeling it too.

At one point he puts his hand on my knee, casually. The bar is crowded enough and we're sitting close enough and he's tentative enough that I don't *dislike* it, per se. It doesn't give me the ick in the way I've felt on some dates with men. But when he does it, my instant, subconscious instinct is to look over to Nico, as though another man touching me has flipped an unwanted switch.

And when my eyes snap to his, for just a second, I see that he's already watching me. *There's* that tension. That's the heaviness. His stare is a furnace on a cold day. I immediately look away.

Beppe's hand doesn't linger, and the moment passes. I have one more drink. I try not to bite my nails. I'm still enjoying the conversation, but now that I've seen Nico looking at me, I don't think I can focus on anything else, and I have to get some air. I need to shake the sensation off me so I can go back to shoving that spark down to where it belongs, buried.

"I'm really glad you suggested this," I say to Beppe, genuinely. I *have* enjoyed chatting with him, even if I'm no longer able to imagine anything more than a drink with him.

"Thank you for taking me up on it," he says.

"I have to work tomorrow, and we both know Gia's not going to let me off the hook for even a second," I say, pumping lightness into my voice as much as I can. "So I should probably get going."

He nods, as though that was a foregone conclusion. He takes my hand and kisses the top of it, like an old-fashioned gentleman who seems to understand that this is where the night has taken us. And of *course* I'm not interested in the chivalrous and apparently perceptive man. No, that has to be reserved for the one person who's *not* interested in taking me out as anything more than *a friend.*

I try to pay for my drinks but Beppe waves me off, standing up to say goodbye while insisting he invited me out. I get two friendly kisses on the cheek, and then I wave goodbye.

I wish I didn't notice that Nico's already left.

Chapter 19

After midnight, I hear pounding at my door. *What the hell?*

I open up to see Nico, hair a mess, fist still held as though he hadn't thought to unfurl it after all that banging. He paces into my apartment before closing the door behind him. I have no idea what's happening right now. But then he turns around and faces me.

"Please don't go on a date with him again. Please."

I stare at him, mouth open in confusion. *That's* why he almost broke down my door?

"It wasn't like a formal date," I finally respond. "We just had drinks. It's not a big deal."

"He had his hand on you," he rushes out. We both stare at each other for a minute, and finally I raise my eyebrows, wondering if he actually expects me to have a response to that. He winces. "I just mean . . . it looked like a date."

"Nico . . ." I say slowly, forcing myself to take a deep inhale so I won't let the frustration that's prickling across my skin take hold. "Whatever tonight was, I'm not really *dating*. As you have pointed out to me so eloquently, I'm *leaving*, and therefore cannot actually date anyone."

I'm not sure if I'm thrilled or embarrassed by the way his eyes widen, my words a straight shot that's landed. But I've never beat around the bush, and I'm sure as hell not going to do it today, when he's barged into my apartment unannounced like I owe him something.

He rejected *me*. He made his feelings exceptionally clear. I'm not going to become a nun just because it irks him unreasonably.

So I keep going. "But even if I *was* to think about a date seriously, you don't have a right to share an opinion on that."

"I know . . ." He sighs. "I know that."

He's looking down now, running his hands through his hair, like a man on the verge of snapping in some way. I can't tell if he's annoyed or angry or something else. It's unnatural on him—he's normally so calm that his mere presence usually calms *me*. And now he looks like a slingshot that's been pulled taut but without any release in sight.

"Well then, what?" I finally say, the edge still in my voice. "I'm not a toy, Nico. You can't tell me you don't want me and then hold me above your head and say, 'No one else can have this.'"

"I know that," he repeats, still not looking at me.

"But it doesn't seem that you do!"

"I never said I don't want you," he mumbles, the words so soft I barely hear them. But even if he's saying them quietly, they still ramp up my own frustration.

"Yes you did," I counter. "And it's fine. It's totally fine. I get where you're coming from. I respect it. I almost agree with you—"

"Almost?" His eyes shoot up, curiosity now winning over his discomfort.

"Well . . ." I sigh again. I'm not used to this. I *never* dance around uncomfortable truths.

I've never had something that felt precious enough not to ruin.

But maybe I need to accept that we've already ruined some piece of it and just be honest.

"It doesn't matter what I think, because you made yourself clear," I point out. "And I *do* want to be your friend. Of course I do. So yeah, in that way I sort of agree with you."

He's not looking at me again. That discomfort roiling within him doesn't seem to be going anywhere. I want to pull his face up and make him look at me so I can scream at him. But of course, because he's Nico,

I don't. He's the only person I've ever been able to stop myself from hurting when he deserved it.

"This isn't fair to me," I finally say, my voice surprising me by cracking. But it's like all my confusion and frustration is beating its way out of me. And that unfairness is the only thing I know that's true in this moment. Tears prick at the edges of my eyes, and now I'm the one looking down.

He takes a step forward and grasps my hands, always so incapable of standing idly by when he sees I'm in distress.

"I know that too," he says with a heavy sigh, pushing his hair out of his eyes.

"So what are you doing?" I ask, my eyes trained on his hands. They're so capable of strength but so gentle when they're on me. He slowly rubs his thumb against mine, and just that small movement makes me want to explode ten times more than anything Beppe did earlier.

"Please don't make me answer that," he says, his voice strained.

"I think you have to," I reply, opening back up the can of worms that was never closed properly.

I can practically touch the desperation radiating out of him. I can feel his eyes on me, even though I'm still looking at our clasped hands. He doesn't want to answer. He's clearly not going to answer.

But when I finally look up, I can read the confusion in his eyes. It makes my heart hurt, seeing him like this.

And it's such a strange feeling to suddenly realize I'd sacrifice myself for someone else.

It's funny, I wouldn't have gone five steps out of my way for John. I've never understood that sentiment of a relationship requiring any sacrifice that matters. But looking into Nico's eyes and seeing that abject defeat, I know I'd do anything to make it stop.

I can avoid going on dates for him. I know it's like a misogynistic whirlpool of nonsense to even consider a self-imposed celibacy on behalf of a *friend*. But I can't stand for him to look at me like that. I can't stand to be the cause of so much confusion in his head.

"It's okay," I say quietly. "Let's just . . . let's just agree to let it go and not talk about whatever ridiculous demand you've stormed in here to make. I won't go on another date."

"You . . . what?" he says, the shock of my capitulation written across his features.

"I mean, I'm not here for long, and I work all the time. It's not like men are beating down my door," I scoff. "It's not worth it."

"Not worth what?" he asks.

I think about what he said to me earlier today when we were in the kitchen together with Emilia.

I just hate seeing you sad.

It's exactly how I feel right now.

"Not worth what, Kit?" he repeats.

"Seeing you sad," I whisper, echoing his words, the truth impossible to keep in.

He nods. He purses his lips and keeps nodding, as though he's coming to terms with everything we've both just said. I'm not getting the sense I've made things any better, but at least he's no longer staring like it hurts to look at me.

"Okay," he finally says and then turns to leave. He hesitates for a moment, but then walks out the door and shuts it behind him.

I stand in the middle of the room, stunned. *What the hell just happened.*

I can't move. It's as though whatever hold Nico has over my mind has expanded, and now it's rooting me to the floor.

This attempt to be friends isn't working. It's getting worse by the day. It was so bad at the beach I had to move away just so I wouldn't have to be adjacent to his torso. When he hugged me today, I held on as long as I plausibly could. And it's not only me, *obviously*, based on tonight's ridiculous display. At this point it feels like slow torture we can't seem to stop.

But before my mind can go any further down that road, the door opens and Nico walks back in.

He strides toward me, a man on a mission.

"Nico, what—"

He wraps his arms around me. "I can't do this anymore," he says.

He pulls me to him, his lips hard and insistent on mine, and I melt. In an instant I open to him, and his kiss is like lightning in a bottle. It's fast and beautiful and a sea of sensation. His hands are everywhere—in my hair, tracing my collarbone, wrapping around my waist, twining with my fingers—as though he's thought about every possibility and now can't choose where to begin.

We fumble backward. Nothing on earth would be capable of stopping the momentum of this kiss now that we've started, but we both seemingly have a mission to get up against something.

My bed seems too far, so I pull him onto my couch, his long frame enveloping me against the cushions. His weight is sedation after all the crackling feelings that've whipped through me since he first walked in the door. It's comforting and grounding. It's stability amid a tornado.

I can't believe I get to touch him.

I can't believe it's instantly this good.

I can't believe my urgency for him.

It's all coursing through me, and I wonder if I had to pull him on top of me so I wouldn't explode from all the wanting.

He sits up, and I whimper from the loss of that weight. He takes off his shirt, and apparently that's all I needed to stop all the madness happening in my brain. His body is like a tranquilizer. Thank goodness I'd already seen his chest at the beach or else we might be here for hours while I simply looked at him.

But if he notices me staring, he doesn't seem to care because he's just as unfocused as I was a moment ago (until I had, *ahem*, this body in front of me to fully focus on). He's attempting to undo his belt; he's pulling at my shirt to get it off; he's running his hands through my hair, only stopping at the base of my neck, where all the strands curl at the end a bit; he's kissing every spare inch of skin he can find. He's undecided and deeply targeted and then back again.

Watching him come so unbelievably undone makes a small smile curve up the side of my mouth. God, I could watch this forever.

I sit up a bit and make quick work of taking off my shirt and bra, and finally that's what stills him. I guess I'm a little bit of a tranquilizer for him too.

I wrap my arms around his neck and pull both of us back onto the couch, wanting that exquisite pressure on me again. Our kiss is deeper this time, slower, but with no less ferocity. Skin on skin is heaven, and it makes me pull him closer to me.

But that frantic urge hasn't stopped; it's only burrowed in deeper. We're both soon pawing at each other again, pants shoddily removed, kisses more urgent, his hands on every new area that's been unsheathed. I can feel him hard against me, and it makes me wrap my legs around him, searching for more. His lips are on my neck and I'm frantic with need, lifting my hips and begging for friction.

"I can't think straight," he says into my skin. "I'm obsessed with the way your mouth moves. The way you breathe. Everything."

"Same," I say, unable to get out more than a single syllable, all that want making my hands move lower to try to peel off his boxers.

That gets some sense of sanity back into his brain, because he pushes himself up onto his elbows and looks down at me, stopping himself when I'm not sure anything else could've.

"We have to . . ." He's breathing so heavily, attempting to come back down from whatever stratosphere we've launched ourselves into. I want to pull him back and make the rationality stop before it starts. But he pushes a lock of hair behind my ear—as though that single gesture will get the wildness of it all to calm down—and puts his hand over my heart. "You have to tell me what you want right now," he says softly. "Because I feel like I'm about to completely lose myself in you, but I'll stop. I promise I can stop," he continues, almost as though he's trying to convince himself too.

He looks gloriously rumpled—hair askew, lips kiss swollen, clothes strewn next to us—with nothing other than his boxers and my underwear between us. Even though he's sat up, he stays tethered, one finger gently circling my hip bone in a gesture that is somehow the sweetest and sexiest way anyone has ever touched me.

"I need you," I hear myself say.

Those aren't words I've ever let slip past my lips. I've never *needed* anything. From anyone. But in this moment, it's palpable how much I need him. How much I need him to touch me, be inside me, whispering more nonsensical devotions into my ear.

And I need to get back to that state of not thinking, because otherwise any thoughts will terrify me.

I kiss him deeply again and pull down my underwear. The movement makes him let out a breathy curse in Italian that I don't understand but instantly love. He plants kisses on my shoulder, a nibble, a lick, as though he just can't decide what would be better.

"I have an IUD," I breathe, hoping that will end the conversation portion of this evening. "What I want is for you to *not* stop. Please don't stop."

When I move my hands to take down his boxers, this time he doesn't hesitate. He lifts up his hips until, finally, there's nothing between us.

There's been so much between us for so many weeks now. We've eroded every layer that we both wrapped ourselves in, slowly unraveling until this became impossible to stop.

When he pushes inside me, it's as though it was always inevitable. We were always meant to be together like this. It's too good, too close, too undeniable.

Those hands that previously were manic and without purpose are now laser focused. That pressure on top of me is now a man determined to make me only think of him.

And when I come undone, I can't think of anything else. When he loses himself, I only want to make him crave me as much as I now crave him. And I'm not sure I'm ever going to be the same.

Chapter 20

I wake up with Nico's legs wrapped around mine, my back flush against him, his lips pressing against my shoulder like he's sleeping mid-kiss. I'm so warm, I never want to move.

At some point last night we'd moved to my bed, exhaustion taking us over even as we kept kissing and touching until we must've fallen asleep tangled up in each other. I move slightly to stretch a little bit, but I feel his grip tighten around me.

"I thought you were a dream," he murmurs into my skin, his voice morning deep, his fingers pressing into my hips as though he's making sure I'm real.

I turn over so I'm facing him.

"Good morning," I say, unable to stop the small smile that's washing over me as his eyes track across my face like a sunbeam. He reaches up and plays with the tendrils of my hair, smoothing some out, then curling strands around a single finger before tracing the line of my neck.

"Good morning," he whispers, still tracing, still touching me softly everywhere.

We stay silent together for a moment, breathing and watching, a visual exploration. I'm relishing getting to see him so close and unguarded with morning light seeping in. Hazy sleepiness and satisfaction line his face, and it's the most gorgeous thing I've ever seen. I find myself reaching for his hair, too, the tactile need to be all over him too great.

"I think your hair is longer than mine," I muse.

That finally creeps a smile onto his face. "I'm obsessed with your hair," he says.

"I've heard you're obsessed with everything about me," I say with a smirk, tugging a little on his waves. He closes his eyes at the sensation, and I automatically angle my hips toward him, suddenly in need of a little friction of my own.

He breathes in deep and then kisses my neck. "You have no idea," he says with his lips still pressed to me. "I could probably talk for an hour just about the way your hair sits on your neck. It's all straight until it gets right to the base, then for some reason right there it curls ever so slightly. It's almost dainty, as though only the back can get away from your attempt to keep it as easy and short as possible."

I pull back to look in his eyes.

"That's the most romantic nonsense anyone has ever said to me." I give him a little push, and he bursts out laughing.

"You don't have to remind me that I'm incoherent right now," he says with a sigh, planting another kiss right on my jaw, as though he couldn't bear to stay away from that particular spot for one more second.

I wrap a leg around his, and he inhales sharply. I can't stop myself from pressing against his body. All this softness from him is stirring up the opposite feelings from me, making me *want* in a way that has me feral. I went from sleeping to practically mauling him in about thirty seconds.

But it's clear it's not only me. I feel him harden against me as he captures my mouth in a kiss. It's a different kind of intensity from last night. Now it's confidence and heat, everything sweet suddenly evaporated. It's still needy, but without the newness.

We kiss with that hunger for a few minutes until I'm reaching down to put him back inside me, needing to be as close as possible, his hands everywhere again as he groans into my mouth. It's frantic and hungry and the air reverberates with our gasps and heavy breathing, so different from the sleepy smiles of mere moments ago. The desperation between us needs release and we both come fast, finding our finish lines easily now that we're wrapped around each other as tightly as possible.

We lie together, unmoving, letting our breathing catch back up with us from the frantic, quick sex that appeared like a bolt of morning lightning.

Reluctantly, I finally roll off him and go to the bathroom. When I come back in the room, his eyes track me, roaming over the view of my whole body appreciatively until I crawl back into bed and snuggle under the covers with him.

He picks up my arm and delicately kisses the inside of my wrist, so much softness once again returning to all of his movements. "I blame yesterday's hug," he finally says.

I raise an eyebrow. "You think the hug where you compared me to a cow made me unable to resist you?"

He snorts a laugh. "Made me unable to resist *you*."

"I don't think you can blame either of us on a singular hug."

He sighs and rolls onto his back, but he intertwines our hands together, like even when he's not looking at me he still needs some tactile reminder. "When you didn't come by Belpagna for a few days, I missed you," he finally says, his voice reflective. "I wanted to go check in, but I didn't want to admit that it mattered that much to me." I squeeze his hand, not wanting to interrupt but not wanting him to feel alone either. "Eventually Emilia insisted we go track you down, and I was more than ready to join her. I intended to stay quiet and only be there, but then Emilia was poking at you and you seemed so sullen and I just wanted to make it better. I didn't really think it through."

"I liked you hugging me." The memory of not wanting to move away from him is still bright in my mind.

"Well, so did I," he chuckles. "But it threw me for a loop the whole day."

He stays staring at the ceiling, and I love being close enough now to see the details of his blush hinting across his cheeks. It's such a delight to be able to stare openly at his profile without having to pretend I'm not; to get to watch that blush creep intimately and see how far it goes.

"I thought about it all day too," I finally say. The admission makes him turn toward me.

"Really?"

"Yeah," I reply. "Although also, it's probably why I said yes to Beppe." He smacks his forehead and I grin. "What was I supposed to do?" I yelp. "I was going crazy! It's not fun to lust after your friend!"

"Don't I know it," he mumbles, and my grin grows wider.

"It was never *fine*, but for a while it was *sort of* fine," I continue. "And then we went to the beach and I had to see you in your bathing suit, and that was a lot."

"You're talking to the person who literally jumped in water to get away from *your* bathing suit," he says, and an unexpected laugh escapes me.

"Okay, so we were a bit of a mess," I conclude.

"Certainly a mess, yes," he says quietly. He traces me again, his finger slowly moving across my arm as he watches, and considers.

I can't stop myself from asking the one question hanging over us. "So what happens now?"

He sighs, as though the whole world is contained in that one breath. "I don't think I could possibly be sorry about last night," he admits in a whisper, like it's a secret he has to get out. "But I am sorry for so many weeks of confusing you, and I'm sorry I got jealous and barged in here and couldn't stop myself from demanding things of you that weren't fair."

I pull myself closer, keeping my grip on his hand. He's so decent to his core. As though *that's* what's bothering me.

"You don't have to apologize for any of that," I reassure him.

"I just made everything complicated." He kisses my palm, another tactile reminder that we're here together, and then places my hand over his chest, grounding me to him.

"It was already complicated," I say. "I don't think a single hug or any one thing was a tipping point that wouldn't have happened otherwise. We gave it our best shot."

He laughs, and the hand on his chest vibrates with his amusement. "We gave it our best shot," he repeats.

"We can still stay friends after . . ." Hesitation lines what I say, not wanting to spook him but knowing desperately in my bones I'm not going to be able to pretend anymore while I'm here.

"When you leave?" he finishes for me.

I nod. "Can't it just . . . be like this while we can?"

He looks at me with that hint of melancholy again, the kind of blink-and-you-miss-it sadness embedded in there every time he's looked at me lately. But before I can study him too much, he pulls me in and kisses me deeply again, holding on tight until I'm breathless. It's care and need and desire all wrapped up in one kiss.

But then he stops, with a kiss to my nose, putting an end to reigniting anything at the moment. I'm embarrassed by the whimper that escapes my lips.

"It's just going to *have* to be like this while we can," he finally says, and the fearful knot that's embedded itself in my stomach unties ever so slightly. "Instead of making ourselves miserable, we might as well enjoy it while you're here. You were always going to leave eventually, but I don't think I had any other option but to fall for you, Kit."

His words ring in my ears as he kisses me again, and I hold him even tighter. My heart is in a blender, mixed up and pulsing and completely unrecognizable in the face of all this sudden openness and honesty.

I want to believe so badly in the pure joy of a summer fling with Nico. I *have* to believe in it because the other option—the option where I care this much after such a short time—is not in my repertoire. It's not something that happens in real life. So I shift his words around in my mind until they're palatable. *Falling* for someone can be a moment in time. It doesn't mean we can't let some parts go at the end of the summer but keep the friendship. It doesn't have to involve anything else. This summer is a respite.

We might as well enjoy it. That's the part I keep repeating to myself.

"Do you remember that the hunters are back tonight?" he says, jostling me out of my spiral.

I'd forgotten that we'd already planned another night of protecting Gia's cows. "Listen, if you wanted to ask me out on a date," I joke, trying to lighten the mood, "you didn't have to go so big as to offer me sleeping on the ground while men potentially shoot at me."

He snorts. "When I ask you out on a date, you'll know it." He shoots me a mischievous look that I feel all the way to my core. "But I am glad I've already conned you into spending this particular evening with me."

"Just promise me this time when I try to kiss you that you won't reject me." His whole body winces. "Too soon?" I ask, and he shakes his head.

"I tried *so* hard to do the right thing."

"In this case the wrong thing," I point out.

"I *thought* it was the right thing," he says. Neither of us verbalize the rest of that sentence that goes unsaid, heavy in the air. Maybe it *was* the right thing. Maybe we've screwed everything up. Maybe we're both setting ourselves up for a nasty fall.

But his words from before ring through my ears. *I don't think I could possibly be sorry about last night.*

It's the only truth that matters. Because it's true for me too. There's no other word but "inevitable" to describe this summer path.

Before either of us can say anything else, my daily morning alarm goes off. "Oh shit," he says, looking over and seeing the time.

"What?" Where could he possibly need to be right now, when usually he's on the way to Belpagna?

"I'm worried about Luce," he says with a grimace.

I sit up, the realization hitting me too. "Oh my god! Luce!" I jump out of bed and walk quickly into the other room, searching the floor for his clothes. I gather them up (we really did get quite haphazard with where we threw them) and then turn around to see him standing in the doorway, smirking at me.

"What?" I ask again, suddenly realizing I probably look a little ridiculous, flitting around my apartment naked while gathering his clothing.

"It's cute that you're *also* worried about Luce." There's affection written into that smirk, and it softens me. I hand his clothes over to him.

"He's probably desperate to know where you are! Not to mention starving—"

"He has food out all the time. He's a weird little grazer. And he has a dog door, so he can come in and out. He's not trapped or anything."

"Well, good," I say, feeling slightly relieved by that. "But you know your absence is noted."

He nods. "I do know that, yes."

"Which is why you're worried," I finish.

"Yes." He pulls me to him and gives me a quick kiss on the lips. "I don't want to rush out on you, and I know there's probably more to talk about—"

"Can we just . . . not?" I blurt out, desperate to end this train of conversation as quickly as it's started. At his confused expression, I rush to clarify: "I don't mean in terms of like . . ." I wave my hands back and forth between us. "This. Us. Not happening. That's not what I mean by 'not.' I just mean in terms of *talking* about it." I pause to see if he's following my nonsensical babbling, but inexplicably he seems to be. "I think we know, Nico. We both know this train has left the station. Whatever is happening between us is happening. If we talk about it, we'll both just get more confused and possibly sad? And I think you're right that we should enjoy the summer and not worry about whatever comes with me leaving, okay?"

I spit all that out so fast. Maybe it's nervous energy propelling me, but for some reason the idea of talking rationally about this irrational set of feelings is practically giving me hives. If we're going to enjoy the moment and ignore the consequences, then let's go all in and fully ignore them. I really cannot imagine exploring what's roiling me underneath.

Nico's eyes are on mine, scanning, trying to read. I wish he could still see the calm from earlier this morning, something in there for him other than *Panic! Avoidance! Sex!* But maybe seeing all of that has compelled him to agree with me, to push our inevitable problems further out and live in the right now.

He gingerly plucks his pants out of my proffered hands and starts pulling them on. "Okay," he says. "'Enjoy the summer' it is. I can do that."

He pulls me to him and wraps his arms around me. I'm already pouty that he has clothes back on while I don't. "I guess this means I'm going to be eating your bomboloni at Belpagna, since you'll be checking on Luce. You're missing out."

His grin is wide and boyish. "I don't think I'd categorize today as me missing out."

I roll my eyes. "Any day without Emilia's pastries is missing out." I try once again to push away the thought that keeps elbowing its way to the forefront—that someday soon that'll be my reality again.

"So bring me some when you come later," he says with a shrug. "It'll be our stakeout snack food."

"You'd rather have Belpagna than whatever dessert we end up making at Pasta Fresca?" I say with mock astonishment.

"Don't make me choose between your food and Emilia's." He wrestles his shirt over his head and slips his feet into his shoes. "I'm happy just with you showing up later. I have no need for any desserts."

"Don't think I didn't notice you completely avoiding the question."

He crinkles his nose with a grin. "See, this is why I like you so much. Nothing gets by you."

He gives me a quick peck on the lips and walks out the door with a chuckle.

Just like that.

Just like nothing's changed and everything's changed. From one day to the next, Nico isn't simply my friend anymore.

I like him too. So much.

Chapter 21

I consider skipping Belpagna, but my need for sustenance before a slammed Saturday is paramount.

Although as I walk the short distance, Palio paraphernalia surrounding me and that same stray cat following along like a shadow ensuring I get to Emilia, I know there's more than just sustenance on my mind.

I open the door, and whatever my face is doing makes Emilia cock her head to the side and examine me with a whisper of a sly smile. She's got on a neon-pink scarf, and I'm not sure today was the day I needed her to be radiating peppiness.

She makes my tea and sets a tart I haven't seen before in front of me. "It's a chunky sweet tomato jam on a shortbread. I'm trying it; it's not quite there yet."

I take a bite and then practically inhale the whole thing. I'm starving from my unplanned extracurricular evening exercise, but that's not the reason I'm already asking her for another one. "When you say 'not quite there yet,' do you mean absolute perfection in every way?"

She scoffs, but I can see the smile she's trying hard to hide. Emilia makes it clear she doesn't believe most people's compliments, but she also knows I don't bullshit. So it squeezes my heart a bit to know that I may be one of the few people whose accolades might tunnel past her skepticism.

"Don't try to change the subject," she says.

My brow furrows. "What subject?"

She circles a finger around my face. "Whatever is happening with you."

"We weren't even talking about me," I say.

"Yeah, but something's up, and you're trying to distract me by talking about the tart."

My mouth is full of tart as I begin denying, so I'm not sure how well that's going to hold up. "You made the tart! It's not my fault it's distracting me!"

"Oh, so there *is* something you want to talk about," she singsongs.

"Not particularly," I mumble through swallowing.

She stares at me, unmoving even as she makes her own espresso. The café is quiet. Saturdays are eventually busy, but they tend to pick up later. On weekends we have the mornings mostly to ourselves, which usually I enjoy. Not today, though.

She comes back to the counter, clunking her tiny cup on the saucer after downing it in one sip. "So what happened with Beppe?"

Oh god. It's like yesterday was the span of an entire year. I've almost completely forgotten what happened with Beppe at this point.

"Nothing," I finally say.

She swats me with a napkin. "Why are you being weird? I know you went for your drink?"

I sigh. Nothing is going to get by Emilia—I'm sure on some level, much like Anita, she's noticed whatever there is to notice. But I also wonder if it's disloyal to Nico to just barge out of my apartment right after he's left and start blabbing to his friend. Yes, she's my friend, too, but she's embedded in this place like Nico is. And while she won't tell anything to anyone else (unlike most people in this town), it feels like breaking a seal of some kind to say it out loud.

"Stop doing whatever calculations you're doing," Emilia says, breaking my spiral.

"I'm not sure it's my place to tell," I eke out, truthfully. I take a big sip from my cup to avoid saying anything else.

"That you slept with Nico?" she says, and I choke on my tea. She hoists herself up over the counter and slaps me on the back, hard, until I stop sputtering.

"What the actual *hell*, Emilia?" I gasp.

"The slapping or Nico?"

"Both?!" I hiss, trying to stay quiet now that a few people have turned around to see what our commotion is about.

"Well, the slapping I could've done with less vigor. Sorry," she says without any actual sorry in her tone. "But the Nico thing was just a guess I wanted to confirm."

I put my head in my hands, absolutely not ready for this conversation being foisted on me. "Emilia . . ."

"You didn't see Antonio out with Nico last night?" she says, and I raise my head to look at her expression.

"Yeah, but that was before . . ." I stop myself.

"Before the sex?" she asks smugly.

I exhale a long breath. "What could your husband have possibly said to you to make you think that's what happened?"

She laughs like I'm the most ridiculous person in the world. "Oh, he came home very amused by Nico."

"Why?" I ask dryly, not ready to admit my curiosity.

"Because he said it was like watching a cartoon character who gets so worked up they eventually have steam coming out of their ears," she says, chuckling.

I press my lips together and try to breathe. She's not making this easy for me.

"Obviously the two of you have the hots for each other," she says casually, as though there's nothing more obvious on earth, and I throw my hands up in exasperation. Is there *no one* in this town who doesn't think I'm completely transparent? *Great.* "But it seemed manageable for two people so clearly in denial. Or sad about their exes. Or determined to stay a little bit tough and miserable." She looks up and squints, as though she's considering which of those is more accurate.

"Get to the point," I finally say, tired of her amusement at my misery.

"Right, sure," she continues, as if this is a totally normal conversation. "So Antonio said Nico left in a huff last night. He followed him out of the bar, but Nico didn't get on his scooter like he usually does. He just went for a walk. That's not like him. And he didn't come here this morning. And now you show up, later than usual, looking both relaxed and perturbed . . ." She shrugs. "Seemed worth testing the theory by asking."

I put my head back in my hands. I'm not sure how to even begin to respond.

"Did you know that for a hundred kilos of grapes, you can get like seventy liters of wine?" she says suddenly, seeming to completely veer away from the topic. I lift my head to meet her eyes, unsure of where she's going. "It's immense. But for olives, if you get fifteen liters, you're lucky. It's just a different calculus."

"What does this have to do with anything?" I ask.

"Most men are grapes," she says. "You can squeeze a lot out of them without much effort; they're pretty easy. Now, maturing them . . ." She whistles. "That takes some skill. But getting started is simple." She rests her elbows on the table and stares at me. "Nico is different. He's like his olives—it takes quite a lot to get something out of him, and not everyone can handle it. But when you do, it's instantly worth it because the result is pretty magnificent."

I soften at her stupid metaphor. Unlike Anita, she's not warning me away (oh *fuck*, am I going to have to tell Anita now?). Or rather, maybe it's a warning of its own kind, but I can tell it's said with a lot of understanding and love.

"I'm not . . ." I start, unsure of what I should even say. "I'm not 'handling' Nico. This isn't going to be a thing."

Her wide eyes get even wider. "Seems like it's already a thing," she says, swiping the biscuit she always lays on the side of my teacup and then shoving it in her mouth, ignoring my protests.

"I'm leaving."

"Yes, obviously no one thinks you're going to stay and be Gia's sous chef for the rest of time."

"So what's your point?" I pout.

She shrugs and walks back to make herself another espresso. I watch her as she moves. Everything is so fluid for Emilia. It's not that she's elegant—on the contrary, she's tall and gawky like me, which I think is one of the things that immediately drew me to her. But it's more that she could do all of this with her eyes closed. She belongs in this space. She knows what needs to get done, what needs to be ordered, who's looking to order something else instead of leaving. The fluidity of this place is in her bones.

I felt that in my restaurant. Maybe not as relaxed as Emilia is, but that sense of being the conductor who could feel the performance of the symphony without even looking. I do miss it.

"It's not a thing," I repeat. "I mean, while I'm here, great. It's going to be whatever it's going to be. But it's not like . . . becoming something."

"I get that," she says, nodding. "But Nico can't just let it go when the summer is over."

My stomach tightens. "We've already talked about it. It's fine."

"Oh okay," she says with a laugh. "You talked about it. It's fine."

"Stop repeating me," I chastise, and I can see her lips almost forming the *s* of "stop" before she thinks better of it.

"Even if that were true"—she rolls her eyes to make sure I'm clear on where she stands—"this town doesn't let anyone forget anything."

I roll my eyes right back at her. "I'm not like his ex-wife who grew up here. People don't need to know about a summer fling."

She smirks. "Oh yeah? You're fooling the old bats who sit out on their plastic chairs in the streets, watching for gossip? You think no one noticed his scooter puttering off home this morning?"

"Come on," I say.

She sticks another two tomato tarts on my plate and then levels me with a stare. "*You* come on. I'm not going to pretend like I don't worry about Nico getting hurt again. But that's not even the thing I'm most focused on right now."

I take a bite of the tart, my desire for pastries overtaking my desire to be petty and ignore them due to Emilia's scolding. "What are you focused on then?" I say with my mouth full.

"On you," she says quietly, and I feel my heart squeeze for a second time today. "Don't you go letting that man come in and hurt you either."

I try to brush off the way my stomach flips. "No one is getting hurt, Emilia." I swallow another bite of tart just to push everything down. "I got dumped by a long-term boyfriend and moved on within a span of days. I'm a big girl. I can have a fling with a friend and then leave it at friends when I'm done."

I can see on her face that she's about to argue, but I'm saved by the bell on the door, which completely changes her expression to one of delight. I turn around and see a tiny woman with a very large baby strapped to her chest.

"Marna!" Emilia cries and pops out from behind the counter to hug her. Very few people get this level of enthusiasm from Emilia, so I'm instantly curious and not at all jealous.

The two start speaking in rapid Italian, punctuated only by the soft kisses Emilia keeps pressing to the baby's cheeks. I've only seen Emilia be indifferent to babies, and she's laughed at the idea of ever having kids herself, so now I'm doubly intrigued.

But after a few minutes, Emilia turns to me, beaming. "This is Marna!"

I look between the two women, frozen by not knowing someone I clearly should have heard of.

"Uhhh," I say, stalling. But Marna laughs.

"Gia only ever refers to me as 'la ragazza,'" she says in heavily accented English, "so you probably have no idea who I am."

I snap my fingers. "You're Gia's sous chef!" I realize, knowing Gia only ever refers to her as "the girl." "Out on maternity leave." I wave my hand toward the baby, and Marna beams.

"Si, I've been with my parents in Umbria, so that's why we haven't met yet," she says. "How is our Gia? I'm relieved she has someone to trust while I'm away." There's so much warmth in Marna's voice that it's impossible not to like her instantly.

I try to imagine this pot of sugar next to the sour lemon that is Gia, and I enjoy the image of Gia being forced to be nicer than she wants to be. Maybe my brashness has been a well-timed little break for Gia.

Emilia asks Marna a question in Italian but then looks toward me and switches to English. "What are you doing in town today?"

"I had some errands, so I made the drive and figured I'd come by and say hello."

I stand up. "I don't want to slow you guys down." It's clear Marna's English isn't as honed as Emilia's. "I should let you guys catch up."

And selfishly, this gets me out of my grilling. I can see the skepticism of that thought pass over Emilia's face, but she's distracted enough by Marna that I think she'll let it go.

"Can I get some extra pastries to take with me?" I ask, thinking of what I said to Nico earlier.

I can see *that* thought is also on the tip of her tongue, but she lets it go as well. I appreciate that she's not going to be the one to start the gossip train, even if she suspects it's not a secret that will be kept easily. She bustles around, making a bag of pastries before she hands it over. I go to grab my wallet, but she shakes her head.

"I know who they're going to," she says slyly and then gives me a kiss on both cheeks.

I resist the urge to roll my eyes again and instead turn to Marna. "So nice to meet you. Will I see you later, saying hi to Gia?"

She snorts a laugh. "Absolutely not. I don't need Gia giving me a lecture on how quickly I can come back."

I nod. "Fair enough!"

And I walk out the door, trying to ignore the persistent thought that's knocking against my brain: I wonder if this is what the town will be like once again when I leave after the summer ends.

Chapter 22

Since I rarely leave my small Cassero radius, it's taken a while to feel at home on my scratched-up little marigold scooter. But flying down the road tonight, past the outstretched blur of wildflowers, I finally am free on it. The warm summer wind is an antidote to the way my body thrummed all day, itching to continue where the morning left off, an unfamiliar sensation of wanting to escape my usually contented confines of a kitchen. As I pull up to Nico's house, that roaring of speed slows and gives way to lilting humidity and the chirping of cicadas and crickets.

It's late, and no lights are on except the small one above the front door. It opens with my arrival, and Nico is framed in the fuzzy halo. He leans against the doorjamb, watching as I climb off my bike, unbuckle the matching yellow helmet I bought, and tousle my hair so it's not so flat.

I walk to him, and that sensation of being allowed to stare still seems brand new and exciting, like suddenly getting to buy a lotto ticket when the clock strikes midnight on an eighteenth birthday.

It's amazing the things you don't see when you're not looking. I'd dulled all his edges out in my mind, protective, placing everything beautiful in the deepest recesses where it couldn't torture me. But now I get to see him in full color. Dark hair rumpled and lightly falling over one eye. The softest-looking dark-blue shirt I've ever seen that curves perfectly over his shoulders. Casually frayed light-wash dad jeans.

End-of-day scruff so tempting I can practically feel it against my fingers just by looking at it. That top lip freckle, slowly rising as he gives me a small lopsided grin.

How on earth was I ever capable of not throwing myself at this man? Being a chef requires a lot of willpower—long days on your feet, avoiding exhaustion and bathroom breaks and outside problems—but maybe all of that has led up to the work of willpowering my way around this.

As I get closer, I'm the strangest version of shy. Our morning bubble popped, the day passed, and now we're out in so much open space. What *are* we now? I try to shake off Emilia's prophesying and focus.

"Hi," I finally breathe, unable to stop my own sheepish grin from forming.

His eyes scan my whole face. "Hi."

We stand there for a moment, goofily watching each other, drinking up this permission to take in all the previously uncatalogued details we'd averted our eyes from.

Luce jumps up on my leg, and it breaks the spell. I crouch down and give him a pet, scratching behind his ears until he starts spinning in an excited circle and he's moving too fast for me to have my hands on him anymore.

I stand up. "So we should probably—"

But I don't finish the sentence before Nico's mouth is on mine. My hand instantly fists into his T-shirt, as soft as it originally appeared. He backs me up against the door and pants my name. He kisses me like he wants me to feel it all the way down to my toes, like he's trying to memorize how I taste and every curve of my mouth. I feel my insides unfurl, that aching need to press against him suddenly roaring back. He's so damn sturdy, and for the first time in my life, I feel delicate, as though I could let myself sink into him.

The thought jars me and I pull back. I hadn't noticed that Luce was barking excitedly at us, so I reach down again to pet him, using that as the excuse as my mind stays as jumbled as the air in my lungs.

"Sorry," he says, as breathy as I feel. "I just . . ."

"I know." I reach out to touch his bottom lip. I can't resist it. And *god*, the way he blushes. I can't get enough of it. "Although we're not going to scare off any wannabe hunters if we're ignoring the world and making out like teenagers."

There's a playful bent in his smile now, his breathing evening, the blush calming. He holds up one of the reflective vests he always makes me wear when we're out here at night. "Think if we both don these fashionable items we'll be more or less likely to stay off of each other?"

I giggle and loop my arms through a vest until it hangs off me, overly large as always. "Are you hoping it's more warning sign than tractor beam?"

He surveys me, lips pressed together in mock seriousness. "I'm afraid to admit that I'm finding it dorkily adorable. I'm hoping the smell of cows makes me capable of not pouncing on you."

"Who assumed the problem was going to be you?"

He laughs, and I love the lightness that's wrapped around him. "I think the evidence of my behavior in the last twenty-four hours isn't great for my case."

My smile grows as I take the other vest out of his hands and pull it over his head. I give him a long look up and down. "It's not going to detract me."

"The reflector vests or the pouncing?"

"Either."

He takes a deep breath and shakes his head, muttering, "Of course helping Gia means I have to sleep outside on the ground instead of in your bed tonight."

I raise my eyebrows suggestively. "Might be the only way we get sleep."

His eyes widen, amused. "You're trying to torture me."

I shrug and reach up to adjust his vest, wanting so badly to kiss him again. But I know we need to get moving. If Tommaso thinks there's a night where he can get away with anything, he will. He'd probably do something at this point just to spite us. I'm still convinced he's the person who messed with the fence, even if Nico has cast a wider net of suspicion.

But as long as the hunters are coming through, we need to keep watch to keep Gia's property safe.

Nico must have the same thought, because he lifts his large duffel bag and then takes my hand, leading me out into the trees.

Our setup is the same as always—Nico sets out the chairs and sleeping bags, and he's got snacks and lamps and our unloaded rifle in his bag. Luce lays down at our feet and falls asleep with a little snort. It's nice to have some familiarity amid all this sudden change in our routine.

We sit down, and he hands me a beer like usual. I take it, the cool drink a balm in an otherwise humid evening. I pull out the pastries from Emilia, and I can see from the look in his eyes that my desserts would never hold a candle to hers.

We sit in companionable silence for a little bit, enjoying the warm air and the pastries and the new comfort that's now looping between us.

"Do you think you'll change your menu when you go home?" he asks out of nowhere.

"I'm always changing," I reply, rolling with wherever he's taking this conversation. "I mean, I've never taken this length of time off of work before—"

"I like how you consider working ten-hour shifts six days a week 'taking time off of work.'"

I scoff. "You know what I mean."

"You're talking to a guy who essentially works six weeks a year." He's picking at the label on the bottle mindlessly.

"I don't think building an entirely new filtration system counts as not working," I point out.

"I'm only saying you could take vacations in the future."

But I shake my head. "I can't, though. This is really only because my restaurant *literally* burned down. There'd be no other excuse for me. They just wouldn't buy it otherwise."

"Who wouldn't buy it?"

I sigh deeply, knowing this answer is so much more complicated. "The entire fucking world of fine dining," I say, lifting my hands in the air. "I have to be in the kitchen, kicking ass, saying hello to the guests, innovating, if I want to stay relevant."

"Come on," he says, looking straight at me now. "So many of those big chefs open multiple restaurants or do TV shows. They're not always in their kitchen." He clearly thinks he's making some wise point. "You could take an extra day off of work or delegate a little bit. Surely you've earned it."

Now I'm the one picking at labels. I don't know how to explain this to him. It's almost like I don't want to burst the pure bubble that he has. I don't even want to look at him. "I don't get that courtesy," I finally say, and he shifts forward to look at me more closely.

"Why?" He's genuinely curious.

"Women in this business always have to work twice as hard." We're both silent for a moment, and I tilt my head up to see the stars dancing through the leaves of the tree. There's a brightness peeking through the darkness, and it's such a beautiful sight to take in. "Women technically can be anything now, sure," I start, trying to think of the right way to say this. "But if you look at the top . . . like of all Michelin-starred restaurants, only six percent are run by women."

"Six?" he says, and I like the twinge of anger that's automatically taken hold in his voice, like somehow he's in this fight too.

"Six. We *can* be anything, but to succeed we have to be *everything*. More organized, harder working, more giving, better mentors. No illness, no weakness, no tardiness, definitely nothing gynecologic. No stagnation. My restaurant burning down was probably the only scenario on earth where I could've left and then eventually come back."

He puts a hand on my thigh and stays quiet. We sit in that silence for a little while, our breathing one instrument among the sounds of all the bugs making their symphonies.

"That's a lot to carry," he finally says.

It's really all there is to say, isn't it? I've been carrying a lot of expectations on my own for a long time. I have myself to blame for a lot of it, but the career I've chosen, the path I want, can also take some of that dubious credit. It's hard to be free and let people in when you need to stay focused to have what you want.

And here's Nico, not judging me, not forcing advice down my throat. Just handing me understanding. I've always assumed I needed to settle for a guy like John because no better man would care as much about the food precision that I'm so passionate about. But Nico upends all my assumptions.

And I can't help it; I have to kiss him. Softly. With so much less urgency than the last few times. I run my hand along that evening stubble and feel him exhale. Let the hoppy taste of his beer linger. Quietly kiss his jaw and nuzzle him before pulling back. Luce opens one eye from the movement, but he promptly rests his head and goes back to sleep.

"What was that for?" he asks.

I shrug. "For always saying the right thing."

He reaches for my hand and intertwines our fingers. We stare at the stars, our beers warm and less frothy now, while I get to know the calluses on his hand that mirror mine.

"What about you?" I ask, the silence between us comfortable enough to have created an opening for more conversations in the dark.

"What about me?" he says, his voice a smile.

"Can you leave more?" He doesn't say anything, so I continue. "Like if you wanted to travel more now, take more vacations, could you?"

Am I picking at him the way we've both lazily worked at the labels of the bottles, trying to see if the condensation has loosened the gluey grip? Are we both grasping at whether this new thing between us can find pockets to exist in the outside world? Or finding ways to burrow into more understanding of each other's lives?

"I do, in the winter especially," he answers. "I visit my mum's family in the UK, and I go see exporters in all the places where they're selling my oil so I can meet with restaurants and shops and let them put a face to it."

"Ever come to New York?" I ask, so obvious.

"I usually do, yeah." He squeezes my hand.

"Good," I reply, not knowing how else to express the way it makes my whole body breathe deeper, the knowledge that at least our friendship isn't rushing toward an arbitrary finish line, even if this particular version already is.

"Would you . . ." I stop, not sure if I can ask the other question that's been on my mind almost as long as I've known him. Out here, with the chorus of nature buzzing around us, it's as though we're in a world that doesn't quite count. "If your ex-wife came back, would you want to be with her again?"

He looks over at me, studying my face again with affection. "No," he says comfortably. "I haven't been in love with her for a long time now." He makes it sound so simple—falling out of love. "I was; I certainly was when we were younger. I wouldn't diminish that. But she hurt me, and we're not the same anymore. We didn't grow together."

"I can see that," I say, even though I know that the one part that separates our stories is that I'm not sure if love was something I ever really felt for John. Lust, friendship, common interests. But never really love. "Would you change any of it if you could?"

"No," he says quietly. He pauses for a moment and then continues, taking a new tack. "So you know when you drink wine and say like, 'Oh, there's green apple in this,' right?"

"Yeah, of course," I huff. "My favorite Instagram account is a woman called Fresh Cut Garden Hose who draws cartoons of the crazy way people describe wine."

"Well, exactly," he says with a smile, even though I'm sure the comment is lost on him—he's never been on Instagram in his life. But he barrels on. "So olives are the only fruit that genetically has the polyphenol of other fruits. Like if you plant an olive near strawberries and almonds, and you get that flavor in it, it's because it *actually* shares some of their DNA. It's got the essence of all the other plants that grow around it. And that's why these older trees are so amazing, because you can shift what you plant in the in-between spaces and fundamentally shift the olives."

"I'm so grateful you get to live in a time where you can be a technology nerd *and* a farmer nerd," I joke, one food nerd to another.

"Except for Instagram," he points out.

"That's not technology you need," I say with a laugh. "That's not as interesting as the altering of olive DNA."

"Very true," he chuckles. But then his expression turns serious again. "But that's why I wouldn't change anything."

"Because you're like an olive, soaking up everything around you?"

He smiles softly. "I'm just saying we wouldn't want to be divided from our past experiences, even if the new ones are what matter in the present."

"You spend too much time with trees," I tease. I don't want to delve too deeply into thoughts of altering DNA.

Luckily, I get that gorgeous grin of his again. "Probably." He nudges my shoulder. "What about you?"

"'What about me?'" I say, mimicking his retort earlier.

"Do you look back? Consider what's behind you."

I shake my head. "Never." His eyebrow raises, and I continue. "I've always been that way. Looking to what's next, finding the next goal, moving forward. I can't get stagnant."

"Is that what happened with rowing?"

"What do you mean?"

"A while ago, you said when you stopped rowing, you went to culinary school. I've been wondering what that transition was like, going from rowing constantly for a decade to something completely new?"

I pause, not having really considered this story in a while, not sure how to contend with that time in my life—the only time I think my dad ever really got upset with me. "Well . . . I got asked to train to potentially join the national team . . ."

"Yeah?"

"I was invited to the Under 23s, and you train with them in hopes of being on the national team by the time the Olympics come around. But it was for a minimum of two years and you have to live in Princeton, New Jersey, and you don't get paid, so you have to find a random job and you obviously aren't even guaranteed a spot. Like, even in the months before the Olympics, they'll have a camp with like seventy people for less than thirty spots."

"You were worried about the odds?"

I inhale a deep breath and then take a moment to let all the air empty out of me, trying to parse that particular moment in time. "No . . . I knew I could get it if I wanted it," I say, truthfully. It's not bravado; I just always have been able to push myself enough to earn the things I want, even if that's hard to articulate. I look over at Nico, and I'm glad to see he isn't laughing that off. "But ultimately, I think I didn't care enough to have it keep being my entire life. I didn't have the passion for it that I'd already realized I had for cooking. I'd set out to be a great rower and reach some pinnacles, and I did it and was done."

"How'd that go over?" It's so Nico to see immediately where the cracks are for me.

"My mom was happy for me, but my dad was disappointed." Understatement of the century. Nico raises an eyebrow, as though he sees right through that statement too. "He felt like it was worth seeing through as far as it could go, but I'd given it so much of my life already and I'd won everything I'd set out to win. I was ready for an actual career and knew I couldn't do well at both if I was doing them at the same time. I'd already applied for culinary school, because when I'd had time off outside of rowing season, I'd worked in restaurants and already loved it—I think I related to the hierarchy and pressure of a kitchen." He snorts a laugh, and I give him a look. *"What?"*

"Hierarchy and pressure aren't usually the standards people are looking for." He gives me a smile and a hand squeeze, making it clear that he's only gently mocking.

"I thrive under that kind of environment, though," I continue. "It brings out the best in me. I want to work hard and know the stakes and have a goal. There aren't a lot of careers where you get that along with creativity."

"Fair point," he says, his mind on something else. He's quiet again for a moment before he turns back to me. "And how was your dad with *that*?"

"He eventually got into it," I say with a casual wave of my hand, ignoring the fallout and instead focusing on his passion once he got on board with my new focus. "He loves the research of it all, so he started looking up where I should do a stage—where I'd learn the most; which chefs de cuisine actually let their line cooks contribute. It was like an extension of coaching for him."

"Did you enjoy it?"

"Enjoy what?" I say, prickling a little bit.

"All of that work? Sounds like you didn't have a lot of time for yourself."

"I don't need time for myself," I say automatically.

The look he gives me is like one you might give to a puppy chasing after its own tail. And it's harder to brush off, since he's one of the few people who's actually scratched below the surface and truly sees what's underneath. All those weeks when I was forcing my heart to say *friends, friends, friends*, it was only the wanting more that was fraught—because friendship happened without effort. I don't let a lot of people in, but Nico slipped in a back door and made himself at home without me even needing to unlock it. He did it so effortlessly I barely noticed that he'd settled in, like a person whose spot was always meant to be occupied.

So when he looks at me with skepticism, I can't help but bristle a bit. He seems to notice it, but that doesn't stop him.

"You can't build a wall on wet cement," he says finally. "You have to take a minute to actually let things marinate."

"Listen, I love a marinade," I joke, trying to lighten the conversation. I know I started it, asking about his ex-wife of all things, but now that the spotlight is turned on me, I want to brush it all off.

He nods in understanding. "I'm glad you're getting this time here, then."

"Me too." He doesn't say anything else, and I put my head on his shoulder, grateful he's letting me off the hook from delving into the past when all I want is to exist in this present.

"The new fencing seems to be holding," I say, changing the subject. From this angle I'm unable to see the patched hole.

He tilts his head. "The seams still bother me."

"Don't be such a perfectionist," I say with a smirk. "You've stopped the wayward fence-breakers; isn't that enough?"

"I'm not convinced they're done messing with us."

"Clearly." I motion around us, the absurdity of another night with an unloaded rifle, camping chairs, and cows obvious.

"I still can't believe you're willing to do this." He reaches over and tucks a tendril of hair behind my ear that wasn't sticking out enough to justify the movement. But considering I've spent the whole evening trying to figure out how to plausibly touch him without any real reason, I understand. His eyes are on my mouth, and I have to shake away my desire to turn this night into something else entirely.

"Well, I'm on Gia's team, and I'm pretty ride or die," I finally say, leaving him out of all my justifications.

"Since being on Gia's team keeps you pretty busy," he says with a smile, his hand still resting below my ear and his eyes still glued to my mouth, "can I claim your one night off on Monday? Since you don't need any time to yourself?" He scrunches his nose like he's enjoying teasing me, like he has no problem calling out my bullshit and already knows it won't bother me.

And it really doesn't. Because I can't think of anything better.

"Is this the part where you're asking me on a date and I'll know it?"

"Yup," he says with a grin.

"Then yes," I reply, because this, at least, really is as simple as that.

Chapter 23

On Monday, I stand in front of the mirror too long, but it's better than pacing my apartment as time ticks by slowly and the sun finally starts to get lower in the sky.

It's only been a day since Nico and I were alone together, but considering we woke up in a field with cows yesterday, it wasn't exactly sexy. I worked late last night and then only saw him at Belpagna with Emilia this morning.

He said he'd pick me up at six, so after getting dressed in a T-shirt and shorts early, I've been fidgeting with eyeliner for at least thirty minutes. I'm not good at it, and I'm not even sure I need it since my eyes already bug out enough. There's a voice in my head that's mocking the low effort I'm putting in while simultaneously running in circles, ringing alarm bells that I'm trying too hard.

It's like my mirror is the edge of a diving board, and I'm staring at it, wondering when someone's just going to push me already. Maybe I've got to be like the kids at the beach who jumped off the rock, even though they were a little bit scared.

But their water was clear. I have no idea what I'm jumping into.

My fingers tap rhythmically in front of the mirror, unable to stop their nervous dancing. This is so unlike me. I don't know if it's because we were friends first or because the attraction had so long to build up or what. Fidgeting isn't something I'm used to.

But before I can delve too far into *that*, there's a knock at my door.

I swing it open to Nico, standing in a shirt I've never seen him wear—an actual ironed button-down that isn't made of flannel. He looks *hot*, and it makes a smoky pressure build in my chest.

He's holding out a bouquet of wildflowers that look like a burst of harnessed sunshine.

"They're from my fields," he says, a hint of a blush rising, and I let myself watch and drink it in.

"They're perfect." I wrap my hand around the stems gently, like they're too beautiful to manhandle even if they're made to survive out in the open, rain or shine.

I grab a vase and pour some water in, taking the moment to not let myself get overheated from the arrival of a seemingly game-on Nico. I arrange the flowers on the coffee table in the center of the room. Everything seems brighter with them here, like an effortless but purposeful addition.

He hands me my helmet. He must've grabbed it from my scooter downstairs.

"You're riding with me tonight. If that's okay," he says.

I nod, sort of stunned into silence at this version of Nico. I think about what he said on Saturday: *When I ask you out on a date, you'll know it.* I thought he'd just meant the asking, but date-Nico is apparently lethal. I might not've noticed the difference if I hadn't already spent so much time with friend-Nico, but date-Nico puts in efforts that simultaneously have no pressure. He's not grandstanding or trying to overtly impress me. But he's done all these small things. Ironed a shirt. Gathered wildflowers. Made a plan. Picked me up at my door instead of having me meet him outside. Grabbed my helmet even before I asked.

And now he's fiddling with the clasp after I put the helmet on, an excuse to touch me again, I think. It softens all my nerves away.

We head downstairs, and his Vespa is right out front. It's such a different sensation, riding with him than going on my own. I don't have to pay attention; I can let him lead and allow myself to go along for the literal ride. I have no idea where we're going, which normally would cause my inner control freak to stand at attention. But with Nico, she's able to stand down.

And instead I'm able to lean into the moment. My arms are around his waist, my head nestled onto his back; the trees I'm now so familiar with line the road like they're waving in the sunset. I don't want to miss the scenery, but I also can't help but close my eyes and breathe it all in.

So I'm surprised, then, when we pull up to his house. Luce runs out the door and bounces around us as though he hasn't seen Nico in years, even if he probably saw him half an hour ago.

"Did you forget something?" I ask as he hops off the bike.

He holds out his hand for mine, indicating I should get off too. "Nope," he says, keeping my hand and leading me toward the house.

"Awfully presumptuous of you to bring me to your house," I flirt. "Buy a girl dinner first at least."

But when he opens the door, all my smart-aleck comments are silenced.

He's set his table for two, with a blue-checkered tablecloth and more of those wildflowers in a small vase at the center. Gentle music permeates the air as much as the smell of garlic, caramelized onions, and a meaty sauce of some kind. It's the date equivalent of everything I've been learning from Gia—simplicity as the root of perfection. There's no rose petals or abundance of candlelight. It's all himself, not overwrought, polished with the shine of subtle effort.

"This is—" I say, not even knowing where to begin.

"I thought, maybe . . . you'd like it if someone else cooked you dinner for once." He shrugs.

It's so earnest. It's so *romantic*. Fuck. I don't think I've ever had a man be romantic. I don't think I've ever given any man the impression that I'd *want* him to be romantic.

And that trips something beyond typical butterflies. It's as though he's reached me below where the butterflies would normally live, dug into the soil, deep inside where I'd thought my senses ended and didn't realize they tunneled deeper than I'd ever known. That sense of being delicate is surfacing again.

I never understood the concept of living rent-free in someone's head, but that's what it feels like Nico is doing to me. It's like I haven't just been thinking about him; he's already in there and at home.

I reach out and touch the pad of my finger to his freckle at the top of his lip, tracing the way the skin curves. I lean in and bite it, gently, the way I've been dying to, and he murmurs a sigh.

"I swear the goal of bringing you here was to cook you dinner," he says, "not an excuse to get you in my house."

"I know." I nod, wrapping my arms around his neck. He kisses me slowly but then pulls back.

"Don't distract me," he says, kissing my forehead with finality while I fight the urge to pout. He pours me a glass of wine and then hands it over while he heads back into the kitchen.

"What'd you make?" I ask, leaning over to try and get a look.

"Don't expect too much of me," he says with a small smile. "I roasted some eggplants, made a salad, and did a ragù for pasta."

"Please tell me it's not—"

"It *is* boar ragù," he says with a chuckle. "But it's because that's what the butcher had and recommended today!"

I can't help but laugh right along with him. "I'm glad you and Gia both trust the butcher, as it should be. But *come on*."

He raises his hands in mock defeat.

"I am but a creature of the town I'm wedded to," he says, a mock sigh added in for emphasis. But then he goes back to cooking, Luce parking himself at Nico's feet, and I decide to take the opportunity to wander around his little home.

The walls are sturdy brick, with decorative arches over the windows and wooden beams on the ceiling. It's rustic in a lived-in way, and the whole house is basically one giant room, with the bedroom raised a bit to delineate the space. As he described, his bathroom *does* only have a curtain. And I can count seven dream catchers on the walls without even looking for them.

His bed looks like a typical man's: He attempted to make it, but the covers are lumpy and a bit askew.

"Why are all men completely incompetent at making a bed?" I muse.

"I blame duvet covers," he shouts from the kitchen.

I wander back over, wineglass still in hand. "What did duvet covers ever do to you?"

"They're ridiculous," he says, tasting a salad dressing he's been mixing. "Why don't they have a zipper down the middle or something? They're impossible to put on."

I snort a laugh. "A zipper down the middle? You'd be so uncomfortable!"

"But I'm already uncomfortable because I can never do the duvet right. It's always more on one side, or I start buttoning wrong and then it's one button off. It's like it's designed to flummox you. Why can we have, like, automatic heated toilets but not an easy duvet cover?"

"Sounds like a project for a man who's already done with the engineering marvel of a new olive oil filtration system."

He shakes his head as he pours the dressing over the salad. "No way. I'm not cut out for the complexity of duvets. Way above my pay grade."

"We wouldn't want scratchy center-zipped duvet covers becoming a thing anyway." I grab the wooden spoons next to him and automatically start tossing the salad.

"*Hey,*" he says, pulling the spoons out of my hands. "No cooking for you today!"

I grab them back. "It's not *cooking* to stir up a salad."

"Kiiiit," he whines in mock annoyance. "Let someone do something for you for once."

"I let Emilia make me tea every single morning!"

I straighten the cutlery he's placed on the table, unable to stand still.

"That doesn't count! You pay her to make the tea."

"Nah, she never charges me for the tea." I grin, loving that I got him on that one.

"You're tossing the salad before I even put the olive oil in anyway," he says, reaching for an unmarked bottle and drizzling it on.

When he sets it back down, I reach out to catch a drip from the side with my finger. I'm about to taste it, but I get the impulse to rub it on Nico's lips instead, and then press my mouth to his. The cooking is briefly forgotten as he leans into it, an herbaceous kiss that neither of us can bring ourselves to stop.

But eventually he reluctantly pulls back. "What did I say about distracting me?"

"I didn't want to waste any of your olive oil," I joke.

He chuckles and pours a little more oil on his finger, then drags it across my collarbone.

"What are you doing?" I squeal.

But his tongue is already on me, licking it off. "Now who's distracting!" I pant. I've lost the battle of sounding indignant to the realities of shallow breathing.

His smirk is downright lethal. And instead of answering, he just winks and turns back to his pasta, leaving me stunned and wondering if it's worth burning dinner in exchange for our own version of skipping to dessert.

But his competence wins out over my lusting. He's not deterred the way I am, which frankly makes him even more attractive as he strains pasta and combines it with the sauce that's been simmering on the stove.

Watching him work is hypnotizing. He's so at ease. Not only in the kitchen but in his whole demeanor. My twitchiness about our new status seems to be the opposite of how he's feeling. For weeks there's been some unspoken tension between us, and now, for him, it appears to have completely melted away. A force field turned off, all his stillness back in order. I envy that. It's how I *should* be. It's how I normally *would* be. I don't get riled up, and I don't ever sweat the small stuff.

But I think about what Emilia said on Saturday. *Don't you go letting that man come in and hurt you either.* There's no world where Nico would hurt me intentionally. But maybe it's *me* who's getting too invested. Maybe Nico has figured out the ease of letting a summer fling happen, and *I'm* the one who's letting it make me all swoony in a way I've never been before.

I'm so unfamiliar with this state of being that I decide to wander around the room again.

I brush my hand along his run-down chair with its matching ottoman. Above it is the photo Nico mentioned, of him as a child on a ladder raking olives. He's so much smaller, but that same quiet confidence is apparent, even as a gangly boy.

I step closer, and my foot brushes a basket sitting against the chair. I look closer and notice it's filled with knitting needles and yarn.

"You *knit*?" I ask.

"Crochet!" he calls back, and I giggle at him pointing out the difference (*What . . . is the difference?*). I pick up the nearest item that he's been working on.

"What are you making?" I ask, unable to suppress the glee at discovering this large man's secret knitting habit (*Sorry . . . crochet,* I internally chide).

"A little rabbit for Marna's baby," he says, and my heart squeezes. I pick it up, a soft turquoise rabbit in front of me, and can't help bringing it to my nose. It already smells like him, his warm hands and woodsy permanent glow. Here's a man spending his free time hand-making a gift for a friend's baby. And I'm just a chump preoccupied with making myself into more of an upgraded cooking robot. No wonder Emilia's more worried about me becoming obsessed than she's worried about Nico.

I put the unfinished rabbit down, knowing that I need to not go deeper into this weird rising neediness that Nico is bringing out of me. I shake off the sensation and grab my wineglass again, taking a big sip and squaring my shoulders back.

I hop up onto the counter next to where Nico is working. I love watching him clock the movement, his eyes roaming down the expanse of my legs that are now dangling in front of him.

"I know I deserve this distraction, but you're killing me," he huffs, and it's adorable.

"This is *not* payback for your olive oil deviance!" I chide. "You told me I couldn't do anything! So this is me waiting!"

"It's still distracting," he mumbles, pressing a kiss to my shoulder like he can't help himself.

I watch as he finishes up. He puts the eggplant and the pasta into handcrafted ceramic bowls that I recognize as coming from a particular local purveyor, and lays all the food out on his beautifully set table. We sit down and eat, and that ease comes back to me now that food is in the equation.

It's actually good—he's a better-than-average cook, and everything he's made has that innate Tuscan simplicity baked in. I have to admit that the boar, cooked down with local peak tomatoes, is the perfect gamy acidic combination with the eggy pasta he's procured. The red wine flows, we get second helpings of the food, and we laugh our way through dinner the way we always have with good conversation and a never-ending enjoyment of each other's company.

He was right before, although apparently I didn't understand when he said it. I definitely know what being asked on a date looks like now.

Chapter 24

"I didn't make dessert, but I did buy gelato," he says after we've cleared the table.

He goes to the freezer and pulls out a Styrofoam container. It's unmarked, but I know it's from Belpagna. I grab two spoons from the drawer, and I love the delighted grin he gives me at the obviousness of my heathen intentions.

I sit back on the counter, and we eat the gelato just like that—together, straight out of the container, no words needed as we enjoy it.

But when he sets the container down and comes closer to me, I already know I'm done for.

I wrap my legs around him. "The goal wasn't to get me in your house?" I tease, my arms propping me up and the torture of not grabbing on to him already exquisite.

He seems to be thinking the same thing because even as he lets himself get pulled closer, he still doesn't bring his hands to me, instead letting them bracket me on the counter. But he does bring his face so close to mine that I can smell the sweetness of the gelato on him.

"The goal was to cook dinner for you," he repeats, not giving an inch.

"And if it just happened to get me into your house?"

"Excellent side benefit."

Neither of us moves, and it's a delicious game of chicken, watching each other and waiting.

He comes closer, still not moving his hands off the counter, but now with his lips next to my ear. "I do like having you here," he says softly.

"Not enough to fix your duvet cover, though," I say, completely distracted by the way he's staying put, his mouth not moving away and his breath on my neck making me shiver.

"If I'd known you'd pay such close attention to my bed, I would've tried a little harder."

"I think it was the perfect amount of trying."

He kisses my neck and nuzzles into me. It's like plucking on a violin string—all that tension suddenly making me vibrate with want. My exhale is shaky, and he chuckles against my skin.

"Do you want me to take you home?" he asks quietly. "Now that dinner is over?"

"No," I rush, the word coming as quickly as it possibly could, my hands finally coming to his chest, as though I want to show him I don't intend on going anywhere.

His hand comes to the top of my thigh, hovering like a question. "What do you want, then?"

I reach for the bottle of olive oil again and drizzle a little bit on my finger. I rub it across his collarbone, like he did to me earlier, and lick it off, slowly. He hisses in a breath but still doesn't grab for me. I take my time with the moment, lingering, relishing. I want him to be at a perfect simmer.

"Just finishing what you started," I say with a smile. "I promise I won't waste any more olive oil."

But he steps back, eyeing me. He grabs the bottle off the counter and pours a little bit on my upper thigh, making me gasp.

"I swear there's never been a better use of anything," he says, kneeling so he can put his mouth right where he poured, his hands gripping the fabric of my shorts, a promise of what's to come. *Oh my god.* I don't think I've ever been so turned on with all my clothes still firmly on my body. He sucks at the skin on my leg and whispers, "*Mine*," and I can't control the sounds that spill out of me.

I'm aching to make him feel as upended as he makes me, and I can't take having him so torturously far away. I grab his shirt, drag him up, and whisper in his ear, "Since your duvet covers are in *such* a state, do you think you could make me forget about them right here?"

He pulls back, and I can see his eyes searching mine, wondering if I meant what he thinks I meant. But I'm done talking and joking and flirting. I need us closer. I reach out to unbutton his pants, and a groan escapes his lips, desperation sounding so *good* on him.

His pants fall to the floor, and he immediately pulls my shirt over my head, then lifts me up as though I weigh nothing and slides my shorts off in one move, taking my underwear with it. He's gotten me naked on the counter in about five seconds, and I'd be impressed if I wasn't so delirious from looking at him right now. I motion for him to remove his shirt as well, my dexterity failing me in the moment, but he takes the hint and unbuttons, that adorably ironed shirt soon joining the heap of our clothes. I push his underwear down, and wow the view is good.

I pull him to me, into me, and I lean back, grabbing on to the counter for purchase. All the lights are still on, but I like it. I want to see everything. I want to *feel* everything. I want his hands and mouth on my skin.

He grabs my hips and moves us close, watching our bodies come together with eyes that look like he's committing me to memory. I want to kiss him, but I don't want either of us to stop watching—one strong arm holding me up, the other touching me in a way that has me gasping, his stomach tightening, my leg hooked around the hard planes of his hips, my hand in the smattering of hair on his chest.

I don't think I've ever been savored like this before, like he wants every inch of me, the last bit of gelato you're scraping from the bottom of the cup so you don't waste a drop. And maybe that's because everything in my life has always been explosive—hard work, big stakes, a fire literally burning things down.

But Nico is the opposite of everything I've known.

He's the slow burn.

He's the luxury of taking your time and letting something melt inch by inch instead of all at once.

But that thought slips away because I'm tipping over the edge. All-consuming need takes hold of me, fingerprints indenting into his bicep while I lose the ability to think straight.

When it's over, we stay still for a moment, breathing each other in, his head resting on my shoulder and my fingers tangled in his soft hair. The backs of my legs are sore from pressing up against the counter, but it makes me feel alive, every inch of me buzzing, awake like I've had Emilia's usual four espressos.

He grabs a dish towel that's in reach on the counter and hands it to me.

"Such a gentleman," I giggle.

"I wouldn't say losing my grip on reality on my kitchen counter qualifies me as being a gentleman." He's fussing with my hair, smoothing it down as though he's suddenly realized I'm disheveled.

"Lose your grip more often, then, please." I hop off the counter, give him a kiss, and pop into the bathroom.

When I come out, he's turned most of the lights off. He takes my hand and leads me over to his bed, pulling back the covers before gently pushing me onto it.

"Duvet problem solved," he says, climbing in with me.

"Because you made me forget about it until you could just unmake the bed again?" I ask.

"Exactly," he says with a laugh, pulling the covers over both of us.

The desperation of the countertop has been replaced by the cocoon of his bed. It's funny that *this* feels more intimate than what we just did—that being relaxed and playful, our guard down, is more personal, more rare. More happy.

He reaches out to push my hair back behind my ear, apparently not content with his work earlier.

"Is it safe to assume I get to keep you here tonight?" he asks.

"Did you pull me into bed so I'd be too lazy to ask you to drive me home?" I joke, nudging him a little.

He pulls me into a hug. "That's only part of it."

"What's the other part?" I ask, the words easier now that I'm not looking into his eyes.

"I want you here," he replies, as simple as the simplest recipe. Then he turns off the one remaining light next to his bed.

I nuzzle into him, the lingering olive oil and his woodsy smell even better this close and corralled under the covers. His arms wrap around me a little tighter, gentle but with clearly no intention of letting go tonight.

I feel Luce hop onto the foot of the bed, circle around, and then plop down. And I know it's only temporary, but I let myself drift off, fully swathed in this little home that so openly wants me in it.

Chapter 25

"I need you to stop whistling," Gia says dully to me, her voice wry and bored.

I snap my head up, unaware I was even doing it. The look Gia's giving me is like what you'd give to a lamb before slaughter. It's pity but also a little bit happiness to be getting it over with.

"Sorry," I say, blowing a strand of hair out of my eyes as I keep dicing the giant bag of onions Gia handed to me a few minutes ago.

The last couple of weeks have flown by on a smooth cloud as I've settled into a new rhythm. Nico and I have been swapping out sleeping over at each other's places, always careful when Nico stays at mine to park outside the city walls, since I know the narrow streets of Cassero would brim with talk of a new Vespa overnight. Perhaps it's naive to think I can leave at the end of the summer without a train of gossip in my wake, but our arrangement also has a side benefit of not upending the other areas of my carefully curated summer life. He doesn't come by the restaurant unless to see Gia for something; we don't sit closer at Belpagna than we did before; he doesn't join me for my morning walks up the stone steps. My internal worry that I might drown in soaking up whatever we're doing is easily nipped in the bud by keeping those lines separated.

I wouldn't put anything past Gia, though. Thankfully, if she had an inkling about what's happening, she would absolutely still completely ignore it. She'd ignore anything personal I didn't bring up. I bet I could walk into Pasta Fresca with a bleeding bandage on my head, and as long as I didn't get any blood on my prep, Gia wouldn't ask me about it.

Happy whistling, though—some embarrassing sex-haze remnant of satisfaction, I suppose—that's apparently a final straw for her.

My phone rings, and I get a more honed look from Gia, as though this is now a plot to make a new kind of noise. I stumble out an apology and go to turn it off, but my hands still when I see who's calling. *John.*

I haven't seen his name on my phone since that last phone call right when I arrived. He's done what I asked of him—he's never checked in, never even sent a text. I knew we couldn't ever be completely out of touch, since his company does own my restaurant, but he's thankfully let other people deal with me. The updates I've gotten on the status of the renovations have been only via email through one of the operations guys. John and I were cc'd next to each other but never truly connected.

So what the hell is he calling me about?

I stand there so long it stops ringing. I can feel Gia's eyes on me, but I don't say anything; I just go back to chopping onions.

Then it rings again, and I hear Gia sigh so loudly that I know I need to make it end. I wipe my hands on a towel, pick up the phone, and barge my way out the wooden door to the alleyway.

"Hello," I say, as plainly as possible.

"Hey, Kit, how's Italy?"

It's so casual and breezy, and I want to slap him through the phone. *How's Italy?* Like I'm just on an extended holiday and my entire world didn't blow up in a single day?

"What do you want, John?" I don't have it in me to make whatever small talk he wants to engage in.

"Ah okay, I see," he chuckles, the overfamiliarity churning my stomach. "So I guess we're staying mad then. I deserve that."

"I'm at work," I deflect, and just the sound of him on the other end of my phone further amps up my annoyance.

"I'm glad you're taking some time to yourself." Even though I know I've described this summer as "time off" to Nico, I hate the way John's ignoring the word "work" and instead is pinning my hiatus to the wall like a mounted insect he's already categorized. "I wanted to catch you up on the renovations, as well as tell you about something new you may want to hear about."

"Mm-hmm," I mutter casually, perfunctory so I don't stall whatever he has to say.

I'm surprised by how little I feel, other than wanting to end this call as quickly as possible. There's no nostalgia from hearing the voice of the man I dated for so many years. If anything, it's like listening to a voice through a window—I can hear it, but the timbre I should recognize feels distant. I'm not sure *what* I thought it would be like to talk to John again, but I didn't expect to care so little. I don't know if that says more about me or him.

"So the investors love the idea of using the reopening as a big marquee moment. With the fire and all the publicity that's generated, maybe you haven't seen it, but there's been so much commentary about you and your career—your consistency, your tenacity—and what's next."

"Okay," I reply. I know this because my dad forwards me every article that mentions me, but I'm not going to say that to John. I've never cared about press and he knows it, so I have no idea where he's going with this.

"One of the things we've been working on is signing the deal to get the exclusive rights to do the restaurants in that new building downtown with the incredible views, the one that's going to be the tallest building since the Freedom Tower. And we're finally ready to close the deal."

"Okay," I repeat, wondering why he thinks I care about his projects anymore, considering I didn't find them that interesting even while we were dating. "Happy for you guys that you secured that project, that's a big one." It's insincere, but at least it keeps this conversation moving. I can't say it to him, but I've got onions to chop and no team of minions to do it for me, and I'm over whatever this story is.

"They want you, Kit."

I don't say anything for a moment. "What do you mean they want me?"

"There's going to be a restaurant at the top, views across the river and over Manhattan, a huge budget, and they plan to make it the marquee of the entire space. They want to give it to you."

"I already have a restaurant."

I've never wanted to be that chef, with a ton of restaurants I eventually don't ever cook in. I want to be on the line, working, making sure every dish that has my name on it is flawless. Sure, I'll admit my ultimate goal is to be an owner someday. But I don't want to expand someone else's empire while diluting my food.

"You have plenty of people ready to step up for you and become chef de cuisine when you're ready," he says, his tone clearly in convincing mode. "This wouldn't be for a couple of years. But it would be *yours*. You'd be a co-owner with serious equity. They want to give you an insane budget—let you build out whatever you want. Style it however you want. Have whatever kitchen equipment and specifications you want. It's a chef's dream project."

I think I've stopped breathing. *Holy shit.* This *is* a dream. I've heard of a few of these types of deals in recent years—hotels looking to lure a top name, iconic buildings that want up-and-coming chefs to make them seem hip again. The money flowing into these projects can really mean a chef gets to take charge. This is a completely different ball game from what I have right now—my name is on the door, sure, and based on press clippings you'd think it was mine, but it's a concept and space planned by others that can override me at any moment. Ownership is the dream. A kitchen of my own design, the budget and the space to do exactly what I want in New York City? It's practically impossible to say no to, no matter the trade-offs.

"What's happening with the renovation?" I ask, trying to not let my voice tip off my thinking. I can't help but be reminded from this conversation of how I felt that last phone call—that niggling sense of always allowing myself to be steered.

"They'll be done the first week of September."

"Actually?"

"Actually. They're saying last week of August, so this is me being conservative."

"Something you've never deigned to do before." I pick at a vine that's growing up the wall just so I have something to do with my hands.

"I want when you come back for you to see I'm deferring to you now."

My hand stops. "Why?"

He laughs and I hate it. He's laughing like we're old pals; like he knows me better than I know myself; like we still share some intimacy.

"I miss you. We had a good thing going. I fucked up. But things will be different when you come back."

"Not a chance," I say quickly, the entire thought repulsing me more than I would've expected.

At the time I *did* think we had a good thing going. And he *did* fuck up. But the fuckup isn't the thing that bothers me now. Nico is what bothers me. I know I don't get to keep him when all this ends—I know that—but he's made me expect something better.

Maybe I won't ever get that in New York. But I sure as hell can't settle for less anymore. I'm perfectly fine being alone; I've always thrived alone. And that's all I can imagine for myself when I'm back home in that kitchen, because anything less wouldn't be enough.

I take a deep breath, trying to not allow the tempest inside me to roil into a hurricane.

"Send me the details about the new space," I say, ignoring the rest. "That's the only part I'm interested in. And get Gavin to send me some photos and a real update on the renovation. I know they've been saying post–Labor Day for a couple months, but no offense, I don't believe anyone in construction until I see something."

"Okay," he says, backing off whatever else he clearly has on the tip of his tongue. "I'll send that all to you by the end of the day. Look everything over—the investors want to pair reopening day in September with the announcement about the future space. So let me know when you're in."

When you're in. So casually, like there'd never be a reason to say no. We both know there *isn't* a reason—that I've worked my entire career for something this big, and it's surreal that it's happening at all, let alone this early—but I hate that the trade-off means he thinks he's got me automatically back, as though I'm exactly the same as when he dumped me on my doorstep.

"Take care of yourself, Kit." And with that, he's hung up, efficient and to the point as always. As *we* always were with each other.

I open the door harder than I intend to, and it makes a noise that causes Gia to look up. I know the walls in these old buildings are probably too thick for her to have heard anything, but she seems to know that I'm a little riled up.

"Renovation update," I say, brushing it all off and getting back to my onions.

Gia nods and we settle back into our quiet work, me with my prep and Gia with her speedy hands making pasta.

A few minutes later, though, Gia starts uncharacteristically talking.

"I was reading the Modernist Cuisine bread book last week," she says out of nowhere.

"Why?" I can't pretend like this is a normal thing for her to just pop out with.

"Emilia finally finished it and she said I should read it, too, that I might find some similarities between bread research and pasta."

"Normal bonding over a five-volume food science book." She gives me a sly smile, and I can't help but internally cheer at almost making her laugh.

The book series she's talking about really is a deep dive into the science of bread-making by one of the most famous voices in food. And it's not light reading you'd just pick up; it's a deeply researched and data-driven tome. She writes it off, but I love knowing that this bastion of tradition and simplicity still wants to keep learning and adapting and fine-tuning. It's what I aspire to be. I can't imagine Gia ever resting on her laurels, and I relate to that so deeply.

It's why John's words have no chance of leaving my head anytime soon.

"I really loved this section about baguettes," Gia continues. "They're only made with four ingredients—flour, water, salt, and yeast—so the writers did this test where they took every written baguette recipe they could find to see if they could get the most common ratios of everything, an average. But there was no average! No clear right way to do things. Temperature vs. containers vs. ingredient ratios vs. hydration . . . The hydration ranged between twenty to one hundred twenty percent. There were so many ways to make a successful baguette."

"And?" I ask, tired of everyone in this town loving a food metaphor rather than getting to the point.

"A baguette is really just anything that looks like a baguette," she says. "There's no right or wrong way to make it."

"So you heard my call then," I say dryly, no longer having faith in the thickness of these particular walls.

"I did," she says without looking up from her pasta.

"You want me to be whatever baguette I choose to be." By this point I'm sautéing the onions and getting them caramelized for later, but I still sneak peeks at Gia.

"Don't be daft," she says.

"I'm the one being daft?"

"It's not about baguettes; who cares about the French anyway?" She tsks, as though bringing up the French was my uncouth idea.

"So what's the point?"

She sets her knife down and wipes her hands on her apron before catching my eyes. "There's so many ways to be great. My way is no better or worse than yours. Take the job in the restaurant that you want. Not what you think you should take."

"Oh, so now you're a wise old lady?" I ask, itching to stay in our kitchen shit-talk pattern and not go out any further.

"Definitely old," she says, going back to her pasta.

"It's complicated," I retort, not wanting to let her dismiss the conversation the way she always does when she's done talking.

"It always is." Her hands move fast across the pasta, the muscle memory making it so she barely has to look at it.

We go back to working, no more words needing to be said. I love this about Gia. She makes her point and moves on. She's not going to try and convince me of anything. I'm not even sure what she wants me to do here. But I respect that she wants to make sure I'm thinking things through on my own.

Once the onions are done, I go to roll out and stamp ravioli for the onion mixture to go inside.

My phone pings with a message, and I pull it out, hoping it's Nico but expecting it to be some more bullshit from John. Instead it's from my dad.

> Just checking in. How's the construction going? Thinking of coming to visit for whenever you open again.

Quite the timing for that check-in. I look up at Gia, still silently making her pasta, and turn my phone over.

I've never been able to keep things from my dad—he's always the person I bounce things off of. But maybe being here under Gia's influence is making me want to not run anything by anyone for once.

Now that I've had some space away from my regular life, the realizations that made me panic when I left no longer seem so daunting.

I'm not going to pretend like I'm not grateful for the way my dad and then John smoothed the past for me so I could focus. I've always been about the work. I don't like any of the bigger-picture stuff. I'm not into marketing or promoting myself or being anything other than the leader of a team. In some ways I've been lucky to have had people to block out the noise for me. When I wanted to be a rower, I had a cheerleader who could also make sure I had up-to-date techniques and equipment and the best training regimen to follow. I didn't need to do any of that research, so I could focus on executing. He transitioned to researching everything culinary and got me from school to internships on the best path.

With John, I got someone who would handle the business so I could make sure all the output was flawless. I showed up for media interviews or picked between new suppliers, and all my mental load could stay on the food.

But I've let them be a crutch.

Crutches can be good while we need them—training wheels or pool floaties or even scaffolding while you're being built. But I need to transition to letting those helpful people be less crutch and more part of the machine—gearshift on a bike, goggles in the pool, or new paint on a building. I need to be ready to make this choice on my own.

I take a breath and finish making the ravioli. I shut everything else out and focus on making the best damn pasta I can make. If I can do anything, I can compartmentalize. I let the question of my future go for the moment and instead put all that energy into my work.

And I can't help but notice later, when Gia puts my pasta in the same drawer as hers for the first time.

Chapter 26

The steps are slick as I walk my usual routine the next morning. Overnight rain and August humidity have created a head-to-toe mistiness that shrouds the town. I imagine it'll all burn off as the sun gets higher, but for the moment, I love the sensation of the moisture holding in the quiet.

With the usual landscape view obscured, I sit on my regular bench and notice again that poem etched into marble next to it, the one that starts with *Ti Amo Maremma.*

I *do* love Maremma. Whether it's draped in the sunset hues mentioned in the poem or misty in the morning, I can't deny this place has worked its magic on me too. It's not like I could ignore it—the signs are everywhere, carved into stone here or as optimistic poems in rocks at the beach. They're everywhere, if you're willing to read them. And I appreciate that I've allowed myself to slow down enough for the first time in my life to actually do that kind of reading.

But ever since I talked to John, my restaurant's resurgence has become a reality. And the creep of missing New York has also started to surface. I miss being in charge of my kitchen. I miss striving for something. I miss the constant fizz of the city. When I arrived here, I was striving to learn again, and I've always been great in the role of hard-charging student. But I know the learning here isn't forever, and it isn't sustainable long-term.

As asked, John emailed me the plans for the new restaurant and also, as asked, didn't request anything else from me. And he got Gavin to send me a comprehensive report on the renovation, including photos, that made it actually seem like maybe I do have a job to go back to in a few weeks.

And both sets of emails got my mind whirring with ideas and menus and the kind of creativity I know I've been missing out on here.

I tossed and turned for a lot of the night. When my alarm went off, I got out of bed quickly, my mind still buzzing and my body ready to start moving.

I can't stay out in this humidity forever, though, so I stand up and make my way carefully down the steps, heading over to Belpagna. As I get closer, I try to shake off whatever stopping to read poetry has done to me, as though I can wring out the sappiness along with my damp clothes.

When I'm inside, I see that the usual regulars are ruminating over their espressos, but Nico isn't here yet—he often slips out to go see Luce and shower at his place in the morning.

I like getting a few minutes alone with Emilia anyway.

She sets my tea in front of me, along with a slice of that apricot ricotta cake I love so much.

"Is it still as vile outside as it was early this morning?" she asks.

"It's barely eight a.m. It's still early morning."

"Not to a baker," she says with a smirk.

She turns around to make herself an espresso, then comes back and leans against the counter to face me. She sees that I've already eaten all my cake and chuckles. "I'm going to have to readjust my quantities when you go back to New York."

My brow furrows. I know I was thinking about going home this morning, but I've never let that inevitable endpoint encroach on my time here.

"What?" Emilia says, immediately picking up on the shift.

"I got a renovation update last night," I venture. Emilia just nods, waiting for me to continue, even while I'm not quite sure what to say. "Everything will be ready again by the end of the month."

"Wasn't that always the goal?" she asks.

"Yeah." I sip on my drink, fidgeting with the tea bag string.

"I'd have thought by now you'd be itching to be back in your own kitchen."

"I am in a lot of ways," I say truthfully. She nods again, the understanding implicit.

She goes to the other side of the counter, grabs my favorite type of bombolone, and puts it on a plate in front of me; I marvel at the small intimacy of having someone know all your little snacks.

"Show me the renovation photos," she says, letting me use that as a distraction. I open up my phone and hand it over. All her comments are the exact ones an anal-retentive restaurant owner would make, so obviously we have the same opinions.

"You'll be ready when it's ready," she says when I finally put my phone away.

I purse my lips, the other specter still looming. "I also got a call from John, my ex, the one who also is the investor in my restaurant." Her eyebrows raise in surprise, but she doesn't interrupt. Instead of explaining, I just click on the email John sent me last night, detailing the space and the offer for the new restaurant. I hand the phone over to Emilia, and she takes her time reading. I watch her eyes to see how they move—where she's surprised, where she's impressed, where she's skeptical.

Finally, after what feels like a torturously long time, she sets the phone down in front of me.

"Well, obviously you're doing this," she says, "so let's not pretend like you're *not* going to."

I chuckle at the brazenness I now rely on. "I wasn't going to."

"Good. I mean, negotiate the hell out of it, obviously. But if this is where they're starting, they clearly want you, and they're willing to build out whatever you want."

"Yeah," I agree.

"What's got you sour?" She slides over a second bombolone, a little more sustenance to keep me going.

"It's just weird to get handed this," I say.

She slaps her hands on the counter. "Who are you?"

"What?" I ask, not following.

"You're Kit fucking Roth. You've worked and built up a reputation that's unmatched. No one is 'handing' you anything. Your stupid ex-boyfriend is smart on one thing, and that's that he invested in you early and has recognized he needs to bring you new opportunities to keep that investment growing. *You* are the asset here. *You* are the talent. I don't want your bullshit false humility here."

The fervor in her voice is surprising for someone who's usually so deadpan. "Why is this your reaction?"

"Don't get complacent here," she says, wagging a finger in my face. "You don't chase accolades, and I love that about you. But this summer is a learning pit stop. Don't question your greatness just because you've taken a minute to reload and a fire messed up your routine."

I put my hand out and cover hers, momentarily a bit overcome by her vociferous defense. "Thank you," I say quietly.

I know she's right, that it's not a question of whether I'll take it. But it's hard to admit when something is scary. This summer was a leap, but it was a temporary one with an endpoint.

Saying yes to a dream restaurant will mean inviting in scrutiny again; it will mean raising my own bar. And while I know I'm ready for it and that I'm the best person for the job, I need to readjust to getting my head back in the game.

Before I can say anything else, the bell chimes on the door, and Nico walks in.

He didn't shave this morning, and the scruff looks delicious. It's impossible not to smile when I see him.

"Hey," I say, and now I get the extra enjoyment of the small blush that creeps up his cheeks from however I'm looking at him.

"Show Nico the email," Emilia says, interrupting my dirty thoughts by handing Nico my phone. Part of me wants to stop her and not let the reality of home problems intrude on this short-term fantasy Nico and I have dug ourselves into. But I do want his opinion.

He scans through the pitch and nods along as he reads. When he finally looks up, I'm like a kid who's been told to wait for a marshmallow, all anticipation.

"This is a great offer," he says. "How do you feel about it?" At whatever look comes over my face, he chuckles and says, "What?"

"Sorry, I'm just used to men mansplaining," I say honestly.

"I'm not familiar with that phrase," he counters with a small grin.

"It's just . . ." I pause, and my smile grows too. I'm enjoying him so much right now. The restaurant can have my attention next month, but for now I want to soak up this sweet man who would rather know how I feel than explain to me what I should think. "I feel good about it," I answer. "But I'll have a lot of follow-up questions. I forwarded it to my lawyer to get her thoughts first."

"That sounds like a great plan," he says, and I wish I wasn't surprised that he doesn't have unsolicited opinions to share. Who knew a man like that even existed?

I must still be looking at him like he's delightful, because he tilts his head, his smile turning curious at my response to him. But he couldn't possibly understand, because how could I explain to him that he makes loving him so *easy*?

Hold on.

Loving him?

Where did that come from.

No.

I shake my head, as though the rain is still caught on me, as though the sappiness has gotten heavy again and I need to wring it out once more. I need to not let sleeping with this man turn me into something I'm not. I'm probably just still not used to the idea that someone could find me attractive, be as interested in work as me, *and* still be a kind, caring person.

I purse my lips, and I can see that he catches my shift in expression. But instead of asking me about it, he reaches into the bag he carried in.

"At any rate," he says, pulling out what looks like a crocheted *something*, "Emilia, I have something for you."

Emilia squeals—a sound I would never have predicted hearing out of her—and holds her hands out with a grabby motion until he gives it to her.

"It's got stretch, so you don't have to tie it, the way you do with your bandanas," he says, and I watch as Emilia takes off the one she has on (turtles, inexplicably, on it today) and slips on the herringbone-patterned one Nico made, varying shades of blue melding together.

"You're the best," she says, pulling herself far enough over the counter to give him a kiss on both cheeks. "I love it."

"I have something for you too," he says to me, and I'm suddenly dreading having something he's *made* for me. I don't know why that's the sentiment that smacks into me, but it's like a raw egg smashed on my head, dripping into every strand of hair.

My instincts are wrong, though, because he pulls out a small spray bottle. "What the heck?" I ask, taking the neon-green container out of his hands.

"For the mosquitos on your patio," he explains. At my quizzical look he continues. "You bought that insecticide, and it didn't seem like you'd actually followed up to ask about real bug spray." He shrugs, like it's nothing.

He makes it so effortless, my brain thinks, and I shake the idea off and shut my mind down again.

"Thanks," I say, gently taking the bottle from him.

Nico and Emilia launch into a conversation about olive oil cake (can those two ever find any other topics?), but my mind wanders.

With both their eyes off me, I study them, the foreign explorer sizing up the locals.

Emilia must've had me pegged more than I thought, because she breezily knew I'd be the one who couldn't handle this thing with Nico. He's all at ease and chatting and nonchalant, and I'm fully tied up over a lack of bad opinions and a bottle of bug spray. I'm the one obsessing; I'm the one who suddenly enjoys gentle care. That's never been me, and I don't think I like this sensation in my gut. I'm already scared enough about this huge new restaurant, and now I'm focused on being scared of batting gooey thoughts out of my mind.

Meanwhile, he's doing the right thing and living in the moment without a care in the world.

I stand up, needing to get my legs moving again.

"Where're you off to?" Emilia asks, breaking her conversation with Nico mid-sentence.

Great. I must've looked like I had some sudden realization instead of just being an emotionally stunted person.

"Oh, nothing." I fidget. "I just thought I'd get home and look some of that stuff over again before I chat with my lawyer later."

"You want apricot ricotta cake to go?" Emilia asks, already grabbing a box.

"Obviously."

She looks in the case. "Ah, we're out—let me grab the fresh one that's cooling in the back."

As she walks away, I sneak a look over at Nico. By his expression, I can tell he's caught on that I'm freaking out a little, but thankfully he seems mostly amused.

"You know, Kit," he says quietly, and just from his tone I already know he's handling me with the kid gloves I deserve right now. "Even when you go back to New York, and we're just friends, I'll always help you out if you need it."

I gape at him. He's so damn good at saying the right thing. It would be annoying if it wasn't so attractive. But my brain catches on the word "need," a twitchy desire to push back. "I wouldn't call bug spray a 'need.'"

I know I'm being a brat and pushing on a bruise for no reason. But I need to say it.

"Of course not," he says, that light smile threatening to break into something bigger.

"I mean, I *will* use it. You've been on my patio."

"I have."

"So thank you. This isn't me not saying thank you. I'm just saying, I don't need stuff. I'm good. We're good. But thank you, that was really thoughtful."

He snorts a little at my incompetence, and I sigh.

I want to lean into him. I want my forehead on his shoulder, breathing in the depth of his scent, calming my nervous system the way it always does.

But I can't do that in Belpagna—I can't upend his easy life. Especially when I'm already, apparently, incapable of not having flares go off in every direction when I think about things too hard.

"I'll see you later," I say, backing up a bit so I don't catch myself smelling him like an imbecile. "Gia actually sold my pasta last night, so my mood will be entirely dependent on whether it was a onetime fluke or if she's actually accepted that I'm a skilled cook."

"Whoa, she accepted money for your pasta?" he asks, genuine joy lining his expression. *Damn it*, here comes that gooey feeling again.

"It's not a big deal," I say, so casual, not a care in the world. He rolls his eyes at me.

"It's not, in the sense that of course your pasta has been great for a long time. But for Gia, that's like the most-earned compliment there is."

I blush. I feel transparent. He's rent-free in my head again.

"I'll come by yours when I'm done at Gia's," I say, this conversation truly too much for my pea-size emotional abilities.

"Okay." That small smile thankfully hasn't dimmed.

And with that, I back out the door before I can think about the kind of man who crochets his friend a bandana so she won't have to tie one herself.

Chapter 27

By the end of August, the entire town has reached a fever pitch about the Palio. The signage has gotten more extreme, the shouting in the street is even louder, and the late-night strategy sessions extend to almost everyone nearby. Emilia, Nico, and Emilia's husband Antonio have made me join in on daily training practices where we all roll barrels for a while until I start complaining.

But it's hard for me to become singularly Palio-focused like everyone else, because I'm in my own fever pitch. I'm channeling my anxious energy about summer ending, the restaurant, and what happens with Nico into late-night activities that distract and comfort.

Being with Nico is like an addiction. And it's not just the sex, although I wouldn't complain about that. But it's all the physicality that exists between us. It's the way he makes me feel adorable when he pats me gently on the head. It's the way he enfolds me in his arms when he reaches fully around me for a kiss and always manages to graze my bottom lip with his hand. The way he mutters Italian curse words under his breath when he tastes food that I've made.

But despite my distractions, the weekend of the Palio—my last weekend here—sneaks up on me, and suddenly I find myself being forced to leave work early on a Friday in order to make the (apparently necessary) presentation of the teams.

I hadn't realized quite how involved I would be, once I was berated into being on Cassero's team. I even had to get a "medical certificate of fitness to practice noncompetitive sports." This was a real thing and not the joke I assumed it was when our neighborhood leader—Flavia, the woman whose missing husband's scooter I'm using—told me I needed to get one and then promptly escorted me to a doctor who would do it. And I had to get Anita's cousin to write me a letter confirming I was paying rent on the apartment, therefore making me a true Cassero resident.

The Friday event is partially a beautiful presentation of the artisans who paint each barrel and partially a chance for each district to try and disqualify each other's strongest barrel rollers.

I spend most of the night trying not to stare at Nico's forearms and running the now-frequent images I have of them rolling a 100-kg barrel (which, when I was initially told this, I googled and learned is a 220-pound barrel. The less exciting part I was instantly made aware of is that I *also* have to roll a 220-pound barrel, since a few years ago the women demanded equality. I was a rower, so I get wanting to go toe to toe, but on the other hand . . . *yeesh*).

Emilia is more pumped up and enthusiastic than I've ever seen her about anything. She's usually so dry that I never would've assumed she had this in her, but for the Palio she's all in, blue/maroon headscarf and all. When Cassero's women's team is announced, she grabs me so we can come to the front together and then insists that I cheer with her at the decibel levels she's deemed necessary.

Our women's team is a little ragtag. You get six people to a team, with two alternates in case someone gets injured. Since you compete in pairs and then change as you go along, the only person who really matters for me is Emilia, since she's going to be my teammate.

Besides us, it's a disparate crew, led by our captain, Martina. Our team pretty much only has height in common and is otherwise spanning a range of generations (we're spread out from age eighteen to fifty-four). I'm a little confused when we're introduced and it seems that three of the six rioni (Cassero, Borgo, and Imposto) all have female captains named Martina, but I guess this quirk has become a rivalry in itself.

And rounding it all out, our Cassero team is fully hyped up by Flavia, who shouts at us in Italian in a manner that I'm guessing is supposed to be encouraging.

The men's team is a little more fully formed. Aside from Nico, I know Antonio, Beppe (back from Rome again), and one of the guys who works at the butcher. Emilia explains the rest to me—only one actually lives in Cassero, and I've seen him around, but the rest are former residents or sons of residents, all people who've come in (like Beppe) to be ringers.

Their age range is narrower than the women's team (the men I don't know all seem to be in their late twenties and thirties). But then again, this town doesn't pretend like the men's and women's events are on equal footing.

I see that in full force the next day, when I learn that the women's event is preceded by a kids' Palio—so women and kids are on one day, and men are on the next. But rather than being able to stay quiet before my own race, I'm dragged out of the restaurant in the early afternoon by Gia, who insists the kids need our support.

"I have to finish helping you prep for tonight," I argue.

"Nonsense, this weekend isn't normal in the restaurant. I don't need your help. Besides, you have to save your energy for your race this afternoon."

"All the more reason I shouldn't be out here watching . . . are those tires?"

We've gotten to one of the town's main squares, and I can see that, while a lot of people are cheering as though this is a major event, I'm really just looking at a bunch of kids wearing the colors of their different rioni, pushing a tire to a finish line. We go stand with the maroon and navy blue Cassero crowd and join in the chanting for our similarly clad kid participants.

They're rolling tires like their lives depend on it, and every adult is jumping up and down, and then within five minutes it's all over. Imposto won, so all the Cassero people are grumbling about how it's all rigged—as though something hinges on a bunch of kids rolling some rubber.

I stand and listen as Martina (the Cassero Martina, and not the now-smug Imposto Martina) starts waxing on about the time Cassero won the kids', women's, and men's Palio in 2018. I wander away and back to the restaurant. Gia might think we're ready for tonight's celebrations, but I'd rather take some time to myself before I have to roll a giant barrel down the street.

I get to the restaurant and wash my hands, working on mentally accepting that I am, apparently, going to be making a fool of myself in about half an hour.

As I reach for a towel, I see Nico walk in.

"I just wanted to say good luck," he says, coming over and kissing my forehead.

Nico's never touched me in the restaurant before, and the way I look around for Gia is automatic.

But I can see from the furrow of his brow that my reaction has confused him.

"Sorry, I . . ." I pause, not knowing quite what to say. "I didn't want Gia to walk in and see this and you'd have to explain it and . . ."

He grabs the towel I'd been looking for on the counter and wraps my hands in it, drying them for me. "I don't care," he says quietly. "I'm sure Gia knows anyway."

I understand that logically he's probably right, but the sentiment still makes me squirm. "I just hate the idea of making things harder for you when I leave."

"Don't worry about me," he says, as if dismissing him from my mind isn't an impossibility.

And then, as though he wants to change the subject, he reaches into his pocket and pulls out something he's clearly crocheted, a small piece of dark blue and maroon against his hands. "I made you something."

I can feel my pulse getting more rapid as I delicately take it from his hands. "It's a bandana in Cassero's colors. I already had the pattern for the one I made for Emilia, and I thought you guys could use them."

I'm left momentarily speechless. It's not a big gesture, but it's surfaced so many emotions in one go: affection for the thoughtfulness; edginess over how much it makes my heart swoop; fear at knowing I'll have a physical object to torture me when I'm gone.

But before I can spiral, he pulls me to him, kissing my head the way only he has ever been able to, a bubble of sturdiness. His proximity makes me momentarily forget my agita, and I nuzzle my nose into his throat. He smells so damn good, always. His arms wrap around me, and we stand there like that for a few moments, the pressure of his embrace calming everything roiling inside me.

Until I realize something. "You're doing the cow thing to me again, aren't you?"

I can feel the vibration of his laugh in his neck, joyful, happy, mischievous. It's impossible not to want to push him against the wall in retaliation, but maybe also to kiss his gorgeous face off.

"I thought maybe you'd be nervous before the race!" he exclaims as I try and squirm my way out of his grip.

"I'm not nervous!" I say, even as I succumb into letting him hold me, the temptation too great, even when I want to be defiant.

"You've never rolled a barrel around a town before."

"Who has?"

"Me and everyone else on your team."

"I meant normal people," I retort, and I love getting the sensation of another chuckle while I'm burrowed into him.

"You're part of Cassero now," he says in my ear.

I wish the sentiment didn't make my stomach inexplicably drop ever so slightly.

I pull back to give him a quick kiss on the lips, shaking off whatever his words and nearness are doing to me.

"I appreciate the pep talk." I grab the towel out of his hand and playfully swat him with it. "But I'm late and need to go meet up with my team right about now."

"You'll do great!" he says sincerely.

I roll my eyes at him with a smile and walk out the door.

Chapter 28

The town is so small that I'm with my team by our designated meet-up spot next to Belpagna within five minutes. Emilia waves me over, and I notice she's wearing her own newly crocheted Cassero bandana from Nico.

Martina leads us in a round of warm-ups, and it feels good to slip back into my competitive athlete skin. It's been so long since I've been on a team. And even though this random hodgepodge may not count in the way other teams I've been a part of did, being surrounded by so many expectant people still gives me the dose of adrenaline I've always thrived on.

I've become familiar with the rules, since Emilia has explained them to me fifteen times already. The race is a six-hundred-meter sort-of circle around the center of town, starting and ending in Piazza Garibaldi with its ornamental fountain. The six teams are broken into three pairs races (since the streets are too small to accommodate more than two barrels at a time). Then the two semifinals have the three winning teams plus the one losing team who had the best time in their first race. And then there's a final race between the last two teams standing.

In our practice runs, I've already gotten used to the slopes, zags, and bottlenecks of trying to push a barrel through an old stone city. I know it'll be different under pressure, but I'm at least familiar with the feel of it. While the men do the circuit twice, the women only do it once—so two of our teammates will take the lead, then they'll switch off about two hundred meters in, and then Emilia and I will bring up the end. Everyone's said that each leg is usually around a minute and a half, so we just have to push really hard for ninety seconds and hope it all goes to plan.

And then do it two more times if we're lucky.

Once we're done warming up, we all walk to Piazza Garibaldi, and it starts dawning on me that I might've underestimated this race. The whole town (and all of its environs) is out, multiplied tenfold from the crowd at the kids' Palio this morning. The edges of the streets that contain the race have barriers up, so people can stand behind them and cheer. Everyone is decked out in the colors of the different rioni, waving flags of every possible size. Our team is wearing matching shirts, and all the Cassero people scream extra loud as we walk by. A giant screen has been erected on the side of the piazza—I guess to show the action as it literally barrels along out of sight.

When we get to our starting line, everyone quiets down as the main referee explains the rules once more in Italian. He points out the twenty-five other referees (and explains what I think are all the various ways to get time penalties), and then it's the moment for everyone to take their places. For this first round, Cassero is racing the Borgo team. Since we'll take over the last leg, Emilia and I will start by running behind the first handoff team, all following behind the barrel.

"You ready to bring honor to Cassero?" she asks with a grin.

"If I'd known you'd have a complete personality transplant around this race, I would've opted out," I tease.

"Come on," she says with a nudge. "This is the right kind of ridiculous." I can't help but grin back at her.

It's true. I never could've imagined I'd find myself racing a painted barrel while a couple thousand people cheered me on for a town I'd never known before a few months ago. But it's everything I love about competition—camaraderie, fun, pushing yourself, adrenaline, reaching a goal. It's hard not to think that my love of competing has been missing lately: that steady drumbeat of knowing you have a job to do and pushing yourself harder to do it.

We get into our places, and I burst forward when I hear the gun shoot off.

Our team rolls ahead of us, and we follow, cheering, encouraging, and (me) trying not to laugh at the absurdity. Every inch of the road is covered with people shouting and clapping. Our barrel runners get to the first curve slightly ahead of the Borgo team. But they get a little stuck on the turn, and Borgo slips in front of us.

"Andiamo!" Martina shouts at them as they finally manage to round the turn. Then the two who have been rolling swap out, and Martina and her partner Gessica are off. They're making good time and rolling along quickly, but it's not quite enough to get ahead. With the barrels, there's a clear tactic to roll as close to the middle as possible so that the other team would have to move over to go around you and waste time (but without going into their lane and getting a time violation for impeding). While I hate to admit it, the Borgo women are mastering that approach beautifully.

But I'm already visualizing the sloping curve of the clock tower, where I know we get to take over. I'm hoping we can use the momentum from the awkwardness that a turn has to go past them.

Martina and Gessica even it out at the curve just as we'd hoped, and they jump out of the way. Emilia and I are up.

Gloves on, heart pounding, sweat already glistening, we're ready.

It's an awkward thing, rolling a barrel while people shout all around you. It's too low to push straight ahead, so you're always sort of squatting and running. You're using arm strength to push it hard, but you don't want to push it so hard that it gets away from you. And you have to communicate with your partner well enough that you're pushing together and not running into each other. I can't help but think it would've been *so* much easier to not have gotten this involved and to be just another Cassero person shouting on the sidelines.

But I'm in it now. Our practices the last few weeks have served us well, and it's clear that having been a rower does have some advantages—being tall and lanky would help regardless, but the mental game of repetitive motion and pushing through the sameness is something I'm used to. Not to mention that I've always been able to block out noise and get into a rhythm. So it's not as smooth as I'd like, since nothing ever is the first time you really do it, but we're pulling ahead the more I get myself into that zone I'm so used to.

We're close enough now that I can hear the shouts of everyone watching on the screen, and as we roll into Piazza Garibaldi, I can see that we only need to make the slight half turn around the fountain to get to the other side where the finish line is. We stumble on the curve a bit, but we have enough of a lead that we make it up and roll across a full four seconds ahead of the Borgo team.

We collapse on the grass as everyone jumps and shouts around us.

"We did it!" Emilia says, flopping onto me with a hug.

"Well, the first round anyway," I say, that rowing part of my brain never able to celebrate a heat when the finals are still looming ahead.

The next hour goes by in a blur. We watch as Fonti takes out Imposto (making our Martina particularly happy to be the last standing Martina). Mulinello gets beaten by Monumento, but since they have the fastest time of the losing teams, they get to make it to the semifinals.

There's only half an hour between the races, and after a breather (and a snack that Gia shoved in my hands before wordlessly walking away), it's time to go again. Fonti had the fastest time, so they're up against Mulinello for the semifinals, and they beat them handily. We get set up for our race against Monumento, and this time it's smoother for our whole team. The curves have been resolved and we're in the zone more, handing off smoothly and staying in an easy rhythm. We beat them handily by fifteen seconds.

The sky has begun to darken by the time it's the moment for the finals. It gives the scene an air of seriousness and mystery while also, wonderfully, cooling the temperature a bit. The cheering has only gotten louder, with more horns and music in the mix. The crowd swells, as though even the people who skipped the first few rounds are ready to watch this one. I'm grateful for the ramped-up energy. I've always fed on that kind of atmosphere. And the buzz and the enthusiasm have put me in the zone to really want to win this now.

As I get into position, I spot Nico for the first time since I saw him at Pasta Fresca before the first race. He's standing by the finish line, not drawing attention to himself, but when he sees me notice him, he gives me a wink.

I try not to react, but the side of my mouth involuntarily hooks into a small smile—our little secret a tether in this increasingly strange day.

But I'm not getting distracted. I've never let a man distract me in any work *or* sporting endeavor, and that sure as hell isn't starting today, when I've got the pride of my entire district on the line right now. (Do I get too into competition? Who's to say.)

I stand back as our leadoff rollers line up against Fonti's. In rowing, there's always a still before the race starts, but this drunken bacchanalia of nonsense doesn't really allow for any of that pomp. Everyone is cheering so much that it almost drowns out the gun when it goes off.

Our women burst forward, and it's neck and neck as they easily round the first curve, passing off to Martina and Gessica. But the barrel goes a bit wonky, and in their attempts to get it back, the Fonti team passes them.

My heart is pounding as we run behind them, waiting for the moment when Emilia and I will take over. The boisterous crowd is so loud at this point that the noise is ringing in my ears, and it seems like night is falling as fast as we're moving.

We go around the last curve at the clock tower, and Martina and Gessica hop out of the way. It's just me and Emilia and at least a two-second deficit.

But the atmosphere has charged me. And nothing gets me going more than starting as an underdog.

"Three, two one, *push*!" I shout in time as we make our first contact with the barrel. If we're pushing in sync, we move more in sync; timing our pushes makes me time my breathing, my steps, my focus. So I keep shouting counts for Emilia and me to stay fully connected. We're on the heels of the final Fonti rollers, and I push myself just a little more, making myself go past the point of discomfort.

We're gaining on them, and somehow, with that extra grit getting us back on track, as we approach Piazza Garibaldi, we've nudged in enough to be neck and neck.

And I can see the finish line. We're so close and I'm so tired and my legs are burning from doing this three times in one afternoon and my back is sore from the weird bending required to reach the barrel. But the win is so close I can taste it; I see the angle where we can do this. Our advantage from being on the right side is going to give us the edge here if we time that half circle around the fountain right. And because it's the barrel that has to cross first, not the runners, we just have to push it at the perfect second to get the momentum.

We round the fountain enough where we're straight again. *"Push!"* I shout one more time, and Emilia and I give the barrel a last, huge heave. That final burst of strength propels it, and our barrel rolls over the line only a second before the Fonti one does.

A sea of maroon and navy blue erupts. The referee is pointing at our barrel, even though I can't hear anything above the madness of the mayhem. Emilia and I are lifted into the air along with our teammates, and everyone is crowding around us and singing in Italian, and someone is throwing a ton of cheap glitter into the crowd and onto me and Emilia. I'm sweaty and exhausted, but it feels so good, like a candle that burned brightly and melted down, and now all that's left is stardust.

I grab Emilia's hand in the air. "You didn't tell me this would be *so fucking hard*!" I shout at her, grinning but still out of breath.

"I heard the hard is what makes it great!" she shouts back, beaming at me.

I snort a laugh. "Anita made you watch *A League of Their Own*, didn't she?"

"Hell yeah!" Emilia laughs, her cackle punching through the air as this madcap night carries us off to celebrate.

Chapter 29

I lost Nico in the sea of celebrations Saturday night. After the presentation of the ridiculous pink trophy, a whole area of the town had been set up with a live band and food stalls and people milling around, drinking—all the inhabitants of Cassero still covered in cheap tacky glitter even hours after it was thrown haphazardly on everyone.

Nico found me there and congratulated me, but with so many people around, we never could find a moment to actually talk. And when he came to tell me goodbye, since he was going to bed early to rest before *his* race, I didn't have a chance to ask if he wanted me to come with him.

I figured I'd take him at his word and that he'd need the rest. After all, I don't think I caught my breath for a full hour after our race finished, and now with Sunday morning staring me in the face (or . . . after looking at a clock, apparently midday), my limbs feel like stiff taffy.

But I don't like how weird it feels to wake up alone.

He doesn't need me to pump him up before a race. And I don't *need* him.

But I don't like the weirdness of the feeling.

I groan as I roll over to get my phone. Texts from Anita parade across my screen.

Anita: We won! You won! You did it!

Anita: My cousins sent me pictures—why was there so much glitter on everything!?

Anita: How many drinks were purchased for you? Are you never going to be allowed to leave?

Anita: I hate not being there for this!

I sit up and stretch, my muscles on fire. I hadn't realized quite how out of shape I was until I attempted to run three races with a barrel in short succession.

Kit: I was hoping you'd explain the meaning of the glitter.

My phone immediately rings, and I pick it up. "Uh hi," I say. "Glitter is all I need to mention to get you to call me?"

"Hush," she says. "It's early here, but I wanted to hear all about it. I don't need your sarcasm."

"But my legs hurt," I whine.

"Your legs don't have any bearing on your mouth."

"So snippy."

She ignores my comments. "I can't believe Cassero won. It's been so long. Do you think the men can win too?"

"Doesn't it count for something that the women won?"

"Not really."

I shake my head and get up, stumbling over to the kettle to make myself a necessary cup of tea. "Well, I'm not a barrel-rolling expert—"

"Except clearly you are after yesterday—"

"—so I have no idea what our men's team is capable of vis-à-vis the other teams. I'm not going to place any bets. And I'm also going to take one fucking second to relish the fact that I practically tore my arm off to secure the victory for your damn neighborhood, and I will not have that be ignored."

"Your neighborhood now," she teases, and I hate that it makes me think of Nico's words yesterday.

"For like half a week," I retort, and that shuts her up.

After a pause she asks, "Have you finalized everything with the investors at the new restaurant?" It's the subject we've mostly avoided, but that little reminder of time apparently puts it back front and center.

"My lawyer's been going back and forth with them."

"John's lawyer," she quips.

"She's my lawyer, Anita," I huff. Ever since I told her about the proposal (and she made me send it to her), she's been trying to insist that I not stay so passive in this process. But I'm not sure I'm ready to face the reality of everything that will come when I officially say yes. I've already had to say yes to the restaurant reopening date, and it's truly official now that the media has been notified. I'll only have ten days back in New York to get my bearings again with the revamped space and make sure the staff is all up to speed again. I know they want to make an announcement about the new restaurant on the same day we're back up, but I've been hesitant to finalize it.

"So why don't you just call them?" she asks.

"Call who?"

"The investors. Shoot them an email, say you want to go over the final details with them and talk through it. You don't need John on a call; you don't need anyone else. This is your name on the restaurant from the start. You're the name that's bringing people in the door. It's not like the last time, where you were brought in and then proved yourself. You're the draw *and* an owner of this new one. They're all working *for you*. Get your ducks in a row and finalize the plan."

"Damn," I chuckle, thinking about having gotten a similar speech from Emilia mere days ago. Maybe growing up together made them more alike than I've even realized. "Isn't it like six in the morning for you? Where are you getting all that fire from?"

"From looking at videos of you hauling your ass down a stretch of Manciano and seeing Cassero's good name honored!"

I sit back down and blow on my tea. I wish Belpagna wasn't closed right now due to Palio prep. Every damn thing in this town is prepping for the main event this afternoon, so I'm stuck with my tea and my stale taralli.

"I know you're right," I say quietly.

"So what's stopping you?"

I haven't told her about Nico, and in this moment he's all I can think about.

In the beginning, my rationale was that it wasn't my secret to tell, when Anita's so connected to everyone Nico knows. But I know it's an excuse, a glaring red arrow, reminding me that Italy hasn't magically cured me of my emotional compartmentalizing. I know I *should* tell her.

But not today. I need to get my head on straight—Nico doesn't have any actual bearing on *this* conversation anyway. Soon this thing between us is going to be over. I'll be back in New York, grinding at my restaurant and talking to media about opening a new one. He'll be here, quietly tweaking his machines and making olive oil. Why should it matter?

I've loved living in this moment, and I'm going to soak up the next few days, but Anita's right. I need to let myself be stronger from this break. I need to take what I've learned, be grateful for it, then get back to what I love. I need to let that fuel me to fully steer my own ship for once.

"Nothing's stopping me," I finally say. "I'll shoot them an email right now."

"Perfect," she says. "Then I'll let you get to it. I can't wait to watch everyone in New York go apeshit when they announce this new restaurant. You deserve all the good things, cara mia."

She hangs up, and I stare at my phone. I shoot a note off to Brian, the lead guy for the property, asking if he has a few minutes to chat about details tomorrow, and I suggest a time. He sends an email back almost immediately with a calendar invite, so I guess this is really happening.

I get myself together and head over to Pasta Fresca. It's hard to imagine a bigger night than last night, but we're prepping enough food for almost double the number of people. More music, more dancing, and apparently more snacks.

At quarter to five we walk over to the edge of town, where a procession is going to begin. There's a lot happening before the race can start. The procession is along the route of the race, and people from each neighborhood come out in outfits with flags and horns and a lot of noisemakers. I'm not sure how people get designated to be in the procession versus a necessary fan on the side cheering, but all I know is that as a member of the Cassero women's team, I'm given no choice but to participate.

I'm in the back of our large crowd but can see Nico up front, made into everyone's favorite flag-bearer because no one could think of anyone better to stand at the front for Cassero. He gets the loudest cheers, old ladies give him kisses on the cheek, and the procession keeps getting slowed down because so many people want to stop him to say hello.

The whole thing takes around twenty minutes to do this tiny loop since everyone's constantly chatting, but it's amazing to be a part of something so competitive and yet so unifying.

After the procession, the teams break off to warm up, and everyone else goes to see a live performance of some local band everyone seems to go crazy for, followed by a very dramatic draw for the teams, and *finally*, the first rounds are set to begin.

When it's Cassero's turn, we make our way back to Piazza Garibaldi, where I spot Nico finishing his warm-up with his team. I'm powerless to not just stop and stare. His floppy hair is being held back by one of those stupid sweatbands that I think usually make people look like douchebags, but in this case it somehow works on him. He's so focused that he's got one side of his bottom lip between his teeth. It's an expression I've seen on him late at night, but from a very different angle. Just the thought makes me involuntarily blush. Usually when we're in public together, he's not like . . . *stretching* and curling the edges of his T-shirt up so I can see every cord of his arm muscles.

I think that's torture enough, but then he catches me staring and breaks out into a grin. And somehow *that* is even sexier than any of the one-step-from-my-personal-porn warm-ups I've been panting over. He's this singular ray of sunshine in a sea of combatants ready for battle. Everyone else is shouting and trying to pump up their teams and getting riled up (most frequently with bottles of beer that someone is selling out of a cooler). But he's simply unfazed, looking over at me like he's spotted me across a café and we're about to sit down for some bomboloni rather than in the middle of a giant crowd of barrel-rolling spectators.

And it's so strange that *that*—that one look—hits me so hard.

Because it's so abundantly clear how much I love him, even if I've tried not to.

And simultaneously I know, because of that, it's even more important that I let him go.

Look at him, so in his element. Surrounded by this town that adores him. This town that leaves him be enough to innovate while staying far enough in his business to make him never feel alone. This town that his grandfather introduced him to but then let him make his own. This town, where his heart got broken but whose residents were always there waiting to put it back together. It's his peace. It's his place.

A better person would think she should've stayed away completely, but I'm not a better person. I'm a chef through and through, and we thrive on ego and overconfidence. I've always gone after what I wanted. So I didn't stay away, and I didn't stop him when he finally kissed me.

But maybe the one thing this town *has* changed for me is that even if my feelings have snuck up on me, I know I'm not going to push any further. This isn't a barrel race where I can dig in harder. I've never been a person who feels peace the way Nico does, but I'm at peace with this. If I tell him I love him, he wouldn't be able to do anything with that. I'm not staying here—I can't stay here. And he belongs here.

That feeling of *needing* him is roiling in me again, strange and unusual.

But I take a deep breath and push it aside. All my years competing have made me uniquely suited to carrying burdens for long stretches of time. So this will just be my burden to bear. I'll love him and I'll pretend to be his friend as long as he needs me to, until maybe one day it can be true again. I've never needed anyone before, and I'll get back to that soon enough. I can do that.

So I keep the tears from forming, grin back at him, and mouth *Good luck.*

And when the gun sounds for the first leg of the first race, he's off, ready to do battle for this town he loves.

I hadn't realized how stressful it is watching people you care about competing in a race you have no control over. I can't believe yesterday I'd even deigned to think it was easier being another Cassero person shouting on the sidelines. Because that's me today, and it's fucking torture.

Emilia and I stand there, staring at the giant screen in the plaza, obviously unable to help Nico and Antonio when it's their turn to roll the barrel. We know how hard it is, how much they want it, and yet all we can do is cheer them on.

Maybe this is why my dad always got so overly involved; I can see the temptation. You want to do whatever you can to clear the path, even when the path can only be taken alone.

I'm so nervous I'm about to bite my nails, but I look down and realize how long they are. Not long by any normal standards (how could anyone use a knife with long nails?), but for chef standards—for *me* standards—they're as grown out as they've ever been. Huh. I guess I hadn't noticed that I'd stopped biting them over the last few weeks.

I put my hands in my pockets, not wanting to mess up whatever streak I've unknowingly been on.

But it's hard to keep them there as soon as the first race starts, because it's tough to watch. They actually lose by a hair, but luckily, as the losing team with the best time, they're able to compete in the semifinals. Then, with that underdog mentality, they crush the second round to make it into the finals. And then the finals . . . well, the finals probably take a year off my life.

Imposto is the favorite going in, having had the best times in both their heats. And it's neck and neck the entire way. The men's teams do two laps, so it's even more to wait for. Watching on the big screen is jarring because we're craning our necks to watch a race on what amounts to a jumpy and sometimes out-of-focus camera feed. Antonio and Nico are the second pair to go, and they start out well—they build up quite a lead right out of the gate. Until one of the Imposto guys "accidentally" trips Nico.

I've gotta say, it's not great to realize you love a guy and then watch him get knocked down so hard his knees and elbows are raw and bleeding. A four-second penalty is called on Imposto, and then we all hold our breaths as the last lap gets underway, Cassero slightly behind but knowing they have the four seconds of cushion.

The last two guys really run their hearts out. They catch back up to Imposto and cross the finish line with them, all of us bursting into cheers immediately since we know we don't even have to wait to see who crossed first because of the penalty.

Nico comes in right behind them, and I can't help it: I run to him, desperate to get my hands on him and make sure he's okay. If I had any hesitation, though, Nico instantly quells it by lifting me up and drowning me in a kiss, like he's been through a battle and I'm his reward.

I hold him tightly, not just because in person I can finally see that he's all right, but also because I hate the thought that this might be one of the last times I get to be this close to him. The word "friends" flicks through my mind like a blinking light, a mockery of the entire idea that I could ever be near him and not want to do exactly this.

If anyone notices, they don't say anything, because within a moment, all the guys on the team have been swept up in the air (although with more than one person needed to carry each of them), and the cheers from Cassero overtake everything.

The trophy ceremony is as over the top as you can imagine, with giant sparklers heating up the already-dry heat of the night as more glitter gets tossed around and horns blare out from every direction. The men lift the barrel over their heads, and our women's team is brought up on the stage, an extra celebration for the Cassero victory.

When the ceremony is over, that's when the real party begins. I have no idea how I get so drunk, but it seems to be the natural progression of things. I drink to celebrate, and to live in the moment and take part in all the vivacity surrounding me. I dance with Emilia and Gia and Marna, who's finally moved back home and is excited and ready to return to Gia after her maternity leave. I let Antonio spin me around, and Martina gives me more hugs than I knew she was capable of. I take every beer anyone hands me and do shots with my teammates, to the cheers of everyone in Cassero. It's too much and not enough all at once. It's abandon that I need.

And when it's almost time for the sun to come up, I don't care who's watching as I drag Nico back to my apartment and make the night stay a little longer.

Chapter 30

If I thought my body hurt yesterday, today is even more of a doozy. I know I had a lot of excuses last night, but I've long past aged out of being able to drink with abandon. Combine that with going to sleep well after morning had already begun, and I am *feeling it.*

Thank god it's Monday, the Palio nonsense is over, and I have the day entirely off.

I look over at my phone and see that it's past 2:00 p.m., along with a text from Nico saying he went home to check on Luce and that I should come by this evening after my call.

Oh, right. The call with the investors.

Thank god that's not until 8:00 p.m. The time difference is really saving me today. Hopefully I can get my act together within the next six hours.

I roll over and let myself lie in the misery of my hangover. It's a gray day outside, with a bit of lightning in the distance, so why should I move at all?

But the longer I lie there, the more everything from yesterday flashes through my mind. Nico's grin. The drop in my stomach when he fell. That damn kiss in front of everyone. The heat of his body on mine late at night (or early morning). The way his hands were gripping me like he never wanted to let go.

I have to get moving.

I take the hottest shower I can handle and let the water run over me for so long it eventually starts to go cold. I make myself do my usual walk (just a bit later than I normally would do it) but skip the vista with its poetry and opportunities to dwell. I grab a cold sandwich and some snacks from the alimentari, since I know Emilia has fully shut Belpagna today in anticipation of *her* hangover. I head home and binge a show I love, happy to veg out for a few hours.

By the time 8:00 p.m. rolls around, I'm almost back to normal, and I can handle being professional for a little bit.

"Hey, Kit, it's great to get you on the phone!" I hear as soon as I dial the number.

This guy Brian is *ready*. He's been ready since the minute we connected. Anita's right that there's really not that much to discuss, since the original offer was meant to go overboard and entice me. We've already done the expected negotiations over ownership percentages and payout structures, so all that's left to debate in the contract now is small-fry items like levels of right of refusal on design things or who the point person on PR will be.

"Thanks," I reply, my professional muscles clearly atrophied from spending too much time with Gia's grunting.

"We looked over everything your lawyers sent, and we're on board with it. We've capped design overages at twenty percent, but obviously we're happy to put language in there about how if the construction ends up taking longer, we can have cost estimates rise with inflation. Does that work for you?"

"Yeah," I reply, surprised that he's so ready to capitulate on everything. It's wild how much money some of these investors are willing to blow to get the prize they want. And I guess I have to get used to being the prize in this scenario.

"John and his team want to get the press release out the night of the reopening," he continues. "We've started working on the wording for a joint announcement. So if you're comfortable signing the version of the contract your lawyer just sent, we are too. And then we can hash out the statement once you're back in New York, since we'll have a few days."

"Oh," I say, shocked that this was that easy. "Well, that sounds like we're ready to announce, then."

"That's what I was hoping you'd say," he continues, earnest excitement lining his voice. "I thought it was a good idea to get on the phone, though, because I want to pick your brain about how much detail you want to share publicly now, or if you'd rather keep things under wraps a little more."

I pause and sit down on my couch. This isn't a position I'm used to being in. My job has always been to stay in the kitchen and execute. The power dynamic has always been lopsided. I'm there to cook and be a show pony when they want to trot me out to the media, but I've never even considered offering my opinions or thoughts on aesthetics or anything related to the business. John always made it feel like he was clearing my way by handling that and not bothering me with it.

This continuing realization makes me sheepish every time I'm reminded of it.

But the more I'm reminded and the longer I've been in Manciano—the freedom that being here has given me—the more I'm ready for this conversation. I'm ready to take more ownership, not just berate myself for not having done it in the past.

The minute Brian and I start talking about early concepts and directions, it's so clear that I can do this. That I'm *ready* to do this in a way I probably wasn't before. Maybe I needed my dad to give me direction when I was young, and then John to oversee my first restaurant. Maybe those were the periods where I was supposed to perfect my craft and ignore everything else.

But it's a new era for me, with new people guiding me. Anita and Emilia hammering at me from both sides has chipped away at whatever was holding me static in the place where I'd always been. This sabbatical has made way for something new.

We've been talking for twenty minutes when I hear my phone beep with another call. I look and see it's Nico. I let it go to voicemail and keep chatting about the benefits of having a wood-burning oven as well as a full-fire wok station (I'm thrilled that Brian is as into this nerdy tangent as I am).

But then the phone rings again. I look at my screen as Brian talks about some Italian artisan who imports ceramic ovens, and I feel the pull. I shouldn't, so I try to ignore it. I can call him back later.

But he's never called me twice in a row.

My finger hovers above the green button to answer, but I don't want to interrupt Brian. This is my future; this is going to be a person who I need to collaborate with, and I'm lucky to be off to such a good start. I need to focus on what he's saying and make sure this conversation goes well.

Then a text pops up.

Nico: I need you.

Tension stills me. I go into autopilot, those three words having flipped a switch. "Brian, I'm so sorry—I've gotta go. I have an emergency."

I don't even wait to hear his answer. I just hang up and pull on my shoes.

I hear my phone ping in my pocket, but I'm already out the door and on my scooter. I fly down the road, and within ten minutes I'm pulling up to Nico's house.

As I approach, it's clear my instinct to hurry was the right one. The sky is lit up, with smoke obscuring the view of flames licking higher and higher. One of Nico's older trees is fully engulfed—leaves, branches, and olives turned into heat and dancing color. Small fires dot other trees and across the ground, stars next to the blazing sun of the central burning tree. Crackles have overtaken the quiet of the night, the sound dry and fast, and the usual music of the bugs Nico and I have heard whenever we've slept outside have been silenced.

"Nico!" I call out, my stomach in my throat. My eyes are watering from all the smoke, but I'm desperately searching for him in the mayhem. The memory of my restaurant's fire spins through my mind, and fear claws at me.

I hear Luce first, his barks cutting through as he runs toward me. He spins in circles at my feet, simultaneously happy to see me while clearly panicking, his manic energy so familiar it almost makes me laugh.

I bend down and let him jump into me, both of us needing the closeness. "Hey, boy . . . hey, you're okay," I say softly as I pet him.

Nico comes up behind him, and I pick up Luce so I can hug them both at the same time. "What happened?" I ask, my face pressed into his chest, my heart rate lowering at simply the smell of him.

"There was a dry lightning strike, and it caught the tree. It hasn't spread much—"

"Because the trees are planted far apart and the cows keep the brush clear," I say, allowing a smile to peek through the madness, remembering what he said the first time I came here.

"Yeah," he says, pulling back to look at me. His face is dirty from soot, and he looks so damn tired. He's got a fire blanket at his feet and a singed set of branches he's clearly been using to try and stop any of the fires on the ground. "I called the fire station, but it's a few towns away and it's going to take them a little bit to get here. I really need to get all the cows into the enclosure and far away from all of this. Can you stay here and just watch? If you need me, either for the fire department or . . ."

His words trail off, and I can see all the panic under the surface of his calm exterior. It's amazing that his natural stillness continues to radiate even in this scenario, but I know him well enough now to know that he's scared. And I'm desperate to find some way to soothe him.

"I'll do whatever you need me to do," I say, grabbing his forearms and trying to give him some solidity to lean into. All I want is for him to have someone he can count on while his world is literally on fire. "I'll keep stamping out the smaller fires when they catch. Do you want me to go get pots of water or anything else? I know how much you love these trees. I promise I'll do anything I can to keep them safe."

He blinks at me, like he almost didn't hear what I said.

"What?" I ask, confused, my grip on him loosening and taking a step back.

"Just please don't try and save anything," he snaps with a force I'm surprised by.

"I'm . . . ?" I don't follow.

But he grabs my shoulders and looks at me with desperation in his eyes, his calm exterior finally snapped. "The trees are not the thing I love here, okay?" he growls out, and my jaw drops.

I have no idea how to respond, and my mind is buzzing, but I know I need first and foremost to just give this man the assurance he's clearly craving so he can go do what needs to be done.

"Okay," I say, nodding, the relief in his gaze palpable. "I'll be careful."

He sighs out the breath he was holding, exhaustion emanating from him, his gaze still pleading with me even as I've said all I can say. "I'll get them penned in quickly, but then I'm coming back."

I nod again, forcefully enough that he takes me seriously. He turns and jogs toward the fencing where the cows have all gathered, clearly not wanting to get any closer to what's happening.

I watch him for a minute, trying to breathe deeper, not sure if it's hard because of the smoke or Nico's words.

Memories of my restaurant's fire surge forward, weighing me down, stilling me with a cold I shouldn't be feeling amid all this heat.

But I know what it feels like to watch your dream burn in front of your eyes; I know how much it can take away. For all Nico's faced, he's never had to worry about *this* being taken away from him. He's hitched his life to his work passion, the same way I have, and it's devastating to be faced with watching it burn.

I'm shocked from my stillness by embers falling off the tree and rolling toward me, catching on the grass. I grimace and look to Nico in the distance, but thankfully he's already leading the cows behind Gia's fence. Seeing him spurs me to act.

I take the fire blanket and throw it on the fire, careful not to get too close. I don't want to break my word to Nico, but I'm also not going to let this get any worse on my watch. There's not a lot of wind, and while the dryness of the trees has created a lot of smoke, the fire's not spreading as much as I would fear. That one tree is still engulfed and the other two near it are also rapidly gaining. But the trees are far enough apart that only falling branches have caught the other trees, so mostly I can keep the smaller fires on the ground from gaining.

But it's not long before Nico's back and we're fighting the spread together. The smoke makes everything hazy, and my limbs ache as we stamp out new fires as fast as we can. Branches that have burned keep breaking off and crashing to the ground, singeing the grass and threatening to take more with them, but we act quickly each time. Everything surrounding us feels flammable—apparently the oil that exists in the olives is also in the leaves and the bark, which means that whenever fire touches anything, it catches almost instantly. The battle seems constant and never-ending.

Every time I get too close to a tree, I can see Nico wince. He stops himself from saying anything—he knows in normal circumstances I wouldn't take well to being treated like I'm somehow weaker—but his silent, pleading expression keeps me back, aching to not make him worry. We've found a delicate dance without talking, containing, minimizing, and praying the fire truck comes as soon as possible.

When I hear the siren, it's like the relief of the cavalry arriving right as the battle is starting to feel lost. I collapse to the ground, exhausted, spent, and coughing. I've been somehow running on whatever fumes I could muster, but the truck's arrival gives me permission to let myself stop. Luce climbs into my lap, having spent the night running around at our heels and now taking his first opportunity for comfort.

Everything next happens in a blur. Men shout in Italian and a hose is brought up, spraying water and dousing the flames. The fire has totally destroyed that one central tree, and three others are in varying states of destruction. Even in the dark I can see all the patches of ground that have been singed, soft grass reduced to soot. But eventually, silence overtakes the sounds of crackles and shouts. There's only darkness and the vestiges of all the smoke that hangs in the air. Nico finishes talking to the firefighters and shakes their hands solemnly. They walk back to their truck and pull out, and then everything is still again.

Nico stands wordlessly staring at the blackened tree at the center of the scene. I get up and go to him, wrapping my arms around his waist from behind.

At my touch, he turns and cups my face with his hands. He breathes me in, looking at me longingly, his eyes so tired and sad that instinct takes over and I *have* to kiss him. He lets out a gravelly sigh at the contact and pulls me closer, as though I'm a blanket on a cold day. He presses his fingers carefully to my jaw, like he wants to hold me in place but I'm too delicate to manhandle.

It's comfort, for both of us. I want so badly to take away the pain of this evening for him. I want to swathe him in bubble wrap and fix the world for him. I want to yell at *him* to stay away from fires and smoke and anything that could hurt him for one more second.

But then he goes deeper, his tongue sliding across mine. One hand still cups my jaw, but the other is grabbing my hip, angling me toward him. And somehow that closeness is like a lightning bolt to my center. All the adrenaline that's been coursing through me all night is awakened with his nearness, like my body is so happy to be present and alive and away from danger that his touch has intensified all my nerve endings. We've shifted from comfort to hunger in an instant. One of my legs has looped around him; I need more of my body to be touching his.

"Kit," he groans, his hand leaving my jaw and tracing down my neck, digging into my collarbone like he's hopeless in his attempts to be gentle but is still holding himself back.

But the sound of his voice makes it so *I* can't hold *myself* back. I push him against one of the trees with a thud, our touches growing more desperate, his mouth firm on mine.

It's automatic, the way I need him now, down into my veins. The way my hands move from his chest down, unbuttoning his pants and mine and practically ripping them both on the way to the ground. My mind is focused only on his body; on his hands; on how he's nuzzled into my neck; on the way his hair falls in his face; on how I'm pulsing with need and desire and gratitude and how much I want him.

In one move he's lifted me up, and I guide us together. He turns us around so I'm against the tree now, and he pushes inside me, his words in my ear a string of expletives and sighs of relief. He kisses me again, hard, like he wants every part of me, his grip tight on my thighs, his movements fast and wild. When I gasp at the press of the tree into my back, he immediately moves one hand up to block it, pressing hard into me but shielding me from battering up against it again.

"I love you," he whispers into my ear, the vulnerability of his words stark against the strength of his body holding up mine. "I'm not sorry I said it before. I can't help it. I love you so much."

There's so much fragility in the rasp of his voice: pained, like he doesn't want to hurt me by telling me the one thing we wordlessly agreed we'd never say. As though he would've broken if he didn't get to explain what he said earlier.

But before I can respond, his kiss is a force again, like he can't bear to see what I'd say back. I'm so close to coming apart that I can't fight him on it, so I try to tell him without words. I tighten the grip of my legs around him, run my hands through his hair, and kiss him fervently, until I can't think anymore. Until the smell of smoke and the reality of me leaving is emptied from my mind through the sensation of his touch. Until every inch of me is liquid concentrate, a firework of touch, and the only word I can say is his name.

Chapter 31

We don't talk about it after. We shower off the dirt and the soot from the fire and then collapse into bed without discussion, letting exhaustion take over.

I wake up the next day with Nico completely wrapped around me, our bodies intertwined as though physical touch is a relief. We stay like that for a while, silent but both awake, holding each other. Eventually his body slips back into mine, and we let that comfort take over, no more words needed, just the feel of each other.

We spend the rest of the morning clearing ash away from the trees that have burned. The damage is, remarkably, not too bad once we start hauling away fallen branches—four trees have major damage, but Nico is confident this will all eventually be a forgotten blip for the grove. We pass the time talking about the trees—how ash is used sometimes as fertilizer, but too much of it shifts the pH of the soil; how older olive trees like these are more likely to regenerate because they have deeper roots.

He talks and I listen, because I don't have the words yet to explain all the thoughts roiling inside me. I want to say how much I feel like these trees. How I've grown here, but *my* pH needs the city and my restaurant and busyness to survive. How I got burned and he helped me regenerate, but my old roots are so firmly planted in New York that I have to keep growing there.

And I know he hasn't asked me to stay. I know he *wouldn't* ask me to, because we're so similar—we both are lucky to get to do what we love in the places that we love. No person could override that.

But among all that love, I know I owe him some words of my own. I have to tell him I feel the same way he does before I leave. He deserves to know how lovable he is, even if there's no happy ending waiting for us.

But that will have to come later. I go home and shower and change so I can show up to work at noon like I always do. I only have a few more days here, and I'm not going to let Gia down after everything she's done for me.

She's already there when I arrive.

"Did you two get the ash off the trees this morning?" she says without looking up, her hands already deep in pasta dough.

Well, *that's* not what I expected.

Gia's property abuts Nico's, but her house is much too far from his for her to ever see anything. There are acres and acres of farmland, cows, and groves between where she actually lives and where Nico's house is. That's why I've never worried about her seeing me as I come and go from his place—they're neighbors, but practically an entire forest separates them.

Although I guess I shouldn't ever be surprised that Gia knows everything. And I'm never going to bullshit her.

"Yup," I answer succinctly, walking over to the sink and washing my hands.

But she's not dropping the topic. "Thank you for keeping the cows safe."

"I didn't do anything for the cows," I answer truthfully, starting to dice onions and now not looking at her as much as she's not looking at me. "Nico got them back behind the fence."

"You know, his grandfather bought me the original Maremma cows I had," she says casually.

I put my knife down with a clang, and that finally makes Gia look up. "Is this Share a Secret Day?" I ask pointedly.

She raises an eyebrow, the deep lines of her whole face rising with it. "I'm not the one pretending the person I'm dating is a secret."

My mouth falls open. *Damn.* We've always played it straight with each other, but that was particularly straight.

"No one's a 'secret,'" I mumble, picking my knife back up and turning to my onions so I can go back to ignoring her.

"Listen, I'm mostly glad you've been able to keep him company, sleeping outside for me. I felt bad about that."

"It needed to be done, Gia."

"You didn't have to," she says, looking up. "Just because I'm too old to fight my own battles doesn't mean you needed to join him."

"I wanted to," I say truthfully.

"For me, or for him?" She smirks, and I just roll my eyes. But she's not done with me yet, apparently. "I bet he doesn't even know I dated his grandfather for a while."

This time, I'm so surprised I actually drop my knife. When I look up at Gia, her smirk has grown wider, loving getting me flustered. "Careful."

"Get to the point, Gia," I say with a sigh, trying to not let my curiosity show.

At the start of the summer, when she said she'd lost her first love young, I assumed she meant he'd passed away. But apparently I'm zero for two on that guessing game. I've *really* got to learn not to assume people have died.

She starts rolling out dough, not looking at me when she begins talking again. "Marcello and I were always a terrible match, but we lived next door to each other. We fought about everything. He was such a stubborn mule, *nothing* like Nico." I can't help the small smile that blooms at that defense of him. "He wanted the kind of wife who stayed home and cooked; he had no energy for a woman who needed more freedom. It was a passionate, tumultuous relationship that took me a long time to get over."

She's still not looking at me. Her movements are always so automatic, I wonder if she ever closes her eyes and keeps working. Her knobbled hands aren't as precise as I imagine they once were, but she doesn't miss a beat. Not even with the kind of admission I would expect to cause emotion in anyone else. But Gia's never been anyone else. She's as matter-of-fact today as I imagine she was then.

"We both married other people, and I avoided him for a long time," she continues, clearly not expecting me to have a reaction yet. "But one day, when I had my first baby—Anita's mother—Marcello came to my door. He brought me two cows. He'd named them Marcello and Gia and said someone else could be stubborn for us. I threw him out the door, and I imagine he laughed all the way home. But I kept the cows. And I really grew to love them. Raising cows is so different to cooking. It has less immediacy. Marcello and I kept avoiding each other after that, but he always left his gate open so my cows could graze on his grove."

"Why did you avoid each other?" I ask, annoyingly invested in this decades-old doomed love story after just two minutes. I'm not a romantic, but come *on*.

"I think when you can't make your first love work, there's never a real end," she says with a shrug. "It never stopped feeling sad to see him. No one else pushed me the way Marcello did, even my husband. He wasn't the right man for me, but I always loved him a little bit. I couldn't just have pleasant chats about the weather or the harvest with him. It was more respectful to what we'd had to not speak at all."

"That sounds pretty dramatic, for you," I admit.

I get that sly smile from her again. "Probably," she says. "We did talk a bit more toward the end. He wanted me to convince Lorena that Nico was too gentle for her. She was always so like me, and I think it scared him."

"And *that* didn't offend you?" I say, shocked.

"No, I kind of agreed with him."

"But they got married anyway," I point out.

She shrugs again. "They were in love. They weren't as strong as Marcello and I were to see they weren't compatible."

Well, at least there's the Gia I know, willing to call anything as she sees it, even if it throws someone else under the bus.

"So why are you telling me all of this?" I finally ask, knowing she's never been one for small talk.

"Love is complicated," she says, pulling out her ravioli stamp and starting to work on the pasta she's rolled out.

I roll my eyes. "That's your entire opinion?"

"You didn't ask me for my opinion. I just wanted to tell you some facts."

I put my hands on my hips. "I'd like your opinion, Gia."

"Are you . . . *asking* for my opinion?" It's a challenge, and she's enjoying it.

"Sure," I say, not quite ready to give in to her but begrudgingly knowing that I *do* want to hear what she has to say.

"Because you know, you never ask anyone for anything."

I groan. I guess I walked right into that. "That's not true," I counter.

"It's absolutely true, you bug-eyed American idiota." She stamps out more ravioli and adds filling to the center, casually insulting me without even looking me straight on. "You think you have to make every decision alone. Anita and Emilia have had to practically drag things out of you. But you're not alone, okay? You can ask me whatever you need to."

Our eyes lock, and I can see she's completely serious.

It's jarring, having that kind of permission. With Gia I know it's earned. It's like my pasta she's now letting get sold every evening (it wasn't just that one night, thank goodness). It's so much sweeter knowing I've earned it. I've earned my way into her heart, and I'm not sure I've ever felt that an accomplishment was so hard won.

And it makes me want to be honest in a way I've never been able to be with anyone else.

"I'm in love with Nico, but I can't stay here," I say quietly.

"That's obvious to anyone with eyes. You'd think your giant ones could see that."

I smile. I'm so glad we're going with insults for this heart-to-heart. I don't think I could handle Gia going all sappy on me.

"So you said you wanted me to ask for something," I say. "I'm *asking*. What do I do?"

"You make the hard choice," she says, this shrug a little wearier than the ones before. "You can't give yourself up for a man. It's not an option for you. It wasn't ever for me."

"That's helpful," I murmur.

"It's not. Not really," she says, pinching the ravioli closed. "But it's helpful sometimes to say it out loud. It saves you from having to buy people cows."

I laugh and walk over and kiss her on the head. She's so small I have to lean over to do it.

"Get back to work, okay?" she says, pushing me away and rolling her eyes. "We've got dinner in a few hours."

And without another word, we both focus on what we do best.

Chapter 32

It's a slow night, with everyone in town still exhausted from the Palio, so Gia insists I leave early.

I ride my scooter over to Nico's, the start of sunset casting a golden glow over the scenery. Across every field I pass, giant wheels of hay are tied up and laid out, as though summer is being packed up and put in its place.

Nico's not home when I arrive, and with Luce also being absent, I have a pretty good guess as to where they've gone.

I don't even make it all the way up the hill before Luce comes running down to greet me, spinning in circles every few steps and barking cheerfully until he reaches my ankles and starts licking. He bounces alongside me as I make my way to the couch perched at the top.

Nico watches me as I approach, the angles of his face shadowed in the diminishing amber light. He looks more serene than I would've expected. But then again, he's always been able to maintain his stillness while the rest of the world runs around like Luce, circling without ever taking a moment to stop.

"Thought I might find you here," I say as I plop down next to him on the couch and lay my head on his shoulder.

He pulls out two little glass containers of Campari and soda, and I sigh with appreciation.

"You'll never guess the mystery I solved today," he says while he pops the tops off both, handing me one before taking a big swig of the other.

"What?"

"I figured out what happened to the fencing."

At that I sit up, and the sheepish excitement to tell me is written all over his face. It makes him look boyish, like life hasn't dealt him any knocks yet.

"Oh, this is going to be good," I say, rubbing my hands together. "Did you catch Tommaso messing with it? Or someone else?"

He shakes his head, relishing the surprise. "I meant it when I said you'd never guess."

"The cows are staging a coup and want to destroy any restrictions on their life?"

He chuckles. "Nope."

"Gia was bored and wanted to mess with you?"

"That feels like something you could've guessed," he points out, and now I'm the one giggling.

"All right, hit me with it then. I give up."

"A previously-thought-to-be-extinct beaver has been chewing it."

I stare at him, gobsmacked. "I'm sorry but . . . you're joking, right?" He shakes his head. "How did you even find this out?"

"I saw them," he says, raising his hands in defeat and taking another swig of his drink. "There's a stream that runs through Gia's property, not far from where the cows are, since that's where they drink. And I guess in recent years there's been sightings of these beavers across southern Tuscany for reasons no one seems to understand."

"Okay, but again, how do you get from 'There's some beavers here' to 'The beavers are hanging with the cows and eating the fence'?"

"When I went to check on the cows this morning, I saw them chewing the fence—"

"All right, I admit that's pretty solid evidence—"

"—so I investigated a bit," he continues, ignoring my nonsense. "There's a whole little den they've built on the stream. And for some reason, they seem comfortable with the cows and the cows seem comfortable with them. But apparently this isn't unheard of—there's actually this viral video from a few years ago of a beaver herding cows."

"This . . ." I put my hand over my eyes and rub my temples for a minute. "This cannot possibly end with a viral video of unlikely mammals bonding with each other."

"Apparently it does," he says, scrunching his nose and holding in a laugh. "I was reading about it, and experts think they both find comfort in the safety of numbers, or something. But yeah. They've been here; they've been casually chewing on the fence when they're stressed or bored. That's the whole story."

"No nefarious plots to screw with Gia."

"Nope."

"Just random repopulating beavers."

"Well, 'random' is a bit dismissive. Technically it's the Eurasian beaver, also known as *Castor fiber*." At my raised eyebrows he mumbles, "I've been googling, and it's interesting!" I shake my head, but he keeps going. "And it's a nice story about nature healing!"

I laugh, doubling over, the whole thing so absurd. We've spent so long plotting and planning and trying to understand motives, and here it is, random all along. We might've had good reason to protect the cows from the hunters, but we were definitely off base about their involvement in the fence.

I guess it's a perfect reminder that you can't possibly guess at or plan for everything.

"Anyway," he continues, "I went and bought some latex paint that they apparently hate and painted the fence. So that's the end of that."

His words sober me. It's so final, so pat. He had a problem, he solved it. I wonder if he'll find something similar to get back to normal after I leave.

"What?" he asks, clearly seeing my change in expression.

"I wanted to, um . . ."

I know what I need to say, but my words are failing me.

I take a deep breath and look out at the horizon as the sun sets. It's not hard to understand why Italians like to memorialize their poetry about sunsets and optimism and forevers when they have views like this. When they have stories of extinct animals coming back. When they have Campari sodas neatly stored in tiny, elegant glass bottles. It's all so romantic you could put it on a postcard.

And yet, for all the beauty of the Italian language, I'm maybe starting to understand that it holds a bit of melancholy in it too. These bright, beautiful vistas can go from light to dark so quickly. They can go up in flames. Nico may have spent his entire career perfecting a filter to keep out impurities, but even he can't stop a fire or rogue animals or people from leaving.

"I do love you, Nico," I finally breathe out. "I know it doesn't change anything . . . but I needed you to know."

He takes my hand in his and watches as our fingers dance around each other's. He traces the lines on my palm, dipping into the grooves of every indent.

"It's funny that you started with a fire and you're ending with a fire," he says quietly.

I snort. "Yeah, it's great to bring destruction wherever you go."

But Nico shakes his head, and I can see the start of tears glistening in his eyes. He doesn't look at me; he's watching our hands, watching as he keeps toying with mine, like he wants the pads of his fingers to brush across every inch of surface area.

"In a grove," he continues, his voice still soft, "with a fire, as long as not too much burns down, once you clear away the rubble, the soil is often actually richer as a result."

I squeeze my eyes, trying to blink back the wetness I can feel forming. *Damn it, Nico.* Stupid Italians and their stupid natural poetics. "You don't have to—"

He lifts my hand and kisses it, stopping me from whatever discomfort I'm trying to wriggle out of. "Thank you for telling me," he finally says. "Thank you for letting me see I can fall in love again. You've made my life richer, and I'm so grateful to love you, even if this part is going to hurt."

He leans in to kiss me, the attempt to hold back the tears failing, small droplets making their way down his cheeks.

I kiss them all. I kiss the tears off his cheeks and on his eyes, and they mingle with mine. My heart somehow is both broken and full, knowing I got to love this man.

I'm trying to be grateful too. I'm trying to remember that I was broken in a different way when I got here—I'd always assumed I couldn't love like this. That I was too fierce, too bombastic, too work-focused, too unapologetic to also have real love. I thought what John and I had was the ceiling for me. And learning that I'm capable of so much more has been a gift.

I want to say *We can make it work.* I want to offer to stay. I want to ask him to come with me. I want there to be some pat solution like the paint for the fence.

But part of growth is also accepting the things that *can't* change. Maybe it was always meant to be like this. And that's okay. I know I would do it all over if I had the choice. I'd knowingly burn it all down again for the chance to get a fresh perspective on who I can be. We'll be stronger because of each other, set aflame and reborn.

The sun flares in its final moments of setting. All the last licks of oranges and pinks in the sky are soon replaced with a dusky blue. The fire's gone out, but a velvet canopy of stars has taken its place.

We're lucky to have burned this bright.

Chapter 33

The next few days are a sad blur.

I finish up my last service at Pasta Fresca, and Gia takes a bottle of grappa down from a high shelf (she insisted on bringing out her mini ladder, even though I could've easily reached it). She pours us both a glass, and then we sit on our stools in the kitchen and drink.

After a few moments of soaking in the quiet, I down the rest of my drink and say, "Can I come back if I need to?"

"No," Gia says without even thinking, then stands up and puts her glass in the sink. She gathers up her things and heads to the door. But before leaving she turns around again. "Marna's starting back tomorrow. You're not a sous chef. Your pasta is going to be a little less terrible after being here, and that's good, but this isn't your place. Time to go home, Kit."

She levels me with a look that says everything without saying it. She's lived her life on her own terms, and she's reminding me to do that too. She makes me *know* I can do it too.

And with that she's out the door.

I wish I could say Emilia's a little less dramatic, but much like with the Palio, apparently she can get emotional when it comes to things she cares about.

Although I have to admit, it warms a corner of my cynical heart to know I could break someone as tough as Emilia.

"The apricot ricotta cake actually lasts a few days if you refrigerate it when you get home," she instructs me, pushing a bag of baked goods into my hands. "So don't eat that first. The bomboloni don't even last the whole day, so those are for the plane."

"I hear you," I say with a small smirk.

"Seriously, don't give any of your New York friends one of my bomboloni twelve hours after I baked them. I don't care if they're picking you up at the airport or whatever. It's too long. Eat them on the plane."

"You know New Yorkers don't ever pick each other up at the airport, right?" I unhelpfully point out.

"Selfish pricks."

I chuckle. "That's the spirit." And I wrap her into a hug.

Emilia is the first female friend I've ever had who has my height, and there's something comforting about hugging someone as equals.

"And don't share them with Nico on the way," she continues, her voice muffled by her arms still around my neck. "He can get them anytime."

"You're bossy today."

"How dare you," she says, pulling back to give me a look up and down. "I'm bossy *every* day."

I laugh and toss my scooter keys to her. "Give these back to Flavia, okay?"

She nods and gives me one more hug. I pick back up the baked goods bag and make my way outside.

My scooter is parked at the entrance. The cat that's been following me around is curled up on the seat. I scratch her behind the ears, but she's already ignoring me. I guess cats can tell when a person isn't worth paying attention to anymore. She's already forgotten me. It's fitting—this millennia-old town puts its own unique imprint on anyone lucky enough to find it, but we can't expect it to keep holding on to us once we leave.

I run my hand along the handlebars of the scooter and give it a pat. My little marigold-colored, banged-up, open-air source of freedom. I'm definitely going to miss having it.

But, as Gia said so succinctly, it's time to go home. Nico's waiting at his car, ready to take me back to the Rome airport.

We spend the hour and a half singing along to music and not saying much. When we pull up to the curb, he gets out with me and helps to put my suitcase on a cart.

When it's time to say goodbye, all the words leave me. I fling my arms around him instead and simply breathe him in. He folds into me and we stand, the world honking and beeping around us while we hold on to the moment. He's solid and still and so perfectly Nico.

"Knock 'em dead," he says, with a kiss on my forehead.

When he pulls back, I see the prickle of tears in his eyes threatening to fall, but I'm surprised when the ones he wipes away are mine.

There's nothing else to say. He gives me a small, encouraging half smile, then turns and gets in his car, and it's really over.

I go to sit on a bench to collect myself before going inside. I'm not going to be the asshole who walks into the airport crying. I give myself a minute and then stand back up.

And then I notice, written in gold across the red bench, another goddamn Italian poem: *Nel mondo si porta la pace con l'amore e non con la forza.*

I pull out my phone and translate it. The tears start again as I laugh, reading the words: "Peace is brought into the world with love and not with force."

I think about the day I arrived in Italy and the words John spat at me. *You can't force it, Kit. You're not going to suddenly find peace in a pasta bowl.*

I hate to admit that John was right. I didn't force peace for myself in a pasta bowl.

I found it with love in an olive grove.

Chapter 34

I'm back in my kitchen within hours of landing. My staff is waiting for me, and once I arrive, we're all automatically in go mode, jet lag be damned.

We have so much to do over the next ten days. We're testing recipes, getting prep going for everything we know we'll need, placing orders to get our suppliers back up and running.

It's consuming. I let it be consuming. I don't see Anita or any of my New York people outside of work. I don't talk to Nico, other than a few texts checking in. For days on end, I don't let myself think about anything outside of the restaurant.

I'm good. I'm getting over it. Manciano is an old photograph, the scenes vibrant but blurry, so I'm not going to focus on it.

And the part of me that's been at rest is suddenly like a muscle flexed. That piece of me feels *good.* That decisive leader, that bombastic creative—she was overworked before, but now she's rested and ready. I know I've got the tools now to not overdo it, but I'm not going to pretend that I've had some massive change of heart about who I am. I want right now to be in a kitchen for fourteen-hour days. I want to think constantly about how to improve a dish. I want to be a cook on the line, living in that flow state when service starts and we've got to make a memorable night for every guest who walks in the door. I thrive on it.

But even though I'm not going to change my pace, I'm already starting to see the ways my time working with Gia has woven itself into me and made me stronger. I've always mentored young chefs, but after having Gia poke and prod me, I understand how important it is to know them beyond cooking in order to push them to find new wells of inspiration. (Did I know that my sous chef Kristen is a huge Giants fan? Apparently I do now, and she's *super excited* for some offensive lineman to be back from injury this season. His name is Cal Durand, and I apparently am capable of caring about this for the sake of my cooks.) I've also let myself go further outside the box on products than I normally would—we're trying out locally milled flours to see if I can replicate what I had in Italy; I let a line cook introduce me to a farmer he's passionate about who's growing specialty lettuces, and then I pulled back on tinkering too much with a salad that sang perfectly fine without adornment.

I'm also thriving on getting ready to announce the next restaurant. Brian and his team have been stopping in, going over plans with me, and running the press release by me. I've never had so much input and so much *trust* in my input. The early renderings have been changed to my specifications, and all the details I've wanted were incorporated. The early imagery is like looking at a dream—the space, the equipment, the view. It's a restaurant with all my fingerprints on it, right from the start. There's tangible energy connected to this new level of creativity.

And most importantly, I haven't seen John. He doesn't butt in. He got the memo and is giving me space to run. As much as he maybe had thoughts about us, he's always thought of me as a chef first. An *asset* first. And for his asset to succeed right now, she needs to not have him around. I'm glad to have him behind the scenes doing what he does best, but I'm grateful he's kept his distance.

Ten days after hitting the ground running, we're ready to reopen and we're ready to announce. At 5:00 p.m. we open the doors, and the publicists hit send on the press release.

I know there's a lot of chatting and glad-handing and talking to media outside my kitchen doors, but none of that matters once I'm in the zone. We're firing dishes and getting prepped for upcoming courses and I'm watching the pasta station like a hawk. We don't get in the weeds or fumble. We're clear-eyed as we make the favorites everyone has missed, and we're nailing the new dishes everyone is curious about.

For five hours we work nonstop. I've got water in a plastic container on the counter next to me, and I need nothing else. It's exhausting, repetitive, and exhilarating. I'm filled to the brim with joy to be back in my space.

Some unwanted thoughts slip in. Luce hopping on Nico's lap. Strong arms carrying my groceries to my door. Cackling laughter. Eyes memorizing me late at night.

My empty bed at home here.

But I let it all move through me. I'm not going to push Nico out of my mind, but I'm not going to dwell. I was lucky to have had him. I'm getting used to missing him.

I'm where I need to be, and he's where he needs to be.

As the night starts wrapping up, I allow a few media people to come into the kitchen to chat and get some quotes for articles that will share the reopening and the plans for what's coming next. There's genuine excitement over the new restaurant, especially over the scale of the project. Most of the food journalists are women, and there's something palpable about the tenor of their questions. One of them mentions a comparative figure for investment in female-run restaurants, and while I hate questions that quantify gender accomplishments, I appreciate that she seems to relish the stride.

I walk outside at the end of the night invigorated, which the energy of New York enhances even more. I could never live without this long-term. I'm fueled by the high of the precision and creativity in fine dining, the limitless possibilities that come with having access to any ingredient and a large team to execute. And everyone else in New York feeds off the same fuel, and it lights up the entire city. I belong here.

Even if my heart still, for the moment, has an undeniable outpost in Manciano.

The articles and social media posts about the reopening and the upcoming restaurant start coming out the next day. They're all glowing about the new menu and the renovations, but more importantly, they're all filled with excitement for the future. I make my morning tea, with a pang for my missing Belpagna pastry, and scroll through.

It feels good to have the confidence of my community behind me. But there's a strange other something lingering behind it.

It's not exactly a feeling—it's almost . . . the lack of a feeling. There's no knot in my stomach, that *need* to prove something. I don't search every word in every post to see if there's some room for instant enhancement. I'm not looking for the expectations in the undertones of what they're writing about the next project.

It's not the same as it was when things started to change for rowing, because I'm not done with cooking. Hardly. But it's the first time in my career I don't find myself craving the achievement for the sake of it. I'm clearly still excited about the restaurant itself; I'm excited about the process of building, the freedom to cook what I want on my own terms. That's been apparent in the days I've been back.

And I'm sure in a few years when the next restaurant opens, I'm going to want good reviews and for people to walk in the door. But if it's anything like now, what I'm really looking for in the stories of people's experience last night is whether they had a good time. Whether they felt fed and happy at the end of the night—that simple experience of sitting down for a meal and having it delight you. Sure, I want them to be surprised and impressed—but mostly I want them to have a really great time with some delicious, well-executed food.

I'm mentally freer to enjoy the process than I ever was before.

Huh.

The answer to *this* unasked question, though, is staring right at me.

I try so hard not to think about Nico. I really do. But this shift in my perspective . . . it's all him. The stillness he's offered to me.

I can't help but think about our conversation last month on the DNA of olives.

It's the joy I remember most from that conversation. His joy at getting to be in a little bubble with another person who found fascination in the makeup of olives. How lucky we were to look up at the stars and have conversations like that.

But the words stick with me too. *You can shift what you plant in the in-between spaces and fundamentally shift the olives.*

At the memory, I put down my phone and step away from my scrolling because a realization has hit me hard. One thing's abundantly clear in this moment.

He's what's altered my DNA.

He planted himself in all the empty spaces in between, and I changed because of his proximity.

I want so badly to be the same as I was before, just with little Italy-centric food-based improvements. But it's more than that. I've absorbed *him*.

I haven't changed completely. I'm not changed enough to want to run back and be the sous chef at an anonymous restaurant and leave my entire career behind. I'm not changed enough to want to sit in a grove and stare at trees all day. I'm not changed enough to not want the energy and life of New York pumping through my veins.

But for the first time since I've shut myself back in my cooking cave, I can see that the changes in me from Italy aren't only what I learned from Gia in the restaurant.

I'm calmer. I'm more at peace with myself.

And somehow that shift in me is the most painful thing of all to realize, because those changes make it impossible not to miss Nico with an ache that seems unbearable.

Chapter 35

"I haven't seen you in almost two weeks, and now you're at my doorstep at eight in the morning?" Anita's looking at me skeptically from behind her door chain lock.

"You already buzzed me in," I say to justify myself.

"Doesn't mean I'm opening the door."

I lift up the paper bags I'm holding. "I got you a bacon, egg, and cheese. New Yorker things. You can't say no."

"You better not have gotten me a shitty street cart BEC," she says, her face closer to the door now that she knows I have treats.

"Hell no." I lift the bag higher so she can see the label. "Daily Provisions. Runny yolk and everything. Come on, have a little faith."

She opens the chain and stands in the doorway with her hands on her hips. "You can't just show up at people's doorsteps."

"Don't be such a silly goose," I say, pushing past her and into the apartment. I park myself at her little kitchen table and start unwrapping our breakfast sandwiches.

"There's no such thing. Geese are extremely serious."

"Really?" I ask, momentarily sidetracked.

"Have you ever met a goose?" she asks. "They look like primordial dinosaur birds. They honk super loud, flap their wings, and they'll bite you. They are the opposite of silly."

"Huh." I take a bite of my sandwich and predictably get yolk running down my arm.

She hands me a napkin, sits down, and begrudgingly grabs a sandwich. "Okay, this is not why you came here."

"You don't think I'm here to discuss geese?"

She narrows her eyes at me but says nothing. She holds her sandwich in such a way that when she bites into it, she makes distinctly less mess than I did. I keep chewing and so does she. I don't know why I'm letting her stare me down—I'm the one who came here. But once again I'm having trouble articulating how I'm feeling. A problem, by the way, I never cared about in my entire life, but recently it seems insurmountable.

I don't know if that new excess of stronger feelings is supposed to be a good thing or a bad thing.

"Thanks for the sandwich," she finally says, breaking the silence. "Now what gives?"

I put my head on the table to avoid looking at her. I haven't said anything to her about Nico since our conversation at the beach where I *assured* her nothing was happening. But that Band-Aid has to be ripped off—I need to stop being afraid to let Anita fully in.

I guess now's as good a time as any.

"I'm in love with Nico, and I don't know how to make it go away," I say into the table.

There's silence, and then an attempt to stifle a laugh that almost immediately loses out.

I look up. "Hey! That's not *funny*?!"

Her lips are pursed, still in an attempt to avoid laughter. "It's funny on so many levels," she says finally.

"What?"

"You're in love with someone you swore up and down you were just staying friends with. Objectively funny." I slump in my chair, annoyed that she's got me so thoroughly pegged. But she continues. "Also, you've never actually been in love, so you're totally flustered and showing up at my house in a panic. That's also objectively funny."

"Someone being in a panic is the opposite of funny."

But she's fully ignoring me now. "And lastly—and *most* objectively funny—you genuinely think there's some magic way to make it go away?"

"Can't there be?" I ask, the desperation seeping out of me.

"Not that anyone's figured out," she says, containing the laugh that's threatening to burst out.

"My sadness isn't funny!" I throw my hands in the air. "This is my real life!"

"I didn't say it was funny!"

"You're holding in a laugh, and you *literally* just said multiple parts of my statement were objectively funny," I whine.

"No," she says, pointing her finger at me. "Your bumbling is the part that's funny. Your sadness is not funny at all."

"Okay, so what do I do with that?"

"I feel like there's an olive tree metaphor here," she says.

I put my head back on the table. "Come *on*, Anita. This isn't the fucking time for that nonsense. You Italians and your insistence on poetic bullshit. I'm having a crisis!"

"You're the olive tree in this metaphor," she barrels on.

"I'm the *olive tree*?" I say incredulously, sitting up. I don't know why I'm offended, but I automatically am because, come on, she's putting me in a damned metaphor.

"Hey, olive trees are so individual," she continues, ignoring my bluster. "They don't need anyone; they survive droughts and even fires. They're perfectly fine on their own. They can make olives and they can be picked or not picked, but it doesn't matter to the tree."

"Oh, so I'm just a loner who can survive drought. My reputation's really skyrocketing here."

"*But*," she says, her finger over her lips to shut me the hell up, "with people they make beautiful olive oil! They're better with humans. They make something great when they involve people."

I'm annoyed because this is akin to my thoughts yesterday, which also means I've succumbed to their absurdity of making everything somehow always about olives.

"I can still involve people and not be in love with a person whose life is thousands of miles away." Maybe I'm trying to convince myself a bit too. "We can still be friends—friends get to hang out, and that's the best thing with him anyway."

"The *best* thing?" she says with a smirk.

I gulp. "One of the best things, yes."

A pang of sadness washes over me because it's pathetic how deep my neediness for him seems to run. I *should* be thinking about sex. But I'd be lying if I said that's the thing I miss most. I miss talking to him. I miss the way he made me feel delicate. I miss having someone I could say anything to.

Anita must catch the look on my face, because her expression softens. "Do you realize how rare that is? To like hanging out with someone all the time?"

"You and I like hanging out." I'm once again in a mode of trying to convince myself.

"But it's not the same, is it?" she says quietly.

I purse my lips. And slowly, I shake my head. "No. It's not."

"So what are you going to do?"

"I don't know, Anita! That's why I'm fucking sitting here!"

Her grin is back. "Oh, you think I can solve this for you?"

I put my head in my hands, needing once again to not look at her. "Just give me some goddamn advice already!"

"You keep this thing from me, tell me nothing, storm into my apartment, and now you think I'm gonna have a solution to a problem you've been thinking about nonstop for weeks?"

"I brought you a sandwich, don't forget that part."

"Noted," she says, and even though I'm still not looking, I can hear the smile in her voice. "But I really can't tell you what to do."

"You told me to go to Italy," I remind her, lifting my head up to level a stare at her.

"I'd say it was a suggestion."

"You practically pushed me onto the plane," I retort, and she grins, not denying it. But I rub my hand across my face, knowing snark isn't going to save me from talking it out. "Come on, this is me being open about my feelings instead of ignoring them and talking to you about the breakfast sandwich all morning. This is me knowing it's not working and gathering the best minds I've got to advise me!"

"Advising doesn't mean anyone else should tell you what to do," she says, eyebrows raised.

I sigh. She can clock me better than anyone.

"I know I've done that for too long," I admit. "I don't like planning. I just want to work. But I have to get better at steering my own path. I know that."

"I'm glad to hear it," she says softly. She reaches her arm across the table to pat me, like I'm a dead man walking and the only comfort she can provide is tactile. She stays silent, waiting, letting me collect my thoughts while her hand stays on me as reassurance.

Maybe instead of letting men steer me, I should've let in more women to stand beside me.

I take a deep breath, not sure where to even begin now that we've at least admitted I'm going to have to participate in my own decision.

"I am sorry I've let you not talk about it," she says, surprising me.

"Well, how would you have known about this," I say, waving her away.

But she shakes her head. "I don't mean this specific thing about Nico. I mean generally. I let my dislike of John and the fact that we never have enough time together make it so I avoided the hard stuff in favor of keeping our time together light. I should've made it more obvious that you *could* talk to me about anything."

"I've always known that, Anita," I say truthfully. "I just took my time realizing I *should*."

She nods, letting the silence sit between us for a moment.

"How'd you leave it with Nico?" she finally asks.

I meet her eyes. I guess there's no avoiding it now. "We love each other. But we live in different places, and we don't want different lives. I love my work and New York, and that's not changing. He loves his work and Manciano, and that's not changing. So we left it where we left it. We said goodbye. We said we'd be friends. What else is there to say?"

"You don't want to fight for what makes you happy?" she asks, although I can see that even she's not convinced that's good advice.

I sigh. "I'm never getting that story."

She crinkles her nose. "What story?"

"You know, I'm not the big-city gal who goes to the small town to roll out pasta and gives up everything for love and a simpler life. I wish I could be that girl in the goddamn Hallmark movie. That girl would stay, because Nico deserves someone who stays for him, and lets Gia retire and rolls the fucking barrel in the quirky small-town race. That girl doesn't mind giving up everything she's built because she values the socially acceptable things like love conquering all."

"I'm sorry, but that's a bullshit narrative that, frankly, is always insulting to the women," Anita pushes.

"Okay, but that's what 'fighting for happiness' looks like in this narrative."

"Bullshit," she repeats. "Those stories always make it seem like one person has to sacrifice to have love. And that makes for a great story. But that's not reality. Reality is messier and bigger, and not *everything* gets to be simple. You should be equals who make choices that make sense for both people's lives."

"Okay, but that's the problem with the options we have. There is no equal option," I say. "I'm destined to be like Gia and give up my great love for my work."

At that she snorts. "I'm sorry, but you're not Nonna. Nonna's amazing and a total badass, but she's from a different generation. She chose from the options that were in front of her. She chose what she wanted and that's worked for her, but it doesn't mean she was otherwise doomed in love. She chose to close herself off after my nonno died. You can admire her, but that's not exactly an example to live by."

"With me and Nico, it's not a choice," I say defensively. I pick at my napkin so I don't have to see the way she's looking at me. "It's the reality of our situation. I don't get to have both. If I need to be here, then I can't be with Nico. That's it."

"He didn't want to leave Manciano?"

My brow furrows. "Obviously he can't leave Manciano."

"Did you ask him?"

At that I stand up. "Did I *ask* him? Did I say, 'Hey, person whose wife left him because she didn't want to live in this small town that you love: Do you now want to leave this town you were willing to lose your wife over?'"

"Don't yell at me," Anita says, not looking offended in the slightest.

"I'm not yelling!" I yell.

"That's a totally misguided way of looking at something that happened like ten years ago," she says calmly. "He was just taking things over after his grandfather died and setting up his own systems. They weren't right for each other anyway, and that just exacerbated all the ways they didn't work. She didn't *want* to make it work." She wipes her hand across her face, thinking. "You really didn't ask him?"

It's like running a light that you thought was still yellow yet has distinctly turned red but it's too late to stop. I hadn't even *considered* asking him.

"What was I supposed to say? 'Hey, want to move to New York with me?'" I ask, trying to sound incredulous but really testing how the words taste.

"In an ideal world, is that what you'd want?"

The thought stops me in my tracks. I see his smile in front of me so clearly I can practically grab it. I see that little freckle above his top lip. I see his hand pushing through his messy hair. His eyes dipping to take me in.

"Probably," I sigh. "I just want him to be where I am." I say it so quietly, but I can see that Anita's heard me. Her expression is some mix of heart eyes and sadness.

"You have to tell him that," she says.

"He would've suggested it if that's what he wanted," I dismiss.

But she shakes her head, not letting me off the hook. "The ball was always in your court, Kit. He couldn't ask you to stay because, come on, as you rightly observed, you never *could* stay there. But he *could* come here. Hell, he basically only *has* to be there in October. And he travels around a lot of the rest of the year anyway, meeting suppliers and chefs and showcasing the oil. He could be based anywhere. He could make that work, if you wanted."

"Again, you're assuming that's what *he* wanted," I say forcefully, pushing away from a too-easy solution that clearly could never be.

"I've never seen you like this," she responds. "I've known you for almost my entire adult life, and you've never shown up at my house distressed. Not when work got hard, not when your family was driving you nuts. And I like this new version of you that seems open to us actually delving into real shit more—I'm *proud* of you. But even in *that* scenario, the idea of you being bent out of shape over a man has never crossed my mind."

"Thanks for reminding me how pitiful my current state is."

She shakes her head at me, although her expression makes it clear she'd rather be shaking *me*. "I'm saying . . . this isn't a thing we're resolving over BECs. This isn't just missing someone. If you're this miserable, he's probably this miserable too. Either way, we're debating what he wants or wanted without actually asking him."

"You want me to just pick up the phone and say, 'Hey, Nico, wanna give up your whole life for me?'"

She cringes. "How bad *are* you at romance?"

I lean over and ruffle my hair in frustration. "Obviously extremely bad! This shit is hard!"

"Nah," she says, and from her sly smirk I already know what she's going to say. "The hard is what makes it great." I groan and she laughs. "But I know what you need to do. I've got a plan."

Chapter 36

I buzz through Sunday night's service.

I'm running on focus and adrenaline to push me. It's something I've always been able to do—cut through the noise and just do the work. You need it in rowing so you don't get distracted by what's happening around you. And you need it in cooking to drown out your personal life and get into a flow when you're having a busy night and can't afford to get behind for even one step.

There's a big part of me that wants to zone out, that wants to think about the flight I'm getting on late tonight. I want to think about what Nico will say when I show up on his doorstep. I want to think about my pronunciation of the poem I've memorized, the one about loving Maremma that I looked at every day from my bench. I want to think about whether he'll appreciate my grand romantic gesture, or if he'll let me down gently.

But there's a reason I've gotten to where I am today in my career. And it's because I'm methodical. I can block everything out. I can get into a rhythm and get the job done.

So I don't think about Nico all night. We do over a hundred covers, and I know each and every one is executed flawlessly because my mind is on the dish in front of me.

But after the final order is out, the kitchen has been cleaned up, and I'm the last one standing, I let my mind finally wander as I wash my hands and prepare to leave. I think about Nico's smile. I think about the straight slope of his nose. I think about wrapping my hands around his waist.

I push open the kitchen door, and now I'm thinking about Nico in New York.

Because Nico's in front of me.

Nico's sitting at the bar, nursing a beer, watching my surprise.

Nico is *here*?

Seeing someone you've been imagining for a few weeks is like getting water after wandering in a desert. You'd binge on it and take in every little detail. That's what looking at Nico right now feels like. It's not the hazy generalities I'd been focused on minutes ago; it's the tangible time-specific realities right in front of me. The fade of the gray T-shirt; the length of his stubble; the way his throat moves as he swallows while he takes me in in all the same ways.

"You're here," I croak, needing to state the obvious to make sure it's actually happening.

"I'm here," he says with a tentative smile. His stillness and calm, like always, calms *me*. I take a deep breath and sit down next to him.

"I was about to go to the airport."

"Oh." He raises his eyebrows. "I didn't mean to stop you. I shouldn't have assumed—"

I put my hand on his arm. Maybe it's to stop his doubts, but it's probably more because I'm desperate to touch him.

"I was going to the airport to get on a flight to Rome."

He closes his eyes and smiles. I can hear the exhale that seems to come from his entire body.

He centers himself, taking a beat, and then finally says, "I didn't think it would be like this."

"What wouldn't?"

He looks me up and down, distracted by my physicality as much as I am with his, and my heart skips a beat.

But after a moment he speaks again. "I ate here tonight—"

"You did?" I beam at the thought. I know he's *here*, but it hadn't occurred to me that he'd had dinner.

"I did." His mouth curves up at my dopey expression. "I love that you seem to be happier at the idea of me eating at your restaurant than you do at me flying four thousand miles to see you."

"I like that part too," I say, and he wraps his hand around mine, a tether after too much time without it. He rubs his thumb along my fingers. I've been so steely the last few weeks, unyielding, trying to be the most singularly focused version of myself. But in an instant, he takes my calloused, burned, tired fingers and makes them feel gentle again. The only person who's ever found the softness on my tough exterior.

"I liked getting to see you through your restaurant," he continues, his eyes back on me even as his hands keep slowly moving. "You're in every bite of the food. All your precision and humor and creativity and boldness. All summer, I loved everything you made, but it wasn't this. Everything that came out of this kitchen is purely you."

I squeeze his hand. "Thank you."

"It's why you need to be here," he says quietly. I feel his words in the pit of my stomach. I wonder what it means for us.

He pulls my hand up and kisses my wrist. "But before, when I was trying to say I didn't think it would be like this, I meant . . ." He pauses, searching for the words. "I didn't think it would be quite so completely impossible when you left. Not simply hard, but totally impossible." He kisses my wrist again. I think we both need to keep confirming that the other is real. "I don't want to be away from you. Life without you is just an empty table."

I pull him into a hug, relieved, because I know exactly what he means. I can do it without him—and I always did before and I've been doing it the last few weeks—but now that I know what life *could* be, everything's been flavorless. Unsalted. Like the first time I went to a fancy restaurant and was gobsmacked that I'd been missing everything food could be.

"I thought I'd throw myself back into work and it would be okay," I whisper against him.

"I only had trees to watch growing, so if it was hard for you, can you imagine how torturous it was for me?"

I laugh, and the sound is muffled because my tears are mixed in. I'm so glad I'm the last person out of the restaurant tonight, because I think I'd die if my whole team saw me in some ridiculous hug halfway between weeping and hysterically cracking up.

"Don't diminish the cows, though," I finally say, needing to find some lightness. "They'd be offended if they heard you saying you 'only had trees.'"

He shakes his head. "I did pay attention to the cows. Although actually, that got me in the most trouble because I was sleeping outside again the other night, and Tommaso walked through and I lost it on him."

My eyes widen. "You did?"

"He wasn't with a group. I think he wanted to get a sense of where the boars were, if they were still around the area for the season. So I saw him alone and I just . . . unleashed. I yelled at him about Gia and his bullying and his lack of consideration for the town. It actually felt really great. And you know what he said?"

"What?" I can't even imagine mild-mannered Nico yelling at anyone, so it must've shocked Tommaso.

"He sat down next to me and asked for a beer." My eyes widen and he nods with a grin, enjoying seeing my surprise. "And we talked about you. He told me if I was losing my temper, I must be going nuts missing you, and when I asked how he guessed, I found out that his wife died a few years ago—"

"Finally a spouse who *actually* died!"

He quirks a confused look at me, and I make a zipping motion with my lips. Clearly *not* the time to share that particular observation.

"Anyway, we started chatting about what it's been like since he lost her, and apparently the hunting trips have been his saving grace.

They've given him purpose in his loneliness. And with sort of a truce on hand, we were able to actually get into the hunting stuff and hash some things out."

I never thought I'd find the emotional intricacies of a small-town hunting dispute hot, but apparently here we are.

"But that's not what's important," he continues, not privy to the depraved direction my mind seems to always take. Instead he squeezes my hand again, another tactile reminder of my presence, which immediately makes me focus. "By the time we were talking, I'd been thinking about you nonstop for days, obviously. But I'd been trying to make myself accept the reality of the situation because so many of the details I love about you are so directly tied to *why* you needed to leave. Your relentlessness, your desire to learn, your ambition."

He sighs, moving his hand up from mine and onto my elbow, like he needs more contact to get all of this out. "I love you, Kit. And I didn't try to stop you leaving because I thought it was what loving you meant. In the past, it was what I thought it meant to love my ex-wife, because she needed to leave, and that was the right choice in the long run for both of us. So I just assumed this, with us, would be the same. It would hurt, but I'd move on. Except right from the moment you left, it didn't feel the same. It was so *wrong*. And talking to Tommaso, every story he told of missing his wife was all about the specificity of *her* . . . And it made everything so clear. I wasn't sad that a relationship had ended or that I was alone—it was you."

He pulls back and wipes the tears off my eyes. His words make me ache because they're exactly the same kinds of realizations I've come to. We're in each other's DNA, and it's not meant to go away.

Although I feel way luckier to have had Anita as my sounding board than Tommaso, but I guess beggars can't be choosers.

"So after that night with Tommaso, what happened?" I ask, knowing that it all led up to him flying to New York, but I'm still totally in the dark about how he got here.

He chuckles. "Well, after not sleeping much that night, I spent the next day doing a *lot* of pacing around the grove. Luce seemed to think I'd lost it. But the trees have always given me peace, and this time of year everything is looking gorgeous, so I thought it would be helpful."

"Did it work?"

He shakes his head. "I hadn't had peace since the moment you'd left, and it wasn't coming back. I'd really always thought Manciano gave it to me. I was happy enough taking over for my grandfather and building on the technology and hanging around with Emilia and Gia and the rest of the nutty people I love there." I'm so grateful to see a smile on him for a moment, completely understanding why that thought is what brings it out in him.

But then he shifts again. "After my wife left, I'd had to rebuild what was lost using the things I loved that had stayed. I associated that contentedness with something I couldn't lose. My peace in Manciano felt so hard-won, and after finding balance again, I was terrified of losing it." He sighs again, and it's bone deep. "But with you gone, it became increasingly clear that my life in Manciano wasn't everything—I'd been happy *enough*, but you seeped into my life in a completely different way."

My heart squeezes at his words—he has no idea yet how much his realizations have paralleled mine. I grip him tighter, encouraging him to keep going, to keep letting out whatever he needs to say.

"I don't need a couch or a sunset or my hands on groves to ground myself," he continues. "You being in front of me gives me that. Manciano is community and support, but you're my home. And I hadn't realized that earlier because it all seemed to fit until you weren't there, until I realized that my table was empty without you. And after hearing Tommaso's grief over not having *his* home anymore, I kept thinking what a waste it is to love someone that much who's still here and not be with them."

He wipes away his own tears, but I stay silent, wanting to let him finish. "I thought maybe . . . I don't have a good answer and I don't know what life looks like, but in whatever iteration, I need my table to include you. I need you. I need to be where you are." I inhale sharply at his words, because they're almost the exact same ones I said to Anita. But he doesn't notice and keeps going. "I don't want you to change, I don't want you to give up anything, I just need you exactly as you are, and we'll work the rest of it out."

Need. That's really all it comes down to, isn't it? Loving him isn't a choice. It wasn't ever a choice. I've always only relied on myself, and I've had other people supporting me and cheering for me, but I didn't *need* them. I wasn't flour and water with anyone else, essential to the entire structure of a dough. Nico intertwined with me and made me into something new. And I can't go back now.

"I was coming to Rome to tell you the same thing."

"Yeah?" he breathes, sounding more relieved than I've ever heard him.

"Well, obviously not the exact same thing, since I didn't have revelations with Tommaso or a grove to wander around." He chuckles and I adore the small sound. "And it was different because, unlike your very rational action to come and have a conversation like an adult, I had a very cringeworthy grand gesture at the ready. I was gonna show up and make you a dinner and recite some Italian poetry and maybe make Luce wear a bow tie . . . It was a whole thing. Anita made me come up with a whole plan."

He shakes his head and laughs that perfect sonorous laugh of his. "I don't need any of that."

"I see that now," I say with a smile.

"Just you."

Just me.

And unlike everything else I've achieved in my life, this outcome has nothing to do with how hard I've worked, how much I've pushed, how far I've tested my limits. It's simply as true as knowing the olives will grow on the tree with or without Nico there to watch them.

He pulls me into a kiss, in the middle of my restaurant, and now I have everything I need.

Epilogue

Three years later

I'm counting on the men to bring this home. I'm still salty about losing our race yesterday. Imposto's Martina hasn't stopped taunting us.

This year's Palio has been plagued by rain, but it seems like the men's teams are getting a break as they're about to start their semifinal round. The weather hasn't hindered anyone from celebrating—the food stalls are still out, the band has set up under a tent, and the people of Manciano are determined to enjoy themselves.

Except, of course, the six men from Cassero and the six men from Borgo who are about to roll a barrel as quickly as they can down wet, slippery stone streets.

"Andiamo!" Anita shouts next to me, while Emilia does that two-fingered whistle I've never been able to master. They are pumped and ready to go. Which is easy enough, since we all have beers in hand and don't have to do anything now other than cheer.

I take in the absurdity of the scene surrounding me—wet people, ecstatic and overhyped friends, good food, and a not-so-ancient barrel-rolling competition—and I'm starting to understand the root of that stillness that Nico's always had. It's as hectic externally as it possibly could be, but inside I'm calm. This is the cherry on top of having what I need.

The last few years have been a whirlwind. Almost immediately, Nico trialed living in New York with me as his primary residence, although he came back to Manciano for the full month of October for harvest and bottling. And then he's traveled a fair amount to meet with clients in the offseasons. He's also submitted a patent for his filter and has spent a lot of time on expanding that. He goes back to Manciano otherwise every couple of months to check in, but, as he said to me the first time I went to the grove, the olive trees don't really need anything from him.

New York didn't faze him, having grown up in Rome, but we were both particularly thrilled to see how much Luce loved his new city life. I guess constant noise and excitement is a way better fit for a small insatiable dog.

My first year back was filled with a double dose of planning as the new restaurant got built out. When summer came back around, and we'd scheduled the new space to open in the fall, I decided to make good on my need for rest and inspiration. I took the whole month of August off and gave over my restaurant to four rising chefs to do weeklong pop-ups instead of our regular menu. It was such a success I've done it every year since. And instead of being judged, other chefs have embraced the concept with open arms—that pressure to always be in the restaurant might be some people's perceptions, but I've stopped caring what anyone other than my diners think about me. I can give back to my community while also staying true to my need to not overdo it.

The new restaurant opened with a smash. *The New York Times* gave us a rave three-star review and said the food and space were "impeccable." We're booked out the minute reservations come online.

But as we've built up, I've also allowed myself to take a day off every week, letting my chef de cuisine run the kitchen, and giving more responsibility to the rest of the team generally—Nico was right, I do benefit creatively from having time to marinate. Gia's been especially smug about inspiring that particular lifestyle change.

So it's my fourth Palio, and at this point I wouldn't miss it for the world. And since I've been coming back for the festivities, it's also nice that for the last couple of years, Anita's planned her annual trip around them too.

Although in this particular moment, I'm wondering why we insist on doing this to ourselves instead of coming during a quieter time.

The gun goes off and there's a scramble. Nico and Antonio are in the second position again, so initially they're just following behind. The screen is harder to see with so much rain still clinging to it, but our guys appear to be behind straight from the jump. They round the corner and take over, Nico and Antonio still in sync after all these years. Emilia and I are holding on to each other, jumping up and down and screaming as though we're WAGs of professional athletes and not the slightly drunk significant others of two dudes in a random barrel-rolling competition.

They've got a decent lead as they pass off to the next men on the Cassero team. It seems like a lock. We're shouting as loud as our lungs will let us, which I'm sure I'm going to regret tomorrow. But it's hard not to let the moment take over.

It's neck and neck coming into the piazza. But with inches to go, I can see that Borgo's starting to pull ever so slightly ahead. It's like watching a car crash in slow motion as they approach the finish line. All four men on both teams are trying *so* hard, and their expressions are so serious you'd think everyone's lives depend on it.

But it's not meant to be this time. Borgo's barrel has a late surge that has them coming in right before ours. Red-and-white-clad people erupt, applauding and spilling out into the street as all our maroon and blue Cassero compatriots dejectedly take swigs of their drinks and start to walk away. Cheers and exhilaration and men on shoulders are in the foreground, while our exhausted warriors slump their way back to us.

Nico's cursing under his breath as he comes to me, and I pull him in a hug. He tries to pull away after a minute, but I keep holding him there, as tight as I can muster.

"You're doing the cow thing again, aren't you?" he asks.

I giggle. "We've already established it's helpful."

"I don't need a cow hug," he sighs. "I need a drink, a shower, and a long nap."

"All of those things can be arranged."

I pull back and tug at his stupid sweatband with a grin. "I'd start with the drink, though, because I feel like this sweaty-barrel-man look is working on you."

I get my own mischievous grin back, all exhaustion immediately out of his expression. "Oh yeah?" he says. "On second thought, let's just go home then."

I give him a kiss on his cheek and grab his hand. "No sore losers at the Palio."

"I'd say trying to get you into bed is the opposite of being a sore loser," he retorts, playfully pulling me back and away from the crowd. "Who can blame me if I want to lick my wounds and also—"

"Can you stop bringing disgrace to Cassero with both your barrel rolling *and* your inappropriate language in public?"

I swivel around and see Gia standing behind us. She's got a wry look on her face that tells me she's heard at least the last few parts of our conversation.

"I expect you to be rolling the barrel next year," Nico says to her, pulling me closer to his side with absolutely no attempt at even pretending we were talking about anything else.

"Pandering is beneath you," she retorts, and his laugh booms louder than the crowd.

Luckily, Tommaso also joins us at that moment. "Gia! I've been looking for you!"

No one was more surprised than me when a couple of years ago, Gia and Tommaso buried the hatchet and actually started working together.

After his night in the grove with Nico, Tommaso softened a bit toward both of them. And it gave him a new idea for a way to bridge the gap with Gia—turns out, he wanted to expand his weekend tourist repertoires to include not just boar hunting, but a much less gun-focused type of hunting: truffles.

When he found out that one of the best forests for truffle hunting was actually part of Gia's property, they struck up a deal. He'd avoid her property entirely with the boar hunters, he could truffle hunt freely on her land, and, in exchange, he'd give her half the truffles he foraged. She got a fresh supply for her restaurant that she didn't have to pay for, and he got a dedicated place to take his people without any competition. Quite the win-win for everyone.

"I dropped today's batch off with Marna earlier," he says. "We had a very successful morning—I think the truffles have been loving the rainy weather."

"Good," Gia says. "Then that means at least Cassero can drown their sorrows in truffles tonight." She gives Nico a pointed look, and I get that big laugh again.

"We can't win every year," he says. "We've had a pretty great run!"

But Gia just rolls her eyes at him and walks off with Tommaso, discussing the rest of the season's truffle schedule.

We stick around for a little bit longer, enjoying the crowds and revelry. We stand together to watch Borgo win the final against Imposto—Nico pretending not to care but secretly breathing a small sigh of relief that the people who beat them beat everyone.

The party starts immediately after, and from one look at Nico's expression, I know it's time for us to go home. I go to say goodbye to Emilia, but she's engaged in some kind of dance battle with a preteen, and I'm not getting in between that. Anita is recording enough video of the entire thing for all of us, so I give her a kiss on the cheek and go to hop on Nico's scooter.

It's freeing, letting myself hold on to him without even needing to open my eyes to see where he's going. He's got me. I can breathe in the timeless, earthy scent of Maremma with the wind on my face.

We pull up to the house and Luce is there, bouncing in circles to greet us. So is one of the cats that used to hang around my apartment and Belpagna, whom Gia eventually decided to officially rescue and keep with the cows. She apparently loves Luce too.

But instead of heading in straight away, we walk into the grove, enjoying the quiet.

We both naturally find ourselves walking to the trees that burned a few years ago. We've come out here a lot over the past couple of weeks. Looking at what stands here now never gets old.

The trees have begun growing back, slowly and steadily. By the winter after the fire, a thicket of shoots was sprouting from the stump where the burned part of the tree had been cut away. And now, three years after so much went up in smoke, the tree has olives again.

It feels like a little miracle. A proof that if you let time do its work, good things will grow.

We sit on the ground—my back against Nico's chest, our hands intertwined—and stare up at the trees, blanketed in the early-evening light.

There's something deeply satisfying about finding the peace to know you have nothing to prove. I can keep pushing and evolving and adapting without needing to win just for the sake of it. I can run a great restaurant and focus on my guests without needing the external validation. And it never stops amusing me that that harmony all started because of fire.

Fire burned down my restaurant; it burned down part of this grove. But from both of those fires, something even more beautiful grew in their place. And now because of fire, years later, I can sit here with the moon shining on me and just watch the slow, simple process of an olive growing on a tree.

Recipes for a Maremma-Inspired Dinner

I love including recipes for my novels, but for *this* book, it felt extra important. This book is rooted so firmly in location and food.

Manciano is a real place that I was lucky enough to spend two incredible weeks in. I love renting houses in off-the-beaten-path locations in Italy, and I'd heard so much about the beauty of Maremma. But it was the luck of the house that brought us to Manciano in particular, which proved to be a total inspiration, the quintessential tiny ancient Tuscan town. They really do host a barrel-rolling Palio that is as hilarious as it sounds. Belpagna and Emilia don't exist, sadly, but there is a café called Belvedere that I based Belpagna on, and it really does have some of the most incredible pastries and gelato!

If you go to Maremma, make sure you don't miss spending time in Pitigliano, Capalbio, and the beach in Porto Ercole.

And a bit farther north, I was lucky enough to also spend time in the groves of Olio Piro, and so much of their process made its way into this book. If you want incredible olive oil, I highly recommend seeking them out.

But since food brings travel to us, I'm really thrilled to include recipes for a Maremma-inspired dinner here, for all the moments we obviously cannot be exploring Italy! You can make this as a single dinner party—the menu includes appetizers through desserts—or make each dish individually for a little taste of some of the items referenced in the story. Maybe we can't have our own Kit or Gia making the recipes for us, but I promise they'll give you a little bit of Italian sunshine of your own.

Gorgonzola- and Rosemary-Topped Figs

If you learn anything food-wise from this book, I hope it's that keeping things simple is often the root of the best kind of food. So this is one of those recipes that is *barely* a recipe, and yet you'll get raves just the same. Please seek out gorgonzola dolce—it's soft, creamy, and delicate. It's mellower than most blue cheeses, and it allows the earthy fruitiness of figs to shine. Topped with fragrant rosemary, this is really a perfect bite. You can also make these on top of toasts if you want to make them a little heftier or if figs are out of season and you want to sub in fig jam.

Makes 20 small bites.

Ingredients

10 to 12 fresh figs
4 ounces gorgonzola dolce
1/2 tablespoon very finely chopped fresh rosemary
Dash of kosher salt
Drizzle of honey (optional)

Slice the figs in half. Top each with a spoonful of the gorgonzola dolce. Sprinkle on the rosemary, along with a dash of salt. If your figs aren't sweet enough, you can add a small drizzle of honey on top.

Shrimp Tartare with Burrata

This is the kind of appetizer that everyone thinks is fancy but is once again incredibly simple, as long as you rely on delicious products. You *can* serve shrimp raw here, but since most shrimp available is flash frozen, we'll quickly poach it a bit to ensure that dreamy tartare texture. Delicate shrimp pairs perfectly with the mildness of burrata, and with a great drizzle of olive oil, you'll have a dish that will transport you to the Italian seaside. This dish can also work as a pasta (over pici! Or spaghetti if you can't find it), or in an endive leaf as a passed app. Once you've discovered this flavor combination, you won't want anything else.

Serves 4 as an appetizer portion.

Ingredients

1 pound shrimp, peeled and deveined
A heavy drizzle of high-quality extra virgin olive oil
Dash of kosher salt
2 balls of burrata
A handful of basil, chopped

Bring a large pot of salted water to a boil. Remove from the heat and add in the shrimp, poaching them until they're opaque and barely cooked through, around one minute. Drain the shrimp and run under cold water. Once they've cooled, chop the shrimp into small pieces. In a small bowl, combine the shrimp with a heavy drizzle of both olive oil and salt.

Cut the burrata balls in half and place each on a plate. Drizzle with olive oil and salt. Add the shrimp tartare onto the burrata and then sprinkle the basil on top.

Handmade Gnocchi with Pecorino

Listen, we aren't going to come close to equaling Gia in the pasta department. But I've found one pasta that anyone can make at home with less than fifteen minutes of effort: gnocchi. This version uses ricotta and then freezes the gnocchi, which ensures they'll remain light and fluffy no matter what you do. You can pair this recipe with almost any sauce—simple butter, tomato, pesto, or even a version of Kit's eggplants if you like. Either way, you'll have the easiest make-ahead meal that'll impress anyone.

Serves 8.

Ingredients

5 cups (32 ounces) firm whole-milk ricotta
2 cups freshly grated Pecorino Romano cheese
1 teaspoon salt
4 egg yolks
1 1/2 to 2 cups all-purpose flour, plus more for dusting
Butter or other pasta sauce (to your taste)

Make sure your ricotta is not too wet. If it is, you can drain it over paper towels on top of a colander or use a cheesecloth and weigh it down.

Once your ricotta is ready, combine it with the Pecorino Romano, salt, and egg yolks. Add in the flour and combine gently. If the dough feels too wet to roll out (either from your ricotta or if you have particularly large egg yolks), add a bit more flour into the dough.

Add a little flour to your surface. Taking the dough into pieces, roll out each piece into a long cylinder, approximately the width and shape of a breadstick, or about 1/2 inch. While you will need to roll the dough a fair amount, try to knead it as little as possible, sprinkling with a bit of flour as needed. Cut the dough into 1-inch pieces and set aside.

To freeze the gnocchi, place them on a parchment-lined pan, ensuring that they aren't touching, and place them in the freezer. Once they've fully frozen (1 to 2 hours), you can either cook them or move them into a resealable freezer-safe bag, making sure to remove as much air as possible. They will stay good up to three months frozen.

Once you're ready to eat, bring a salted pot of water to a boil. Add the gnocchi into the water and let them cook for 2 to 3 minutes, or until they start to float. Remove the gnocchi from the pot with a slotted spoon and immediately combine with butter or sauce.

Almost Boar, Almost Ragù over Polenta

I love the perfection of a long-simmering ragù, but this recipe takes my imagined version of Gia's and makes it suitable for everyday cooking. I think the combination of beef and pork provides the perfect in-between to the gaminess of boar. Using ground meat speeds everything up, but I think the hefty doses of anchovy paste and tomato paste provide the requisite depth of flavor you'd normally get from a long cooking time. If you're even lazier (as I often am), you can also use polenta rolls instead of making the polenta from scratch. But either way, this recipe will give you a taste of the countryside, no matter your setting.

Serves 4.

Ingredients

1 cup polenta
3 teaspoons salt, divided, plus additional
1 large Vidalia onion, diced
10 cloves of garlic, minced
Drizzle of olive oil
1 pound ground pork
1 pound ground beef
1 tablespoon anchovy paste

1/4 cup tomato paste
2 teaspoons thyme
2 teaspoons oregano
1 cup (or more!) grated Pecorino Romano

Bring 4 cups of water (or stock if you prefer) to a boil and add the polenta and 1 teaspoon of salt. Turn the heat down to low and let it simmer, stirring occasionally for around 30 minutes or until the polenta is cooked.

While the polenta cooks, heat a large sauté pan on medium-high heat. Add in the onion and garlic with a drizzle of olive oil and a dash of salt. Cook for 5 to 7 minutes, stirring occasionally, until the onions have begun to soften.

Once the onions are ready, add in the remaining salt, pork, beef, anchovy paste, tomato paste, thyme, and oregano. Cook for 7 to 10 minutes, stirring occasionally, until the meat is cooked through.

To serve, stir in 1/2 cup of the grated Pecorino Romano to the polenta. Top it with the pork and beef mixture, and then add the rest of the cheese. Serve hot.

Apricot Olive Oil Ricotta Cake

I don't think I could ever live up to Emilia's fictional bomboloni, but nothing's easier than an olive oil ricotta cake. There are no two better items for keeping a cake moist than the Italian duo of olive oil and ricotta. When you add the tart delight of apricots to the equation, you have a can't-miss combination. I like using self-rising flour for its ease, but if you don't have it, just use 2 teaspoons of baking powder mixed with regular all-purpose flour. Either way, you'll have a cake you can eat from breakfast to dessert.

Makes one 9-inch cake.

Ingredients

1 cup fresh, full-fat ricotta
3/4 cup extra virgin olive oil, divided
3/4 cup granulated sugar, divided
2 large eggs
1 1/2 cups self-rising flour
1 teaspoon salt
6 medium apricots, halved and pitted

Preheat your oven to 350 degrees and place a 9-inch cast-iron pan inside.

In a bowl combine the ricotta, 1/2 cup of olive oil, 1/2 cup granulated sugar, and eggs. Whisk well. Add in the flour and salt and *very* gently fold it in (you want to stir as little as possible to keep the batter light).

Remove the cast-iron pan from the oven. Add the remaining 1/4 cup of olive oil to the pan and then sprinkle the remaining 1/4 cup of sugar on top. Add the apricots, evenly spaced, cut-side down. Don't worry about crowding the pan; you want to nestle in as many apricots as possible. Put the batter on top of the apricots (it doesn't need to be completely even, since it will all even out when it cooks and this is a pretty thick batter, so just do the best you can) and place the pan back in the oven. Bake for 35 minutes, or until a toothpick comes out clean.

Remove from the oven and cool for 10 to 15 minutes, then turn the cake out of the pan, apricot-side up.

Acknowledgments

This book is dedicated to my mom, but I'm still putting her first in my acknowledgments as well: Hi, Mom! Love you.

Sometimes the ideas for books take time, and others hit me in an instant. This book was the latter type and is majorly indebted to Olio Piro, especially Charlotte and Roman Piro. A few years ago, I went on a work trip to Tuscany to see how their olive oil is made, and this story jumped into my brain and wouldn't let go. I felt instantly inspired, and not just by their oil—which is incredible, and they really do use an unparalleled filtration system that I based Nico's on—but also with their adoration for the process of making something beautiful in the world. And while the imagery of sunset-drenched hills and craggy groves has stuck with me, it's the kindness of the people there that will always be nestled into my heart.

Speaking of amazing people, I have the absolute best in my writing corner. Wendy Sherman, maybe you're sick of me saying this, but it's your fault, because now I've been able to write it into four books—thank you for being the best agent and friend. You dish up honesty with love, and I couldn't be more grateful for you.

Lauren Plude, let's never stop being bonkers together. Thank you for letting me tell this story that you knew I'd never let go of. Every conversation we have brings me so much joy—I don't take for granted that that's a giant publishing rarity. And likewise for Lindsey Faber. I've never met someone who so many authors claim as their personal favorite miracle worker. You have a true gift in bringing out the best in people, and I'm so lucky to have your fingerprints on every book.

Thank you to Jessica Brock and Allyson Cullinan for letting me run with my bananas ideas and for getting my books into so many people's hands. I appreciate everything you guys do! To Katrina Escudero—man, I cannot *wait* for the world to see what you've done. I'm in awe of you!

Thank you to Bill Siever for not writing me off as a stalker after I wrote a book about falling in love with copy editors. Your keen eye and humor make the editing process a true joy, and I'm so grateful to have you back for this one. Brenna Bailey-Davies and Tristen Bakker, thank you for your keen proofread and cold read! And Andrea Nauta and Angela Elson, thank you for shepherding this book through production.

I'm really lucky to have friends who are willing to read my messy first drafts. Matthew Kane, thank you for being the friend I can trust to hold my heart and take it seriously every single time. Juliet Izon, I don't think I could do this without you?! Thank you for deep-diving every part, including the sex scenes (true friendship). Now everyone please order her debut novel, *The Encore*—it's amazing.

Thank you to Tarah DeWitt for letting me constantly bounce plot thoughts for this book by you (and every other demented thought in long, rambling voice notes). Thank you to Ali Hazelwood for insisting on being my Italian sensitivity reader and giving me a blurb, despite the fact that you already are basically shouldering being the hype woman for the entire romance industry. I hope Nico drinking Campari instead of Aperol is a good start for my gratitude. Lauren Kung Jessen, I so appreciate you reading an entire book just to answer basically a single question I had right at the end. Thank you to Charlotte Druckman for looking out for Kit. Our walks make everything better!

So many wonderful people helped ensure this book was accurate in all the places it needed to be. To Anna Grace Robinson, you marveled at Manciano with me and loved all her quirks as much as I did. I hope Emilia is exactly how you imagined our Fleabag! Thank you to my father-in-law, Yehuda, for surviving the road to Saturnia with me—yes, that really happened, and yes, we stayed calm and made it out! Thank you to Alex Hammer Ducas for explaining the intricacies of rowing to me, even though I promise I was paying attention when we were younger. Hillary Sterling—thank you for letting me pick your brain on the business of restaurants. And, you know, for being a chef whose food I'd follow anywhere. Now everyone go to Ci Siamo (in New York or Boston!). Thank you to Alex Roth for letting me use your last name! And thanks to Deb Perelman for encouraging my deranged Swiftie Easter egg (if you clocked it, you're welcome).

Thank you again to my parents for always supporting me with such open hearts, along with my siblings, Annie and Will, and their spouses, Jon and Skye. And my other family, Yehuda, Natalie, and Aaron (and always Rachel). Love you all.

Like Kit, I love cooking, Italy, and New York, but nothing beats my three kids. My son, Guy, is my best reading buddy. I feel so grateful that we share that love together. And to my daughters, Joy and Rae—I hope I'm role modeling the type of ambitious and kind woman I like to write about.

And finally, to Daniel. I promised you over twenty years ago I wouldn't drive a Vespa again, but I hope you'll forgive me for resurrecting that little marigold one in my writing. Thank you for perfecting the art of hugging me like a cow. I love you.

About the Author

Photo © 2022 Melanie Dunea

Ali Rosen is the bestselling author of *Recipe for Second Chances*, *Alternate Endings*, and *Unlikely Story*, described in a starred review by *Kirkus Reviews* as "a swoonworthy romance reminiscent of a Nora Ephron movie."

Aside from loving escaping into fictional worlds, Rosen is also the Emmy Award– and James Beard Award–nominated host of *Potluck with Ali Rosen* on NYC Life, as well as the author of cookbooks including the bestselling *Modern Freezer Meals*, *15 Minute Meals*, and *Bring It*. She has been featured everywhere from the *Today* show to *The New York Times* and has written for *Bon Appétit*, *The Washington Post*, and *New York Magazine*.

Rosen is originally from Charleston, South Carolina, but now lives in New York City with her husband, three kids, and rescue dog. She can usually be found wandering the Union Square Greenmarket or curled up in a chair reading a romance novel.

Connect with her online at www.ali-rosen.com or via Instagram @Ali_Rosen.